From **PRETZEL LOGIC**
   Whatever the thin
shadows and the eye's periphery ...
and it used them with speed. Eyes couldn't see it, their gear
couldn't track it but Rascal could, a bit.
   He could know where it would probably strike in any case,
seconds before the hit. If the damn jarheads (were SEALS called
jarheads?) had just listened, three of them wouldn't be chunks of
sliced meat now. Three dead in fewer seconds than it took to say.
Rascal was damned sure he wasn't going be Corpse Number
Four.

From **COVENANT OF SALT**
In her mind, she pictured herself standing on the Garment Club's
tiny stage, facing a room full of people excited to see her. It was
her dream venue—the kind of hole-in-the-wall place that knew
how to spot talent. She imagined the dingy crimson walls
decorated with autographed photos of respected performers
who'd gotten their start there, the scuffed wooden floor, the plain
yet well stocked bar...
   She was so lost in her head, she didn't see the enormous
blond woman approach until the latter had grabbed her arm.
   Jojo opened her mouth to cry out.
   "Keep quiet, Sarcastic Fringehead, or I'll rip your arm off,"
the woman growled, her green eyes glinting.

From **COUNTER ATTACK**
Automatic locks clicked, and the rear door rolled open, letting
Reese make the short jump to the ground.
   So far, the exoskeleton had been behaving smoothly and
making all the right whirring noises. The next-gen enhancements
improved flexibility and response time, making them better for
combat than the CED specs.
   "I'm five by five," Reese announced.
   "I'll be monitoring your vitals from here," Greene said,
opening a laptop and accessing the signals emanating from the
tech buried throughout Reese's body.
   Reese began moving toward the scene of destruction...

PHENOMENONS
THE WIND AND FIRE

EDITED BY

MICHAEL JAN FRIEDMAN

CRAZY 8 PRESS

For our friend Brian Augustyn, who taught me a thing or two about pulling together a superhero universe.

CONTENTS

Phe-nom-e-non \fi-ˈnä-mə-ˌnän, -nən\ *n, pl* **phenomenons** : an exceptional, unusual, or abnormal person, thing, or occurrence (Merriam-Webster)

FOREWORD

I'm not gonna lie: This Phenomenons book was tougher to put together than the two that came before it. It's one thing to present a collection of only tangentially related tales and another to drive story after story, chapter-style, toward a satisfying, novel-like conclusion.

Fortunately, I had a dream team of ridiculously skilled and motivated writers working with me, determined to make this edition of Phenomenons the best of the lot—among them my pal Peter David, with whom I plotted out an arc for his character, Professor Paracelsus, well before he ran into his current medical difficulties.

The late Brian Augustyn, to whom this book is justly dedicated, once told me: "If you pick the right horses, all you have to do is let them run." It was the best editorial advice I've ever gotten.

Much better than: "You, Friedman? *You're* going to edit a superhero anthology? I mean...*seriously?*"

If you enjoy *Phenomenons: The Wind And Fire*, you can whisper a little thanks to Brian. I know I will.

—Michael Jan Friedman

PRETZEL LOGIC

BY GEOFFREY THORNE

1: SAVE POINT

Carmody went down, screaming.

It was an incongruously high-pitched sound, coming from a man that big. He'd been one of those meat sacks whose every move screamed Navy SEAL or Special Forces or some other of those government-sanctioned murder squads they make movies about. Rascal hadn't liked him on sight. He never did with that type–schoolyard bullies who tracked themselves into lives and jobs where using a gun was a perk second only to snapping a neck by hand. The party line was those sorts of kids grew up to be criminals, menaces to society. Turned out there were equal measures of brutality and violence on both sides of the legal fence.

At least outlaws are honest about who they are, Rascal had always thought.

Even so, Carmody hadn't deserved to go out like that–squealing like a slaughtered pig, in two big chunks, as his life spewed out on the tiled floor. Or, maybe, he had. Rascal didn't know his pedigree and didn't care to know it. He'd warned him. He'd warned them all, the whole squad, but he was just a criminal on a leash to them, only valuable because their boss said so and barely that. So, they'd barreled on through, unheeding, seeing nothing, hearing nothing, dismissing him.

Idiots.

Whatever the thing was—barely visible, rippling through the shadows and the eye's periphery—it had claws, maybe teeth too, and it used them with speed.

Eyes couldn't see it, their gear couldn't track it but Rascal could, a bit. Somehow as he could with the strangely shifting dimensions of the rooms and corridors, he could sense the thing, sort of.

He could know where it would probably strike in any case, seconds before the hit. If the damn jarheads (were SEALS called jarheads?) had just listened, three of them wouldn't be chunks of sliced meat now.

Three dead in fewer seconds than it took to say. Rascal was damned sure he wasn't going be Corpse Number Four.

"Back," he said, his voice like a knife, cutting. "Fall back to the sec-station."

No one had to be told twice. As a single body, they moved back to the rally point, only sliding once on the bloody floor. Not one slip resulted in a fall and nobody stopped to recover the weapons of their morgued comrades.

The interior of the Arkworx Unlimited facility had been both more and considerably less dangerous than everyone had expected, going in. The team's leader, a frosty, obviously ex-spook calling herself "Miss Metal 'had sent in and lost several teams prior to this one. As no bodies had been found, her analysts had chalked the losses up to the constant dimensional shifting the facility's interior had displayed ever since returning from...wherever.

Maybe those first few tries had ended that way. The shifts did remove or deposit walls, desks, bits of floor and any other kind of matter in the place, seemingly at random. No reason it should treat a human being any different than a lamp or a begonia. On the other hand, maybe, all the shifting had done was clean up the mess.

The killer, whatever-it-was, seemed to be moving independently of the shifting he was able to easily track. It seemed to constantly be transforming itself, somehow. If it was, that explained how none of the squad's hyper-tech gadgets could track it nor anyone's eyes see it, while Rascal's abilities could lock on, albeit too late to save lives.

So far. Rascal himself was still in the game and meant to keep it that way.

"This guy's useless," said one of the jarboys (Rascal was calling them 'jarboys' now). Aside from skin color–this guy's was sandy brown, rather than the pink-white of his dead fellows–the jarboys were identical. They might as well have been CGI stuntmen in a crap action movie for all the personality they shared. "We barely made it up an extra floor before that thing–"

"Stow it, Bailey," said Miss Metal in a near growl. "You secure that mouth or I will."

She was a tall woman, with severe features that only doubled down on the frosty attitude she flexed on the world. On their first meeting Rascal had pegged her as just one more spook in a suit, whose obvious fitness was the result of hours spent on some workout club treadmill, largely for show. Tricked out in the same tactical gear as her jarboys, it was clear to anyone looking that Miss Metal was as lethal as any of them.

Bailey's mouth snapped shut as Miss Metal's cold gaze centered on Rascal.

"What about it, Mr. Eaves?" her tone and look reminded Rascal too much of a cobra setting up for a strike. "We're trying to save the world here. Thinking about holding up your end anytime soon?"

Rascal's end was helping the crew of killers, and they were all definitely killers, he decided--through the shifting maze of corridors to the facility's core, where they would do whatever they'd planned to shut down of the expanding effect of the M-brane Bridge. He and the other Midnight Ramblers had been sent in to steal the thing when all this mess had begun. The irony of his current position was not lost on him.

When the disaster happened that forced this place into its constant dimensional shifting, Rascal had been the only one lucky enough to make it out. His friends, Marry, Deacon, and Runaround, hadn't been so fortunate.

He pictured them all, screaming, dying, dissolving in the shimmering tidal wave of light and noise that had taken everything in this place except himself away to some other place or energy state and left a couple acres of glass sheet spread across the landscape.

He blinked the vision away, focusing on the now and the here. He'd had too much practice with that in the last couple years. Since the...event...he'd had to train his mind to do that almost to the point of obsession.

There were two reasons Rascal had agreed to this nakedly suicidal mission. The distorting, obliterating effect that had given him his mojo and taken Arkworx and his friends away was expanding. If that couldn't be stopped, what was happening here would be happening to everyone in the world. It wasn't the version of Armageddon every religion had predicted was eventually coming but it was Armageddon nonetheless.

Rascal didn't much like the majority of people who lived in the world, but he loved the world itself. It was where he lived, after all. The other reason Rascal agreed to do the Sacagawea bit for Miss Metal's lethal expedition was the very off chance he might find his friends here, even only one of them, still alive. It was a longshot, but he had been the king of beating odds even before he got his mojo.

Metal thought his end was making sure she and her team accomplished their mission–to find and shut down the M-brane Bridge–and get out of this place alive. His payment for services was his being allowed to keep breathing as well. Rascal had serious doubts about Metal being square on that count but that was a five-minutes-from-now problem."

"Your boys croaked it because they don't like to listen," he said, facing her. "They didn't jump when I told them and they got morgued for it. That's a whole bunch of not my problem."

Her gun, a modified Desert Eagle with some sort of extra tech attached to the stock, was inches from his left eye in a flash.

"Beg to differ," she said as if she were discussing the Times crossword puzzle with a stranger. "Your life expectancy lasts as long as you're useful to this operation, Mr. Eaves. Based on current performance, I'd say your clock is very much ticking down."

The other guns, more of those modified assault rifles these people called shatterguns, came up as well. The threat wasn't unexpected. The more time Rascal spent in Miss Metal's company, the more he was sure she and her crew weren't government. He'd known she'd likely try to murder him once the gig was over and been willing to bide his time until he found a moment to E-X-T-E-N-D his way out of her clutches. Currently that didn't exist.

No matter how far he E-X-T-E-N-D-E-D there was no scenario in which he got out of this room without their weapons turning him into bloody cutlets. He had to bide, keep the timer ticking.

"Easy, Sis," he said. "I got you this far, didn't I?"

"And no further." Like her tone, the guns didn't waver. "Why is this room stable and the others are still blinking and ghosting around?"

Rascal shrugged. He'd taught himself the necessary conceptual physics to get a handle on his new abilities but, beyond that, he wouldn't even qualify as a Poor Ma's Schoedinger.

"No clue," he said. "And no idea what any of this is, anyway. You brought me along because of what I can do, not so I can give a science lecture."

"I say we smoke this scrub," said Bailey through his teeth. "Cut bait, set charges, blow the site."

"And that's why we don't pay you to think, Bailey," said Miss Metal.

Slowly, far too slowly to Rascal's mind, her pistol dipped, then swiveled down to her side and the tiniest bit of steel melted out of her gaze. She was mulling something, Rascal could tell. As the men lowered their own weapons, Miss Metal reached into one of her thigh pockets and withdrew a small metal sphere.

"Take this," she said, handing it over. It didn't weigh much in his hand, about the heft of a baseball. "You remember the map to the central lab?"

Rascal did. He remembered the maps from every job he and the other Ramblers had ever taken. Things were a little off, what with the walls and floor moving, vanishing or turning into pottery at seeming random but, overall, the floor plan here had proved relatively static.

"Yeah," he said, rolling the thing between his hands, locking in on its feel. "What about it?"

"You're going to take that to the central lab," she said. "Whatever you find there, you're going to set it down somewhere in the middle of the room and you're going to press this."

One of her hands was on his, moving his fingers with hers until he noticed a slightly depressed circle in the ridges of the sphere's surface.

A button? Okay. Missed that on the first look.

"Then what?"

"Then, all of this," she gestured around with her gun hand, clearly meaning the whole structure, 'is nobody's problem anymore."

"What is it?" he said, examining it more closely. The surface wasn't smooth at all, was it? It was a lattice of circuits so densely spaced that they only seemed to present an unbroken skin. The sole deviation was the single tiny button and that could only be found by knowing where to look. "Some kind of bomb?"

"It's a solution," she said. "It's the solution. Now, move your ass. If you make me do this myself, it will be over your dead body."

2: LEVEL TWO

Rascal moved much faster through the space without the jarboys slowing him down with their creep-along pace. The dimensional shifting increased as he went deeper–walls and floors becoming bookshelves, becoming stairwells, becoming soda machines becoming nothing at all–but it was not as random as everyone had first guessed.

He couldn't quite describe the pattern, couldn't put a number or any verbal description on it but it was there, perceptible by the same part of him that allowed him to E-X-T-E-N-D. It was if a tuning fork was there inside him that pinged and shivered according to the size and scope of any impending shift.

He knew Miss Metal would be watching his progress on the internal monitors, if she could. If those systems were still up, she would get what he and Marry had gotten when they'd watched this whole mess start. She would see Rascal, sure, but she'd see him doing any one of twenty different actions on twenty separate monitors. She would be confused; maybe she'd think it was some trick he was playing and start planning contingencies. If she was smart, it might give her a better clue as to how his own mojo worked. Miss Metal was definitely smart.

Something for later, he told himself as he leaped over the sudden deadfall. A nanosecond earlier that had been a section of floor. Now, it was basically an empty elevator shaft going down, down, down. He'd make it to the central lab in under two minutes at this rate. The shifts were actually kind of pretty once you knew how to see them, a sort of rainbow shimmer, sliding across and through the ghosting surfaces like rainwater on a wall. Rascal relaxed. He could do this. Tuning fork pings, jump. Tuning fork vibrates, duck. Rinse, repeat.

Easy.

Now that he was away from Miss Metal and her kill-squad, his escape options expanded back up to more than sixty safe getaways. Hell, he could be out of here and halfway to Memphis before they knew he was gone.

He was allowing himself a little half daydream about QUINN'S OLD TIME BBQ on East McLemore and that deadly sweet sauce when the tuning fork screamed.

Before he could move, before he could think or blink, the thing was on him. It appeared from nowhere as it had before. As it had the first times, it seemed to swim through the solid walls and settle on open air as if the floor that had been there was now absolutely not.

This time, instead of the shimmering, almost perfectly invisible presence, the thing was a thousand choirs screaming in his mind, in his ears, filling the whole universe around him. This time, it was a million clawing fingers, a thousand taloned hands slashing at him, pulling at him, trying to rip him apart. This time he had no moment to react, no time to dodge, no chance to run or to fight back. This time, it was Rascal who'd die and he knew he would be screaming.

On instinct, he did try to E–X–T–E–N–D his way free but, somehow, the thing's attack cut off all the possibilities he might exploit. There was no space to find a weapon, no line where he hadn't encountered the creature and no moment where it wasn't trying to rip him to bits. Somehow it was everywhere at once and Rascal was soon to be nowhere.

Oddly, he thought of something Proud Marry had said once after a particularly energetic barroom brawl.

Some assholes just don't know when to let things go.

It was one of the only times he'd seen her with a full-glow smile gracing her face.

Then there were hands on him, pulling him away from the attack, away from that point in the corridor where the creature dominated. There were flashes of color, streams of what might have been abstract wall art or strange machinery or the wireframe outlines of all the objects his gaze fell on.

There was a sort of wind he could hear as well, a cyclone breeze rushing past yet leaving no sense of touching him. He couldn't credit any of it. His body was in so much pain, bleeding from more places than he'd have thought possible. His mind was little better. The creature was still screaming in there, howling from a million mouths in rage and, maybe, pain?

All at once everything was still and the hands that had pulled him away were now laying his body gently on some sort of low couch and pulling away. His vision swam and Rascal knew he didn't have long to save his life. He had to focus, concentrate.

"Holy shit," said a voice too familiar for him to believe he was hearing it "It's Rascal."

"Figures the little bastard would still be in the mix," said another familiar voice, a low bass rumble he never thought he'd hear again.

I'll give you 'little bastard,' you oversized heap of–

"He's bleeding out!" Now there was panic in the first voice. "Look at him; he's goddamn shredded."

Don't stress, baby. Just give me time to...

Harnessing every inch of will and focus he could to get past the pain from his destroyed body, Rascal E–X–T–E–N–D-E-D again. The strange physics and flickering geometries of this place made it hard, but he pushed through. Here was a thread where he died during the monster's attack. No. Here were several where he lost a limb and crawled off to die in a corner. No. Here was one where he anticipated the attack, not quickly enough to avoid damage but nowhere near the murder-in-progress he was trying to escape. Good, closer.

"Look. Holy shit, look," said the first voice. From the sound of her, she seemed to be hovering somewhere between shock and horror. "What's happening to him?"

"Think I know?" said the lower voice in an equally grim confusion. "I don't even know what happened to us."

Here was a thread where he'd got hit, got hurt but was pulled away before the monster could do more, could kill him. Got it. Rascal reeled it into himself and smiled as ninety-five percent of the wounds he'd just suffered vanished.

He pulled himself up to his elbows and took in the scene. He'd been laid on some sort of low couch, the sort one might find in a medical waiting area. There were machines he could identify as computers on one wall and host of others he could tag dominating the rest of the space. He'd seen this before. He knew where he was.

Central Lab, check. Weird little contraption he remembered as being the M-brane Bridge sitting on the center table, check. The blood that had gushed from his many gaping wounds? Gone.

He was only a little scratched and bruised now. The tactical uniform they'd force him to wear–sans gun or communication device, natch–were barely torn. Rascal took the win. He'd made it and, bonus, these were people he knew, friends he'd never expected to see again.

"Guess he got some extra juice out of this too," said Deacon Blue, a big grin splitting his massive brown face. He was just there, wearing the same suit he'd had on that night, and not looking too much the worse for wear. Not bad at all for a dead man. "Hey, Rascal."

Runaround was the same, just exactly the same as he'd last seen her, as she'd stayed in his memory these last two years. Sure, she looked a little scuffed around the edges, but she was breathing and smelled so good and she was alive.

Runaround just grabbed him and hugged him so tight he thought his ribs would crack. He'd forgotten how strong that small frame of hers was.

"OOF, Susie. Ease up, baby. I'm not a hundred percent, y'know?" he said. Then, with a smiling glance at his other friend. "Hey, Deac."

Runaround Susie did relax her grip on him and, when she looked at him, he could see the pools of happy tears welling in her eyes.

"You're alive," she said. "Holy shit, you're ALIVE!"

"So far," said Rascal, kissing her cheeks and her forehead softly. "Glad to see you both skated."

"Skated? Dunno about that," said Deacon, his grin faltering to a frown. "We're still stuck in here, mate. You made it so, yeah, That's good, but—"

"But the danger is worse than anyone comprehends," said a voice Rascal did not know.

He swiveled in Runaround's grip. Apparently, she wasn't quite ready to let go of him yet. Stepping into the space from a doorway he hadn't noticed before was a smallish, slender Asian man holding a mug of what smelled like coffee. He wore the same Arkworx Unltd lab coat Rascal remembered and his face sported a sad half smile.

"I gather you're the fourth member of the thief quartet," he said, taking a seat on the high chair near the center table. "My name is Dr. Michael Woo."

"Rascal," said Rascal. "And it's Midnight Ramblers, Doc. Get it right."

"Point taken," said Dr. Woo. "No disrespect intended."

"So, how about it," said Rascal. "We walking out of here or is it, y'know, kaboom?"

"The answer to that depends on a host of variables, Mr. Rascal," said the scientist, blowing steam off his coffee and taking a sip. "Not the least of which, I think, is you."

3: RESPAWN

Ultimately Runaround did relax her grip on Rascal enough for him to stand and join Deacon and Dr. Woo at the table. She didn't let go, though, only looped one arm around his waist and moved with him, staying close. Rascal was surprised to find how much he appreciated that possessive familiarity.

None of the Ramblers would ever submit to anything as restricting as official couple-hood but they were all close and had shared enough skin and sweat to be considerably more than friends. Strange as it was to admit it to himself, Rascal had missed Runaround in his heart, which was something he hadn't thought himself capable of. He wrapped one arm around her waist in return and felt her body relax into his just the tiniest bit more.

"You may find this a common story," said Dr Woo. "And myself not a little naive to have fallen into it the way I did. I suspect you people live a much more complex life than I can imagine. You'll be much more sanguine when it comes to lies and subterfuge."

"You imagined this M-brane Bridge thing," said Rascal. "Pretty sure none of us could do that."

"Yeah, what even is it?" said Runaround. "We been so busy keeping those things off us we haven't had time to–"

"About that," said Rascal, cutting in. "How are you still alive in here? I mean, I guess you all had cafeteria food and maybe some vending machines but…enough for two years?"

"Two years?" said Deacon. "What are you on about? It's been, maybe, ten hours since everything went tits up."

Dr. Woo sighed and pinched the bridge of his nose like a man who had been thinking about too many things for too many hours to have one more dropped on his plate.

"Time distortion and dilation was always a concern," he said, finally. "It makes sense as a tangential effect to the ongoing dimensional and spatial shifts."

"So, what, time's going slower in here, than outside," said Runaround.

"Got it in one," said Dr. Woo. "For criminals you are all surprisingly quick on the uptake."

"*Criminal* don't mean 'stupid,' Doc," said Deacon Blue. "We all got brains, innit."

"Corrected and chastised, Mr. Blue," said Dr. Woo. "I will remember."

"Wait," said Rascal, his mental rewind kicking in. "You said *keeping those things off you? What things?*"

"Perhaps, I should start at the beginning," said Dr. Woo.

"Sure," said Rascal. "Not like there's a clock ticking on us or anything."

"A clock?"

"I didn't get in here on my own, Doc," said Rascal. "Somebody out there wants that Bridge thing either in their hands or nobody's, ever. Get me?"

From his expression, it was clear Dr. Woo got him.

"I will dispense with a recap of the decades of physicists contributing to and shoring up the multi-worlds theory of the universe," the scientist said, after another sip of his coffee. "Suffice to say, branched realities exist but we were having a devil of a time providing any form of observational data.

Here and there, a quantum experiment would shift the position of a particle or two, supporting all the math and making everyone very hopeful. The real get would be to look into one of these branches, to actually see alternate versions of our world progressing in their own directions, independent of ours. So, I created the M-brane Bridge to do just that. Well, I theorized the device. It wasn't until Arkworx Unlimited approached me with funding that I was able to build it."

"Let me guess," said Rascal. "They did you dirty."

"Well," said Woo without adding the obligatory ahem, for being interrupted. "They meant to. You see, my Bridge began life as nothing more than a window. The initial plan was simply to create a means of looking at the reality branches and keeping a record of what was seen.

"It quickly became clear the field created by the M-brane Window allowed far more than just watching. We learned we could interact. We could literally reach into the branched version of this reality to lift out, say, an apple, and return with it wholly intact."

Deacon whistled.

"See where this is going," he said. They all did. They'd been to the movies. There was no way the giant corporation, presented with this amazing new wrinkle, would not instantly figure ways to monetize it. And after that, it was a short step to weaponization.

"How soon did the military complex kick in?" said Rascal.

"Oh, instantly," said Dr. Woo. "Arkworx's CEO called someone at the Pentagon while I was in her office. I told the man my findings, what my window had already allowed us to do and he was, shall we say, over the moon. He wanted a new prototype built, one that could be used to allow something the size of a tank to be able to pass into the branched reality and back. I suggested we start small."

"Wait," said Runaround. "*Small?* But you already built the small version, right? That's this thing. The window thing."

"Correct, young lady," said Dr. Woo. "But, if I've gleaned nothing else from my dealings with CEOs and heads of governmental departments, it's that they neither know nor care how science actually works. They're only interested in capitalizing on it, in one case, and weaponizing it in the other. My proposition was only to stall for time."

"The size of the device doesn't matter, does it?" said Rascal, chewing the story in his head. "It just generates the field, according to how much juice you pump into it. The more, the bigger, yeah?"

"Exactly! Exactly right," said Dr. Woo, a real smile spreading across his face. It was like the sun coming from behind a cloud and made him seem much more a human being than the brain with legs Rascal had taken him for. "After all, it's the field generated by the M-brane Bridge that has caused all this trouble."

"You were monkeywrenching," said Deacon in his low rumble. "Trying to throw a spanner in their plans."

Dr. Woo gave a curt nod as he ran a proprietary hand over the weirdly innocuous device.

"We could have applied the Bridge to world hunger, overpopulation," said Dr. Woo. "Colonized the solar system. Returned extinct species. Ended all dependance on fossil fuels and reversed climate change."

"Paradise in a shoebox," said Rascal. "But your bosses just wanted better guns, right."

"They wanted every dystopian, authoritarian fantasy written about in a science fiction novel," said Dr. Woo. "And they knew I knew it."

Deacon pulled the contract to steal this thing off the Counter, Rascal thought. *An anonymous client, big bag of money for the Ramblers to split, minor threat profile at the target site. Gold.*

It had seemed too good to be true, right at the jump, but greed and Runaround's pleading had bought Rascal's 'yes' vote. He resolved to trust his guts going forward, regardless of how willing and bendable Runaround promised to be.

"I was in the midst of sabotaging the Bridge when you broke in," said Dr. Woo, with a sheepish little smile. "My hands were shaking, I was so nervous. This entire disaster happened because my fingers slipped."

"That Shimmer Wave thing we heard on the warning PA."

Again Dr. Woo nodded.

"Everything caught in the wave was... altered," said Dr. Woo. "The building, yourselves, everything. Except me, it seems."

Rascal flinched inside, remembering the feeling of that weird energy washing over him, moving through him, making changes. It hadn't hurt, not exactly, but it had been so strange, as if he'd been solid one second, liquid the next, and all of him made of tiny sparkling lights.

When the wave passed, he was himself, his friends and the building were gone, and it was all he'd been able to do to keep from going freaking insane on the spot.

The first time he'd E-X-T-E-N-D-E-D it had been on instinct, trying to get out of the path of an oncoming car. He'd seen his death zooming his way and just...flexed something inside him, something new and surprising. Suddenly he'd been presented with a host of possible cars all coming his way in some fashion. There were alternate cars, alternate streets, alternate cities around it all but only one Rascal, always himself, right at the center.

In most of the alts, the car hit him, dead on. Sometimes he was crushed, sometimes spun to death, sometimes splatted on impact, sometimes lingering for minutes, bleeding out on the pavement to the sound of rubber tires grinding far away.

Only in a few did the car miss him entirely or only strike a glancing hit. Only in one was there no car at all.

Again, on instinct, Rascal had pulled the position he occupied in that alt into the actual world.

A kid on a City Scooter had sped past and Rascal had watched him go, safe, now standing near the bus stop, waiting for the red DON'T WALK to switch to green WALK.

As far as the universe was concerned, he'd always been there, never in danger of death by hit-and-run. That was Rascal's mojo. He spent the following year using it, testing it, learning its limits. He spent the year after that refining and employing it to stack cash, to stay out of trouble and off everybody's radar.

He related all this to Runaround and Deacon, who took it in with simple nods of understanding.

"We didn't have all that time," said Runaround eventually. "But, yeah, me and Deacon got the mojo too. I mean, not like yours, but–"

"Runaround, she flickers," said Deacon. "Like watching a strobe, yeah? When she stops, she's in another spot. Could be ten foot away, could be another room. Either way, it takes about a second."

"Deacon changes, like, the world, I guess," said Runaround, moving closer to the big man. Then she faltered a little, obviously not knowing how to relate what she meant.

"Nah, nah, nah, luv," said Deacon, gently placing his hand on hers. Just bits of it. Like, if the walls need to be concrete instead of plaster, I give it a little think, a bit of a nudge and, poof, they always were concrete and never nothing else."

Jesus, thought Rascal, as visions of gold and cash flooding the world took over his mind. Jesus H Christ.

"When we get out of here," he said aloud, grinning the way he hadn't in two years, "the Midnight Ramblers are going to feast."

Dr. Woo cleared his throat.

"Yes. About that," he said. "There's a problem. More than one, in fact."

It was at that moment Rascal realized Proud Marry wasn't with them. He was puzzled and a little nervous that she hadn't even crossed his mind. He hadn't quite forgotten her, not exactly, she just sort of wasn't. She occupied a strange non-place in his memory that he now had to actively look at to see.

"Yeah," said Deacon, seeing the realization wash over his friend. "Wondering about Marry, innit?"

"Where is she?" said Rascal. "She was right with me when the wave hit. If I'm here and you three skated..."

"Unlucky," said Deacon Blue. He sounded like a coffin lid coming down. Runaround looked like every widow at every funeral in the history of the world.

"Well," said Rascal, feeling himself falling into that granite state of mind he had for dealing with tragedy. "Somebody, tell me what happened to Marry."

4: BOSS

Proud Marry led the Midnight Ramblers in nearly every way except name. The Ramblers were all equals, a pure democracy, each with their own special talent none of the others could match and never tried, but it was Marry who drove.

Amazonian in stature, with the focus of a laser, she was that sort of player with that sort of personality and, most important, that sort of mind.

Of course, she would be followed over most hills even when leading the tiny herd of cats constituted by the Ramblers.

Her head was always cool, her tactics unassailable, and her ability to mete out debate-ending violence on anyone who crossed her or them unparalleled.

When the Shimmer Wave passed and the world outside had gone away, apparently taking Rascal with it, Proud Marry never blinked. She accepted the new state of play as unavoidable but determined she would damned well make it as temporary as she could.

She made her way to the central lab where she found Deacon and Runaround, picking up the pieces of themselves as well as an extremely unsettled Dr. Woo, now frantically working to reassemble his damaged M-brane Bridge.

It quickly became clear that, while both her compatriots had acquired some new talents, Marry and the doctor had none. Again, Proud Marry didn't blink. She spent the first hour putting together and implementing a battle plan.

Scout the site, locate and seal any vulnerable spaces, lock down food and medical supplies and do anything necessary to help Dr. Woo get them all the hell out of this place.

The next hour was spent putting her plan into motion. It was simple, sensible, easy to enact and went straight to hell the second they stepped out of the lab.

There were things out there in the corridors, deadly, vicious things, invisible to any surveillance, impossible to fight. The first attack took the three Ramblers totally unawares and, before Runaround could get them all out, Proud Marry had been taken.

"Wait," said Rascal, interrupting the tale. "What do you mean, taken?"

"Don't know what else to call it," said Runaround, miserably. For, her these events had taken place only in the last few hours. "We could barely even see them. They came out of the walls, and the floors, and everywhere."

"Burn when they touch you, don't they?" said Deacon Blue.

"Marry told me to get Deacon out but I couldn't just leave her," said Runaround. "While we were arguing about it, Marry got distracted, and one of them—one of them--"

Runaround wilted then, pulled down into herself by emotions too big and unfamiliar for her to process.

"It touched her, didn't it," said Deacon, his tone flat. "Touched her and she got pulled into it, pulled away. Apart, maybe. Anyway, old girl is gone."

Except...

Except Rascal didn't think she was. It didn't make sense the three of them got the mojo but Marry hadn't. Maybe there was something hinky about where the Doc had been standing when the wave hit but Marry had been right with Rascal. The wave had molded him, right through the pile of protective jumpsuits he'd slid under. Marry had just been standing there, naked in the face of that chaos.

"So...what are we doing here?" said Runaround after she'd zipped them back to the section of the building where she'd found Rascal. "Besides making my skin crawl."

"Couple things," said Rascal, already casting around the nexus of five corridors. He was sure it had been a T-junction his last time through, but he was equally certain this was the right spot. "One, I'm gonna find Proud Marry and two, if I say "bolt 'you're out of here, yeah?"

"Hey, I love the rescue Marry part," said Runaround, also swiveling her gaze. They'd fallen into the mutually defensive back-to-back stance out of habit. She had her knives in her hands though. What she meant to do with them Rascal couldn't guess. "Her not being dead would be cake and icing."

"But...?"

"No way I do a dash and leave you to get gutted," said Runaround. "I go, I'm pulling you out with me."

"Nix," said Rascal. "Either I'm right and Marry's coming home or I'm not and anyone here in...about fifty seconds...is a bloody corpse. I don't love that for you, Susie. Sorry. You gotta break out when I say."

Her hand was in his then, and she was yanking him towards her, smashing hard hot kiss into his mouth, grinding her body against him like they were both teenagers in somebody's hay loft

"Runaround," it had taken him a second longer than he liked to break the kiss and now he was gasping a little. She had that effect. She always had that effect. "Susie, what the hell?"

"I love you, you stupid, sideways shit," she said, whiplash grin and all. "And I love Marry and Deacon the same. I'm more likely to eat a gun than leave you jammed up and you know it. And I'm never eating a gun."

She wouldn't leave and they had ten more seconds, give or take. The walls were already starting to shift and flicker, the air around them was already getting sticky and sharp. So he told her.

He told her what he was guessing about the mojos they'd all got, how they were all variations on the same theme and, if what he'd felt on his last dance with the monster was what he thought, Marry had not come through the wave unaltered.

"You can see the thing?"

"Not see, exactly," he said. "Not feel, exactly, either, y'know?"

She seemed to get it. The way she could move now was nothing like running anywhere, was it? There weren't the words to say what it actually was, but her mojo was enough like Rascal's that she could sort of grasp it.

She was about to ask him what he actually planned to do when the things–or the one thing–showed up, and it was all too late.

The world kaleidoscoped around them. The floors were suddenly walls, the walls were suddenly waterfalls, and the air was suddenly molasses and a rainbow of colors never seen in this world.

The monster—or monsters—was the center of that storm at the same time it was every edge of it and a cyclone pushing it along. Did the monster roar? It did not.

The monster—or monsters—screamed and howled, a choir of anguish and rage. Runaround flickered and was at the far end of one of the corridors for just a second before she screamed from something slashing her from a direction Rascal couldn't describe. She flickered again and was back with him, down on one knee, a massive bloody gash bleeding rivers down her side.

"Holy shit," she managed to rasp as she pulled herself back up to her feet. "You better be right about this."

He was doing better than she was, able to sense the strikes before they hit, able to leap clear before the monster—or monsters—erupted out of a surface that was suddenly no more solid than mist.

It couldn't surprise him again like it had before, he could sense the non-shape of it, like the taste of impending rain on his tongue. If he was right, if he timed it right, he might just be able to–

"Susie," he yelled over the din. "Take my hand!"

She did, without hesitation, and he was leaping forward, pulling her along into the heart of the maelstrom of claws and scream. His freehand was outstretched in front of him, reaching trying to touch. When the thing—or things—bit him, it felt like it was taking his arm off at the elbow.

Rascal did scream, of course he did. The touch of those claws was like being bitten by teeth made of lightning. So, Rascal did scream but he didn't pull away.

Rascal E-X-T-E-N-D-E-D.

Rascal E-X-T-E-N-D-E-D and the rainbow cyclone stopped, froze in place around them. Runaround flickered violently but she didn't vanish. She didn't speak or let loose of his hand either. Despite her seeming to be in some sort of constant motion, it was clear to Rascal that she couldn't move.

Then his reach hand found fingers reaching back. The fingers had a hand attached and they grasped, pulling him forward hard and fast. Runaround came along with him, her fingers on his other hand vise-tight and the rest of her flickering away like mad.

The maelstrom was still everywhere but this little pocket had a floor and normal walls and one of his only friends, looking weary and battered as he'd never seen her.

"Well, goddamn," said Proud Marry. "Took you long enough."

"Everybody thought you were dead," said Rascal, not releasing her hand. A little electric sizzle had passed between them when they touched and he wasn't sure it was a good idea to break the connection. Not yet.

"That's what I thought of you," she said, allowing the tiniest of grins on her lips. "Ramblers die hard, I guess."

"Seems that way," said Rascal.

"What's that lightshow attached to you?"

"That's Runaround," said Rascal, and watched Marry's face crumble a little, just enough to show just how much toll all this was taking. Until that moment he'd have bet all his money nothing would ever rattle Proud Marry.

"Is she–" Marry struggled to hold tight and get the words out. "Is Susie—"

"She's fine," said Rascal, hoping it was still true. "A little weird for wear but who isn't, y'know?"

"Deacon?"

"Deacon too," said Rascal. "We're all good, Marry. We made it."

"Where's Deacon," she said, pulling it together. Rascal smiled a little watching her rebuild her mask. When she'd reset her normal stoic façade, it felt like coming home. "Why's he not with you?"

"Deacon's on the other side of that," Rascal nodded at the frozen maelstrom. "He's protecting the mad scientist."

"Didn't think there was anything on the other side. Not anymore."

"There is. The whole facility is basically intact," said Rascal. "Doesn't like staying in one place for too long and it keeps changing its floor map but–"

"Protecting a scientist?"

Rascal nodded.

"Protecting from what?"

It was weird, just standing there, holding hands, talking with the chaos of color, shape, and sound frozen all around them. To Rascal it was as if they were in the eye of the sculpture of a tsunami made of rainbows.

But he didn't let go of Marry's hand and she never pulled back from his. On some instinctual level they both knew, right here and now, that would be a monumentally bad idea.

"Those things that got you," said Rascal. "They keep coming at Dr. Woo. And anybody else who comes in here. Killed at least ten guys, from what I know. Deacon's keeping them off the doc while he works on a way out of this."

Rascal told her about Miss Metal and her mission and about Dr. Woo and Arkworx screwing him over and how the whole world was in danger from the effects of the M-brane Bridge, and that they all needed to get the hell out of this quicker than yesterday.

"And, with all that, you came back for me?" said Marry in a voice Rascal had never heard from her. It was equal parts gravel and roses and from it, he knew she loved him and that she knew he loved her. "On a hunch?"

"Not a hunch," said Rascal. "More like a feeling. I didn't know what it was the first time I got attacked but, now that I'm here, now that I touch you, I'm dead sure."

"Sure about what?"

"There's no monster, Marry," said Rascal. "There's no monsters."

"Pretty sure you're wrong on that," she said but she still didn't release his hand. If anything, her grip got a bit tighter. "I think, if I wasn't holding your hand right now, they would come for you, and you wouldn't get away."

She meant the maelstrom and she was right. Even in this weird still point they occupied, even with the chaos congealed like gelatin all around them, unmoving, maybe unable to move for the moment, he could feel its anger. He could feel its screaming desire to lash out, to rend, to bite and tear, to trample the whole world in an avalanche of rage.

"You're right," he said at last. "All that already tore chunks out of me and Runaround. And all those guys. It keeps trying it with Dr. Woo and Deacon. But not you, Marry. It took you but you're fine. Why's that, do you think?"

"I don't–" She faltered. Proud Marry was a lot of things—thief, sometime killer, bar brawler, and a bonafide super-genius, but she was not a liar. So it was sort of amusing watching her try to lie to herself for the first time. "I don't understand what you're saying."

"Come on," said Rascal in the soothing tone one may have kept for a wounded pet. "You know. Same way I know exactly how many ways we could all die here if you don't admit it. Same way Runaround can, well, run around anything, anywhere. You know. The Shimmer Wave gave us all the mojo, baby. This one is you."

She did know. Maybe she'd suspected ever since she got pulled away from the others. Maybe she'd just been resisting the idea that what she thought was the death of her friends and maybe the world beyond was all her fault.

Of all the Midnight Ramblers, Proud Marry was the one who never ever lost control of herself. She was the one who finished brawls but never started one even once. She was the last punch, the end of the line for any static that came her way.

He'd once sat terrified in a stolen Humvee as Marry drove them clear of a job gone bad. Never mind she'd never actually driven a Humvee. Never mind it was the middle of the Balkan night and she didn't know the road that wound around the edge of some particularly ugly mountains. Never mind every turn was a hairpin and she never lifted the pedal off the floor. Marry never flinched, never blinked, never broke a sweat. Marry drove them clear, in the dark with no headlights.

Marry was in control. Marry had to be. He life before the Ramblers was a shitstorm of beatings from her father and that first couple of boyfriends until she'd had enough. It was at least two attempted rapes after she'd thought herself free of that first cadre of dirtbags. No one would ever see those men again, not even the many pieces of each of them she'd scattered all over Belgium.

Marry never flinched. Marry never blinked. Marry was never anything less than in total control of herself, one hundred percent of every day.

Rascal had wondered, early in their association, why? Why so tight? Why all the time? Even her lovemaking was…not restrained exactly but planned, almost choreographed. Not like Susie, who was a carnival of improvisation between the sheets. He'd talked with Deacon about it once and all he'd said was, "Marry burns, mate. Can't you tell? That woman's got enough Pissed Off in her to fry the whole damn world."

They never discussed it again. All the Ramblers had their things, their scars, their buried malformations. Rascal's was trust. He didn't, not anyone, anywhere, anytime, except the other Ramblers. They held everything good about them in their hands and none of them had ever dropped it, not once, not ever. Runaround couldn't be on her own. For some reason that she would never reveal, she needed to be amongst people, her people, nearly always or she would fold up into herself and maybe not come out again. Deacon Blue carried sadness with him like a conjoined twin.

Oh, Deacon laughed and he danced and he flexed his little black book of contacts to get the Ramblers the things they wanted and the places they wanted and the lives they wanted. He kept them safe from all predators, criminal or otherwise, but Deacon's sadness was as real as the black lion tattoo that covered his back.

The world had done all of them wrong enough that, in the end, the Ramblers belonged to the Ramblers and no one and nothing else.

"It is me," said Marry at last, her gaze locking on Rascal's again. "They're all me. How?"

"Dunno," said Rascal. "Don't care. All that matters is you need to reign it in, like we do with our mojos, so we can all get the hell out of this."

"Gonna ask again," she said. "How?"

He thought for a second, then, "When I do my thing, I call it *extending*. Like I'm stretching me out into that other direction, the one with no name? Like I'm spreading myself over all these alternatives, possibilities. Like I'm stretching all the way out. Maybe, with you, you need to pull it in?"

He watched her think about it for all of two seconds. He watched her chew it. Her hand squeezed his, hard. Proud Marry nodded one sharp nod and her brow furrowed in concentration.

At first, nothing happened.

Then Rascal felt it. It sparked in his fingers, that strange electricity flowing between them, pinpricks at first now surging over his hand, across his body and into Runaround too. They were a circuit of something now.

"Rascal?" said Runaround and he could tell, without looking, the flickering was done. She was herself again. "What's happening?"

He didn't know, exactly, but the electricity was ramping through him and her and back to Marry like a river. All around them, the maelstrom shrugged itself to motion. He could hear the screaming choir, first at a seeming distance, then louder and louder. The walls and floors quaked and shimmered. It seemed the entire structure was fighting against collapse.

"I'm doing it," said Marry, through gritted teeth. "I think I'm-I'm-"

There was a horrible flash of thunderous light, that same prisming of colors when Runaround had dragged him clear of the monster—Marry's– attack. The lightning in their bodies seemed to be screaming too, wanting to erupt out of them and, yes, damn it, it hurt now!

Rascal felt his body fall to its knees, never letting go of either hand. He felt Runaround drop behind him. He looked up at Marry, suffused in the rainbowing glowing lights and what seemed to him like the onslaught of a million of her ghostly reflections being pulled into her body.

Marry screamed without sound.

The whole world seemed about to explode.

Everything was burning, blinding white light, and then...

And then...

And then...

It all stopped. The maelstrom, the burning electric current threading through them, the pain wracking his nerves, all of it gone in an instant. And there was Marry, on her knees as well, gasping for air as if she'd run five marathons in ten seconds.

For a moment he saw her shifting, her shape flickering, growing bigger, smaller, monstrous, beautiful, naked, armored, holding a vicious-looking serrated ax, holding a pistol that looked like something out of a sci-fi movie and then, finally, just Marry, only Proud Marry kneeling on the floor of a refreshment alcove beside two of her best friends.

"Marry," said Runaround in a tiny voice. "You okay, baby girl?"

Proud Marry took a moment, just one more heartbeat, to pull herself together and, when she looked up, she was cool and calm and everything she'd ever been to them.

"Come on," she said, letting Rascal's hand go as she got to her feet, "Let's get the hell out of here."

"It should work," Dr. Woo told the reunited Midnight Ramblers. "Now that I've had some time to observe you all and to think, yes, it should work."

He'd explained it but, of the Ramblers, only Rascal really had a handle on what was about to happen. Marry was smarter but she had no experience yet with how her mojo really worked.

Each of them was somehow connected to the clusters of branched reality that sprouted from every moment, every decision made or not made. It manifested differently in each of them but the connection was the point.

"So, what," said Runaround. "We all just flex out powers and we poof out of Oz, back to Kansas?"

"Essentially," said Dr. Woo. "With the Bridge repaired, it will act as a sort of anchor or stabilizer. When I activate it, you four will...'flex'...and we should all return to normal spacetime."

"What about this place," said Deacon Blue, swinging one big hand to indicate the whole facility. "This all coming back too?"

Dr. Woo actually shrugged at that.

"Possibly," he said. "I just don't know. This is all guesswork and hope as much as anything else. It depends a great deal on the timing."

"All at once or we get nothing, right," said Proud Marry.

"That's about it, young lady, yes."

Rascal smiled. If there was one thing the Midnight Ramblers did well it was work in perfect synch. If this escape hung on that, they were home free.

He thought about Miss Metal and her surviving mercs, waiting for him to "solve the problem" of Woo and his little gadget, and his smile broadened. There was no way the little sphere she'd given him wasn't some kind of bomb and the odds of this stun bringing back anything beyond the five of them were low. If everyone got back at once and in one piece, Miss Metal would have a lot more problems handling the whole crew than she had with just Rascal alone and that had been nearly too much for her. If only Woo and the Ramblers made it back, Metal and Arkworx would be stuck together in whatever this non-place was, outside time and space, with no way to get back.

Rascal liked Door #2. Yeah, he liked it lot.

"So, we doing this or what?" he said.

"We are," said Dr. Woo. "There's no time like the present, I always say. When you're ready, we will go on my count."

Rascal nodded and took Runaround's hand, which took Marry's, which took Deacon's, which took Rascal's other, forming a ring around Dr. Woo and the M-brane Bridge.

"Ready," said Rascal.

"Right," said Dr. Woo, his hand poised over the activation key. "Five, four, three, two"–

Later, years later, when Rascal had a minute to think and more to jot, he'd call it the Psycho Calliope because that was the closest he could get to a description of that awful moment outside of proper time.

Light and color.
Strobing.
Flickering.
Screaming.
Howling.
Sobbing.
Singing.
Down.
Into.
Out of.
Over.
Down
and
down
and
down through a whirling cyclone of shapes and feeling and time ticking-tick-ticking in his head like a cathedral bell, like a thousand.

Forty fingers reaching, falling away from each other, becoming smoke, inside mist, inside fog, eyes bleeding tears, throats screaming fire, the terrible melody of despair and regret and then...

and then...

and...

Glass, cool and smooth beneath him, supporting his prone body without crack or collapse. He knew it was glass, the same he'd seen before all this, before he'd found the Ramblers and lost them again. It was thick, solid, and strangely comforting in its persistent reality. That much glass, spread over such a space should not have existed at all yet, it did, and it would and there wasn't a damned thing anybody was doing about it.

He pushed against it, slowly, quietly, lifting himself up. His sense of absolute exposure was almost a physical sensation in him. He felt like a fish who'd suddenly found itself transported from cool dark ocean depths to the dry, glaring death of the Sahara.

If Miss Metal's boys were watching, if there were rifle sights trained on him already, he'd be morgued before he could blink.

Rascal blinked.

Rascal blinked again.

After the third one without parts of him being exploded by bullets passing through, he risked standing up. He looked around and, sure as hell, that football field of new perfect glass covered the same area it had, right down to the edge of the Potomac. The KEEP OUT fence was still up and from the hint of a deeper chill in the Autumn air, Winter was still coming.

Otherwise, Rascal was absolutely alone.

It was a simple matter to E-X-T-E-N-D his way back to Miss Metal's little secret base—cleared out completely now, of course. The structure under the house was there, but anyone looking would find only an oddly complex concrete bunker and a small network of corridors and tunnels, some leading up to a hidden drive-out in a nondescript alley, but no sign of any occupant or goods ever stored inside.

Crazy rich people do nutty things with their money, would likely be the consensus.

Rascal stayed in the empty bunker for some time, weeping quietly, thinking what the hell he was going to do next, then weeping some more.

Arkworx Unlimited was gone again, probably never coming back, never unboxing any of the poor souls trapped inside—not Dr. Woo, not Miss Metal and her mercs, and not his friends.

He'd lost the Ramblers. Again. His friends were gone, again, this time with no means of getting them back. He was nearly ten hours into his grief before he realized that wasn't exactly true, was it?

Rascal might not have the tools or the skills to re-open Dr. Woo's M-brane Bridge—but somebody out there did. Somebody must, he thought.

Miss Metal's crew weren't spooks, meaning they worked for somebody and that somebody had resources, records, and, very probably, some sort of big ongoing scheme. They must have all that or they couldn't have grabbed Rascal in the first place, could they? No. They'd hunted him, stalked him, and found one way to partially thwart his ability to get away. None of that could have been easy.

Yeah, somebody out there had a plan and, having spent all that time and effort already, was not likely to give it up. No, somebody would pivot, figure a new tack and keep moving.

Good advice, Rascal thought, and more importantly, feeling like himself again.

They'd hunted him. Now he would be the hunter.

They'd screwed the Ramblers. Now they were the ones who could expect some payback.

He would find whoever was at the bottom of this. He would break every plan, every asset, every god damn rule, written or unwritten, and he would bring the Midnight Ramblers home.

Failing that, somebody would learn just how creative Rascal could get with his mojo, and just how much better it would have been to just suicide out and go straight to hell, instead of facing the torments he would visit on them.

You took your best shot, whoever the hell you are, he thought. *Now, it's my turn.*

PHENOMENON STORIES, PART I

BY MICHAEL JAN FRIEDMAN

Traction—Matthew Wang, underneath his mask—had underestimated the competition.

It wasn't a mistake he'd made in his youth as a world-class soccer player, when the slightest miscue could have resulted in a goal for the other team. And it *certainly* wasn't a mistake he'd made as a costumed Phenomenon, when lives—his own included—depended on the way he applied his friction powers.

Yet it was a mistake he'd managed to make just moments earlier, when he reduced the friction under his heavy-duty boot treads so he could accelerate his assault on the seven-footer who'd dragged an elderly man out of his car in midtown, then threatened to kill him if a Phenomenon didn't't show up 'freakin' *now!*"

Traction had been only a couple of blocks away, making an appearance at a firehouse fundraiser, so he'd volunteered to respond. "I've got this," he had told his United Front teammate Scopes.

"I'll send backup," Scopes had told him over the comm device in Traction's mask.

But Traction hadn't waited.

After all, he'd fought his share of bad guys in the years he'd been a member of United Front. And by using his mastery over friction, he'd always gotten the best of them.

Accelerating as he approached the giant with the bulging muscles—that was a tactic he'd used to good effect more times than he could count. It was a solid idea, one that always worked.

Because his adversaries never moved fast enough to get out of the way of his friction-minimized attack, or to grab him as he went by. Unfortunately, this one *did*.

Which was why Traction found himself dangling from the giant's fist by the fabric of his tunic, his feet a foot and a half off the ground—as the giant pulled back his other fist, presumably to reduce Traction's face to a fine, bloody pulp.

Luckily for Traction, he could do more with his powers than make himself accelerate. He could make it impossible to hold onto something—in this case, his uniform. Which he did, the skinniest fraction of a second before his adversary could plant his knuckles in Traction's mouth.

"Hey!" the big guy cried out as Traction slithered from his grasp.

He tried to get ahold of Traction a second time. But by then the Phenomenon had touched down and was off again—this time accelerating *away* from his adversary.

But only for a moment. Because there was still the elderly guy to worry about, and any other bystander the bruiser could get his hands on.

Traction had never been much of a planner. On the soccer field, he'd always gone with his instincts. And there at an intersection in midtown Manhattan, he did the same thing.

He applied the brakes to his progress, skidding to a halt. Then he turned and went at the giant again. Except this time, he made the asphalt slippery under his enemy's boot soles—so much so that when the guy reached for Traction, his feet would shoot out from under him.

That was what was supposed to happen—but it didn't. Too late, Traction realized why. *Some kind of anti-slip tech*, he had time to think.

Then he was in the worst possible place—the bruiser's wheelhouse. At the last possible moment, Traction used his

power to turn his face super-slick—enough to make his adversary's fist slide instead of catching him square.

But the big guy had gotten enough of Traction to send him reeling, his face half-numb with the impact he'd absorbed.

By the time he stopped rolling, his adversary was almost on top of him again. He tried to get his feet under him, to find his balance. But it was no use. His legs had turned to rubber.

One more shot—this one on target—and Traction would be a goner. Even though his fog, he knew that with a certainty.

Then he heard something. Something sharp and piercing and high-pitched.

A siren, he realized. *The police...*

Traction turned to face his adversary again—but the giant was gone. *Thank heaven*, Traction thought, and sank to the pavement.

A moment later, a face swam into view. A woman. A police officer. "You okay, bud?" she asked.

Traction coughed up some blood, wiped it from his lips with the back of his hand, and rasped "Truthfully...? I've been better."

LA SOMBRA RETURNS!

BY ALEX SEGURA

SOMBRA JOURNAL - 4/14

Martinez's birthday is like any other day for me. A chance to hit the street. To put force behind my words. To wash away the grime and blood coating this neighborhood with my own kind of justice. A justice without conflict. I do the real work. I get my hands dirty. Nothing else matters.

I let out a dry laugh.

Martinez's birthday? A day for work, nothing else.

Or a night, I should say. Martinez called it early today, exhausted from a long, drawn-out City Council meeting, a barrage of interviews, and a tedious phone call from her mother. An idealistic paper-pusher with little power to make actual change. She's always tired, her mom complained. Of course she was. Because when Queens Councilwoman Andrea Martinez closed her eyes, she didn't shimmy off to dream land.

She became someone else.

But enough about her. She's just the vessel—a means to an end. I have work to do.

I'll report back later.

***

Andrea Martinez groaned as she watched the coffee machine drip its final delivery into the waiting pot. Before it could beep to alert her it was done, Andrea grabbed the pot and filled her waiting mug. It was almost eight in the morning and she was running late. Andrea hated being late.

Her head was pounding, but this was standard. Every few nights, she'd wake up feeling like she'd gone twelve rounds with George Foreman—aches, pains, a few cuts and scrapes. And the clothes—battered goggles, a lengthy purple scarf, and a billowing coat that felt like something out of a pulp novel. She'd find pieces of what she realized over time was La Sombra's costume spread around her apartment like breadcrumbs for Andrea to chase down.

She liked to think she'd settled into this routine, but that felt like insanity—hell, it was the definition of insanity. But what choice did Andrea have? She was an elected city official, trying desperately to represent her constituents in spite of the various corporate, criminal, and political interests stacked against her. She didn't have time to figure out what was wrong with her brain—why she felt the need to dress up like a crimefighter while in a fugue state and do God knows what. It'd been months of the same thing, but she knew it wouldn't last. The world wasn't built to keep secrets, especially when the people trying to do it were famous. And Andrea Martinez had become famous.

Just a few months earlier, before Andrea had even been sworn in, her predecessor—a hack and corrupt politico named Paul Persinio—had been snagged in a complicated scam to frame Andrea for the hit-and-run murder of a child on Halloween. The evening crime had never been solved, but Persinio had managed to doctor photos to make it look like Andrea was the culprit. If not for the interference of local *Queens Beacon* reporter Will Shriver, Persinio might have succeeded. Shriver and, of course, La Sombra.

Andrea rubbed her temples and closed her eyes. These were the moments that bothered her. The moments she could feel and almost see what La Sombra had seen. She remembered standing in Shriver's sparse newsroom. Recalled the reporter turning and telling her he knew who she really was. Warning her to stay on the right side of the law. But as quickly as the vision formed in her mind's eye, it dissipated—like a puff of cigarette smoke catching the wind.

"Say again?" Will Shriver asked, wheeling his desk around to look at John Nacinovich, the latest intern-turned-reporter at The Queens Beacon. There'd been another round of layoffs just the month prior, and the small local paper had gutted its political section, losing two reporters and merging the editorial oversight under one staffer. Will had seen this program before. It sucked.

But some losses become other's gains, and in this case, Nacinovich was the beneficiary. A sharp, diligent, and hardworking college grad, the guy had an idealism and drive Shriver thought long gone. He wanted to like Nacinovich. But with that drive and idealism came a lot of questions, and Will Shriver was too tired to play mentor to another generation. He'd tried that already.

"I asked if you'd looked at those notes I sent you," Nacinovich said with a smile. "About the bodies. The murdered migrants. I have a theory-"

Shriver let out a long sigh and spun his chair back around. He grabbed the neatly stapled stack of pages he'd set aside and turned to face Nacinovich.

"These? No, I haven't. I don't know if you've noticed, John, but--"

"We are understaffed and overworked, yes–I have noticed," Nacinovich said, still smiling, but the joy long gone. "But I'm chasing this story and I think there's something there. You know better than most that all the institutional memory in this place is gone. You're the only person who's been here longer than a few years."

"It's my cross to bear," Shriver said with a shrug. He could almost see Nacinovich biting his tongue.

"Mr. Shriver," he said through gritted teeth. "I could use your help. Can we touch base on this later? I'd greatly appreciate it. I need some support, and my editors only talk to me when they want me to run out to a crime scene. But this feels bigger. It's important. These people are coming here and they have no support system. They're ending up dead on our streets and no one is speaking for them. I just need time to work on the story. Time and guidance. I feel like it's tied to something bigger. If I just had the pieces, I could see the bigger picture. You know that feeling, right?"

Shriver did. And he actually had read Nacinovich's notes. But he wasn't sure he could bring himself to help the guy. Because if he did, it'd bring him back to the one ethical decision he'd made as a reporter that kept him up most nights. A choice he'd made not long ago—one that he'd thought would protect a friend.

But may have released a monster.

***

"So they pay this person, who then gets them here to the U.S., without any papers, and then they owe that person what? Hours? Days of their lives?"

Andrea's question hung between her and her chief of staff, Arturo Arbona. He shook his head gently and continued. Arbona was her rock. Organized, methodical, driven, and passionate, Andrea knew she was lucky to have such a solid number two watching her back. But she also knew the time would come when he'd want to embark on his own, perhaps run for office himself. She'd been meaning to ask him, too, but it always got too busy. Why would someone so talented not run, she wondered? But the question kept getting deferred. His voice snapped her out of her brief mental detour.

"They pay them ten thousand up front, then once they get here, however they get here, they have to start paying the rest of the balance," Arbona said.

"The vig," Andrea said, absentmindedly. "They have to cover the vig."

"What?"

Andrea shook her head. She didn't know where that word had come from. She was certain she'd never read it or said it aloud.

"Sorry, never mind. Keep going."

She rubbed the bridge of her nose as Arbona resumed reading from his notes.

"The term for this kind of—well, operator, is "snakehead. ' They find a way to bring in someone illegally and then profit from the work they do in this country." Arbona said. "It seems like a percentage of the new migrants we're seeing come in are doing it this way."

Andrea leaned back slightly in her chair. She tried to focus, but could feel her vision blurring. She'd spent extra time trying to dab over the scrapes and bruises, especially the slight shiner on her left eye. But she knew it hadn't been enough, based on the look Arbona had given her when she stumbled into the office that morning. She felt like everything was unmoored. But she had to work. She had to help the people in this neighborhood. She could figure out the other stuff, the Sombra stuff, later.

"Do we have any idea who this is?" Andrea asked "This "snakehead'?"

Arbona flipped a few pages in his notebook. "You know that organic health food store on Lefferts, by the movie theater?"

"Thistle?" Andrea said. "You're kidding, right? The guy that owns that place is a...snakehead, or whatever you called it?"

Arbona shrugged. "That's what I'm hearing. Feds haven't returned my calls or emails. Local PD has nothing to say. But if you believe the papers, the guy who owns the place—Diego Carranza—isn't just making bank selling tofu sandwiches and green juices," Arbona said with a scoff. "He's tapped into some kind of infrastructure that allows him to stow these poor people away. On boats, mostly. Many of them die on the way.

Some arrive owing thousands. You can imagine what happens when they don't pay."

"What do you mean?"

"They get hurt, Andrea—or worse," Arbona said.

"The murders then, those migrants that have ended up dead," Andrea said. "He's the one taking them out. People who just want a fresh start. People desperate for some kind of hope."

Arbona tapped his pencil in response.

"Carranza isn't just trafficking people here. He's killing the ones that can't pay the bill."

Andrea nodded. But she wasn't listening anymore. Her mind was somewhere else.

***

SOMBRA JOURNAL 4/16

The glass shattered with ease. My boot hit right at the center of the door's lower pane. I could hear bustling on the other side. No, scurrying. Feet on linoleum. I moved fast. Unlocked the storefront door from the inside and stepped into the darkness. Even in the pitch black, I could see him—could smell his vile stench. The smell of the guilty. Of someone who knew they were being hunted.

I leapt over the boxes. Strewn on the floor to impede my progress. I ran down the center aisle, knocking over vitamins and paper plates and whatever else had been stacked to prevent me from finding him.

I hear a low yelp and pivot left. A crack of moonlight shines through the store's main window and I catch sight of him, trying to get his basement door open. He never will.

I tackle him, feel his body slam into the wall behind him, hear his head thump against it, then against the floor. Then an unexpected crunching sound, a scream of pain. I try to pull away, but I can't. I'm tangled in the person, struggling for purchase.

Then the screams stop. The arms pushing and pulling at me go limp.

I stand up and look down.

I see a dead man.

John Nacinovich didn't believe in coincidences. He wasn't the spiritual type, though. He believed in the reach of power, and that tiny things happen because big things are put into motion by powerful people. Tonight was one of those moments, as he sat at his—well, anyone's—cubicle in the cramped Queens Beacon offices. He heard the crackle of the police band radio. The hurried call for a squad car and an ambulance. The familiar address on Lefferts. The name said hastily.

It felt too convenient, Nacinovich thought.

He jotted down an address, grabbed his coat, and left.

***

Andrea Martinez woke up on the floor. The room was dark and her face ached. She got up slowly, feeling every pop and pinch in her body as she straightened up. The throbbing in her knee. The still-healing cut down her left forearm. The bruise she knew was forming on her forehead.

She was in her apartment. She knew that much.

She reached up to the light switch in the foyer, but hesitated before flicking it on. What would she see? Who would she find?

She closed her eyes as the overhead lights came on. Then, slowly, she opened them.

It wasn't as bad as she thought. That's what ran through her mind first as she assessed the damage. She was wearing clean clothes. Pajama pants and a tee-shirt hastily chosen. But that was only the surface. She walked down the hall, wincing with each step, and looked at herself in the long mirror next to the coat closet. A black eye. A nasty-looking bruise on her forehead. Dirt-caked cuts on her arms and legs. Scratches and scrapes. She felt like she'd just run through a giant meat grinder, and felt worse. She felt her eyes welling up. Andrea Martinez looked away, unable to see the tears begin to streak down her face. But she felt them. And she knew something was very, very wrong.

"Who am I?" she said aloud.

No one was there to hear her.

***

Will Shriver heard the jangle of the bar's door as he brought the pint of Guinness to his lips. He swallowed and let out a brief sigh. He knew, he just knew, that whoever was coming into Cobblestone's Pub was coming to look for him.

And he was right.

He turned his stool slightly to see the familiar face of John Nacinovich, file folders clutched close to his body as he scanned the sprawling bar. Cobblestone's had been a hole in the wall a few years prior—the best kind of dive bar. A spot that felt lived-in and familiar. Recently, the owners had knocked through a wall and bought the adjacent space, sprucing up the place with a new paint job, better lighting, and a complete and utter loss of personality. Shriver wasn't sure why he still drank here. Maybe part of him was hoping he could manifest it back to what it once was. He knew that wasn't possible.

"Will?"

Nacinovich's words snapped him back to reality.

"Hey, John," he said. He'd only had a few rounds but tried to be mindful of his mannerisms. He didn't want the rookie to see him slurring his words. He was better than that. "What brings you here?"

"Well, I know this is your spot."

"My spot?"

"Larry on the press said you usually…end up here."

Shriver nodded. Larry was a prick.

"What do you need that can't wait until tomorrow?"

Nacinovich looked around, trying to get a sense of who could hear what he was about to say.

"I have a theory and I need your help," he said.

"The notes you sent?"

"It's more than that," Nacinovich said, eyes darting around. "Can we get a table?"

Shriver motioned toward the tables in the rear of the large bar."

"After you."

They walked through the mostly empty bar and found a booth near the back, adjacent to the bathrooms. Nacinovich laid out his files and looked up at Shriver.

"I think we need to talk," Nacinovich said slowly, like an HR rep before they laid you off.

Shriver slid into the seat across from her and took a long pull from his beer.

"Just get to it," he said. "I'm off the clock."

Nacinovich flipped through a few pages and stopped before looking up.

"You covered the Persinio case, right?"

Shriver nodded. "Yeah, so? Is this what's driving you to interrupt my--"

Nacinovich gently raised a hand. "I'm sorry to bother you off-hours, but I need some clarity. I've got all these details staring back at me, and I can form a solution, but I want to check with you before I--"

"Just cut to the chase," Shriver said. "What do you think is going on?"

Nacinovich sighed and dropped his notebook atop the files. He slid them off to the side.

"You sure?"

Shriver shrugged.

"I don't need the bread crumbs," he said. His voice sounded dry and tired. "You want to say something to me, say it."

Nacinovich tilted his head, as if trying to get a better look at him. "You know who she is."

Shriver met the other man's gaze but said nothing.

"You know who La Sombra is."

Shriver leaned forward. "Whether I know or not doesn't matter," he said, his voice a sharp whisper. "What does matter, kid, is if you know."

Nacinovich leaned back, his eyes still on Shriver, his disdainful frown saying more than he could put into words.

"What, you're judging me now?" Shriver said.

"You don't need me to judge you to feel bad," Nacinovich said. "But, to answer your question—yes, I have a very good guess. No alibis. Lots of coincidences. Still a guess. But I'd bet my car on it."

"Yeah?"

Nacinovich nodded.

"And you know what, Will?" he said. "Your knowing is a problem. Because if anyone else but me finds out you've been sitting on this nugget because of some twisted loyalty, then you might get an early drop-off in the next round of layoffs…or worse."

"Is that a threat?"

Nacinovich let out a humorless laugh. "Come on, Will. I'm not here to hurt you. I need help, dude. That's why I'm here."

Shriver shook his head. Now he was really confused.

"I need you to help me because someone is out to get La Sombra," Nacinovich said. "And they're about to frame your girl for murder."

Andrea heard the buzzer and almost jumped out of her fresh clothes.

She took a few deep breaths and scanned her living room for anything that might scream "vigilante crime fighter." Finding nothing, she walked toward the door and waited.

"Yes?"

"It's Arbona."

Andrea opened the door slowly and watched as her chief of staff walked in, not meeting her eyes yet. He seemed more wound up than usual.

"Diego Carranza is dead," Arbona said, turning around now and finally meeting her eyes. He then looked her up and down, his expression morphing from stoic determination to shock. "What the hell happened to you?"

Andrea looked herself over. She thought she'd done a good job of covering the major bruises and scrapes, but it'd been hasty and the lighting in her tiny Queens apartment was bad on a good day.

"What do you mean?"

"You...your arm is all cut up, and you look like you pancaked makeup over a black eye," Arbona said, stepping toward Andrea to get a better look. "What happened?"

Andrea backed away, hands held up defensively.

"I'm fine, okay?" she said. "Tell me about Carranza."

Arbona pulled out his phone and tapped the screen a few times. Then he handed it to Andrea. She took it hungrily. The top of the Queens Beacon website said it all.

VIGILANTE HERO TURNING INTO COLD-BLOODED KILLER?

Before Andrea could tap on the headline, Arbona took his phone back. He shook his head as he slid it back into his pocket.

"You believe this shit?" he asked, incredulously. "Not only do we have to deal with everything else—but now there's a killer in our neighborhood?"

Andrea's head was spinning. Visions crashed into her mind. She could see herself smashing into the store. Her fists swinging at a faceless man. The crunch of her knuckles making contact with cartilage. The soft moan as a life whooshed out of her target.

La Sombra was a killer, she thought.

Did that make Andrea one, too?

She shook her head, pushing and willing the thought away. There was so much she didn't understand. So much that she'd avoided. She couldn't ignore this anymore, she realized. But she needed to think.

"I need some time alone," Andrea said, motioning for the door. Arbona nodded. "I'll circle back with you later today."

"Get some rest, boss, you look...well, I'm worried," he said, a pitying expression on his face. "It's none of my business, but...if you need help, well--"

Andrea let out a dry laugh.

"I'm fine, Arturo, seriously," she said quickly. Once she saw how stricken he was, she course-corrected, placing a hand on his arm. "But thank you. Not sure what I'd do without my right-hand man."

He gave her a warm smile before turning to leave. Andrea watched as the door closed behind him.

She walked to the door and flipped both locks. She felt her heartbeat quicken. She had to deal with this. She had to face the dark, festering secret inside her. The shadow lurking above her that she'd tried so hard to ignore. But she couldn't anymore. Not if that part of her—that shadow-self--had done this. Or anything close to it.

She pulled out her fading green yoga mat and unfurled it across the floor of her living room. Andrea crossed her legs and sat, closing her eyes. She took in a deep, long breath and cleared her thoughts. She let herself drift, absorbing the sounds and sensations of the world around her. She tried to keep her mind empty, open. Not nudging, not forcing anything. She wanted to embrace whatever came, to welcome whatever other part of her hid behind her subconscious. She wanted to face this person. She wanted to talk.

Then she let out a long, pained scream.

***

SOMBRA JOURNAL 4/16
Martinez is foolish. Idealistic. Tries to do good within the system. The system is broken. A festering wound that can't be cured by esoteric means. The limb must be cut off. Cleanly. She doesn't understand that.
Can sense her anxiety and fears. People are getting close to the truth. Her double-life. But her double-life isn't mine. I am one person, La Sombra. I have my methods and whatever happens to her won't affect me. All that matters is my mission—and keeping it alive.
Arbona did something. Feel an imbalance. When he showed Martinez that image—that headline--it blurred something. I can see her now. She can see me. Have to fix that. Later. Now I need to do something else.
I need to find the truth.

"You're telling me this guy is innocent?" Shriver said, taking a long sip of his bodega coffee. He and Nacinovich were seated in the front seat of the guy's cluttered Prius, which was positioned across the street from Thistle, a health food store on Lefferts Boulevard. It was very late, and there was little activity on the street, which cut through the heart of Kew Gardens, Queens.

"Innocence is relative, I guess," Nacinovich said, looking out the driver's side window at the storefront, which was unlit and empty. They both hoped that would change soon, if Nacinovich's research proved to be right.

"But he's not dead, that's for sure," Nacinovich said, jostling in the cramped front seat, reaching across Shriver to grab a notebook from the glove compartment. "For some reason, though, people want us to think he's dead—and to think La Sombra had something to do with it."

"Hard to frame someone for murder when the vic is alive," Shriver said with a scoff.

Nacinovich looked at the older man and scoffed back.

"You'd be surprised," he said.

Suddenly, a tall figure stepped up to Lefferts from the LIRR train platform near a tax preparer and another bodega. They were dressed completely in black--cap, hoodie, pants…and mask. Whoever this was didn't want to be recognized, and seemed willing to go to great lengths to keep that from happening. Not exactly the epitome of innocence.

"Looks like we have a visitor," Nacinovich said.

"And another—look over there," Shriver said. He was almost leaning over Nacinovich, straining to point up above the storefronts that were all part of the same long building that ran down Lefferts Blvd. Nacinovich saw it after a moment. Or, rather—saw her.

Shriver looked at Nacinovich, a devious smile on his face.

"Ever talk to a real-life superhero before?"

***

SOMBRA JOURNAL 4/16

My head is throbbing. Every movement aches. Like something—someone—else is pulling at me. Stopping me from acting. From fulfilling my mission. I can hear her now— Martinez--in my head. Screaming to be let out. Angry. She can see me now. Can feel me controlling her—my—body. No matter. I can push through it. I can force her down. I have to deal with something first. An immediate problem. My wolf in sheep's clothing. My hidden enemy.

***

The man in black used a key to enter Thistle. He knew how to act in situations like this. Quickly, calmly, behaving like you belonged. Like you should be there, even if you were wearing a mask over your face and every inch of your clothing screamed "interloper." It was late at night. There wouldn't be anyone around. But still, the man in black knew how to behave. And he wouldn't be here long. He'd gotten the call from his informant at Forest Hills Hospital an hour or so ago. Carranza would be fine. He'd been badly beaten, but there would be no lasting damage aside from a few broken ribs and a sore jaw. Whoever had come at him had done it fast and hard. The man in black shook his head. He'd hoped for the reality to inch closer to his ruse, to buy him some time. To finish the work he'd taken on from the boss. That's what he called her, at least. But life never worked out the way you wanted it, and he had to act fast.

He made his way through the long aisles of the health food store to the tiny office in the back. That door was unlocked. He flicked the light on and started rummaging through the papers strewn about the small desk jammed into the corner of the phone booth-like space. Invoices, delivery orders, receipts. But the man in black knew what he wanted. What he needed, really. The manifest.

A few weeks ago, a raggedy transport vessel known as The Wager had made a hasty landfall in the Rockaways, abandoning hundreds of migrants from all corners of the world. Central America. China. The whistle stop tour the ship had been on had taken months, avoiding surveillance, a false flag and registration getting it past most checkpoints. It promised to be a huge pay day for the man in black—and it had been. Hundreds of thousands of dollars. Desperate cash collected by people clamoring to leave their homelands for a shot at the American dream, a dream that might not even exist anymore. The man in black had been diligent, too—collecting the fees like a zealous creditor. But he'd been in this game for a while, and he knew for every batch of timely payments, there would be stragglers. The people begging for more time. The excuses varied, but the message was the same: Just gimme a few more weeks, boss, then we'll be square. Illness, job woes, family problems. The man in black had heard it all. But at a certain point, he had to show strength. Because all the man in black had was his reputation, and if people felt like they could get past him, what would that mean for the next boat? If he let three pass this time, next time it'd be ten. Then twenty. Pretty soon, the entire operation would leave him in the red. So he took care of business. He hadn't been hasty about it. Carranza had served as a nice patsy. The store a serviceable front. All the evidence pointed to him and his tiny operation. The man in black was not connected to any of this by name or on paper. Except for one document. The reason he was here. His one mistake.

Then he saw it—tucked in the back of the unlocked safe, in a thick manila envelope loaded with cash. The man in black smirked. Even capable Carranza was not without vices. Even the best employees skim and scam, he thought. He stuffed the cash in his hoodie pocket and looked at the manifest and let out a long sigh of relief. There it was. His name in big, bold blocky letters—confirming the shipment of people, but a shipment nonetheless. The point of contact in the U.S. was the man in black.

Arturo Arbona.

Now he was just the man in black, he thought. His double life was secure.

It'd all started innocently enough, he mused. A phone call from someone—his mysterious new benefactor. It was like she already knew him. At first, Arturo had balked. But he soon got over the awkward outreach and started talking. He appreciated the secret friendship. Something outside of work, outside of his daily life serving Andrea's every whim. He respected Andrea Martinez, had once admired her. But over time, especially once she'd been elected, Arturo began to feel taken for granted. His boss was clearly grappling with something, he'd thought. At first it seemed like drugs—though he'd never even seen her take as much as a drink in the years he'd known her. But something was messing with her. She would show up late, disheveled, to events. She was distracted and groggy in meetings. Most people didn't notice, but Arturo knew her well.

It'd all clicked into place after Paul Persinio, Andrea's predecessor, was arrested for fraud. Caught by that new vigilante, La Sombra, in the act. Arturo had come to Andrea's apartment unannounced, a box of doughnuts and some coffee in hand. It was time to celebrate. But when Andrea opened the door, her eyes bloodshot, a dark bruise on her face and—most tellingly—a dark cloak and purple scarf strewn on the floor of her apartment's entryway…that was when Arturo started to realize that there was more to his boss's demeanor. And that was when his new friend started to point out just how unfairly Arturo had been mistreated.

"You deserve better—you should be in charge. Why is she telling you what to do, when she's actually out there breaking the laws she claims to uphold?" she'd told Arturo. And his new friend was right.

This had continued apace over the last two months, Arturo feeling his bond with his new friend always getting stronger. Slowly, she 'feed him information, little nuggets of detail that not only fueled his resentment of Andrea, but gave him insight into what she was dealing with. The dual personality. The struggle for her own self. Openings for him to manipulate and benefit from. He was open and pliable. Ready to do what his new boss wanted. So when she finally did ask him to do something—something Arturo had never considered himself capable of—he hadn't hesitated to say yes. The request had come over drinks, probably one too many for Arturo, and he'd sometimes wondered if she'd slipped him something that night. But those thoughts were fleeting and easy to ignore, overwhelmed by the rush of power and adrenaline that came with each act of murder. With each chip and dent in Andrea's armor. Soon, the mission would be complete, too—with Andrea revealed as La Sombra, Carranza taking the fall for the deaths, and his entire snakehead business proceeds funneled to his boss. Arturo had done well. He was a good man. He would be first in line when things changed.

"Back away from there."

The voice startled Arturo, the man in black. So much so that he fumbled the manifest, only regaining control of the sheet of paper after some struggle. He felt his face redden as he turned to see who had spoken the words. But he knew the answer before he saw her. He had recognized Andrea Martinez's voice. What surprised him, though, was what she was wearing.

La Sombra stood before him.

But that couldn't be right, he thought. He knew, of course, they were the same—at least in body. But when La Sombra took over, Andrea Martinez was gone. Everything about her changed—her voice, her mannerisms, her presence.

"Not anymore," La Sombra said. Andrea's voice was there, but it had more bite to it—slightly lower. As if the two beings had merged into one. Arturo had not expected this. "I'm not two people anymore, Arturo. I know what you've been doing. How could you?"

Arturo didn't hesitate. He wasn't a fighter. But he was prepared. She—his mysterious benefactor—had prepared him for this eventuality. He tapped the fob in his hoodie pocket.

"How could I?" Arturo said with a jagged laugh. "How could you, Andrea? Jumping from the rooftops like some comic book hero, ignoring the laws you claimed to care about. You're a joke."

La Sombra leaped at Arturo, her movement fast and targeted. He felt himself tumble back as she slammed him further into the tiny office, his head crashing into the far wall. She was close now, her breath hot on his face, her hands grabbing his shirt roughly.

"You lied to me," La Sombra said, her eyes wide. He could see them past the dark goggles and purple scarf. He could see his former friend. And she was very mad. "You told me Carranza was dead. Showed me that false headline. Why? Did you think it'd break me, Arturo? It did the opposite--"

She sent a knee into his midsection, bending him over in pain.

"It made me stronger."

Arturo felt his body slide down to the floor, his midsection burning in pain. He tried to wrap his arms around to dull it, but couldn't. He'd never been hit so hard. He felt weak. Pathetic. Heard a whimper leave his mouth as La Sombra turned around and grabbed the manifest from the floor. She took a step toward him.

"You came here for this?" she said, her gravelly voice more confident now "Did you think this would save you, Arturo? You're too far gone, man. It's over."

"Could...could say the same...about you," Arturo said through gritted teeth. "You'll be revealed by morning."

"Maybe," La Sombra said, walking out of the tiny office. "But at least I did what I thought was right. I didn't sell my soul to the devil."

SOMBRA JOURNAL 4/16

I leave Arturo sobbing in pain in the back of the store. I have no more use for him. I got the confirmation I needed. Arturo betrayed me. He'd actually been the snakehead all along. Killing the people who didn't pay in cold blood. It was hard to believe, but we live in a hard-to-believe world.

I feel different now. More complete. Like I'd subsumed a part of my mind that I can see now. Arturo showing me that headline—a fabricated image that he hastily pulled away— snapped something into place. He'd made me believe La Sombra had crossed a line I couldn't allow. Next thing I knew, I was swimming through my own mind, struggling with a mental projection of La Sombra, a dark and brooding figure so unlike me—but also part of me somehow. I don't remember what happened after that. Only snippets. A battle. A conversation. A decision. In sequence and all at once. The only thing I did know, was when I awoke, soaked in sweat, collapsed on my living room floor—I knew I was alone. There was no other. I was La Sombra. And La Sombra was me.

Shriver watched as La Sombra stepped out of the tiny store, a sheet of paper in her hand. She looked around, trying to locate them. Nacinovich waved her down. As the vigilante started to walk toward them, the world seemed to explode behind her.

The fireball burst out of Thistle, sending glass, debris, and a fair share of gluten-free products all over Lefferts Boulevard—and jettisoning La Sombra clear across the street. Shriver's hands instinctively went to his ears as he and Nacinovich ducked down behind a parked car. He watched glass from the car's windows sprinkle the grimy pavement around them, the sound of the explosion ripping across the usually quiet Queens block.

When his hearing returned, Shriver started to make out some sounds—sirens, in the distance, but louder. Nacinovich, babbling something, and a low, pained moan.

Shriver got up slowly and looked over the car. The block looked apocalyptic. Windows shattered. Fire dominating the center of the street. Dust and smoke floating around them. It felt familiar to Shriver, who'd spent his fair share of time abroad in war zones.

"You think anyone survived--" Nacinovich started to ask.

"In there?" Shriver asked, eyes wide. "No way."

Without another word, he darted into the street toward La Sombra, who was slowly getting up to her feet, the familiar black and gray costume covered in soot, tattered and torn. Shriver tried to help her up but she waved him off.

"I'm—I'm fine," she said. "Arturo…he's in there."

Shriver placed a hand on her shoulder. "No way he survived that," he said plainly.

La Sombra's shoulders sagged.

"Do you, uh, know those guys?"

Shriver and La Sombra looked at Nacinovich, who was a few feet in front of them. The reporter was pointing down the street, at a group of four tall, well-built men approaching them from Austin Street. They were all dressed alike, walking in unison. And they were damn fast.

"I think I've seen them before," Nacinovich shouted. "Or someone like them—they took on Traction. Sent him packing, too."

La Sombra had never been one to follow the Phenomenon on the news, so she didn't know who these giants were or why they would be going after the Phenomenon called Traction. But one thing was clear—the four of them were coming her way now. And it wasn't to make friends.

She tried to move, but winced at the pain it cost her. Shriver put an arm around her to provide support, but she pushed him away.

"If they beat Traction," Sombra said, "not sure what…what I can do."

The giants were moving faster now. They'd be in front of them in seconds, Shriver thought.

"Bring the car around," Shriver yelled at Nacinovich, who nodded and darted in the direction of his wheels.

Shriver prayed the engine started. As Nacinovich got behind the wheel, Shriver grabbed La Sombra. She didn't resist this time, matching him step-for-step as they crossed the street. He looked back. The quartet reached Thistle and seemed distracted, a few of them stepping into the still-burning inferno. That's when it hit Shriver. These were not normal, fit men. They were something else. Something more.

Nacinovich stopped the car next to them and they piled into the backseat, the car moving before Shriver could close the door behind him. Through the car's back window he watched as one of the giants noticed them. Shriver had let out a sigh of relief as the car crossed the next light, thinking it impossible for anyone on foot to catch them. But then the giant started running. As Shriver screamed for Nacinovich to step on it, he watched as the man—this superior man—almost reached the rear bumper. But it wasn't the car's speed that dissuaded him. He stopped, as if hearing a command from far off, like a kid recognizing his mom's voice in the distance. The next thing Shriver knew, the big guy had spun around and made his way back down Lefferts.

"Guess we weren't worth the effort," La Sombra said.

Shriver looked at her face. It was covered in dirt and dust, her sharp jaw tighter than usual, her dark eyes reflecting the fire in Thistle. She turned to meet his gaze.

"Guess you guys have no choice this time?" she asked.

"This is a big scoop for you. Local politician moonlights as vigilante, can't save her treacherous chief of staff in massive explosion. I won't hold a grudge."

Nacinovich looked at them through the center rearview mirror. "We always have a choice," he said. "And I know what mine is."

La Sombra—Andrea—looked back at Nacinovich, then to Shriver.

"And you?"

"I made my choice already," Shriver said with a smile. "Seems the world's getting a helluva lot more dangerous."

"Sure is," Nacinovich said. "And we damn well could use some more heroes."

COVENANT OF SALT

BY MARY FAN

"You said you had nothing to do with your mobster uncle!"

Jojo Fang hurriedly used saltwater to corrode the handcuffs binding Michael Donnelly to the ferry's passenger seat. She yanked him to his feet, thoroughly ticked off. Who wouldn't be after discovering that their friend had orchestrated his own kidnapping in order to bring down a rival mob boss?

"You told me your parents moved out of Queens to get away from him!"

"They did!" Michael drew a sheepish hand through his mop of brown hair. A nasty-looking black eye marred his pale complexion. "They—"

"One sec!" Jojo whirled as a man appeared in the doorway to the passenger cabin, struggling to maintain her balance on the rocking ferry. At least the rough, storm-shaken East River gave her plenty of ammo. Feeling the salt within the surges, she commanded a giant wave to crash over the edge of the deck behind the man—one of Hera Buchanan's nanotech-enhanced goons. The tech gave them regenerative abilities that prevented her from lowering their sodium levels, but she had other ways of knocking them out.

The wave hit the man so hard, he slammed into the floor and lost consciousness. Jojo waved her hands and sent the water back into the river. She didn't want to sink the ferry, after all.

This is not how I planned to spend my Saturday afternoon. I was supposed to be practicing for our band's audition!

She spun back to Michael with a scowl, her rainbow bob whipping across her face. A few damp strands stuck to the black mesh mask covering her nose and mouth. Her soaked rainbow leggings and black mini-dress clung uncomfortably to her skin, and her black boots felt twice as heavy as usual. Her Sarcastic Fringehead get-up wasn't exactly waterproof.

She couldn't believe she'd taken a cab all the way across town, stolen a kayak, and used her control over saltwater to speed it to the ferry where Michael was being held captive after getting kidnapped—again. He'd managed to text her with the words *HELP, kidnapped*, and *Buchanan*, before the bad guys had chained him up. Fortunately, they'd left his phone on, and she'd been able to track him using her Find My Friends app. Except she wasn't sure if he counted as a friend anymore.

She'd had her suspicions after she'd freed him from Buchanan's clutches last time, though she'd dismissed them, thinking her slacker-y classmate and bandmate couldn't possibly have done something so nefarious. Now, she realized, she'd been in denial.

"What the hell is going on?" she demanded.

Michael gave her a helpless look. "I was visiting friends in Hoboken, and when I got on the ferry back to Manhattan—"

"Yeah, yeah, the whole thing was crewed by Buchanan's goons. I figured out that part! Also realized the ferry was heading downtown and that it was gonna round the tip of Manhattan and go up toward Queens, which is why I was able to beat it to the East River. What I wanna know is—Dammit, where do these guys keep coming from?"

She'd already washed several goons overboard. Yet either two had climbed back on board—she had a hard time making out their faces since no one had bothered turning on the passenger-cabin lights—or they'd emerged from a lower level.

With a great cry, she summoned the most ginormous wave yet and struck the goons as they passed under the doorway, sending them to the ground. While she had all that saltwater handy, she used it to corrode their weapons. In case they came to, they'd be a lot less dangerous without them.

Outside the wide window, distant blue lights flashed from approaching police boats. Thank goodness she'd had the presence of mind to call the cops on the wayward ferry before going after it. Though she didn't want to be around when they arrived.

"All right, I'm out." She put her hands on her hips. "You've got thirty seconds to tell me everything if you wanna come with me."

Michael glanced anxiously at the blue lights. "Okay, so I figured out you were Sarcastic Fringehead a while ago—"

"How?"

"I followed you the night you told off Elena Chu. Uncle Ken wanted me to gather intel on my classmates and their families, since, you know, everyone at St. Kinga Academy has got some powerful connection or another. You'd been acting kind of funny, so I wanted to see what was up. But I didn't tell him right away… thought it wasn't the thing to do."

"Oh, how noble. Where does the staged kidnapping come in?"

"It wasn't staged—not exactly. Look, Uncle Ken wasn't exactly impressed by the stuff I gathered before, and he gave me an ultimatum: bring him something useful, or he'd cut off my allowance."

"You gave away my secret identity over your allowance?!"

"It was for our band!" Michael spread his hands. "Who do you think pays for our rehearsal space and our equipment? Do you know how much a good microphone costs?"

Jojo narrowed her eyes. "Thought those came from your parents."

He shook his head. "They don't exactly approve of my rock-n-roll dreams… or of my grades."

"So you turned to Uncle Mobster."

"I didn't hear you complain about the new amp I got for your bass guitar!"

Jojo huffed. She'd assumed that Michael's parents, like most parents of preppy St. Kinga kids, had infinite money to throw at their son's artistic ambitions. She wished she'd questioned their supposed magnanimity sooner.

Thirty seconds had come and gone, and those police boats were getting too close for comfort.

"So, are you gonna leave me here?" Michael asked nervously.

Jojo hesitated for a moment, then said, "You can come with me, but you'd better keep talking!"

His shoulders sagged in relief as he followed her out of the passenger cabin. "It was Uncle Ken's idea to bribe one of Buchanan's goons into kidnapping me. He knew you'd come save me. That's why he had it happen during our school's talent show."

"He wanted the Phenomenons to take down his rival." Rain pounded down, plastering Jojo's hair to her face. She'd have to recolor it after this mess. "And you played along."

"He didn't give me much of a choice!"

Jojo raced down the ferry's narrow deck to where she'd left the kayak, then glimpsed the bridge above. Her eyes widened.

Hera Buchanan herself, a full-figured woman with bright red hair that Jojo recognized from the news, stood at the controls, yelling into her phone, probably summoning backup. *She must be pretty down on her luck to be doing her own dirty work.*

Jojo whirled to Michael. "Is this one of 'Uncle Ken's' plans, too?" Lighting streaked the sky, and she had to shout over the pounding rain. "A way to finish off Buchanan?"

Michael shook his head. "This one was real. Buchanan wanted revenge. The only reason I'm not already at the bottom of the river is because she thought I'd make useful leverage."

She didn't know if she believed him. *Maybe I should tell the cops everything and get him arrested.*

But if she did that, My Bedroom Panic would be down a lead singer. And with their audition for the small yet prestigious Garment Club coming up in a week, they wouldn't have time to find a new one.

Guess I'd better save him, then.

Maybe that was a stupid reason for doing what she did next, but it was better than no reason at all.

Enough river water had already splashed onto the ferry that she didn't need to summon any more to corrode the metal supporting the bridge's window pane.

The salt ate away at the metal, and the pane fell out, leaving Buchanan exposed to the elements. The woman drew her weapon in alarm. Jojo sensed the sodium in the woman's body, and though she wasn't sure if it would work, she tugged at it. Buchanan swayed, and the weapon dropped from her hand. Whatever enhancements Buchanan had used on her goons, she apparently hadn't taken for herself. Probably because they were still experimental, and she didn't want to take the risk of something going wrong.

Your mistake. Jojo smirked as the woman fell unconscious on the bridge.

By then, the police boats had surrounded the ferry, and an officer was yelling commands over the loudspeaker.

Jojo rushed into the kayak and motioned for Michael to follow. He jumped in behind her. It was a tight—and awkward—squeeze.

She first commanded the river water to spray upward, forming a nearly opaque wall of mist, and then summoned a wave to carry the kayak off the ferry's deck and toward Manhattan. *Good thing it's a stormy day… this would be a lot harder to pull off on a clear one.*

The cops had been searching for Buchanan, and Jojo had handed over the mob boss on a silver platter. That had to be a good thing, right?

Yet knowing that she'd also helped the notorious Kenworth Clark eliminate a rival left her with a sick feeling in her stomach.

***

The school bell rang. Jojo slammed her locker shut and trudged toward her first-period Art class. Though it was Monday, she was still exhausted from her adventure on the East River. It didn't help that she'd spent the previous day volunteering at the Chinese community center where her grandmother played mahjong with a bunch of other old immigrant ladies.

Man, I miss the days when all I used my powers for was taking down schoolyard bullies for a price.

At least Jojo's growing reputation as Sarcastic Fringehead meant those gigs, when she got them, were easier to pull off.

She resisted the urge to scratch at her wig of boring, shoulder-length black locks, which covered her rainbow-colored hair—a compromise she'd made to blend in at her prep school.

"Hey, Jojo!" Michael rushed toward her.

"Oh, it's you," she grumbled.

"Um… we good?" He gave an awkward smile. The concealer over his black eye hid the injury pretty well, and Jojo would have bet her bass guitar that his mother had done it for him.

"I'm coming to band practice after school, if That's what you mean." She stomped toward the Art classroom, which was on the ground floor. "I'm not gonna let a stupid thing like you being a big fat liar get between me and the Garment Club. We've still got our space, right? Considering Hera Buchanan got arrested, that place better be paid off for the next decade!"

"Yeah, We've still got our space." He rubbed the back of his neck. "Look, I know I was doing stuff for my uncle, but I'm not, like, evil or anything…"

"The show must go on. That's all I've got to say to you." Jojo marched into the classroom and took her usual seat.

Annoyingly, Michael took his normal spot as well: the desk right beside hers.

"Good morning, class." Eric Mesa, the art teacher, glanced around the classroom from behind his desk, and his dark eyes warmed. A neatly trimmed beard framed his mouth. "Today, we begin our unit on Cubism."

Jojo smiled back. She was looking forward to spending the next hour thinking about early-20th-century paintings instead of all the ways in which being a Phenomenon had screwed with her life.

Mr. Mesa stood slowly, gently pushing his chair back as if worried it might shatter. His jaw tensed, and Jojo furrowed her brow. *Is he okay?*

"We all know about Picasso, of course." Mr. Mesa gingerly picked up a dry-erase marker from his desk. "Today, I want to talk about some of the other pioneers who shaped the movement."

He turned to the whiteboard and started writing, but only made it as far as *Ge* before the tip snapped off the marker.

"Dammit!" Mr. Mesa hollered. He threw the broken marker onto the floor. It landed behind his desk, and the loud popping noise it made reminded Jojo of a gunshot.

She gasped.

Mr. Mesa glanced back at the class and gripped his dark hair with both hands. "I'm so sorry, class…"

One of the reasons why Mr. Mesa was Jojo's favorite teacher was because he'd always been chill. This wasn't like him. Worry bit her chest.

"I… can't be here." Mr. Mesa spoke through gritted teeth. "Use this period as a study hall. I-I apologize…"

He rushed to the door, reached for the knob, then hesitated. From the caution he used to exit, one would have thought he was an archeologist handling a fifty-thousand-year-old Neanderthal skull. He left the door open behind him.

The entire class sat in stunned silence.

Jojo sprang up from her seat and ran for the door. "Mr. Mesa! Are you all right?"

By the time she reached the hallway, he was no longer in sight, though she could hear his rapid footsteps sprinting away in the distance.

Whispers peppered the classroom—*What's wrong with him?* and *That was so weird!* and the like.

Jojo reentered the classroom, confused. She approached the teacher's desk. The broken marker lay shattered by his chair—near a deep dent in the linoleum floor.

"Whoa."

Jojo jumped at the sound of Michael's voice. "Don't startle me like that!"

"Sorry." He stepped back. "Mr. Mesa must be *Phenomenons-strong* to break the floor."

Mr. Mesa, a Phenomenon?

Jojo's mind flashed back to how one of Buchanan's goons had injected Mr. Mesa with nanotech that both controlled his mind—forcing him to kidnap Michael—and gave him extreme strength and endurance to pull it off. *Clark wanted me to witness it so I'd run to the rescue… Mr. Mesa just happened to be MC-ing the talent show…*

She glowered at Michael. "This is your fault," she hissed.

"Huh?" He gave her a clueless look.

Aware that the rest of the class was watching, she reached toward the ground. Enough sodium lay in the sediment beneath the floor for her to manipulate the small patch beneath the cracked linoleum to rise up and flatten the dent. *At least it looks less dramatic now… Like anyone could've done it if they were mad enough.* "I think the nanotech's still messing with Mr. Mesa," she whispered.

Michael shook his head. "No way. It's supposed to go inert after a day. None of Buchanan's goons who got arrested kept their powers."

That's true... Jojo returned to her seat, frowning. Maybe Mr. Mesa's strange behavior had nothing to do with the nanotech. She hoped that was true.

Because it wasn't, then it would mean that someone innocent had gotten hurt because of her being a Phenomenon.

***

With school done for the day, all Jojo wanted was to jam with her bandmates. Though she hadn't had a chance to learn the new song yet, she planned to get to the rehearsal space early and speed-learn her bass riff.

She strode down Amsterdam Avenue, her instrument strapped to her back; she'd swung by her Upper West Side home to grab it and ditch her backpack.

In her mind, she pictured herself standing on the Garment Club's tiny stage, facing a room full of people excited to see her. It was her dream venue—the kind of hole-in-the-wall place that knew how to spot talent. She imagined the dingy crimson walls decorated with autographed photos of respected performers who'd gotten their start there, the scuffed wooden floor, the plain yet well stocked bar...

She was so lost in her head, she didn't see the enormous blond woman approach until the latter had grabbed her arm.

Jojo opened her mouth to cry out.

"Keep quiet, Sarcastic Fringehead, or I'll rip your arm off," the woman growled, her green eyes glinting.

The scream froze in Jojo's mouth. Since she was still wearing her plain black wig—she hadn't bothered changing out of her school uniform—the attacker must have figured out her identity.

The woman looked nearly seven feet tall, with shoulders three times broader the Jojo's and the muscles to match.

Jojo reached out with her powers, but though she was able to grasp the sodium in the woman's body, she couldn't manipulate it.

She then grabbed at any salt she could reach—leftover rock salt from a late-season storm, particles pulled from food trucks, whatever sodium lay in dirt and dust of the street. Though the minor storm she summoned caused several passersby to cough or stumble, it had no effect on the attacker.

The woman gave a cruel smile. "Your little tricks won't work on me, Salt Girl."

Tears filled Jojo's eyes. "If this is about Buchanan—"

"Who?" The woman arched her brows. "I don't care who you've beaten in the past, kid. You're a Phenomenon, and That's all Boss Lady cares about."

"Who are you?"

"Epsilon. Now, come with me."

Seeing no other choice, Jojo walked beside Epsilon. *Is she taking me to another lab where they'll experiment on my powers? Or is she planning to kill me and just doesn't want to do it in the middle of Amsterdam Ave at rush hour?*

A terrified sob escaped. Jojo used her free hand to wipe her eyes, but they kept leaking more tears.

"Stop your blubbering!" Epsilon gave Jojo's arm a squeeze, and it was all Jojo could do to keep from crying out in pain.

"I'm trying." Noticing all the concerned eyes shifting in her direction, Jojo stopped trying to hold back. A waterfall ran down her face, and she let a few high-pitched whimpers escape her throat.

"She's fine," Epsilon said to a particularly worried-looking old lady, giving an uncomfortable grin. "She was just talking about her break up. Teenagers and their relationship drama, you know?"

Apparently, even Epsilon knew that story wouldn't fly with her fist clenching Jojo's arm. Epsilon moved to hold Jojo around the shoulders instead.

Jojo took advantage of the brief opening and dropped into a crouch, making herself as small as possible. Epsilon reached down, but her prodigious height proved to be a disadvantage. She stumbled.

Jojo knew better than to think she could fight Epsilon. Her only option was to run. And though it pained her to ditch her precious instrument, survival mattered more. She slung the bass guitar case off her back and dumped it on the sidewalk.

Then she sprinted down Amsterdam, dodging passersby. She didn't have to look back to know that Epsilon was close behind. Jojo knew she couldn't outrun the woman—her powers didn't extend to speed, and she was notorious for cutting gym.

Her eyes fell on the 96th Street subway station, bustling with a weekday afternoon commuter crowd. *Maybe I can lose her in there!*

For once, Jojo was grateful for the boring look she'd been forced to sport in order to adhere to her school's dress code—not just the plain wig, but the generic slacks and button-down shirt. She rushed into the station, wove her way through the crowd, and jumped a turnstile.

Epsilon pushed past alarmed commuters and smashed through the turnstile. She shoved people aside in pursuit of her target, knocking several to the ground.

Jojo ran deeper into the station, until she arrived at the subway platform. The downtown train just happened to be there when she arrived. She shoved past the crowd and slipped through the doors right before they closed.

The train started moving, and Jojo exhaled.

But then it jolted to an abrupt stop. She gasped and looked out the train's window.

Epsilon stood on the platform several feet back, gripping the train's roof. A wicked grin spread across her mouth, and she took a step toward the nearest door.

Jojo looked around wildly. If Epsilon made it onto the train, then Jojo would be trapped. *What do I do?!*

Just then, several members of the NYPD arrived on the scene and drew their weapons.

Epsilon scowled. She hesitated for a moment, then released the train to confront the authorities.

The train bolted forward, and Jojo grabbed a pole to avoid losing her balance. Her heart pounded, and sweat trickled down her face. She couldn't tell if the world was spinning because she was so scared or because she was breathing so fast that she couldn't get enough oxygen.

She closed her eyes and exhaled deliberately, trying to calm herself. *I'm fine... I got away...*

Yet she knew it was only because of dumb luck that she had. If the train hadn't been there, if she'd been at smaller station that didn't have a police presence...

She wished she could attribute her escape to her own strength or cleverness. Knowing it'd merely been fortunate circumstances left her feeling helpless.

***

Police Seek Fugitive Who Terrorized 96th Street Station. The headline blazed across Jojo's phone, alongside a collage of low-res stills of Epsilon taken by a security camera.

As Jojo headed toward her locker, she quickly read over the article. All it said was what she already knew: that Epsilon had escaped, and that the authorities were actively looking for her.

Surely, the cops or the United Front or someone would catch Epsilon soon. Jojo had considered searching for Epsilon herself then realized she hardly had the experience or the resources to conduct a manhunt. What could she do that the NYPD couldn't?

Epsilon might have gotten away, but she'd be forced to hide now that the authorities were after her. Or, so, Jojo had to believe. Because nothing was more terrifying than an enemy who was after you not for anything you'd done, but for what you were.

In any case, Jojo wouldn't let fear stop her from living her life. Which was why she hadn't told anyone about the attack. The last thing she needed was her parents squirreling her off to some remote location for her safety. She still had that audition for the Garment Club, after all.

She only hoped that her bass guitar would be fixed in time. Fortunately, living on a swanky Upper West Side street meant that the person who'd stumbled upon her abandoned instrument had returned it to the address written on its tag; Jojo had gone home to find it waiting at the front desk with her building's doorman. Unfortunately, she'd busted it when she'd thrown it off.

The repairman said it'd be ready for pick-up by Thursday, and the audition's not till Friday. It'll be fine. She could always rent an instrument, as she planned to for the next day's rehearsal, but she'd much rather use her own for something so important.

"Where were you yesterday?"

Jojo spun to find Amaya Wilson, My Bedroom Panic's guitarist, striding up to her with Bethany Hawthorne and Stephen Peterson—the drummer and keyboardist, respectively—close behind. All held accusing looks on their faces.

Jojo tilted her brows into an apologetic look. "Sorry I missed rehearsal. I… got busy."

Bethany gave her an incredulous look. "That's all you have to say for yourself?"

"Do you even care about the band?" Stephen crossed his arms. "You barely come to practice anymore, and we lost our last gig because you didn't show up! What was your excuse then, again?"

That I'd just been kidnapped and experimented on by a creep who messed with my powers? Jojo couldn't say that aloud. Though so many people knew about her secret identity, she wondered why she bothered keeping it anymore.

Then she glanced at Amaya, Bethany, and Stephen in turn. As long as there was some chance that the day's baddies might leave her friends alone because they didn't know about their connection to Sarcastic Fringehead, she had to try.

"I'm sorry," she mumbled. "Like I said… busy."

"We're all busy." Amaya threw up her hand. "Clubs, sports, test prep, volunteer work, all the other crap our parents make us do so we'll get into Ivies… you think you're the only one who has to deal with that?"

"But we make it work." Stephen glared. "Why can't you?"

Jojo shook her head, unable to answer.

"Hey, lay off her." Michael approached. "She's got a lot going on, okay?"

"And we don't?" Bethany demanded.

Jojo recoiled. She didn't need Michael, of all people, defending her. "I'll do better, I promise."

Annoyance filled Amaya's face. "Just make sure you're at rehearsal tomorrow. It's our last one before the Garment Club audition. You remember that, don't you?"

"Yeah, of course," Jojo grumbled.

Michael stepped toward the others. "We can rehearse Thursday, too, you know. I've got the space booked—"

"We've got conflicts, remember?" Bethany gave him an incredulous look. "We agreed on this rehearsal schedule months ago to accommodate all our wild schedules! The rest of us have respected it—why can't you, Jojo?"

Because people keep needing saving, or those who want to hurt the world come after me so I can't save it. Unable to say that, Jojo only shrugged. "Sorry."

"Not good enough." Amaya pointed a stern finger at her. "I hate to do this, but the others and I came to a conclusion: If you don't make it to the Garment Club audition, we're getting a new bassist."

Jojo's jaw dropped. "You can't—"

"If you can't do your part," Bethany said, "we'll find someone who can."

"Guys, please," Michael mumbled. "I didn't agree to this." The others ignored him.

Stephen gave Jojo a sad look. "None of us wanted to do this, Jojo, but we're tired of being blown off. This is important to us."

"It's important to me too." Jojo's voice shook. Yet she couldn't blame her bandmates. If she'd been in their position, she'd have been pissed too.

The bell rang.

Jojo marched off to Art class, even though she hadn't had a chance to change her books. Amaya, Bethany, and Stephen had different classes, but Michael walked alongside her.

"What really happened yesterday?" he muttered.

She shot him a poisonous look. "That's something I'd only tell to someone I trust."

Chastised, he looked away.

Jojo sped into the Art classroom. Instead of heading for her usual seat, she took one in the back. Michael settled into his normal spot and glanced at her with a wistful look.

The desk at the front of the classroom was empty. Jojo didn't think much of it at first—maybe Mr. Mesa was running late.

But then a man she'd never seen before entered.

"Hey, kids!" the man said, sounding too chipper. "My name is Paul Balze. I'm your sub today!"

Sub? Jojo raised her hand so high, she practically jumped out of her seat. "Where's Mr. Mesa?" she demanded before Mr. Balze had a chance to call on her.

"Oh, he's not feeling well," the sub answered. "Anyway, I believe you were discussing Cubism?"

Jojo had about a million questions, but Mr. Balze wouldn't be able to answer them.

As Jojo grabbed her notebook from her backpack, she couldn't stop thinking, *Something's wrong with Mr. Mesa. What if the leftover nanotech's hurting him?*

Whatever was going on, all she knew was that she had to help.

***

Jojo had hoped that Mr. Mesa would come to class on Wednesday and prove that he was all right after all, that'd he'd needed a day off because of the sniffles or something. If it hadn't been for the nanotech, she wouldn't have worried too much when he didn't show up again.

Yet she couldn't stop picturing the weird ways in which he'd acted on Monday—how nervous he'd seemed, how he'd suddenly freaked out, how he'd put a dent in the floor.

She'd told Michael that the nanotech thing was his fault, but in truth, it was hers. Michael's mobster uncle had only come up with the plan that used Mr. Mesa because of who she was.

Unable to stand not knowing anymore, Jojo reached out to her friend Jess Dorian, a.k.a. Black Hat, and asked her to find Mr. Mesa's home address. The future-tech-powered hacker responded with the answer about thirty seconds later.

Of course, the guy had to live in Jersey City of all places.

Jojo marched up Columbus Drive, her phone pressed to her ear. It was a testament to her desperation that she'd actually *called* someone.

"You gotta tell them, Michael," she pleaded. "No one else would even pick up. They must think I'm blowing them off again, but I swear, I have a really good reason for missing tonight's rehearsal."

"Well, what is it?" Michael demanded.

"Mr. Mesa! But you can't tell them." She approached the high-rise in which Mr. Mesa resided. She found his apartment number on the buzzer and pressed it, but he didn't answer. She pressed it again, with no response. "They can't know about this Phenomenons stuff, or your mob stuff, or any of it! I don't want anyone else I care about to get mixed up in this crap! Promise you won't tell them!"

"But you *do* want me to tell them that you're missing rehearsal again," Michael grumbled. "The last one before our audition."

"Oh, don't you guilt-trip me!" A resident of the building opened the door and exited. Jojo caught it, and the other ignored her as she entered. She stepped into the elevator and punched the button for the seventh floor. "*You* are the reason Mr. Mesa got flooded with nanotech against his will! So just tell the others I won't be there tonight and convince them that I have a legit excuse, okay?"

"How do you expect me to do that?" Michael sounded frustrated.

"I dunno! You're the one who's good at lying!"

"Hey!"

The elevator arrived. The door with Mr. Mesa's apartment number was right across from it. "Anyway, just—"

A muffled cry rang out from behind the door.

"Mr. Mesa!" She punched the doorbell. "Are you all right?"

He didn't answer, only cried out again.

Alarmed, Jojo shoved her phone into her pocket, reached into her backpack, and grabbed a water bottle. Since she hadn't known what she'd find, she'd come prepared. She opened the bottle and drew out the saltwater, then used it to corrode Mr. Mesa's lock.

She shoved the door and burst in.

Unfamiliar tech that looked like it'd been Frankenstein-ed together, connected by thick cables and flashing with colored lights, covered a six-foot-tall bookshelf near the back window. A metal piece protruded outside. Mr. Mesa sat in a wooden chair, and wires snaked from the contraption and into nodes attached to his arms and forehead. Electricity zapped down those wires, and bolts wrapped around the art teacher, whose eyes were squeezed shut. He gritted his teeth, but a pained groan escaped.

"Mr. Mesa!" Jojo rushed to him and reached out.

Mr. Mesa's eyes popped open. "Don't touch it!" he cried.

She froze, staring in shock and alarm. What was Mr. Mesa doing? Where had all this tech come from?

She suddenly recalled him telling the class that before he'd become an art teacher, he'd studied engineering and worked at some pretty top-tier labs. *I guess he built it himself? But what is it?*

The machine wound down, and the electricity faded.

Mr. Mesa exhaled, then looked up with a stern glare. "What are you doing here, Jojo?"

"I was worried!" Jojo answered.

"I appreciate that, but this is highly inappropriate. I must ask that you leave at once."

Ignoring his comment, Jojo approached the machine. "What is that thing?"

"It's a private matter." Wincing, Mr. Mesa removed the nodes from his forehead and arms. He started to stand, bracing his hand on the back of the chair. "Now, please—"

The chair splintered, crushed by his touch.

Mr. Mesa stumbled and caught himself on the wall. A crack appeared, and he cursed.

Jojo reached out with her powers, thinking maybe she could at least calm Mr. Mesa, but found each time she tried to move the salt in his system, it snapped back. "It's the nanotech, isn't it? It's still messing with you."

"Please, Jojo, you must leave—"

"I'm so sorry, Mr. Mesa!" she wailed. "I should've been better about hiding my secret identity! If I had, this wouldn't have happened to you!"

His brow crinkled. "What are you talking about?"

Jojo hesitated, then decided it was time to come clean. Realizing she'd never closed the front door, she glanced back. To her relief, it'd swung shut on its own.

"I'm Sarcastic Fringehead." She reached out for the salt in her backpack, drew some out of its container, and swirled it over her hand. "Surprise."

Mr. Mesa stared in disbelief.

Jojo directed the salt back into her backpack. "You know, you were the one who made me realize how much my powers could do, when you told us about all the things salt is capable of."

"I… see." Confusion remained plain on Mr. Mesa's face.

"I only did small stuff under the radar at first, but then… I dunno, things kept getting bigger, until Michael's uncle had someone nail you with nanotech to stage his kidnapping, knowing I'd go save him and take down rival mobster Hera Buchanan." She drew a breath. "Hey, I know what it's like to suddenly have powers you can't control. I was kidnapped not long ago, and they messed with my abilities."

"You were *what*?" Alarm filled the teacher's face.

"Don't worry, the Phenomenons saved me, and I'm back to normal now." Jojo waved her hand dismissively. "Actually, I know someone who can help you out, too. Want me to put you in touch? Or would you rather keep zapping yourself?" She gave the machine a doubtful look. "What were you trying to do?"

A wry smile twisted Mr. Mesa's mouth. "I was hoping to rid myself of the remaining nanotech. An x-ray revealed several particles still in my body, and though they were no longer functional, I feared what the long-term health implications might be. Of course, this isn't the kind of issue that most medical doctors know how to deal with, but I recalled a few tricks from my engineering days and thought I could handle it myself. The device required an enormous amount of electricity—more than the city's power grid could handle—and so I took advantage of Saturday's storm." He gestured at the piece sticking out of the window.

"You purposely got struck by lightning?!"

"It's a little more complicated than that, but essentially, yes. Something went wrong, though. Instead of ridding me of the residual nanotech, the machine seems to have mutated and multiplied it."

"That's why you keep breaking things. You've got super-strength now, only you don't know how to handle it."

"I don't want it." Mr. Mesa glanced at the machine with a sigh. "This second experiment seems to have failed. I had a feeling it wouldn't be powerful enough, but I didn't want to wait until the next storm... I need this extraneous strength gone, so I can return to my life. I had to ask my wife to go stay with her parents because I was afraid I might hurt her by accident. I took leave from the school so I wouldn't jeopardize the students. Until I return to normal, I'm afraid I'm trapped in here."

"You know, tons of people would kill to have super-strength. Maybe you don't need to get rid of it. You just need practice. Hey, Picasso didn't invent Cubism overnight, did he?"

"Picasso did not 'invent'—" Mr. Mesa broke off, and his lips twitched. "I see your point. And I appreciate your checking in on me. However, I must ask you to leave. As I said, this is highly inappropriate."

"Yeah, sorry." Jojo gave a sheepish grin. "I promise I won't invade your privacy again, now that I know you aren't dying or anything."

"Also, please don't tell anyone about what you've witnessed here. I don't want any trouble."

Jojo made a zipping gesture across her lips. "Not a peep." She headed to the door, then paused and looked back. "I didn't choose to have superpowers either. But hey, if I could figure out it out, then anyone can."

Mr. Mesa smiled, but a disturbed look remained in his eyes.

***

Jojo slumped into the apartment, relieved that her parents were out at a business function. She was in no mood to figure out a lie for why she was home so late. She couldn't't give away Mr. Mesa's secret, and she'd never had a chance to rent a bass guitar, so she couldn't use practice as a reason.

Exhausted—more emotionally than physically—Jojo made her way to her room and dumped her backpack on the floor. Her phone buzzed, but, fearing it was her bandmates yelling at her for missing rehearsal again, she couldn't bring herself to look at it. Guilt gnawed at her. With her instrument still at the repair shop, she couldn't even practice her parts on her own.

Jojo's grandmother appeared in the doorway, dressed in a flowery muumuu with her white hair in rollers. *"Chi fan la ma, hai zi?"* *Have you had dinner, kid?*

Jojo shook her head. "Not hungry, Laolao."

Laolao sat down on Jojo's bed. *"Zen me le? Wei shen me bu e?"* *What's wrong? Why aren't you hungry?*

Knowing the question had nothing to do with food, Jojo plopped down beside her, glad that she'd never had to hide anything from her grandmother. Unable to hold back, she confessed everything that had happened over the past few days.

She finished with, "I wish I'd never gotten my salt powers. They're nothing but trouble! I just want to make music, and because of these stupid abilities, I can't even do that!"

Laolao frowned. "I thought you were finally embracing what you were capable of. Weren't you the one who faced a Bronx Bruiser to return the tiger artifact to our village? And weren't you the one who chose to help when Torque lost control in Chicago, thereby exposing yourself to a much wider group of people than when you were simply taking on schoolyard bullies?"

"Maybe I shouldn't have done that," Jojo grumbled. "It used to annoy me that no one had heard of Sarcastic Fringehead, but now, I wish I could go back to being nobody."

"Oh, so you would have let all those people in Chicago get hurt? Just so you could play in a rock band more easily?"

"Well, when you put it that way..." Jojo stared at her hands. "It's not fair. You told me that tons of people from our ancestral village touched that tiger hoping to gain powers, but didn't. Yet I just happen to be born with them because it altered your DNA in a way that got passed down to me? Why'd it have to be *me*?"

"Perhaps it was meant to be you." Laolao's dark eyes crinkled kindly. "No one understands the technology that powers the artifact, but some believe it has a will of its own. It protected our village for centuries, and those who gained powers from it before all became great heroes and leaders. Not once did someone who received powers from the artifact turn out to be corrupt. How such a mechanism might work is beyond our scientific understanding, but our spiritual one says that it chooses those who are worthy. Even though you were a generation removed from its physical presence, it might still have exerted its will."

Jojo snorted. "Yeah, right."

Laolao gave her an annoyed look. "I know that you young people valorize being 'bad'"—she waved her hands mockingly— "and that being good isn't 'cool.'" She crossed her arms and lifted her chin with her thin eyebrows tilted, mimicking a pose so often struck by musicians on album covers.

Jojo couldn't help chuckling.

"However," Laolao continued, "you can't deny your nature. Everything you do—it isn't about you. It's bigger than you, and even those you help. You might sometimes pretend not to care about anything, but you obviously have a deep desire to help others, whether it's a friend who lied to you, a teacher you only know from school, or even complete strangers like Torque."

Jojo recalled how she'd used her powers to calm the Phenomenon whose powers had gone awry. That had felt pretty good.

Laolao leaned in closer. "I think that even if you didn't have these powers, you would still have tried to help people, and you would still have found yourself in this situation. Face it, Josephine. *Ni you yi ge do fu xin.*" *You have a tofu heart.* In other words, *You're a big softie.*

Jojo made a face. "I never wanted to be a superhero. Sure, I helped some people in Chicago, but there were other Phenomenons around to do that. Meanwhile, my teacher is stuck with nanotech he doesn't want, my friend dragged me into his uncle's mobster crap, some nutjob called Epsilon is after me for reasons I don't even know—I mean, I got kidnapped and experimented on! Other than getting that bronze tiger back for our village, this whole Phenomenons thing has only ever brought bad things to me."

Laolao's thin lips quirked. "I wouldn't be so sure."

***

The rest of My Bedroom Panic might have been too busy with other activities to practice Thursday night, but Jojo was not. She had her bass guitar back from the repair shop, and she was determined to play catch-up. *I'm gonna nail those bass riffs if it's the last thing I do!*

Since her parents were hosting an elegant dinner for their fancy corporate contacts that night, she'd had to seek a rehearsal space other than her bedroom. Laolao had escaped to the community center, preferring Tai Chi to the stuffy affair.

The studio Jojo headed toward was so far west, it was practically in the Hudson River. It was the only studio with a spare practice room on short notice that didn't cost, like, a million dollars.

She'd ditched her school clothes, opting to free her rainbow hair and wear ripped jeans like she might at a gig. Her instrument case rubbed against her back as walked down the long, long, *long* block between avenues.

She'd been told she'd have to show her ID to the security guard when she arrived at the building, so she was surprised to find the front desk unmanned. *Maybe they're on a bathroom break?*

She waited for a few moments, then, impatient, continued around the corner to the elevator, which would take her to the studio's third-floor reception area and the individual rehearsal spaces branching off from it. If anyone had a problem with her, she could flash her ID then, plus her email confirmation that she'd booked the space.

She should have found it weirder that there was no one at reception either. She should have been more creeped out by the fact that the space was completely empty and silent, even though all the other rehearsal spaces she'd been in had, despite the best efforts of the sound-proofed walls, buzzed with the pounding of dancers' feet, the warbles of musical theater ballads, the thumping of electronic beats.

Instead, she was so single-mindedly focused on the bass riff in her head that she waved it all off until she pulled open the door to her rented practice room—and found Epsilon waiting inside.

The woman gave a cruel smirk. "Your parents were right about your band being a distraction. Did you really think I'd give up so easily?"

A startled cry escaped Jojo, and she stumbled backward.

Epsilon took a menacing step toward her, fists raised.

"Okay, okay!" Jojo held up her hands in surrender. "I'll come quietly. Just let me put down my bass, okay? It got wrecked last time and… well, if I don't make it, at least she should."

"'She'?" Epsilon barked out a laugh. "Yeah, fine. That thing'll just get in my way."

Jojo ducked under the strap of her bass guitar case, then gently placed the instrument against the wall.

What Epsilon didn't know was that JoJo's pockets were full of salt.

Jojo seized every grain she could and threw them into Epsilon's eyes. Maybe the woman was tough enough not to feel the sting, but the sheer quantity would create an opaque white barrier. *She can't get me if she can't see!*

With one hand holding the salt before Epsilon's eyes and the other commanding more to trail after her, Jojo sprinted out of the practice room and looked around wildly. Waiting for the elevator would be stupid. Thinking she could outrun Epsilon down the emergency stairs was even stupider. And the reception area had no windows.

She glanced around at the various doors. A sheet of paper on one indicated that the rehearsal space had previously been reserved for a ballet troupe. *If any place is gonna have windows, it'd be the dance studio.*

Jojo ran at the door and was relieved to find it unlocked. She shoved it open. Several wide windows marched behind the ballet barre.

She didn't have any water on her—nor did she have time to find some and dissolve the salt swirling behind her. So she wound up with all her strength and shoved the white minerals at the glass as hard as she could.

It wasn't strong enough to break the glass, but it weakened it enough that when Jojo picked up a chair and threw it, the glass shattered.

Behind, Epsilon's lurching footsteps pounded toward her. Though Jojo worked hard to keep the salt-mask in place over the woman's eyes, it wouldn't hold her forever.

Jojo gathered all the salt she could feel and leaped out the window.

She blasted downward with her hands, shoving the salt into the ground below. For a moment, she thought she'd gotten away. She could fly, and Epsilon couldn't, and—

A great force knocked into her middle, and she cried out. Epsilon gripped Jojo around the waist—the woman had leaped out of the window, apparently not caring that she'd fall straight to the pavement.

Jojo cared. She didn't have any kind of invulnerability, after all.

She used her salt blasts to slow both their descents. Maybe that was what Epsilon was counting on. Or maybe the woman didn't give a damn if Jojo got flattened.

The two landed roughly on the pavement, Epsilon still gripping Jojo around the middle.

The woman stood, bringing Jojo with her. "Nice try, kid."

Jojo scrambled for a solution. She could blind the woman again, but what good would that do when she was nowhere near strong enough to break free from her hold?

Epsilon squeezed Jojo so hard that, Jojo thought her ribs might crack.

Then the woman slapped a hand over Jojo's mouth to stop her scream. "Let's try this again. Nice and quiet, right?"

Tears welling in her eyes, Jojo nodded.

This was it. This was all being Sarcastic Fringehead would lead to: Jojo getting dragged off by some goon, for some demented reason that she didn't even understand.

A van sped toward her and came to a screeching halt by the sidewalk. The door slid open, and half a dozen bruisers leaped out. Their heights and genders varied, but each was bulging with muscles.

They had to be with Epsilon. That van was meant to carry Jojo away—

Except the bruisers swarmed the large woman and pounded her from every direction while, somehow, avoiding Jojo, who was still pressed to Epsilon's torso.

Epsilon hollered and kicked. Finally, she was forced to release one arm from around Jojo to sucker-punch a man who'd been pressing his thumbs into her eye sockets.

Two others took advantage of the moment to yank Epsilon's other arm off Jojo.

Jojo rushed away so fast, she tripped and fell on the sidewalk.

"Hey, Jojo!"

She looked up with a start.

The van's window was open, and beyond it, she glimpsed Michael behind the driver's wheel. He gestured rapidly. "C'mon!"

"Michael?" She stood in shock. For some reason, the first thing that came out of her mouth was, "You can drive?!"

"Got my permit last month. You coming?"

Not needing to be asked twice, Jojo leaped into the back of the van, and Michael sped off.

"HEY!" Jojo clung to the back of the passenger-side headrest. "Close the door!"

"Sorry!" Michael pressed a button, and the door slid shut.

"What're you doing here?! Who are those goons?"

"They're my goons, and they've got the super-strength nanotech. They'll do whatever I say, and I told them to save you!"

"*You* have goons?!"

"I convinced Uncle Ken to assign me a squad as a reward for taking down Hera Buchanan."

"Um, excuse me, but *I* took down Hera Buchanan."

"Do you want credit, or do you want me to have goons?"

She crinkled her nose. "Depends on what you do with them."

"Well, right now, they're saving your butt!"

Jojo looked out the window and glanced back. Epsilon ran after the van, but the six bruisers kept throwing themselves at her, nailing her with punches and kicks and elbows and knees.

One fired some kind of weapon at Epsilon, but when it did nothing to penetrate her skin, the woman settled for grabbing Epsilon under the arms instead, putting her in a Full Nelson.

Jojo spun back toward Michael. "How'd you know I was here?"

"I had a feeling you were in trouble after you were acting weird in school, so I ordered one of my goons to tail you—"

"You what?!"

"—so I'd know if you were in trouble! I know being Sarcastic Fringehead comes with lots of enemies, and... Well, I didn't wanna miss out on another gig because our bassist was kidnapped." He threw her a lopsided smile.

Jojo had no idea how to feel about that. On the one hand, the idea that *Michael Donnelly* had his own squad of nanotech-enhanced goons was beyond weird.

On the other, hand... well... her friend was in the middle of saving her, even though she'd never asked for help.

The van ground to a halt, and Jojo slammed against the seat. Terror seized her chest. She knew what she'd see before she looked out the window, but still, the sight of Epsilon gripping the back of the van made her face go cold. The vehicle tilted; Epsilon had picked up its back wheels.

The six goons lay on the pavement behind Epsilon. Even with their superior numbers and nanotech enhancements, they'd been no match for the woman.

Where did she come from? How's she so freaking strong?

Some of the goons—*should I call them "goons" if they're on my side?*—picked themselves up, but they were clearly winded, despite the nanotech's regenerative powers.

Epsilon shifted the van in her grip and made her way forward. Any minute, she would rip open the door and grab Jojo.

I'm not going down so easily!

As Epsilon seized the handle to slide the back door open, Jojo climbed into the front seat, shoved open the passenger-side door, and jumped out.

Epsilon whirled to face her, dropping the van, and grasped at Jojo, who dodged and seized whatever salt she could sense.

She shoved down with all her might and shot herself twenty feet into the air.

Epsilon bent her knees, preparing to jump. *Would she be strong enough to leap so high?*

Two of the bruisers seized Epsilon, but the woman easily threw them off.

Jojo's arms shook, and she looked around at the surrounding buildings. Maybe she could reach a porch, or even a rooftop, but how far could she get?

A blur of motion appeared in the street below and threw itself at Epsilon, knocking the woman flat.

Epsilon roared and threw off her attacker, who landed on his back.

"Mr. Mesa?!" Jojo blinked, unsure if she could believe her eyes.

"Oh, yeah!" Michael called up to her. "You never hung up last night, and I heard everything! When the lady I had tailing you called to say you were in trouble, I called him for help. Figured having an extra bruiser around might be helpful, and after his freak-outs, I figured he'd be good at this stuff!"

"Show some respect, young man." Mr. Mesa jumped up. "I'm still your teacher!"

"Sorry, Mr. Mesa!" Michael said.

Still holding herself aloft, Jojo summoned a cloud of sodium-containing sediment to attack Epsilon's face. This time, she covered the woman's nose and mouth as well as her eyes.

It seemed like a nasty way to fight, but it was effective. Unable to see or breathe, Epsilon wasn't strong enough to resist as Mr. Mesa and Michael's goons overwhelmed and restrained her. A man retrieved a pair of handcuffs and slapped them onto Epsilon's wrists, then pressed a button that sent a bolt of electricity through them.

Epsilon spasmed, then went still.

"What is that?" Mr. Mesa demanded.

"Relax, it only stuns people." Michael climbed out of the van. "My uncle wouldn't trust me with anything scarier."

"I should hope not." Mr. Mesa gave him a chastising look, and Michael shrank. Mr. Mesa pulled a phone from his pocket. "I'm calling the police. I will only tell them that the fugitive Epsilon was spotted at this location. It's up to you whether you want to stay."

Jojo lowered herself to the ground, looking around in disbelief. It was over. Epsilon had been defeated, and the authorities would be there soon.

Michael gestured at the goons. "C'mon, let's get out of here!" They jumped into his van, and he sped away.

Jojo thought about running off too, but it didn't seem right to leave without at least talking to her teacher.

Mr. Mesa, his conversation with the police complete, turned to Jojo. "I'll remain nearby," he said, "though out of sight, until the authorities have Epsilon firmly in custody."

"Thanks for coming to my rescue," Jojo breathed.

"I could not in good conscience have refused." Mr. Mesa looked at his hands. "Perhaps these new abilities aren't so bad after all... I told my wife what was going on. She said she'd never forgive me if I didn't help a student in need."

Jojo gave a grateful smile, then glanced down at Epsilon, who lay at an awkward angle—facedown but with her hips turned to the side, her legs splayed and her arms bent. "Nice work, Picasso."

"Picasso?"

Jojo stuck her nose in the air. "You deconstructed and rearranged your subject in an unexpected yet aesthetically pleasing manner."

Mr. Mesa chuckled. "I see you've done the reading. I hope that means you're prepared for next week's quiz."

"Quiz?!"

"Come, now, Jojo, you've been in my class long enough to know that I always quiz the class the week after introducing a new unit."

Jojo sputtered. In the distance, sirens wailed.

Mr. Mesa retreated into the shadows and nodded at Jojo, as if to say, *Go on.*

Jojo ran back toward the rehearsal studio. Not only because she had to pick up her bass guitar, but because if anyone spotted Jojo Fang, all they'd know was that she'd had a legit, email-confirmed booking at the nearby rehearsal space.

As she rushed down the sidewalk, a strange yet warm feeling filled her chest.

Two new heroes had shown up to save her that night.

One was a kid who'd only looked out for himself before, but who'd leveraged his nepo-baby status into saving a friend from certain doom. Jojo still wasn't sure how she felt about her friend having mobster-supplied goons. But considering how many baddies were bankrolled by Captains of Industry, maybe it wasn't such a bad thing to take advantage of an insider.

And the other hero? A mild-mannered man who'd found himself with an unwanted power, yet stepped up when someone needed help. Jojo had no idea if Mr. Mesa would keep his power for good or continue seeking a way to get rid of it, but his actions that night confirmed what she'd always known: that he was one of the good guys.

Maybe that night's action would be the end of both heroes. They'd retreat back to the holes she'd inadvertently yanked them out of.

Or maybe they'd help others as they'd helped her, and choose to continue helping others for as long as they could.

And maybe those others, whether superpowered or not, would choose to help more still.

Everything you do—it isn't about you, Laolao had said. *It's bigger than you, and even those you help.*

Maybe that was the true point of hero-ing. Not just helping others in the moment, but showing them what was possible, so they might radiate that goodness out to the next person, who'd pass it onto the next person, and the next…

She reached the practice room and opened her bass guitar case. Epsilon was finished, and Jojo had paid for the space, after all. She plugged in her instrument, closed her eyes, and started to play.

What it meant to be a superhero, what made it worthwhile or not... Those were bigger questions than she cared to answer. She was content with deciding she didn't regret having powers after all.

***

Jojo was the first one to arrive at the Garment Club on Friday. Standing outside the Midtown club with her bass strapped to her back, she tapped her foot deliberately as the others pulled up in a shared cab.

"Oh, look who decided to show up," she said with a teasing grin.

Amaya narrowed her eyes. "You'd better know your part."

"Know it? I'm gonna kill it! We all are." She glanced up at the Garment Club's sign. Though it looked dull in the daytime, having been denied its evening LED glory, its stylized letters still sent a chill down her back. My Bedroom Panic had played a handful of nightlife venues before, but the Garment Club was special. Every member of the band could name at least ten indie musicians they admired who'd stood on the tiny stage they were about to step onto.

Amaya held her irritated glare for another second, and then her expression melted into a smile. "Let's go in there and rock their socks off!"

With a whoop, Bethany yanked open the door, and all five of them strode into the club like they owned the place, even though half an hour remained before their turn to audition.

As they waited, Michael glanced at Jojo.

"We good?" he whispered, though he needn't have bothered; a metal band was in the middle of auditioning.

Jojo pretended to hem and haw, then let her face warm. "The show must go on." Which meant, *Yeah, we 're good.*

Michael nodded in response.

She panned her eyes across the tiny stage, the plain chairs and tables presently stacked in the corners, the no-frills bar, the signed photos of musicians that hung lopsided on the dusty walls…

The metal band finished, and after two singer-songwriters who crooned about their feelings and a weird band filled the space with alien-sounding synths, it was My Bedroom Panic's turn.

Jojo took her place on the stage, her fingers tingling with anticipation.

"A-one, two, a-one, two, three four!"

Even before Stephen counted them off, even before they dove headfirst into their bold new song, Jojo knew they'd get the gig. And she let the music carry her away.

Plenty of musicians had day jobs. Being Sarcastic Fringehead just happened to be hers.

MEMORIES OF A RED SKY

BY MICHAEL A. BURSTEIN

My name is Jeremiah Singer. I'm a 24-year-old physics graduate student. I need to hold onto that.

My other identity is Red Sky. I'm a Phenomenon. I spent my life training to fight. But I also have a special power. I can take myself back in time fifteen seconds to correct a mistake. Or at least I could before my power went all wonky.

The last thing I remember is following a clue to an old, abandoned warehouse, one of the oldest clichés when it comes to bad guy hangouts. But I knew that the conspirators who messed up my power were planning to do other, far worse things, to other Phenomenons. I had no time to contact any of my compatriots. I had to stop the bad guys right away, before they could do anything else to anyone else.

So why can't I recall what happened next?

Jeremiah is seven years old. He is playing in a wide concrete alleyway near his house with five neighborhood friends from their yeshiva in Brooklyn. Apartment buildings stand on either side of the alleyway, and the alleyway itself has a row of garages all on one side. Most of the garages are closed, but one near the end is open and empty. An odor of oil and gasoline emanates from it.

Jeremiah and his friends don't have a lot of options for a softball field, so they have turned this alleyway into a makeshift game space. They have chosen places to serve as bases, including a garage door on one side and a chunk of rock in the short concrete wall on the other. They have no designated teams; whoever is not batting has to serve as one of the fielders, whether at a base or as pitcher or catcher, and if the bases ever end up being loaded it means fewer players to tag someone out. The score is kept sporadically, if at all, for each player, but they really have no way to decide easily who won or who lost.

Jeremiah doesn't care. He loves playing with his friends.

He is at bat and about to swing at a pitch when suddenly he hears a noise, a clink from the ground near the rock they've designated as third base.

His friend Eitan, who is pitching, pauses. "What was that?"

All of them stop and listen. They hear another clink, then another. Jeremiah's friends in the field put down their gloves and Jeremiah puts down his bat.

They walk over to the third base rock in the wall, and as they do, they hear more clinking sounds. But just as suddenly as the sounds started, they stop.

"Look," says Eitan, pointing down.

On the ground near the concrete wall, there are a bunch of clean, shiny pennies.

"Where did these come from?" Lev asks.

Jeremiah looks up at the apartment building. "Maybe some kid is pushing them out one of the windows," he says. "We should pile them up on the wall and see if anyone up there knows.

His friends agree. They bend over to collect the pennies, twelve in all, and make three piles on top of the wall. Meanwhile, Jeremiah keeps looking up, scanning the windows above. It takes a moment, but then he thinks he sees a flick of a curtain.

"Hey! I see someone!" Jeremiah shouts.

All his friends start shouting as well. "Hey! Up there! Can you help us?"

At first, it seems as if they imagined the movement of the curtain, but then they see the face of an adult, mostly obscured, looking down on them. "What?" says the adult, quietly but loud enough for them to hear.

Jeremiah points to the piles of coins on the wall. "Do you know anything about these coins?"

The adult, who seems to be a woman although she keeps hiding behind the curtain, quickly shakes her head.

"We think a kid is knocking coins out of their apartment," Jeremiah says. "We want to return them."

The adult in the window frowns. "Return them?"

"Well, yes," Jeremiah says. "Do you know of any kid in one of the other apartments who might have pushed these out?"

The adult's eyes look wary. She shakes her head again.

"Well, if you think of anyone, let them know. We'll leave the pennies here."

It isn't until that evening, when Jeremiah tells his parents about the incident, and the two of them share a sad, knowing look, that Jeremiah comes to understand that more was going on. And it isn't until years later that he hears of the antisemitic custom of a non-Jew pitching pennies at Jews, leaning into the stereotypes that Jews were greedy and cheap. Jeremiah was glad that they had told the person they were hoping to return the pennies, but–

Wait a moment. Jeremiah was still standing with his friends, why was he remembering the future? How was he remembering the future?

I'm seven years old, he thought. *I'm a kid. I'm–*

There's a flash of light.

***

Jeremiah found himself floating, which felt strange; as far as he knew, flight was not one of powers. He looked down and through a fog saw himself in full Red Sky costume: masked and cowled, red spandex covering his body and red boots on his feet, with a red starburst against an orange background on his chest. But the Red Sky he saw wasn't jumping from rooftop to rooftop or stopping a mugging in an alleyway. The Red Sky figure below him was strapped onto a metal bed. A whole bank of computer monitors circled his head. Other electronic devices surrounded his body. Despite the fact that Jeremiah worked in a lab, he didn't recognize most of the equipment.

Wait a moment? I work in a lab? Aren't I just seven years old? No, wait. I was --

The fog began to dissipate. Jeremiah looked beyond his unmoving body and saw a slight woman in a white lab coat accompanied by a hulking figure of a bald man in a jacket and tie that hung loosely on him.

Am I dead? Should I be trying to recite the Sh'ma?

No, wait, I remember now. That woman is Kate Burns. She's a scientist, studying Phenomenons. Works for–for someone. And the man–she called him Bob. He's the one who knocked me out. He's a–a Counter, I think she called him.

The two figures approached the unconscious body of Red Sky. Jeremiah quieted his thoughts and listened.

Kate Burns glanced over at one of the monitors. She walked around the metal bed and checked the readings on another monitor.

"Are you done yet?" Bob growled. He pulled at the knot in his tie.

Burns glared at the Counter, despite her nervousness. "No, I'm not done yet," she said.

"Soon, Doc?"

"Don't call me 'Doc.' Didn't Georgina tell you to give me all the time I needed?"

"Yeah, but I've been wanting to squish this guy." Bob stared at Red Sky, an excited look on his face. "I'm looking forward to killing him as soon as you're done."

Burns grimaced but kept her face toward the monitor. "You'll wait until I tell you I'm done with him. Not a second sooner."

Bob grunted. "What exactly are you doing? Why's this guy so important?"

Burns adjusted her glasses. "He's important because he's a Phenomenon. And what I'm doing is enhancing his power."

Bob looked startled. "This guy has powers? I knocked him out with one punch."

Burns sighed. "Yes, I know. He has one power that we know of, which Georgina found out thanks to Parallel."

"Parallel?"

Burns looked chagrined, as if she had said more than she should have. "One of his enemies. It doesn't matter."

"So what is it? What's his power?"

Burns flipped a few switches next to one of the monitors. "Not that it matters, but time travel."

Bob's jaw dropped. "This guy can travel through time?"

"Sort of." Burns studied one of the monitors that displayed Red Sky's vitals. "Blood pressure, temperature, both normal," she said to herself.

"What?" Bob asked.

"Sorry." Burns walked over to one of the devices sitting next to the bed. It looked like a laser. "He can apparently repeat his last fifteen seconds, although there are limits. He can't do it more than once for any period of fifteen seconds."

Bob whistled. "Still seems useful to me."

"Yeah, That's what Georgina thinks. She wants to figure out a way to copy his power."

"And give it to me?" Bob asked.

Burns paused. "Sure," she said quietly. "Or to any of the Counters."

"Well, what are we waiting for?"

"I can't just snap my fingers and make it happen," she said. "His power has already been affected. I need to fix it, enhance it, and then extract it." She tapped on the device that looked like a laser. "The problem is, when I send the chronon waves through his body to try to extract his power, it sends him places. And then I have to wait for him to return."

"Where?"

"Not where. *When.* His body stays here, but his consciousness, well, it gets unstuck in time. I'm not sure where–I mean, when–he is right now."

Bob nodded. He walked over to what Jeremiah, his consciousness floating above, now realized was the chronon emitter. "Well," Bob said, "maybe if you do this thing again now, it'll bring him back."

"Huh," Burns said. "I hadn't thought of that. I don't think it can hurt him, and Georgina does want this done as soon as possible…"

She pushed a button on the emitter.

Jeremiah saw a flash of light–

***

Jeremiah is fourteen years old. He is in ninth grade at a public high school. This year, despite his family's devotion to Modern Orthodox Judaism, his parents pulled him out of the yeshiva system and sent him to the local Brooklyn high school. They thought it would be a good experience for him.

Jeremiah is sitting at a lunch table on his first day of school, a Mets cap on his head. He was invited by a bunch of the other Black kids at the school to join them. They sit at their own table. Jeremiah looks around. It seems as if there are many other Black kids at the school, but they all sit at tables by themselves. Jeremiah also sees tables of Asian kids and white kids.

He knows there must be other Jewish students, but he can't pick them out. It perturbs him for a moment to realize that he instinctively looks for white faces. Internalized racism.

Jeremiah eats his sandwich that he brought from home; his parents had little idea how available kosher food would be at the school. Normally, given that the sandwich has bread, Jeremiah would have gone through the ritual of washing his hands with a blessing before eating, but he's trying to stay under the radar. He whispers the blessing over bread under his breath before taking a bite; the other kids don't notice.

He is only half paying attention to the conversation. He hears the other kids complain about school and about family. And then he hears one of them say something insulting about his family's landlord. And then the kid shakes his head and concludes:

"Jews are cheap, man."

The other kids at the table nod in agreement.

Jeremiah is shocked. He's not sure how to respond. The conversation around him continues. He thinks, and chooses his course of action.

Jeremiah removes his baseball cap. Even now, he wears his hair in a short afro and temple fade but he also wears something else on his head: a round, blue kippah, clipped to his hair as best as he can.

The other Black kids fall silent, one by one, as they spot the kippah. They stare at him.

Jeremiah picks up the remains of his lunch and his backpack. He gets up from the table and walks to the door.

There is a flash of light.

***

Jeremiah closed his eyes, shook his head, opened his eyes, and looked around. He found himself sitting at a table at one of his favorite restaurants, Talia's Steakhouse and Bar on the Upper West Side. Across from him were his old college friend Gail Morse and her fiancé, Gregorio Camus. On the table was a stack of three small plates and a basket of pita, accompanied by a larger plate with hummus, baba ganoush, beets, and assorted vegetables.

"Um," Jeremiah said. "What?"

A glance passed between Gail and Gregorio. Jeremiah had the impression that they had been having a casual conversation a moment ago, but now both of them looked shaken.

Gail cleared her throat. "Gregorio, I think it's happened."
Gregorio nodded.

"Hi, guys," Jeremiah said. "Did I miss something?"

"You just thanked us for deferring to you and your need to go to a kosher restaurant," Gail said. "You also mentioned that you know Ephraim, the owner of this place."

Jeremiah nodded. "I do," he said. "But I don't remember anything from before a moment ago." He pulled one of the small plates off the stack, reached for a piece of pita bread, dipped it in the hummus, and then paused. "Did I wash?" he asked.

Gail laughed. "Yes, you did."

"Good. I'm starved." Jeremiah's stomach felt as empty as it did on Yom Kippur. He took a large bite of the pita and swallowed; it was delicious.

"Okay," he said. "So, what's going on?"

Gail cleared her throat. "Jeremiah, listen carefully. You've become unstuck in time."

"Unstuck in time."

"Yes. You seem to be visiting your past." She gestured around. "Do you remember this at all?"

"It seems familiar," he said, slowly, "but I like this place. I come here a lot." He paused. "In fact, I suggested we come here to celebrate when I learned about your engagement."

"That's tonight," Gregorio said.

Jeremiah nodded. "Okay, so if I am unstuck in time, how do you know?"

"You told us," Gail said. "I mean, you will tell us. About a week ago."

"I *will* tell you...a week *ago*. So you're telling me something that...that I haven't told you yet?"

Gail flashed a brief smile. "Yeah, when you told me that I was confused too." She reached into her purse, pulled out a small notebook. "I took notes."

"Of course you did," Jeremiah said. "So what did I say?"

"You gave us the information we needed to tell you to help you break free and return to your normal time. You said that you need to concentrate on one memory. But then you only had time to tell me one word to give you the clue."

"What was the word?"

She held up the notebook and showed him. "Moshe."

"Moshe," he echoed. "The Hebrew name for Moses."

"Yeah, we know."

Jeremiah's face turned hot. Gail worked at the General Research Division of the New York Public Library; she would have looked up the name had he not had time to tell her the meaning. "Sorry."

"It's okay."

"So what now?" Jeremiah asked.

Gail shrugged. "I guess think about Moses?"

"Moses. Moshe. Moses. Moshe." Jeremiah paused. "Gail, did I ever tell you about the time that I played–"

There was a bright light.

***

I am six years old and in second grade. I'm in a school play. We are little kids pretending to be the Israelites. We stand on a stage all together. We each get only one line. All the roles are small.

But I get to play Moshe, the lawgiver, the lawbringer. I remember now. One of my teachers pushed for me to get the role. My parents will tell me later that some families complained. I won't understand why.

The other kids have made fun of me because of my brown skin. I don't yet realize that there is a world of antisemitism out there, but among my fellow Jews I have sadly already learned about racism. It's one of the reasons why my parents plan to pull me out of the yeshiva system later in my education.

This school is a bad one anyway. One of the teachers was warped by her experiences in the post-Holocaust world, and she shares some strange ideas with the students. I remember coming home one day in tears because she warned us that if the scroll in the mezuzah on our doorpost were faded, when we went to touch it on our way into our home, our hand would burn off before we had a chance to kiss our fingers.

But that's not what's happening now. Now I am on stage about to play Moses. To be Moses.

And now I am thinking about racism and antisemitism. And I'm thinking of all the people who are kept down by The Man.

That's why I'll became a superhero. The injustices I feel, the racism and antisemitism I experience. No one should feel alone and ashamed. Everyone should feel protected. In the same way that I feel protected by God, by HaShem. A cyclotron explosion may give me my power, but even before that happens I'll train myself to be the best fighter I can possibly be.

A fighter for justice.

It is my turn. I say my line, "Al tira'u." Do not be afraid. *I grab the Torah scroll and as I walk in front of my classmates, I hear them singing "Torah tzivah lanu Moshe"–the Torah that Moses commanded to us. The same Torah that includes the idea of loving one's neighbor as you love yourself.*

At the end of the stage is a portal of light. I've never seen anything like it but somehow I know what to do now. Carrying the Torah scroll, I step directly through the portal, and leave my memories behind.

***

It was Jeremiah Singer who entered the portal, but it was Red Sky who suddenly awoke. He tensed his muscles and broke free of the straps holding him down to the metal bed. Fortunately, Dr. Burns and Bob were facing away from him. It took them a moment to realize that he was free.

"Bob!" shouted Dr. Burns. "Grab him! Don't let him get away."

Bob sprinted toward Red Sky, and Red Sky was astonished. How could a man so large be so fast?

Red Sky dove away as fast as his athletic training would let him. But it was of no use. Bob was too quick for him. The Counter grabbed him around the waist and began to squeeze. They were going to capture him again, experiment on him again. There was nothing he could do.

If only I had my power, Red Sky thought. *If only I could still chronoback*–

Suddenly, the world took on a red tinge and the usual odd, eerie silence fell on his ears. More importantly, Bob began to loosen his grip on Red Sky's waist. And most important of all, Red Sky was able to jump away from Bob.

Yes!, he thought. *My power is back. Whatever that scientist did must have restored it. Thank HaShem.*

When his power had gone wonky, he had still been able to go back in time fifteen seconds, but he couldn't move around and change what he had done before. But now he was no longer constrained that way. The rest of the world had to move back to where they had been fifteen seconds ago, but he could move anywhere he wanted. So he had fifteen seconds to–to do what? That was the question.

Let's see, fifteen seconds ago, I was over there. He looked at the spot where he had been standing, right where Bob had grabbed him. He watched Bob moving backward, back to where he was before he grabbed Red Sky.

So let me position myself over…here.

Red Sky backed up a few paces, and made sure to face the Counter. He reached into his utility belt and pulled out a small bag of sand and a bag of ball bearings.

Three…two…one…

Just as normal time resumed, Red Sky threw the handful of sand directly into Bob's eyes and the ball bearings at his feet. The big man spit, screamed, and rubbed at his face, and then slipped and fell.

And Red Sky ran. It was not his favorite thing to do–heroes, he believed, shouldn't run away from danger–but he knew that he couldn't handle this guy on his own.

He managed to make it many blocks away before he had to stop to catch his breath, and he once again thanked his past self for all the athletic training. It was the middle of the night, and fortunately the neighborhood was mostly deserted. He scaled the side of an apartment building using his special suction cups and caught the rest of his breath while sitting on top of the roof.

He had time to think through all the experiences he had just re-lived. It took him a moment to realize that he didn't recall giving Gail the clue that would free him from the time slipping. Did that mean he would time slip again at some point? Was he going to have to figure out a way to trigger it on his own?

No matter. Time travel meant he could worry about it later. For now, there was something more vital he needed to take care of.

Jeremiah pulled out his cell phone from its utility belt compartment. He pushed a button to dial one of the other Phenomenons, Luminosity, someone he knew well.

Of course, she didn't answer. He waited for the beep.

"Luminosity," he said, "it's Red Sky. Listen, I've just escaped from a scientist who had me trapped in my own past. I don't get it either, but somehow her experiments restored my chronobacking power. I'm able to relive those fifteen seconds again, as before.

"But…she had some brute helping her out, some guy called Bob. He's enhanced: super strong, super-fast, and with super endurance. No way I could have defeated him. I barely escaped with my life.

"I think we need to gather United Front."

HIRED HELP, PART I: S.O.S

BY RUSS COLCHAMIRO AND HILDY SILVERMAN

Georgina Pinkerton reclined in a supple leather chair behind the ornate custom desk in her Lower East Side office. Just outside the window, a beautiful day gleamed. Not a single cloud dared obstruct her sunny view.

She had the Phenomenons on the run.

Yes, they'd proven more formidable than she initially anticipated. But she'd studied their ways. How they fought, how they planned, how they worked together... and yet how disparate and unorganized they really were. That was their greatest weakness. Easy to exploit.

These powered people, these abominations, these domestic terrorists, were set apart from the rest of humankind. With unnatural physical and psychic abilities, given license to fight for their self-defined, self-serving, arrogant, and myopic views of how they defined *humanity*.

Despite horrors inflicted by these radicals upon legitimate and rightful citizens, the authorities and public at large—those not directly impacted by what were clearly egregious acts of domestic terrorism—excused the collateral damage as the price of having "heroes.'

Georgina shifted her gaze to one of three large screens on her desk. A structural engineer by trade, who understood the intricacies of how to efficiently design, build, and finance real estate development, she scanned each of her New York City properties through a viewscreen.

From the exterior, the nondescript low-rise building in which she sat on the Lower East Side was easy to overlook, with a laundromat, pizza joint, and *Chita's Nails* on the ground floor. Pulsing within the building's interior, however, was the heartbeat of her operation.

She relished how her global network of power, technology, and wealth, and her clandestine private army of customized powered beings had arguably made her the most influential person in the world.

She also remembered the event that had led her down this road. Yes, wealth and power had awaited. But she never forgot the horror that drove her there.

When Grey Guardsman battled the Dark Tide and Jonesy more than a decade ago, they took down the affordable housing project Georgina had worked on as a mid-level structural engineer for Peachtree Construction. Eighty-six low-income residents were either killed or severely injured.

Georgina later discovered Grey Guardsman, in his reckless indifference to safety, also punctured an underground gas main a block away. The pressure had built up and followed a trail to a building that had nothing to do with the battle. An inconvenient fact left off the official report, chalked up as an accident in service of the greater good.

The building she resided in at the time. Where her ten-year-old son, Dennis, had just returned after school that day, bubbling about how well he'd pitched during baseball team tryouts.

She'd crawled out from under the rubble, battered but alive.

Dennis did not.

Georgina had been an idealist before that day, but the devastation broke her spirit. Psychically traumatized her. When she protested, *begged* for justice for her lost son and the other innocents wounded or killed, nobody listened. Nobody cared. At least, no one who had the will and the power to do anything about it.

Not even Robert Pinkerton, her then-boss, with whom (during one night at a business conference when too much liquor flowed) she'd conceived Dennis.

No options. No support.

No problem. She'd found a way to settle accounts herself.

With poised and deliberate clicks of the mouse, Georgina now observed activity at the South Street Seaport, Brooklyn Bridge, and Wall Street. Then, one by one, the remainder of the city's neighborhoods throughout Brooklyn, Queens, Staten Island, and The Bronx. The city populated in total by millions of unsuspecting citizens who spoken hundreds of different languages and prayed to every form of deity humankind had invented to appease their anxiety, fears, and impotence in the battle for existential purpose—or control those with whom they disagreed.

They sure as hell listen now, she thought. *And they sure as hell care. And soon, real soon, the Phenomenons will all be gone.*

And the world will be mine.

Georgina felt a minor tremor, as if an underground subway was rumbling nearby. It vibrated through the solid-oak floor reinforced with nine inches of concrete and a patented, nigh-impenetrable metal alloy, covered in a Flokati rug from Cyprus.

One of her three oversized monitors glitched, replacing her view of Bellevue Hospital with static. The image reappeared. She swiveled her chair, then peered through the third-story window with its tinted, blast-proof glass. Usual activity outside. Honking cabs, clunking delivery trucks, and pedestrians walking with the guarded aggression and determination you find only in dense urban landscapes.

No reason to feel threatened. To worry. But Georgina hadn't amassed this much power and wealth by ignoring molecular nuances and liminal shifts in energy. No matter how seemingly inconsequential the event, if every action had an equal and opposite reaction, then she was sensing a reaction.

Which meant there was a precipitating event. Cause and effect.

She swiveled back to face her computer station. On the second monitor, subdivided into a dozen six-inch-by-six-inch frames, were the secret laboratories she financed and operated throughout the world. Where her handpicked teams of revolutionary geneticists, researchers, physicians, and engineers dissected and experimented on captured Phenomenons to better understand, and thus control, the mechanisms of their powers.

Thanks to the data gleaned from those unholy creatures, her lab teams had been able to ply otherwise normal humans with genetic manipulation, technology, nanobots, cybernetic augmentation, and (for all she cared) dark magic, to create her own enhanced warriors.

Loyal only to her, with specific powers targeted to counteract those of individual Phenomenons. And if those experiments resulted in failures along the path to success, including grotesque and horrifying mutations and unstable soldiers? So be it. They were all disposable. Even failures could be used to serve her purpose.

Lab Number Eight, fifty-six feet beneath a soybean farmhouse on the outskirts of Whitley County, Indiana, went dark. Georgina sucked in a breath.

"Turn," she said through the intercom. "Everything okay out there?"

Tyler Akinomi, aka Turn, did not respond. His lab-created powers enabled him to turn any corner, at any angle, regardless of resistance, speed, or narrow field of vision, all without losing his balance, timing, or coordination.

But not always. And never without a long period of blackouts afterward.

"Turn," Georgina repeated.

No answer.

Another rumble. Only this one vibrated up her left leg, the one mangled when her apartment building collapsed from Guardsman's gas explosion. The titanium pin in her knee pinched, triggering a merciless wave of pain that blinded her for several seconds.

She regained her sight just in time to watch another lab on the view screen go dark, the one secreted behind a walk-in freezer of *Bango 's Fish Market* in Brisbane, Australia.

Same again with labs hidden in unremarkable locations in Detroit, Tempe, Arizona, Ettlebruck, Luxembourg, and Mongu, Zambia.

Hot flash. Tacky mouth. Adrenaline. Her voice quivered as she spoke again through the com.

"Darla One," she said to one half of her security team.

On the third desktop screen, she beheld ten red dots—each representing one of her Counters, her latest and most powerful generation of soldiers—clustered in the main hall.

This was never supposed to happen. She took great pains to keep her creations separated from one another, avoid any camaraderie or sense of team. Bonding would inevitably lead to confiding in one another, sharing expressions of resentment against management, labor organization.

Other unpleasantries.

Georgina hadn't feared for her safety in years. She had security redundancies. "Darla One. Darla Two. What's happening on the…"

Flutter in her chest. As always when she was alone, she had her financials up on the widescreen mounted in the wall across from her desk, so she could monitor her investments and the global markets in real time. Millions, sometimes billions, gained or lost in less than a second. Timing was everything.

Multicolored lines, graphs, and charts were displayed against a black background. A ticker scrolled along the bottom of the screen. As of 7:42 a.m. EDT that morning Georgina had been one of the largest single shareholders in Langston

Chemicals, valued at $237.32 per share. The stock was down to $53.29 per share and dropping precipitously.

A Cayman Islands bank account with more than $3 billion flashed onscreen. The cursor blinked four times. Then a notice appeared: *ACCOUNT DEACTIVATED.*

Georgina had spent more than a decade consolidating power. And control. In a flash, it was all slipping away. A festering pool of panic roiled in her gut. "What in the Sam Hill is *happening?*"

A second account in The Republic of Seychelles was also deactivated. Another $7.35 billion gone.

In rapid succession, four more of her experimental labs went dark. Multiple large-scale trades were authorized from her account to buy stocks in poorly managed companies on the fast-track to bankruptcy. Three more of her offshore bank accounts were deactivated.

She was being demolished.

The building rumbled again. Only this time, it wasn't a tremor. The floor buckled.

Whatever the cause of these attacks, Georgina still had access to her privately financed satellite system that gave her global access to communications networks. She tapped the keyboard. The screen that had been focused on her local properties switched views.

Data, charts, and graphs displayed. Video feeds. Audio files. It was all there.

She was still in control.

Georgina pressed a hand to her chest, felt her heart thunder beneath her sternum. She drew a deep breath. In and out. *Slow. Easy. Calm.*

The satellite network mattered most. So long as she had eyes and ears everywhere...

Her feeds shut off.

As a woman accustomed to controlling her environments and everyone in her ecosystem, she was suddenly without recourse. She trembled, keen mind all but paralyzed by confusion.

There was no way to ignore the truth.

The most powerful, fortified woman in the world was under attack. In her own bunker.

A voice crackled through the com, barely audible. Darla Two. "Ms…" Garbled noise. "There's been"—more static—…breach." Thunderous gunshots. Chaotic screams. "Get to…!"

Silence.

Georgina pressed a button on the underside of her desk. From the top of the doorframe, a metal alloy shield that put titanium to shame slid down to the floor. Same again with the windows.

She crossed the room and tilted the painting of a half-felled peach tree with an ax buried in its stump. Behind the painting was a thumbprint and retinal scanner.

She activated the mechanism. The door to her panic room slid opened. After she dove inside, it closed.

Locked.

Sequestered in her impenetrable fortress, Georgina's priorities changed radically. Rather than plotting the next move in her quest to eradicate all Phenomenons, her revised and refocused goal became clear and simple: Live to see the end of the day.

Because one blistering arrow of reality pierced her veil of fear and humiliation.

The Phenomenons were good. But they weren't *this* good. There was only one way she could have found herself in such a precarious situation.

Somehow, someway, and against all odds, the unthinkable had occurred.

Her creatures had betrayed her.

***

There are panic rooms and there are panic rooms. Georgina had a panic suite.

Her reinforced bunker was decked out with a command center computer station, cameras, vault, full kitchen, 90-day rations of food and drink, queen-size bed, clothes, laundry, and bathroom with a steam shower. A presidential suite within a bunker.

She had long been disrupting society's rhythms and patterns. Knew full well the vibrations she triggered might someday reverberate. She was waging a war that absolutely had to be won—and she *would* win. The course of human civilization depended on it.

Her son's ghost demanded it.

There were real and frightening monsters on the loose who had no regard for common decency. And monsters rarely went down easy.

The irony wasn't lost on her that the war she had waged against these inhuman creatures, the Phenomenons, was borne from the terror, the profound loss, she'd suffered as a victim of their collateral damage. Yet in her pursuit to eliminate them... was it possible she'd become a monster herself?

She acknowledged the collateral damage recorded on her side of the ledger. She accepted, at least on some level, that *what comes around goes around* applied to her too. But now that it was all falling apart...?

She had never believed she'd actually need this panic room. Now it was the only physical barrier protecting her from the very creations she'd manipulated to serve at her behest.

The entire building shook again, as if an earthquake had erupted along a fault line. She stumbled, fell into the command center chair, clutched the armrests. A part of her wanted to throw a tantrum, rail against this contemptible turn of events. But that wouldn't solve her very real and immediate problem.

Survive first. Revenge later.

Georgina activated her computer terminal. Cameras switched on. They ran on a separate network only she knew about. She couldn't see them in the frame, but from within the building, she heard aggressive, violent howls, smashing wood and glass, and multiple gunshots.

Ophelia and Smith were both on the second floor, directly above the laundromat. Georgina had hand-selected those two and one other to serve as her personal guards.

All of Georgina's Counters had been injected with a nanobot tracker deep into their bone marrow. The ten invaders were each represented by a red dot on her screen, her elite guards by yellow.

Georgina watched the yellow dot representing Ophelia. A former tattoo artist, her cybernetic implant gave her lightning-quick reflexes and logic-response times, and the ability to interface with all manner of technology. She was retreating toward the southeast wall near the windows overlooking the alley.

"Ophelia," Georgina said, her voice raspy. "Report."

Five brutal gun blasts echoed in her ear. Georgina winced. *"Under attack."* More gunfire. *"Trapped. Can't—"*

"Ophelia," she repeated anxiously. "Ophelia!"

A second yellow dot moved toward the center of the room. A lethal fighter with expertise in a dozen styles of martial arts, Smith had been injected with a virus that mutated her genetic make-up, enabling her to release a paralytic nerve agent through her breath.

In a tight, military formation, red dots on the opposite side of the room appeared onscreen. Three. Now five. Now eight. Ten.

"Code Black!" Smith shouted. "Code Black!"

"Code Black." Georgina said aloud, mostly to herself. *Infiltration. Prepare for extraction. Impossible.* Then she remembered something Robert had said. *"The insidious nature of conviction is that it blinds you to your own weaknesses— and realities you'd rather not face."*

Still, she could not accept that the infrastructure she'd planned, financed, and executed at great pain and sacrifice was falling apart. No one else on Earth had her combination of intelligence, willpower, focus, determination, and vision to see it through.

"*Perhaps*," she'd responded to her then-boss and future husband, "*but the empowering nature of conviction is that, despite long odds and in the face of adversity, you power through while most others would surrender, retreat, or take the coward's way out.*"

From her neck dangled a gold locket. Inside was a photo of Dennis, one month old, perfect, and cherubic. Along with a single pill.

Georgina cradled the locket between her thumb and forefinger. She thought about her baby, her unplanned but beloved son. How he'd looked when the morgue attendant pulled back the sheet for her to make the formal identification. Half of his face had been sheared away. Every still-growing bone crushed. His smooth flesh rendered a twisted and torn sack.

She never forgave Robert, the weak-willed, selfish old bastard, for refusing to stand up and be a man, to ID their son's remains or exact vengeance against Grey Guardsman and his ilk. Because he "*didn't have the heart.*"

Then he'd had the unmitigated *gall* to tell her to stop being hysterical. That it would be bad for business to go after the Phenomenons. "*They're too popular with the people*," he'd claimed. "*And I've got too much to lose.*"

That was the moment. After that, it had been simple enough to weaponize her grief. She'd also lobbed a strategic and not-so-veiled threat to reveal to the press the circumstances under which their son had been conceived. And her husband's callousness about the inconvenience of it all. About the child he never wanted. To avoid a scandal, the rich geezer finally divorced Wife #2 and married Georgina.

She had set the long game in motion. Georgina systematically insinuated herself into his businesses, gaining control of his networks and finances, until *he* was nothing more than the inconvenience. Then she removed his odious presence from her life. Permanently.

The floor of Georgina's office rumbled again, returning her attention to the here and now. The walls shook.

She shut her eyes as she clutched the locket, as if the tighter she squeezed both, the further she could suppress those memories. Instead, the more forcefully she applied that resistance, the gold trinket digging into her palm, the more intense the resurfacing memories became.

The blood. Her son's screams. Innocence destroyed.

Emboldened to do it again and again, the Phenomenons were heralded as champions rather than as the vicious, reckless, and self-aggrandizing terrorists they actually were. Society had lost its collective mind. It was up to Georgina to restore sanity.

Another possibility crested the edge of her consciousness. In her quest to save society, had she lost herself along the way? Had she become a cliché? Was her cure worse than the disease?

How many mothers now mourned *her* collateral damage? And if she were to blame for their agony, did that mean…?

It shamed her to think it. To allow herself to consider, even at the periphery of her tainted soul, the idea that *she* might have become the villain she'd set out to destroy. That whatever was happening now might be someone else's idea of justice.

Reality shook her from her despondency.

Screams and gunfire echoed through the speakers. A seam in the wall buckled.

Her heart gave a single thump, a beat of primal fear. Dark, oily bubbles obstructed her sightline. Black pools of defeat infiltrated her soul. She nearly blacked out.

Until she remembered who she was. And why she could not allow herself to fail.

She called upon her third inner sanctum guard. "Lampkin," she said through the com system. "Can you get behind the intruders?"

On her screen, a third yellow dot appeared. Slowly it encroached, as the red dots fanned out from the center of the room. Ophelia and Smith were being backed into a corner. Nowhere left to run.

"Lampkin," Georgina repeated. "Can you—?"

"In position," Lampkin said, her voice silky smooth. "Get ready."

Hope flared anew. Lampkin was her greatest experimental achievement before she developed her Counters. Fused with octopus genes, Lampkin had sprouted eight tentacles, four each on her front and back torso. When dormant, they appeared as nothing more than functionless nipples. When activated, however, they were something more.

There was still a chance.

The yellow and red dots converged. The battle began.

While she didn't have a visual on the melee, Georgina envisioned the scene. Smith exhaling her paralytic nerve agent through her breath. Lampkin's tentacles squeezing the life out of her opponents, injecting them with a fast-acting toxin through the suckers. Ophelia unleashing her brutal combat skills.

The building rattled. Through the coms, Georgina heard soul-piercing shrieks. Agony. Terror. Gunfire. Explosions. Shattering glass.

The red and yellow dots merged onscreen to the point it became impossible to see one behind the other. Until one red dot vanished. A Counter was dead.

One monster down, nine to go.

Another red dot gone.

Yes, Georgina thought. *Making progress.*

A third red dot blinked out.

Then a noise. A grotesque explosion of meat and matter. A yellow dot vanished.

Lampkin. Tentacles and all likely smeared across the walls. *No. You have to fight! You have to…*

Another yellow dot blinked away. *Ophelia.*

Georgina fell back into her chair. It couldn't go down like this. It just couldn't.

Her coms crackled. Smith's com. Only it wasn't Smith's voice.

"Mrs. Pinkerton," Maître d said.

Maître d had worked in an upscale restaurant before being arrested for scamming customer's credit card numbers. Pinkerton's team of researchers had made him a Counter. But this was early in the process of creating the Counters, so one of her researchers had innovated, injecting Maître d with an experimental nanobot protocol that allowed him to infiltrate the banking system through an access rod he could extrude from his left forefinger. He was also a highly organized, competent planner and a skilled motivator.

Banking system. Planning. Motivation. Georgina realized what was unfolding. *Well, shit.*

"We have your pets with us," Maître d said. "Or should I say, we *had*. I'm not sure there's enough of Ophelia and Lampkin left to identify. But Smith here, well… she won't be paralyzing anyone anymore. Not without her tongue."

Georgina heard muffled, choked grunts through the coms.

"Did you really think you could keep us on a leash?" Maître d inquired. "You might have the vision, the money, and the contacts. But us Counters?" Georgina heard more noises. Shuffling feet. Smith's desperate moaning. "We have power. Power you gave us, whether we asked for it or not. And That's the thing about power. Once you give it away, it's no longer yours to control. Because once you switch it on, it's almost impossible to switch off."

Georgina couldn't make out what was being said in the background, until she heard two names mentioned: Argyle. Kennel.

Argyle had the ability to shift their skin tone to red and white argyle patterns, eliciting intense, fast-acting vertigo to anyone in their sightline. Kennel had been fused with eleven strands of canine DNA. He was as strong and vicious as a tortured pit bull with razor sharp teeth, and a jaw powerful enough to crush a cinderblock.

Maître d was back on coms. "Rather than respect us like the warriors you said we would be, you treated us like lab rats. For those of us who survived." Whispered discussion. "Demonstrate to Mrs. Pinkerton how mistreated employees react to indifferent managers."

Tightness in her chest. Georgina struggled to breathe.

As did Smith, who sounded like she was simultaneously plummeting into a swirling pit of darkness while being ripped apart by a snarling, psychotic beast. Georgina envisioned crunching bones, exposed organs. Heard slobbering. Throaty howls.

Maître d cleared his throat. "No one of us could have crossed you alone. You could've switched us off. Fortunately, it never crossed your mind that, if enough of us banded together, we could neutralize your countermeasures. That we could neutralize *you*."

Georgina scrabbled at the control panel on her desk. She'd had individualized explosives, poisons, and genetic autoimmunity triggers implanted within each of her creatures, specific to their powers. One press of a button and they'd be dead. This lot represented a significant return on investment. But if it was them or her, sacrifices had to be made. Sunk costs.

She activated the kill switches. All ten.

The red dots remained.

"That's the problem with trying to conquer the world," Maître d said. "You were so convinced of your righteousness, of your absolute control and power over the inhuman creatures you consider us to be, that you ignored our still very human desires. Never even considered we might have plans of our own."

With a trembling forefinger she pressed the button to activate her com. "I didn't…," she began weakly.

Maître d was right. In a flash, a series of seemingly unrelated moments coalesced in her mind. Whispered conversations, silence when she entered a room. Minor delays in the transfer of lab equipment, money, or personnel. All chalked up to the reality that no single operation, no matter how well conceived or managed, ever functioned perfectly.

She'd seen it in real time but hadn't connected the dots. Her Counters must have been plotting against her for months. She'd overlooked the warning signs at her own expense. Her quest to dominate left her exposed.

"Everything you built, everything you planned, now belongs to *us*." Georgina cringed at the smug satisfaction in Maître d's voice. "The world isn't ready for what we can do. Which will make it so much easier, and a lot more fun, to topple their empires. And rule our own."

Georgina was accustomed to heft in her own voice. Gravitas. Conviction. It was all gone. But she couldn't let them hear it. So, she summoned as much confidence as she could, and hoped it would buy her time.

"It's never as easy as you think," she said firmly.

"Don't worry about our problem. I'd worry about yours."

"Well then…"

A final screech from Smith, an unholy squeal that carved a gaping wound into her soul. Georgina had lost the battle. Maybe even the war.

Maître d offered one last commentary. "And this is what happens when you neglect the hired help."

* * *

Georgina had made many sacrifices. And she'd sacrificed so many. All in the name of eradicating the Phenomenons.

She had nearly pulled it off. She'd had plans. Backup plans. And backups to the backups. Yet they'd all been thwarted, from within, all because she lost sight of where she came from. Forgotten what it was like to be powerless.

Ordinary people, the citizens of New York and the world over, were more important than the powered monsters who ran amok in the name of whatever righteousness ruled the day. She herself had no enhanced powers, but she may as well have given all she'd accomplished.

Only now did she realize that she'd been too focused on fighting to renew humanity, writ large, rather than forging alliances. Permitting her creatures to take advantage, and fight for themselves.

Which hit Georgina where she lived. Because no matter where her quest had begun or why, she'd fallen prey to one of the oldest temptations in the history of humankind: She'd become a true believer in the virtue of her cause. The ends justified her means, no matter how deliberately cruel or casually indifferent. God and Baby Jesus were surely on her side.

Exactly what she despised most about the Phenomenons.

And now hubris was biting her in the ass.

Footsteps thundered from outside the panic suite. Her monsters were pounding on the walls, trying to break through. She'd had the suite reinforced so that neither Phenomenons nor rogue creations could break through. Theoretically, at least.

The lights flickered off and on, off and on. The floor rumbled. The monsters were shouting at each other, and at her. She knew it was their way of trying to rattle her nerves, to get her to make a mistake. She couldn't let that happen.

Still, she was terrified.

She couldn't stay in the panic suite forever. She needed another way out. A new plan. Even the tiniest opening to exploit.

Fortunately, she was good at finding those.

The way to defeat and ultimately eradicate the Phenomenons had been to rip them apart at the seams. They tended to work alone or in pairs, only occasionally as a larger unit. But mostly they were rogue agents, individual terrorists.

Which meant they had no overarching plan. Only the façade of being a united force. They didn't understand the strategic value of the long game.

Georgina did. And it started with a single Phenomenon. One who, thanks to a tech-powered bodysuit, could shift her form at will, sneaking around in plain sight with none the wiser. Unless you knew what to look for.

About a year earlier, Silvercat had been patrolling a bodega in Flatbush, Brooklyn, taking it upon herself to act as the neighborhood's crimefighter, to thwart low-level criminals.

Georgina had sent one of her monsters into a bodega to test his recent implants. That particular subject hadn't been the sharpest tool in the shed. He loved to play with his food. Using her own tech against her, he would have killed Silvercat there and then. Only the shapeshifting pads Georgina gave him failed, turning the bodega into a bloody, gruesome horror show when his body literally exploded.

Losing one of her lesser monsters had been a small price to pay. His failure had prompted Silvercat to go on the prowl. No longer solely motivated to simply protect her neighborhood, she'd wanted answers about her assailant, and who was behind his attack.

With Silvercat hooked, Georgina set a new plan in motion. Through back channels, she then tipped Silvercat off about an invitation-only sex-and-politics party she regularly hosted at the Latham Institute, a Gilded Age mansion near Central Park. The parties were a gold mine for blackmail, access, and influence.

Which made it a high-value target for Silvercat. A chance to track down the brains behind the Phenomenon-hunting monsters cropping up around the country.

Overeager to infiltrate Georgina's operation, what Silvercat hadn't realized was that Georgina had set her up, had used her to manipulate two other Phenomenons into attending the party. Together, the three of them had gained access to one of Georgina's less-productive experimental labs and some of her more… disappointing specimens.

Which was when Georgina had the mansion blown up with Silvercat still inside. It had the desired effect. It took Silvercat off the board and destroyed the will of the other two Phenomenons who'd inadvertently led their companion to her death. Ending their inconvenient investigation and teaching them a valuable lesson: Never go up against Georgina Pinkerton.

Even in death, Silvercat continued to serve a purpose. She would save Georgina's life.

The lights went out.

Georgina reached into her desk drawer. In the back was a metal box with a latch lock. Inside was her last chance to survive before her creations tore her to pieces.

Or worse. If they were of such a mind—and some of them likely were—they very well might be inclined to kidnap and torture her instead, perhaps even subject her to the very same experimentations she had conducted on them.

I can't let that happen. She set her jaw in grim determination. *I won't.*

She tapped the locket around her neck. One pill. It would all be over. Quick and painless.

No, she thought. *This will work. Because I know who they are and what they're about.*

BAM! The outer wall shook. *BAM! BAM! BAM! BAM!*

Sledge, one of her strongest Counters, was trying to penetrate her bunker. She doubted he could get all the way through the wall on his own, but halfway might be enough. Then the other Counters and those who'd thrown in with them could find their way through the seams.

Just like she would.

"These walls won't hold," Maître d shouted. "And neither will you."

Georgina did something that even hours earlier she would have deemed unimaginable.

After the fire at the Latham Institute, she'd had Silvercat's surviving tech pulled out of the rubble. Georgina had held onto it, with the hopes of discovering its secrets. And a gut feeling it could serve another purpose, even if she hadn't been entirely clear what it might be.

She knew now.

One of her engineers had been able to reactivate the power source. The growth/shrink components, the ones that enabled Silvercat to shapeshift, had been damaged beyond repair. But one element was still functional.

The homing beacon. With an S.O.S. code. Which she activated, gambling that two very specific people would be unable to ignore the call.

Alone in her panic room, there was nothing left to do but wait and pray that Penetrable and Syntax, two Phenomenons, two sworn enemies who hated her with a fierce and fiery rage, got the message.

Because for Georgina, the would-be mastermind of humanity's salvation, time was running out.

HIRED HELP, PART II: INSIDER TRADING

BY RUSS COLCHAMIRO AND HILDY SILVERMAN

Penny Trouble sat slumped over her usual table at Mike's Tavern. The former private investigator cradled a glass of rotgut whiskey in one hand while the wrapped stump of the other rested on the graffiti-etched table. Useless. Pointless.

Much like herself.

"Is it self-pity o'clock already?" Deisha Carlyle strode to the table, glared down at Penny the way she would at gum stuck to the bottom of her Louboutin. She raised her wrist to one ear, shook it, and tapped the face of her gold watch. "Hm, coulda sworn that wasn't for another couple hours."

"Bite me," Penny said without an ounce of feeling. She hadn't been able to summon any emotion for... she'd lost track, but it had to be at least a month.

Everything was gray, inside and out. In a way it was a comfort not being able to feel the losses of her client, her friend, her hand, and her powers anymore. In the weeks since the Latham Institute blew up, she'd been all but paralyzed by the searing physical pain and smothering guilt of her colossal failure.

The painkillers she'd been on after the amputation of her mangled hand had taken the edge off at first. The pills finally ran out. The alcohol did not. Neither did her self-pity and depression.

Much to her surprise, Deisha reacted differently. Despite her prior insistence that she was and would never be a hero, the con artist had become the crusader. As far as Deisha was concerned, she and Penny had a duty to avenge Silvercat and nail Georgina Pinkerton, their true enemy behind the Phenomenon-hunters and the destruction of the Latham Institute.

Since the explosion, there had been no missions, no team-ups. Penny had blocked Deisha's number and stopped answering her door. So Deisha found Penny where she'd been every day since. Alone, anesthetized, and leaning head-first over a pit of despair. Deisha sat down, uninvited.

Woman can't take a goddamn hint, Penny thought.

"How much longer you gonna keep this up?" Deisha sighed. "What's your plan, what's your endgame, Troublemaker?"

Penny flinched. She'd always hated that nickname. She also knew Deisha was using it to get a rise out of her. "What's yours?"

"Huh?"

"You heard me." Penny looked up to meet Deisha's gaze and her former partner flinched. Penny could imagine what she must look like—chestnut-colored hair hanging in unkempt strings, eyes bloodshot, new lines in her face that had nothing to do with laughter. She managed a humorless chuckle. "You're trying to save me. I don't want it."

"Don't want what, exactly?" Deisha tossed her long braids behind her shoulders. She'd pulled off her share of cons and more, word-twisting her victims to the point of no return. For money, for revenge. This didn't seem to be a con though. "To finish the job? To pull your shit together? To stop wallowing—"

"Any of it!" Irritation seeped through a crack, threatened to surface. Penny quickly tossed back her drink to suppress it. "I don't want to remember, okay? I don't want to think about it, don't want to feel it. And most importantly, I don't. Want. *You!*"

"Well, too bad, 'cause you got me!" Deisha drew a deep breath, closed her dark brown eyes briefly. When she spoke again, her tone was calmer. "Penny, this ain't you. It's gotta stop. You're gonna drink yourself into the grave."

"Sounds like a plan." Penny raised her stump to draw the bartender's attention. "Hey, Junior! Get me another, will ya?"

"You think she'd want this?" Deisha said softly.

"Don't. Don't you…" Penny shook her head hard. Other feelings threatened to ooze through the seams Deisha was trying to tug apart. Tears stung her aching eyes.

"Silvercat's death wasn't your fault." Deisha reached across the table, tried to take her hand. Penny pulled it away before contact could be made. "It's all on Pinkerton."

"Who got away with it. Like always."

"Yeah, we had a setback. A bad one." Deisha sat back in her chair and folded her arms under her breasts. "But you're a private eye. And you know, better than most, that punishing yourself won't stop Pinkerton and it won't bring back Silvercat. But what we *can* do is honor her sacrifice. We need to finish what we started. And the people in the labs, in those horrible tanks with those unholy experiments and… Penny. I didn't want this life. Until you showed me my purpose. You have a purpose too. Don't drown it out. Don't let yourself forget."

Penny shuddered, bile surging into her mouth. It tasted of cheap whiskey and failure. Swallowing it back down, she whispered, "I'll never forget. Any of it. The torment. The flames." With her good hand, she pawed at the one she'd lost in the Latham battle, leaving her with a cauterized stump. She felt phantom fingers. And pain. Always pain. "Jessup hanging there, broken, bleeding black. See it every time I close my eyes."

Their former client, Roland Jessup, had ended up in one of Pinkerton's tanks. It was a gruesome affair.

Deisha nodded. "Same same. Like it or not, we're the ones who know the truth about Pinkerton. She's hunting us. Phenomenons. One by one. If we don't stop her…"

"*How?*" Penny slammed her right hand on the table. The handful of other afternoon patrons in Mike's glanced toward her then went back to drowning their own sorrows.

Lowering her voice, Penny continued. "We got *nothing*. No evidence, no leads, no witnesses. Just our word. Pinkerton saw to that by blowing it up—the lab, the Institute, Jessup." She tried to swallow the boulder in her throat. "All those people…"

"We'll connect the dots. Other labs, electronic trails, paperwork, witnesses. No matter how long it takes. The proof's always there. We just need to find it." Deisha hesitated, then chuckled.

Penny accepted a fresh drink from Junior, paused before knocking it back. "What's so funny?"

"I sound like you. Well, the old you."

Penny sighed, held up her stump. "Don't have it in me. I'm useless."

Deisha rolled her eyes and caught the bartender's sleeve before he walked away "Junior, bring me whatever she's…naw, scratch that. Bring me somethin' decent. Mid-shelf, at least." He nodded and walked away. "Look, I get it. You say you ain't even tried to ghost since…"

"Since."

Deisha leaned across the table. "But your brain still works, right? When it's not bein' pickled. You can still investigate, follow the clues."

Penny raised her glass. Deisha caught her wrist, forced her to lower it back to the table. "And you still got me. Like it or not."

"I," Penny started to retort, but then her phone rattled in her pocket. She released the glass, pulled her wrist free of Deisha's grasp, and fumbled her phone out onto the table.

And stared at the impossible on the screen.

"What?" Deisha leaned over. When she saw the image, she sucked in an audible breath and dropped back into her chair. "Is that... what is... *how?*"

An image of a cat blinked on the screen. Not randomly, but in a pattern: *S.O.S. S.O.S.*

"No." Penny shook her head. "That's impossible. It can't be her. We saw..."

"I know what we saw! But That's Silvercat's signal. Maybe she shapeshifted before the building went down. Maybe she escaped. Maybe she's hurt. Either way... That's her."

Penny couldn't deny it, impossible though it seemed. No one had the signal but Silvercat. It had to be her. Didn't it?

She bit back a sob as more emotions slithered through the cracks in the fortress around her heart. Most of them stung, but there it was, an emotion she'd never expected to feel again.

Hope.

***

"The hell is this place?" Deisha looked dubiously at the nondescript low-rise in front of her and Penny. Just past nightfall on the Lower East Side, a couple of parking lot lights barely illuminated it, but that was enough to reveal it looked like at least a hundred other bland brick buildings in the city. Generic storefronts on the bottom, offices or residences on top. "What woulda brought Silvercat here?" She eyed the first-floor laundromat. "To do a load of whites?"

Penny stood beside her in silence studying the place. "No idea." Neither of them was convinced the signal belonged to Silvercat, but if there was even a grain of possibility, they needed to see it through. "But if she's hurt, recovering, not a bad place to lay low."

"Yeah." Deisha nodded. "Maybe."

Penny pulled a small, folding pair of binoculars out of her trench coat and aimed them at the building. A moment later, she lowered them. A crease formed between her eyes. "Hm."

"Hm what?"

"Hm, that." Penny gestured to the top story with the binoculars.

Deisha squinted in the low light. It took her a few moments to realize what had caught Penny's attention. "Windows are barred."

Penny handed her the binoculars and Deisha looked through them. "Not just barred," Penny said. "Shielded completely. Solid metal shutters."

Deisha handed her back the binoculars. Nodded. "A bit much."

"Notice anything else?" Penny tucked the binoculars back in her pocket and nodded toward the building. When Deisha shook her head, she continued. "Security globes there, there, and there. But no fire escape. Pretty flagrant code violation, don'tcha think?"

Deisha nodded slowly. "So we approach with caution."

"Extreme."

Keeping to the shadows, they circled around to the back of the building. Usual dumpsters in the alleyway, along with an overturned recycling bin and assorted trash littering the ground. A steel back door was set in the brick. But instead of the expected padlock-and-chain these places usually sported, this one had no door handle and no visible lock. No way to access the interior. Only a retinal scanner set into the brick next to the door.

"Bougie," Deisha said. She glanced over at Penny. "Well? Go on."

Penny just stared at her. "Go what?"

Deisha waggled her fingers at the door. "Ghost through. Open the door. Let me in."

"Can't, remember?" Penny's tone was bitter.

"I remember you ain't tried," Deisha corrected. "We don't have time for Penny's Pity Party. If Silvercat's in there—maybe by choice, maybe not—we owe it to her to try. Unless you think she ain't worth it."

Penny grimaced, then closed her eyes, inhaled deeply. Released her breath in a slow, low hiss. She went to the door, pressed her right hand against it. It faded briefly, just around the edges, but then she yanked it back. Even in the dim light, Deisha could see her trembling from head to toe.

PTSD was a bitch.

Deisha gripped Penny's shoulder. "You can do this..."

Penny choked out a laugh. "Don't think I can." She faced Deisha, eyes so wide the whites were visible around her light brown irises. "You don't know what it was *like*, pushing and pushing to get through all that solid mass. Couldn't breathe, couldn't see or even think, just pushing one more step, then another, not knowing if I would ever get out. If I'd get stuck between matter. And then..." She held up the stump of her left hand.

When they first met, Penny had deflected Deisha's opposition, finally convincing her to join a cause bigger than herself. Become more than a rogue con woman only out for herself. In a twist of fate Deisha never saw coming, their roles were now reversed.

"I hear you," she said gently. "I do and I'm sorry. But either we go in... or call the cops."

Penny all but snarled. "Yeah. Don't think so."

"United Front then. You still have friends there, right?"

"*Friends* is a generous description. And what would I even say? I got an S.O.S. from beyond the grave?" She snorted. "They *might* consider sending an intern. Next month. Maybe."

Deisha threw her hands in the air. Gave Penny an exaggerated bug-eyed glare.

Penny sighed. "Okay. You're right." She frowned in thought, then reached into an interior coat pocket. She withdrew a bobby pin, held it tightly between thumb and forefinger.

Penny mumbled something under her breath that was either a prayer or a string of cusswords. She tentatively pressed her hand against the panel around the retinal scanner.

Her good hand wavered, as if being viewed through water. Then it disappeared into the wall.

Deisha nibbled a hangnail on her thumb. Penny was far from full strength, but Deisha believed her partner could maintain her ghosting powers, phasing through the solid brick. At least, Deisha hoped so. She wasn't conning her partner, exactly, but she wasn't *not* conning her either.

Sometimes we all need to be messed with for our own good.

Deisha heard a sound. A hiss of a circuit shorting out. Then the door slid into the wall.

Penny yanked her hand free, gasping. She cradled it like a baby, resting on the pillow of her left stump. Stared as though she couldn't believe it was really there.

When Penny looked up again, the relief on her face was damn near beatific. "I... I did it."

Thank Christ! Deisha thought, resisting the urge to hug her. Instead, she simply said, "You comin' or what?" and walked inside.

Chuckling, Penny followed her into the darkness.

***

"Well, shit," Deisha muttered under her breath.

"See 'em," Penny confirmed.

They huddled just outside a palatial office space, which was completely incongruous with the rest of the building. Inside were seven people, a few of whom looked perfectly ordinary while others had been obviously augmented.

The remains of others were splattered across the walls and floor. No way to discern how many from the pools of blood, mangled organs, and severed body parts.

One of the figures still breathing was a giant of a man with dark hair slicked back over his skull. He and two others were wholly focused on a sealed set of doors. Slicked Back was pounding a sizable dent into one and swearing like a sailor whose shore leave had been cancelled.

A fairly ordinary looking man clad in an ugly argyle sweater and wearing a loaded toolbelt strapped to his waist was using a highly advanced-looking drill on the hinges. It raised a lot of sparks, but that appeared to be all.

Meanwhile, a third man elongated and flattened himself. He kept trying to squeeze through the tiny gap between the doors and the floor, to no avail.

Another big man sat behind a computer terminal on a large, fancy desk and appeared to be holding a plug into the docking station. He looked over to snap, "Get it done already!"

The brains of the operation? The boss, Penny suspected.

Get It Done pressed a button and spoke into an intercom on the desk. "This only ends one way! If you open the doors like a good girl, we might make it quick. Well, quick*er*."

Penny curled her fingers into a fist. They hadn't known exactly what to expect. It was possible that Silvercat had somehow extricated herself from the Latham Institute rubble. And that she'd received medical attention but had been too injured to reach out sooner.

Or maybe she'd crawled out, wounded and alone, and was in hiding from Pinkerton's forces. It seemed clear now which was the likelier scenario.

Penny regretted having brushed off Deisha's suggestion to summon the United Front. But at least she'd restocked, loading her pockets with useful tech. They'd been left to her by her dear slain friend, Keith, aka Ranger Moon, a fallen Phenomenon.

For Penny, his will had stated. *For investigations that get real.*

"What's our play?" Deisha whispered.

Penny mentally ran and discarded a handful of scenarios. "Get past 'em. Get Silvercat out of here."

Deisha hissed, *"That's* your plan? Seriously? We're outnumbered and down a good hand. Girl, they will *crush* us! This crew's above our paygrade. I'm down for the cause, but I'm not down to get dead."

She was right. If Pinkerton had sent in this squad, as suspected, they were very likely the Counters she'd been deploying against Phenomenons. Sending her thugs with abilities that were equal to, but opposite those, of powered and tech-supported heroes.

Traction had almost been killed in one encounter. And there was an attack on Sarcastic Fringehead. And they'd almost lost Red Sky as well. But if they backed off and left it to United Front, the heroes wouldn't arrive in time to save Silvercat.

Assuming That's who was on the other side of those doors.

There were no other options.

Penny studied the room again. Get It Done on the computer, but weirdly not typing. Almost looked like he was jacked in directly. The images of what appeared to be stock trades and other financial activities fluctuated wildly on a large wall-mounted screen. A slight man with comically oversized glasses hovered behind the apparent hacker and watched the screen intently.

Across the room, a husky woman rifled through file cabinets, tossing manila folders onto the floor, muttering to herself. A guy with a massive jaw fussed with a scanner set in the wall, a torn and broken painting at his feet. He snapped his teeth like an enraged Pitbull and punched a hole in the wall.

They're stressed, Penny thought *On edge. Determined. Some on the tech, the others on the door. Which means they're after something specific. And not expecting us.*

Penny met Deisha's gaze and her partner nodded.

They could work with this.

She pulled two pairs of infrared glasses out of an inner pocket in her trench coat, handed one to Deisha. "Distraction first," Penny said. "They're all about to snap. This," she said, and withdrew a pair of what looked like game dice, "will make it worse."

"Turn 'em against each other." Deisha grinned. Confusion was her wheelhouse.

"If I've assessed right, this should take out the leader." Penny held up the dice. They began to hum. "In the confusion," she nodded to indicate the sealed doors. "I'll slip in and through those doors."

She hoped Deisha didn't notice the shudder that went through her at the thought of having to ghost through reinforced steel or whatever those too-solid looking doors were made of.

Penny rolled the dice against each other. Her heart thrummed in her chest. They had one shot at this.

She leaned across the threshold dividing corridor from office and rolled the dice inside.

The hum quickly became a high-pitched whine as the devices rolled toward the center of the room. Before anyone inside could react, they exploded.

Brilliant flash of light. Deafening boom. The lights inside went out, courtesy of an electromagnetic pulse. Those who'd been standing staggered around, clutched their ears, swore, and shouted in dazed confusion.

Penny donned a pair of infrared glasses. The computer and overhead screen went down. So did Get It Done, who flopped to the floor, limp. She was pleased her assessment that he'd been directly jacked into the system had been accurate.

Deisha put on her glasses, started to rise. Penny caught her by the shoulder, handed her a small earpiece. "Keep in touch. And be careful. If they spot you—"

"Stealth mode. Promise." Deisha tucked the earpiece into her right ear, stood. "Don't worry. I got this."

I hope we both do, Penny thought.

***

Deisha moved in, low and fast, careful to avoid the temporarily blinded and partially deafened goons. Despite her parting bravado, her mind was all but shut down by fear.

This is the job, Syntax, she cajoled herself. *Do your thing.*

She scrambled over to the desk with the computer terminal, careful to avoid the unconscious hacker's body. Dazed from the EMP, the little guy who'd been watching the screen was blinking rapidly and pounding keys on the console, trying to get the screen active again. It slowly came up again—probably some kind of shielded battery backup activating. But all it displayed was a *Connection Lost* message and a string of error code. Fortunately, that would be enough.

"C'mon, c'mon," he muttered. "Show me the money!"

Deisha was happy to oblige.

As he looked up, she twisted the error messages. While the actual text on screen showed nothing abnormal, what he saw, thanks to Deisha, was an SEC warning. Accounts draining funds. Random accounts filling. Stock transfer messages.

"Shit. What is… no, no, no!" the slight man cried, pounding the keyboard with both fists.

The man with the enormous jaw stormed over. He tripped over the fallen hacker, yelped, and kicked his body across the room. "What's your problem, Frankie?"

"The trades, Kennel, the transfers—everything! They've been cut off, re-routed from our accounts. The SEC's onto us!" He jabbed a finger at the screen. "All the funds. We're screwed!"

Kennel looked up at the screen, scowled. "What in the hell you talkin 'about? I don't see nothing about any SEC or whatever."

Those where his exact words. But Deisha plied her word-twisting powers, so that what Frankie heard was, "Don'tchu worry "bout it. Everything's goin' according to plan. *My plan.*"

"Plan? Whadaya mean plan? What did you...?" Frankie stood up so fast he knocked over his chair. "You sonuvabitch. You greedy sonuvabitch. You took it all. You ripped us off!"

"Me?" Kennel growled. Grabbed Frankie by the lapels and hoisted him until Kennel's slavering oversized mouth was inches from Frankie's nose. "You been up Ma Matre'd ass since we got here. You two were rippin' *us* off!"

The heavy-set woman stumbled over from the file cabinet. "Can't see a frigging thing." She pawed at her head. "What's going on?" she demanded.

"This little weasel's stole our shit," Kennel snarled. "He set us up!"

"Not me. Him!" Frankie shouted. He jabbed a finger toward the screen, where Deisha made sure the crawl continued to lie. "Don't you see?"

"Bullshit!" Kennel opened his mouth wide, preparing to bite Frankie's face off.

Frankie's glasses began to glow. "*You want to put me down. Back up. Right now.*"

Kennel stiffened as though struggling with himself. Ultimately, he obeyed.

Frankie's glasses seemed to have some kind of tech that allowed him to bend others to his will. *Damn,* Deisha thought. *Scary power. Could use a pair.*

The husky woman let out a rumble. "I should've known better than to throw in with you lot. Let Matre'd convince me there was strength in numbers. That we could take down the Queen. But it was all just a scam. You were always gonna burn me."

Kennel tried to placate her, get her on his side. But Deisha made sure what the big woman heard instead was, "*There ain't no scam, you stupid bitch. Unless you're the scammer.*"

The woman did not take that well. She balled a giant fist and piledrove Kennel to the floor.

Kennel whimpered, but quickly scrambled back to his feet. "Ursa," he started. "You lost your goddamn mind?"

Meanwhile, Frankie slowly backed away from the pair. But his foot brushed Deisha's. He peered down at her through the darkness. "Who the hell are you?"

Shit, shit, shit.

"I said, *tell me who you are.*" His glasses began to glow again. Deisha felt a sudden compulsion to answer. "*And why are you here?*"

Deisha would never intentionally betray Penny. But she couldn't help it. Without knowing how or why, she wanted to confess. More than she wanted to draw another breath. "I… I'm Deisha Carlyle. I'm here to…"

No! If she'd learned anything from her years on the con, it was the necessity to pivot in real-time, reconstituting the plan on the spot. She clapped both hands over her mouth, so her response was too muffled to understand.

"*Put your hands down,*" Frankie commanded. "*Answer me.*" But as he repeated his questions, Deisha pushed back and twisted his words so that despite what he said aloud, what Kennel and Ursa heard was, "*I told you. We steal the funds then shut the place down!*"

"So, this *was* you and maître d." Kennel lunged at Frankie, snapping.

Ursa roared. She'd had a few chunks bitten out of her while tussling with Kennel but didn't seem overly bothered. "Spare the lies, dog breath. You're all in it together!"

As Kennel pounced on Frankie, sending the latter's fancy glasses flying, Ursa charged Kennel.

Deisha didn't wait to see the outcome. She tucked and rolled away, but before she got to her feet, she spotted Frankie's glasses. Almost instinctively, she snatched them up, then sprinted toward the doors.

Four down. Three to go.

Deisha huddled behind a credenza near the guy in the argyle sweater. To his credit, he kept his cool and switched from his plugged-in drill to a handheld pneumatic saw to hack through the hinges. He'd also donned a headband with a bright light mounted on it to illuminate his work area.

The same could not be said of the giant with the slicked-back hair. He was whipping around blindly and shouting, "Maître d! The hell's going on? What's happening? Are we still a go? *Somebody! Talk to me!*"

Argyle heaved a sign. Turning off his drill, he said, "Sledge. Chill out. Stay on task. We're almost through."

As soon as Argyle began speaking, Deisha grabbed his words and twisted. Hard. Something about taking both their cuts and using the money to defile Sledge's mother.

Sledge snapped to attention. "I'm gonna kill you!" He lunged for the bewildered Argyle.

She couldn't be sure what Argyle's abilities were, but they seemed to disorient Sledge enough that he staggered past his target and face-planted on the floor. Which only infuriated Sledge further. He sprang to his feet with impressive speed for a huge steel-skinned creature, grabbed Argyle by the ugly sweater, and yanked him clean off his feet.

Roaring, Sledge spun Argyle like a caber and sent him flying ass over teakettle.

Argyle slammed into the reinforced metal shutters covering the windows. His terrified screams cut off abruptly.

Surrounded by chaos and violence between those who, until now, he had considered allies, the rubbery man who'd been failing to slide under the sealed doors snapped his body back into human form. He bolted toward the door leading out of the office.

Deisha pressed her earpiece. "Penny," she said. "Stretch. Headin' your way."

"Copy that," Penny replied.

Deisha blew out a breath. She had to trust her partner could handle the fleeing goon alone. Because Deisha still had one large and angry problem to contend with.

The filing cabinet she'd been hiding behind raised up and flew halfway across the room. She looked up and beheld Sledge squinting down at her. "Hey! I don't remember you on this team."

There was no one left to speak. No words to twist. Which for Deisha, meant only one thing.

I'm dead.

"You workin' for *the Queen*?" Sledge grinned, teeth gleaming in the infrared light. He cracked his knuckles and it sounded like a string of M-80s exploding. "I used your buddies to redecorate her office. You're next."

Deisha backed away. "Now c'mon, big guy. I'm sure we can work it out." She raised her hands—and noticed what she was still clutching.

Terror triggered inspiration. She swapped her infrared glasses for Frankie's mind-controlling lenses. *Hope they're switched on.*

Sledge reached for her with one long arm while raising the other to strike. "Maître d called me in," she cried. "He needs your help. The doors are too thick. But he's got an idea."

Sledge hesitated, lowered his raised fist slightly. "What the hell are you talkin' about? We don't need more ideas. Just more time. I've nearly punched through."

Deisha had no clue how the glasses worked or whether they'd work for her. But her word-twisting ability was limited without someone else available to speak, to have their words manipulated. Her plan was going to work. Or she was in real trouble.

Deisha focused her ability on her own words and spoke. "*Headbutt the door. You'll break on through. Which means the Queen is all yours. You know what she did to us. Time for some payback.*"

Sledge nodded slowly. Muttered, "Of course…my *head*. That's the ticket. Gonna make that bitch scream."

He stomped back to the battered door, arched his neck back, then slammed his forehead into it. Again. And again. And again. The sound reverberated throughout the room.

Fifteen seconds later, he dropped, out cold.

Deisha nearly collapsed with relief. She glared down at Sledge. "Dumbass."

***

Penny stood, back pressed against the wall opposite the office door. She pulled a black glove on her good hand. When Stretch came pounding out of the office, she extended an open-palm strike to his sternum. The glove sent a hundred thousand volts of electricity into his gut.

He formed and re-formed into some very interesting shapes before he collapsed, twitching and drooling.

Penny removed the glove, which needed to recharge. *I'm up*. Her gut churned as she passed through the office door.

Skirting the carnage, she made her way over to Deisha and the sealed doors. *You're okay,* she coaxed herself along the way. *You ghosted through the panel and you're still in one piece. You've done it before, you can do it again. Your powers are back.*

She met Deisha's gaze on arrival. "Nice glasses," Penny said.

"Thanks." Deisha grinned. "They're new."

Penny started to ghost.

Panic struck.

The fear flooded her mind, told her that she could not, *must* not risk it again. She'd lost one hand already. These doors were solid, reinforced metal. Who knew how thick they were? How deep they went?

She panted. Her vision shrank to a black-tinged tunnel view of the doors. She felt steel closing around her, crushing her, no end in sight…

A voice in her ear. "You *can* do this. Mind over matter. Or in your case… through it."

Penny squeezed her eyes shut. Her teeth chattered. The terror flashed through her again. Getting stuck in the Latham walls. The panic. The loss of control. "No, not like this. I can't. I just can't." She doubled over, clutching her midsection. "Gonna be sick."

Deisha's hand pressed against the middle of her back. "I'm sorry. I really am. But we don't have time for this."

Penny's eyes welled up with tears. "I can't do it."

"You can and you will. Walk through that wall. Now."

There was suddenly nothing in the world Penny wanted to do more. Without further hesitation, she stepped forward, ghosting her entire body straight through the door.

On the other side, she found herself in a large, well-equipped room. And there was a woman, but not the one she expected. This one had faded blonde hair and cornflower blue eyes. She spoke with a raspy Southern drawl. "Well," the woman said. "It is about time."

Anxious, Penny looked around. "Where is she?"

"Where is… oh. Right." The woman smoothed her wool skirt and plucked lint off the sleeve of her silk blouse. "Your friend, Kitty Cat—"

Penny grabbed the blonde by the throat and swung around, pinning her flat against the wall. "Silvercat," she snarled. "Where. Is. *Silvercat?*"

Despite the metric ton of Botox rendering her middle-aged face smooth as a baby's bottom, the woman's eyes crinkled at the corners. "Bit hard for me to tell you, Miss Trouble, whilst you are choking me to death."

Penny squeezed tighter. But just as her good thumb was about to pop the woman's trachea, Penny reluctantly released her grip. "Just who in the hell are you?"

The woman's voice was raspy. "Oh, bless your heart." She coughed a few times until her normal tone returned. "I would have thought that'd be obvious."

Penny froze. Because she knew. "Georgina Pinkerton."

Pinkerton nodded and stuck out her left hand, then made a show of noticing Penny's missing left, and extended her own right. "Pleasure to finally make your acquaintance, Miss Trouble. Now, if you would kindly get us out of here, I am ready to accept my fate."

Penny struggled to keep her temper. "What do you expect That's gonna be?"

"Why, justice, darlin'." Georgina batted her false eyelashes. "I am ready to turn myself in."

Deisha found herself in the most luxurious panic room she'd ever seen. The doors shut behind her to keep out the battling goons—the ones still on their feet anyway.

Penny glared at her so hard Deisha nearly ran back out of the vault. "I don't know how you forced me through that door," Penny growled, "but that was some next-level shit. We're gonna have another talk about boundaries after this."

Deisha swept off Frankie's glasses and stuck them in her back pocket. "One thing at a time," she said. Then she shifted her attention to the other woman in the room.

Deisha knew that rescuing Silvercat—her supposedly dead friend—was a longshot at best. But she hadn't anticipated finding a Martha Stewart stunt double. It didn't take a genius to figure out who she was.

"Georgina Pinkerton. Damn." Her heart pounded. The old Deisha would have clawed Pinkerton's eyes out. But there was too much at stake. And, as she had a moment to think, to consider the variables, her own conniving mind saw the long con play out. But not the one she thought. Deisha turned back toward the steel door, and realized why Pinkerton was hiding in a panic room. "Your monsters turned against you. You didn't take them out yourself, you didn't call in a hit team. This is more than going rogue. They *toppled* you."

Deisha looked to Penny, thought more, than turned back to Pinkerton. "*And* you called *us*. Which means…"

"You're totally screwed," Penny said with a vindictive smile.

"You have a delightful interpretation of events," Pinkerton said. "I am far from screwed, as you so eloquently described. I am, in fact, just getting started."

Penny got in Pinkerton's face. "Tell me why I shouldn't just rip out your heart."

Pinkerton shifted her gaze to Penny. "It's not in your nature."

Penny slapped her hand against Pinkertons chest. "Don't tempt me."

"Penny," Deisha said. "Don't. She *called* us because she *needs* us. Which gives us leverage."

Penny ghosted her good hand, millimeters from Pinkerton's sternum. "It would be so easy… and the world would be so much better."

"That, Miss Trouble, is where we disagree. You slipped past some of my lethal monsters. But there are dozens more just like them. And without me to keep them on a leash, they'll become mad dogs on the loose."

"Which means you have a problem," Penny said.

"No," Pinkerton corrected, "it means *we* have a problem. So for you and you only, I have a proposal."

"Proposal?" Penny felt like her face might burst into a fiery ball of rage. "We're not—"

"You take me to the United Front. I will go willingly. I will turn over whatever research is still available to me. I will relinquish my remaining funds. And, most importantly, I will assist in neutering those mad dogs. Because they will only get bolder and more dangerous. You need me as much as I need you. But if it assuages your ego… yes, I need your help."

"Help you? *Help* you?" Penny raised her ghosted hand up to Pinkerton's blue eyes. "I should *kill* you! Where's Silvercat?"

"Temper, temper, darlin'."

"Don't talk to me about my temper." Penny's ghosted fist was a millimeter from Pinkerton's face. One push and she'd have a handful of brains. "I'm gonna—"

"No, Miss Penny. You are not going to kill me, and for three very good reasons." Pinkerton raised her index finger. "One, you aren't a cold-blooded murderer." She raised her middle finger. "Two, you have a whole lotta questions only I can answer." She held up her ring finger. "And three, if you do, you'll never see Silvercat again."

Penny stiffened. Deisha cocked her head to one side. "I call bullshit."

"Then do your worst." Pinkerton shrugged. "If my time has come, so be it. But you'd be leaving quite a bounty on the table." She waggled her fingers toward the doors. "My labs did more than just create new powers. We also... resurrected them."

"Now I really call bullshit. There's no way..."

But was there a way? Was it possible, through Pinkerton's twisted science, to resurrect powers?

To resurrect the dead?

"We've seen your experiments," Deisha said. "I'll never sleep right again. But even you can't—"

"I don't know," Penny said. "She did reach out to us. Using Silvercat's tech." Her expression was pleading. "Which means she found Silvercat. And if she *found* her, is it possible, as crazy as it sounds, that she saved her? Or even"—Penny blinked twice, then held her stare—"brought her back to life?"

Pinkerton reached into her desk drawer, then held out a badly dinged-up communication device.

Penny sucked in a breath. She snatched the device from Pinkerton's hand, examined the tech. "This was Sylvie's." Her voice cracked on her friend's name.

"Not *was*," Pinkerton said, almost kindly. "Is. She *is* alive. Not well, by any means—she's healing. Slowly, but she's healing. I've got my top team working on her. I can take you to her. But to go *there*, we need to leave *here*."

Penny was too close to the situation. It was on Deisha to be the voice of reason. Game recognized game, and Deisha knew in her heart that Pinkerton was working a con. A long, insidious con.

"How do you figure?" Deisha asked. "Your empire collapsed. You're in hiding from your own monsters. If you still have a team that good, you wouldn't have called us."

"You know what they say." Pinkerton regarded her with a glimmer of respect. "Necessity is the mother of all invention. And in your case... in Silvercat's case... we are long past necessity. We have urgency. You can't afford to ignore my offer." She walked over to a large computer on a desk. "I can understand your reticence. So don't trust *me*." She pointed to the screen. "Trust your own eyes."

Penny went over. She leaned in close then gasped. "Jesus!"

Pinkerton smirked. "More like Lazarus, darlin'."

Deisha joined them. On the screen was a series of large glass pods, eerily reminiscent of the ones in the Latham lab that had been filled with mutated human specimens. Floating within, attached to several tubes and wires, was a nude woman with what appeared to be an oxygen mask covering her mouth and nose. The hair, the visible features, however, strongly resembled those of the woman she'd known.

"Sylvie," Penny murmured.

Deisha saw what Penny saw. But she couldn't accept it. "That could be anyone—"

"Look at her!" Penny waved at the screen. "It's her. It's definitely Sylvie."

Deisha hesitated. It was true that Penny had known Silvercat for years and Deisha had known her only a few weeks. But she couldn't help but wonder if Penny was only seeing what she desperately wanted. "I dunno."

Penny grasped her hand, stared deeply into Deisha's eyes. Her own shone with unshed tears. "I know it's insane…" She glared over at Pinkerton, who stood impassively next to the computer monitor. "But it's Sylvie, Deisha. It's Sylvie." She sighed desperately. "I don't know. Maybe it is, maybe it's not. Maybe she's just messing with my head. But if there's even the *slightest* chance…?" Tears leaked from Penny's eyes. "I have to know. I have to."

Deisha nodded slowly. It couldn't be Silvercat. It defied all logic. *But what if,* she thought. *What if it's real?* It was only now that Deisha finally understood what it felt like to be on the receiving end of a con. Caught between buyer's remorse… and doubt. Either way, you come up short. And hating yourself for it.

She addressed Pinkerton. "So we get you outta here, you give us Silvercat. That the deal?"

"That is indeed the deal." Pinkerton grinned. "You escort me to safety, and in return, I'll help you track, capture, and eliminate my monsters. Whatever is still mine will be yours. The Phenomenons are simply ill-equipped to defeat them on their own. I, however, know *exactly* what to do."

"The problem," Deisha said, "is that I still don't trust you. How do we know you're not—?"

"Deal," Penny said and extended her good hand.

Pinkerton smirked, shook hands.

Goddammit, Deisha thought. *You don't take a deal unless you've vetted all the terms. But still…*

It was time to get out of there. Penny called into a contact with United Front, laid down Pinkerton's offer. Better Angel and the others would have no confidence that the mogul was being sincere, but having her in hand, regardless of how or why, was simply too critical to pass up. They would treat Pinkerton like the person she was—the most dangerous criminal alive. And if there was even a shred of truth about Silvercat… they had to check it out.

A team showed up within minutes—Traction, Scopes, Yoga, and Revek. Pinkerton's remaining monsters put up a hell of a fight. But the chaos gave Penny and Deisha cover to slip out down the back stairwell, hiding Pinkerton in a clothes bin from the laundromat, which they wheeled into the service elevator and out into the back alley.

Waiting there was a dingy white van. But the interior was a United Front control center replete with unbreakable shackles fastened through an eye hook bolted to the floor.

Pinkerton sat on the metal bench, her wrists clamped in a metal alloy. "Where's Grey Guardsman?" She rested her now-cuffed hands in her lap.

"Busy," Yoga said. "But you'll get your chance. There's a lot to talk about."

"Well then." Pinkerton gave her a polite nod. "As they say, take me to your leader."

Deisha wondered if anyone else noticed the undercurrent of rage in the woman's tone. They may have had Pinkerton in custody, but their time with her was far from over.

WE INTERRUPT THIS APOCALYPSE

BY PETER DAVID AND MICHAEL JAN FRIEDMAN

Perry Casey, highly regarded professor of archaeology at New York University, sat back in his chair and watched the scene unfolding on the wall-mounted television in his office—the newly elected president of a small African country coming out onto a flower-festooned balcony in that nation's capital city, smiling and waving to the crowd gathered below him.

To the rest of the world, this man was his country's savior, the charismatic, Western university-educated fellow who would bring his people out of the depths of hunger, ignorance, and hopelessness into the light of modernity and prosperity.

However, this man was not what he seemed. As far as most anyone knew, he had risen to his country's highest office— one formerly occupied by a violent bloodsucker of a tyrant— through hard work and the purest of motives.

In fact, the fellow had become president by virtue of hundreds of foreign campaign donations, which had enabled him to hire a veritable army of canvassers—many more than any of his opponents possessed. These canvassers had gone door to door, extolling their candidate's virtues, "getting out the vote."

And every one of those campaign donations had been the work of Perry Casey. It was a simple task for him to generate wealth, after all.

But then, Perry Casey wasn't just a college professor. He was also the Phenomenon known as Professor Paracelsus.

And he had a plan. One he had thought out, and carefully implemented over the last several years, and continued to implement.

He hadn't spent his days sitting around like other Phenomenons, waiting for something bad to happen to the people of his city so he could swoop in with flowing cape and matching goggles and save them in dramatic fashion. He had gone out into the world—the entire world, not just his corner of it—and established the kind of network only the Captains of Industry had formerly enjoyed.

A network that pursued the objectives he had laid out for it, even if no one could tie him to it. A network more imposing and far-reaching than most of the nations in which it operated, though no one except Paracelsus had any suspicion that it existed.

A network made possible by his unique abilities, which enabled him to transmute base metals into their most precious counterparts—which could, in turn, be used to mold the futures of the most backward nations as well as in the planet's most venerable seats of power.

And why not? Why should the Captains of Industry—the greediest and the most ambitious of all creatures walking the Earth—have been the only ones capable of gathering wealth and using it to mold the affairs of the world?

So when a costumed hero saved the lives of a sardine can full of overworked commuters trapped on a runaway bus, Paracelsus didn't feel admiration for that hero. He felt pity if he felt anything at all. Pity for the limited vision that kept that hero from seeing beyond the current emergency to its underlying causes.

If the Phenomenons really wanted to help people, they would have spent their time looking into the maintenance practices of the bus company, where corners were cut savagely and purposely on a daily basis. Or the disdain for safety measures in the city's residential buildings, which saw one deadly fire after another. Or the gala events of the wealthy class that sapped the manpower of the police force, which might have otherwise protected the city's citizens from a surge of muggers and gangbangers.

Armed with that kind of knowledge and insight, those costumed heroes might have made some headway. But as far as Paracelsus could tell, only *he* was inclined to operate proactively rather than reactively. Only *he* was willing to embrace the enemy's methods and meet them on even ground.

Then again, it was more than an inclination…wasn't it? *If I'm honest with myself,* Paracelsus thought, *and I must be, I'm better equipped than most to establish points of influence around the globe.*

And not just by virtue of his powers.

Because Better Angel was just a child, innocent and unsophisticated, when one stripped away her physical capabilities. Red Sky knew Queens as well as anyone, but he wasn't a traveler with a sense of the globe entire. Even Grey Guardsman, the Phenomenons champion of champions, seemed pitifully limited in his vision.

Only Professor Paracelsus had the intellect, the constitution, and the experience to do what he had done.

And that should have been enough. It *should* have. And it *would* have, he was certain, if his daughter hadn't been shot to death at that stupid, unnecessary protest in Virginia.

A protest against Ortega, the very South American tyrant that Paracelsus had put in power. *Ironic*, he thought. As ironic as anything in the history of mankind—a topic on which he was an expert, so he knew.

Penny's death had cut the ties that bound Paracelsus to the real world. It had left him adrift, talking to ghosts and ghosts of ghosts—him, a man of science, who had until that moment believed only in himself.

Oddly, in a way he still didn't understand, the loss of his daughter seemed to have transformed the gem in his palm from red to green. One moment it was as ruby-red as the moment he found it in a cave near an Algarve fishing town. The next it was a brilliant green, like the aurora at its most vivid, on a night when the sky was clear and dark, and the magnetic currents surrounding the Earth lined up just right.

That shade of green.

The stone hadn't changed otherwise. It still had the same properties, still gave him a remarkable range of abilities. It was just a different color. Or maybe it had changed after all, and Paracelsus just didn't know how yet.

At any rate, he had recovered from Penny's death. Not from the fact of it, because that would linger with him forever. But from the shock, at least.

He was in control of himself again. Capable of furthering his plan, manipulating the pieces he had placed on the board, moving the world inexorably in the direction of the future he saw for it.

Once had thought that future more important than his daughter. He wished—desperately—that he could reach the point where he thought that again.

Casey used his remote control to turn off the video screen. After all, he was still a professor. He had duties to perform in that regard.

It was with those duties in mind that he sat down at his computer and activated it. After a moment or two, the machine's screen should have shown him a prompt, asking for his password.

But it didn't. Not even after thirty seconds or so had gone by.

The screen remained dark. As dark as the sky on Flores Island the night the Paluweh volcano went off and blotted out the stars with thick plumes of smoke. Yet the computer was on. He could feel its vibration under his fingertips.

Turn it off and start it up again, Casey thought.

That's what he had been instructed to do on other occasions when his computer seemed less than cooperative. So he indeed turned it off, and turned it on again. But the result was the same.

The device was on. It was just the screen that wasn't.

Casey knew a lot of things—not only all there was to know in his chosen field but also the intricacies of other disciplines, like phylogenetics and theoretical physics, which he had picked up as a member of a intellectually vibrant university faculty. But if there was a gap in his education, it was in the area of computer technology.

He hated the idea of being a stereotype, but he couldn't help it. He was unequivocally that fellow who could perform complex mathematical calculations with ease but had no aptitude for the workings of a Mac.

Casey knew one thing: He didn't have time to tinker with the device.

So he turned it off again, left his office, and started in the direction of the university's faculty club, which had a whole bank of seldom-used computers. If there was a bug in his office machine, or something even more pernicious, he would avoid it by resorting to the club's computers.

The walk outside his building was full of students. They came out in the nice weather, and this was one of those days when the campus was treated to an early taste of spring.

"Hey, Professor!"

With a sigh, Casey stopped in his tracks and turned to look back, and saw Lenny Rock hurrying after him. Lenny was a student in Casey's Intro to Archaeology class. One of the more promising students in that section, actually, despite his penchant for consistently turning in his assignments after they were due.

Casey wanted to get to the faculty club as soon as he could. However, his position as a professor was useful to him, as it provided a cover for his other activities. And any professor at NYU who ignored a student calling to him in public wouldn't remain a professor much longer.

"Hey, Professor," Lenny said, red-faced with exertion as he caught up with Casey. He held up a thin sheaf of stapled papers in front of him—a sheaf Casey had taught long enough to recognize as a term paper. "I'm so sorry," Lenny continued, "but I wanted to get this to you before you left for the day. I thought your office hours went until—"

"Five," Casey said.

"That's what I remembered," Lenny said. "So, if you don't mind…" He offered the professor the term paper. "Or would you rather I left it in your mailbox?"

"What I would prefer," Casey said—genuinely without rancor because, truth be told, he couldn't have cared less when Lenny Rock or any other student turned in his assignment—'is that you hand in your papers on time. This one, for example, was due yesterday."

Lenny turned an even darker shade of cherry-red. "Right. You see, I—"

Casey removed the paper from his student's hand. He'd heard so many excuses since he'd begun teaching that he could have published a leather-bound volume of them. He doubted that Lenny's excuse would be any more intriguing than the others.

And he wanted to get to the faculty club with all possible dispatch.

"Excuse accepted," Casey said peremptorily. "*This* time."

Lenny's relief was evident in the smile that spread across his face. "Thanks," he said. "No wonder everybody says you're the best."

Casey had never especially cared what everybody said about him, and since his daughter's death he cared even less. But he mumbled something along the lines of "Thanks," stuffed the term paper into the inside pocket of his blazer, and resumed his trek.

The faculty club was housed in a stately brick building a couple blocks away. It took him just a few minutes to get there, make his way to the room where the club maintained its bank of computers, and sit down in front of one.

As Casey had done in his office, he turned the machine on. This time, the screen illuminated, offering him a chance to use the password assigned to him by the university.

But when he did so, the screen went dark again. As if the computer had realized it was him, somehow, and was part of some plot to keep him from doing his work that day.

So it wasn't the machines the professor was using. It was *him*. Or at least the *him* they recognized.

But he could hurdle that problem, couldn't he? All he had to do was employ the password used by his old assistant.

As he thought that, the strangest feeling came over him...the sense that as he looked at his computer screen, the screen was looking back at him.

But he hadn't engaged any facility that would have enabled such a thing. The little green light positioned above his screen—the one that lit up when he was connected to a conferencing program—was dark.

Damn it, Casey thought.

Did he dare ask for help from a student? He was a popular lecturer. Any number of students would have flocked to help him if he but asked.

John Fitter came to mind. Chris LaBanca. Joe Peluso. James Louie. Any of them would have been happy to give the professor a hand.

But what if in helping him, they caught a glimpse of something Casey wanted to keep to himself? Something, perhaps, that suggested he was more than he seemed?

Could that happen? He didn't know—and he couldn't chance it. Not if he wanted to keep his plans for the world a complete and utter secret.

"Everything okay?" asked a feminine voice from behind him.

The professor turned and saw Amanda Cherry, a graduate assistant in the History department. She pointed to his computer.

"You know," she said, "with *that*?"

Casey thought again about what he had to hide, and how much more important that was than any work he had to do for the university, and said, "I'm fine."

Cherry looked at the darkness on his screen, then at him. "Are you sure?"

Something snapped in Casey then. He had no idea why.

Cherry was a lovely person, after all. As pleasant as anyone he knew, within or without the precincts of the university. And she was just trying to be helpful.

But something about what she'd asked, or maybe the way she asked it, evoked a surge of guilt and regret and sorrow in him that broke down the dam he'd constructed for himself and overwhelmed him—a surge that pushed him inexorably, arms and legs flailing, over the edge of some psychological precipice.

"Professor?" Cherry said, looking concerned.

He looked away from her and repeated, "I'm fine."

Cherry stood there for a moment. Then she said, "Okay. If you need something, just let me know."

Casey nodded. "I will."

Cherry waited a moment longer. Then she walked away, leaving him sitting there with his unresponsive screen.

He was about to get up, to leave the place and try to figure out another way to get access to his work, when he realized the little green light above the screen…was *on* now.

As if someone or something was watching him. Just as he'd felt earlier—except now there was evidence it was actually happening.

Someone else might have freaked out at the realization. But not Perry Casey, and definitely not Professor Paracelsus. He drew a steadying breath, as the monks in the Tibetan village of Zhangmu had taught him, and sat back in his chair.

And saw something crawl across his otherwise still-dark screen: A string of bright golden letters forming six words and six words only.

He watched the words shuttle by over and over again, always at the same speed and in the same sequence. *A greeting*, strangely enough, though it didn't say from whom. And an invitation:

Hello, Professor. We need to talk

OVERSIGHT

BY GLENN HAUMAN

<null> sat back from his laptop, stretched, and gazed out the window of his motel room at an apple tree that had seen better days.

Even in its wizened state, it would produce apples—perhaps not as many as it had in its youth, but some. And those apples would contain seeds. And seeds…produced other things, <null> knew, some obvious and some not so obvious.

He frowned and returned his attention to the screen of his laptop. What he hadn't told Paracelsus, or by extension the United Front people Paracelsus was tasked with contacting, was how he had come to an understanding of what they had to do—and who had to do it.

He'd been conducting an experiment, the kind he undertook from time to time. The kind he felt *compelled* to undertake, in part because no one else was doing so. These experiments made use of artificial intelligence and its ability to extrapolate—to take existing data, examine its interactions, and predict outcomes based on it.

This particular experiment, the one he'd been conducting much of the night before, had involved Georgina Pinkerton and her Counters. After all, they promised to be the cause of so many effects these days.

At least, it had seemed that way to <null.> But it was only after he ran his simulation that he could be sure of it. *Horribly* sure. Nor was there any way to misinterpret the results of his analysis.

Pinkerton's Counters were on their way to creating a bleak and oppressive future—not only for the Phenomenons or New York City, where the Counters were focusing their efforts at the moment, but for the entire world.

There were precious few scenarios in which that future did not materialize—precious few out of billions and billions of possibilities. In all of them, the United Front dispatched an oddly constituted team to a particular location.

Six names kept popping up on that roster, and only six. Grey Guardsman—the newcomer, strangely enough, rather than the man who had made the name and the shield famous. Professor Paracelsus, despite his personal demons. Colosa and Particula, the most seasoned crimefighters in the group, but prone to sister issues that could be bigger than Colosa herself. Lipstick Lily, whom most people had never even heard of. And of course, Scopes.

The addition of any other Phenomenon doomed their effort to failure. And if only five of them completed the trip to their remote destination, their odds of success were drastically diminished.

<null> could only hope all six of them reached their destination. And if they did, that they followed his instructions to the letter.

Especially when it came to the dog.

At least, <null> thought, he'd gotten the ball rolling in time. He'd moved Paracelsus in the right direction before the United Front could move in the wrong one, and he'd done so while the world could still save itself.

He was congratulating himself on that count when the news from New York City appeared on the screen of his laptop…and he realized, numbly, that his intervention hadn't been as timely as he'd hoped…

BLINDED BY THE LIGHT

BY KEITH R.A. DECANDIDO

Friday, 9:47pm
Fifty-one minutes after the disaster

Luminosity found that just the act of lifting her arm to point at the large piece of metal that had once been a support beam for Madison Square Garden to be a near-Herculean effort. After more than half an hour of doing so, her arms felt like they weighed a thousand pounds each.

But she managed to raise her arm once more, point, and say, "Over there" to indicate the beam, which was but one piece of rubble among many.

Sarcastic Fringehead swallowed audibly and spoke in a ragged tone. "There is *no way* I can rust that out." Her ability to manipulate salt had been useful in speed-corroding some of the metal rubble, making it easier to move, but she had her limits.

With a sigh, Luminosity said, "That's what I thought. Where the hell is Jansson?"

"Right here."

Luminosity turned to see Thomas Jansson approaching. At this point, the pants Jansson had shown up in were covered in dust, the jacket and tie long since abandoned, the shirtsleeves rolled up, the top three buttons unbuttoned, revealing a rather hairy chest. Luminosity was also covered in dust, but she'd used her light-controlling powers to render all the dust invisible, so her white outfit with the prism motif was fully visible. (She no longer bothered to make her hair purple and her skin pale, as her true identity as Lucia Maldonado, former assistant district attorney for Bronx County, was now public knowledge.) People wanted to see bright, shiny heroes rescuing them, not dust-covered messes.

Pointing again at the support beam, she said, "We've got two people trapped under that—can you move it?"

"I can try." Jansson's prior answers to that query had been confident affirmatives, but he was starting to reach his limits.

In Luminosity's considered opinion, the enigmatic wealthy man wasn't used to admitting to having such limits.

Jansson went to squat down in front of a part of the support beam and got a grip on one edge of it, when Sarcastic Fringehead interrupted.

"You should move down about ten feet to your right. The leverage'll be better," she said.

Jansson shot her a look.

"What?" the teenager said, throwing up both hands. "It's physics!"

Grumbling something under his breath, Jansson moved ten feet to his right. Then he took a deep breath and heaved the support beam up.

As soon as he did so, Luminosity made the whole area as bright as possible. The two victims—both men, one Black, one Latinx—blinked and held their arms up over their eyes against the brightness, but also looked relieved.

"Can either of you stand?" Luminosity asked.

"Maybe?" the Black one said.

Through gritted teeth, Jansson said, "Take your time!"

Luminosity and Sarcastic Fringehead ducked down to help both men to their feet. The Black one had what seemed to be a busted leg, so he leaned on Luminosity. The Latinx one was more mobile, and Sarcastic Fringehead just guided him out.

"Was anyone else with you two?"

The Latinx one nodded. "We were both in the men's room, and there was a homeless guy there, too."

Once they were clear, Jansson dropped the support beam, which made a loud crashing noise and kicked up more dust. Both victims had coughing fits.

As recently as an hour earlier, that crashing noise would have scared Luminosity. Now she barely registered it. She'd been hearing too many loud noises tonight….

With Luminosity providing full illumination all around them, they led the two victims to the command center. Located just past the perimeter of the disaster on Eighth Avenue and 30th Street, there were hundreds of EMTs waiting to treat more victims that were brought up.

La Sombra was walking away from one of the EMTs. She had just arrived out of nowhere and offered to help shortly after Luminosity and Sarcastic Fringehead had, and right before Jansson's appearance. "What's next?" she asked in a voice that sounded like a truck driving over broken glass. Still, she'd been a lot friendlier than her reputation.

Luminosity turned and concentrated, pulling the light that reflected off an area of buried rubble that made it visible and putting it in front of all of them. This time she focused on the area near where they'd rescued their latest two, hoping to find the homeless guy they'd mentioned.

She found him, but he had a very large piece of rebar sticking through his chest.

"Oh, God!" Sarcastic Fringehead cried out.

Wincing, Luminosity cast the image aside as fast as possible. Sarcastic Fringehead had seen way more than most teenagers thanks to being a Phenomenon. This was her first direct experience with corpses, however, and this one was particularly gruesome. Her exclamation didn't sound like the confident teenager Luminosity had gotten to know since the kidnapping incident that had brought them together a while back, but rather like a very frightened little girl.

Luminosity tried another area nearby, and found a woman and an infant, the former looking dazed, the latter crying.

"You okay, kiddo?" she asked Sarcastic Fringehead.

The rainbow-haired girl nodded quickly, palming the tears from her face, and managed to put her yeah-whatever teenage voice back on. "I'm good. Really."

Luminosity somehow managed to force her face into an encouraging smile, then looked at La Sombra and Jansson. "Let's go."

Friday, 6:20pm
Three hours and thirty-four minutes before the disaster

"Well, *you* look like ass," De'Andra Jones said without preamble as Lucia Maldonado walked into the large space on Commerce Avenue that served as De's place of residence, her lab, and Luminosity's headquarters.

And, ever since she outed herself as being Luminosity, Lucia's temporary home as well, as her apartment was a target for the fourth estate.

Heading straight for the fridge for a beer, Lucia said, "Thaaaaaaaaanks, De. I took care of the car theft ring, but I had eight thousand paparazzi waiting for me outside the chop shop." She pulled out a beer bottle, opened it, and took a swig.

"How the hell'd they find you?"

"Damned if I know." She collapsed on the couch next to De and took a longer sip of beer. "I'm just glad I can make myself invisible. Though honestly? I think That's why they keep tryin' to find me. Nobody can get a pic, 'cause I go transparent soon's I see them. So now it's a challenge for them." She sighed and gulped down the rest of her beer in one shot.

Then she released a giant belch.

De laughed. "Real smooth, Looch."

"That's me, the dignified Phenomenon," she said, returning the laugh. "God, I need a break."

"So you ain't goin' to the concert?"

"What concert?"

"Don't you read your damn e-mail? My Bedroom Panic's playin' the Garment Club."

"Um, okay. And I care about this, why?"

"You *are* tired. That's Sarcastic Fringehead's band."

Lucia's eyes widened. "Right! Forgot the band name. And I did say I'd go to the gig, didn't I?"

"Yup. Have fun."

"You're not coming?"

De just gave her a look.

"Right, I forgot, I was talking to Ms. I Don't Listen To Any Music Made After 1972."

"Hey! That ain't right!" De grinned. "It's *Doctor* I Don't Listen To Any Music Made After 1972. So unless SF turned it into a Motown cover act since she shared the band's music files with us, I'll stay home, thanks."

Friday, 10:02pm
One hour and eight minutes after the disaster

"You up to this, kiddo?" Luminosity asked. She'd started calling Sarcastic Fringehead by that nickname, as her superhero name had too many syllables and she respected the teen's desire to keep the fact that she was really Jojo Fang a secret. *Kinda wish I still had a secret identity*, she thought wistfully, but dismissed the thought. Thomas Brincefield had learned who she really was, and she outed herself to get ahead of the story and so that Brincefield and his fellow Captains of Industry wouldn't have anything on her.

For her part, Sarcastic Fringehead was staring at the sheet of metal that was currently standing between them and four more victims, who were all huddled together under the metal, seemingly unhurt, but also unable to move.

"Yeah, I got this," Jojo said with a ragged confidence.

Luminosity was worried that the teenager was doing too much—it took a *lot* of salt to rust away metal. "Just focus on one area that can make a hole big enough for them to crawl out of."

Nodding, Sarcastic Fringehead got a look of concentration on her sweat-and-dust-covered face.

Pulling salt from any number of places, including some rock salt left over on the roads from a late winter storm, Sarcastic Fringehead pelted a spot in the middle of the metal sheet.

Luminosity had spent a lot of time in the last hour watching Jojo do this high-speed rusting thing, and it never failed to captivate her, as it looked like a video on super-fast-forward.

Eventually, it was a fully oxidized circle, and Luminosity heel-kicked it at the center, and the corroded metal crumbled away.

Hearing the coughs and shouts of surprise from the trapped teens, Luminosity called down, "Sorry about that! You should be able to climb up out of there, but please do it slowly—the edges of the hole we just made are pretty sharp."

She reached out a hand, and one of the victims' hands came up through the hole to clasp it. Luminosity started to pull, and a young girl with dark skin and a dot in the center of her forehead came up out of the hole. She was very skinny, and in no danger of hitting the sides as she came up.

"I knew it!" the girl said as she stepped off the metal sheet. Calling down to the hole, she said, "I told you the United Front would rescue us, Leilani! It's Better Angel and Scopes!"

As she pulled up another teenager, Luminosity sighed.

Friday, 8:48pm
Six minutes before the disaster

The last time Lucia was in the Garment Club was in law school, when she and some fellow aspiring lawyers had come to see Tedious Jello shortly after the semester ended. A lot of indie bands got their big break after playing the Garment Club on Eighth Avenue, just west of the Garment District (hence the name). Like most New York City clubs, it was a dimly lit hole in the wall. On the right was the bar, while the left-side wall was covered in photographs (many of them askew) of several of the bands that had played there and moved on to bigger and better things. Wormhole Death Cannon and Alabama Meth Gators were both there, and Lucia was thrilled to see that Tedious Jello had a picture now, too, right between Situationally Meatless and the Satanic Atheists.

Most of the crowd was about the same age she'd been when she'd come here to see Tedious Jello back in the day. But none of them recognized her, which was what mattered. Of course, like any good club, the place was *very* dark, with bright lights shining on the stage.

My Bedroom Panic was supposed to go on at eight-thirty, so of course, they hadn't actually started yet now at ten of nine, but they were setting up. She saw Jojo tuning her bass, her rainbow hair reflecting magnificently under the stage lights.

The bar's PA was playing a song Lucia didn't recognize, which was interrupted by a voice saying, "All right, put your hands together New York—it's My Bedroom Panic!" over a staticky sound system.

The drummer counted off, and they dove into their first song. Unfortunately, the crappy sound combined with the singer's shouty vocal style to keep Lucia from understanding a word he said. But the music was good—Jojo kept a solid bass line going, and she was in sync with the drummer, which was important. The keyboardist sometimes got a little too cute, and the guitarist's solo wandered a bit, but they were overall pretty solid.

Truthfully, they were a helluva lot better than Tedious Jello were back in the day…

Then the entire club was rocked by a massive boom that sounded like it was very far away but also right on top of them. The entire club shook like it was an earthquake, but only for a second.

What the hell was that?

Then the power went out.

Friday, 10:21pm
One hour and twenty-five minutes after the disaster

"Back to our top story: both Madison Square Garden and Penn Station have been destroyed. At eight-fifty-four this evening, the Garden collapsed by means as yet undetermined, with the ground under it compromised, and the rubble of the arena falling through to the train station. Very few people were in the Garden, as it was being prepped for a Billy Joel concert tomorrow night, and it was past rush hour, so Penn Station was less crowded than it was earlier in the evening. Nonetheless, the casualty toll is high, with this being spoken of in the same breath as 9/11 and the Triangle Shirtwaist Factory as one of the worst disasters in New York history. Let's go to Len Dvorkin, who's live on the scene. Len?"

"Thanks, Amalia. Several Phenomenons have been aiding NYPD and FDNY in rescuing people buried underneath the rubble. I've definitely seen Luminosity and La Sombra, who are both pretty far from their usual stomping grounds in the Bronx and Queens, respectively, but I guess it's all hands on deck? Anyhow, there are two others, a woman with rainbow hair and a man in a shirt and pants, who also seem to have powers. According to a couple of the rescued people I've spoken to, the man has incredible strength, and the woman with rainbow hair has some kind of corrosive ability. The four of them have been working tirelessly."

"Thanks, Len. We'll have more from Len Dvorkin on site and also here in the studio as this crisis goes on."

Friday, 8:51pm
Three minutes before the disaster

"I was so sorry to hear about Arturo."

Councilwoman Andrea Martinez screwed a smile onto her face, as that was about the five thousandth time she'd heard that since her chief of staff, Arturo Arbona, was killed in an explosion, and at least the twelfth time she'd heard it just tonight.

She was holding a glass of sparkling mineral water close to her face as she nodded and said, "Thank you" by rote. Arturo was a hair shy of a slave trader, and also a murderer, and while she was sorry he was dead, she wasn't sorry that he wasn't her chief of staff anymore.

Tonight was one of the rare occasions that she wished she was a drinker. Alas, she found the taste of alcohol—*any* alcohol—to be revolting, so she'd remained a teetotaler.

Her fellow City Council member Chris Carothers was giving a speech to some lawyer organization or other. Mayor Wolf had made it clear that the entire council was expected to attend. Several lobbyists belonged to the organization in question—Andrea couldn't even remember its name—so Wolf thought it was important to have the entire council attend the speech and the reception afterward.

But not the mayor himself, of course. That would require effort. Though Andrea would have thought the open bar would have been enough to get him here…

One of Andrea's great frustrations with the job had been getting Wolf to commit to—well, anything. And most of her fellow councilors were unwilling to push.

Carothers himself was approaching her now, and she screwed the smile back on. "Chris—very nice speech," she lied. The speech was droning and dull and she remembered not a single word of it.

"Thanks, Andrea. I was so sorry to hear about Arturo. He—"

A massive boom, and then the building shook.

The event was on a high floor of the Empire State Building, with a window that provided a view of everything west of them: the Garment District of Manhattan, the Hudson River, and the eastern coast of New Jersey, including Hoboken, Weehawken, and Union City.

But what quickly got everyone's attention was the plume of dust and smoke that billowed upward from a spot about halfway between them and the western coast of Manhattan Island.

"Oh my God," someone said, "I think they blew up the Garden!"

Andrea put her water glass down. "I have to go."

Friday, 10:32pm
One hour and thirty-six minutes after the disaster

Jansson had cleared away some rubble, then moved on to another spot to help out some firefighters. The strongman's efforts had cleared the way for six people to clamber out into the open air, one at a time. Luminosity stayed behind to use her powers to allow them to see their way out. Power had yet to be restored in the area, so the portable lights NYPD had brought were the only thing providing illumination besides Luminosity herself—and the NYPD floodlights didn't reach this far down into the rubble.

"That's it, come on through," she said as she guided the fourth person, a Black woman in an NYU sweatshirt and jeans, out.

"Thank you," the woman said. "You're Luminosity, right?"

She nodded.

"Figures they need the Bronx to help out."

Behind her, La Sombra said, "Queens, too." She was helping the trio who'd already come out, making sure they were up for the trek to the perimeter and the EMTs.

Luminosity attempted a smile. "Sombra will help you."

"Okay. Thank you. I don't care what your real name is, you're awesome."

Nodding, Luminosity silently helped the woman toward the other hero.

She didn't even have the energy to thank her. All her focus was on keeping the area lit.

The fifth person, a pale, redheaded Caucasian woman, came out and jerked a thumb back behind her. "He won't come out."

Luminosity nodded, guided the redhead to La Sombra, and then peeked down the makeshift passageway. "You okay down there?"

"I ain't movin'!" came the response.

Luminosity looked back at La Sombra, who had the other five all around her. "Go ahead and get them to the EMTs. I'll take care of this."

"You sure?"

"I got this, and they need to get looked at." She made a shoo-ing gesture with both hands. "Go!"

La Sombra stared at her for several seconds, then finally said, "I'm too tired to argue with you." To the others, she said, "Come on," and they moved up the pile of rubble.

Luminosity peered back down the passage. "What's your name?"

"Say what?"

"That's a funny name, Say What. I'm—" She hesitated, then: "I'm Lucia."

"My—my name's not Say What."

"I know, it was a crappy attempt at a joke. Crappy's the best I can do right now." Luminosity gathered up the tattered remnants of her focus and brightened the light in the passage so she could see who she was talking to. He was a short Black youth with his hair in braids that flopped over his eyes. He wore a dark blue hoodie over a black T-shirt. All of the above was covered in plaster dust. "What's your actual name?"

"Z-Zane. And I ain't movin'. I move again, I'll die."

"Why do you say that, Zane?"

"The ground don't feel that great. It was fine before, but it feels all loose now. I don't wanna move!"

"Zane, you can't just stay there."

"Watch me."

"No, I won't either. Look, Zane, I've been here for an hour and a half, and there are still hundreds of people that I can save—including you. Now let's go."

"Nuh-uh."

She sighed. On the one hand, she couldn't leave him there. On the other hand, she had a lot more people to rescue, and she couldn't afford to spend very long on just one of them.

"I'm gonna come down there," she said.

"No! You can't! You're Luminosity! You'll die if you come down here, and that ain't right!"

"How'd you know I was Luminosity?"

"Duh, you can make light. Who else'd you be? And you said your name was Lucia, and everyone knows that Luminosity's real name's Lucia McDonald."

"Maldonado, actually," Luminosity said. "Look, Zane, I won't let you die. And I won't die, either. Now I'm gonna come halfway, and I want you to grab my hand, okay?"

As she spoke those words, she crawled down the passageway that Jansson had made.

"C'mon, Zane, you can do it." She reached out toward him. "Grab my hand."

Zane just stared at her for several seconds.

Then he closed his eyes, whispered something, and did as she said.

Slowly she backed up the passage, pulling him along, until they were both in the open.

"Shit," Zane said. "We're still alive."

Luminosity grinned. "Yup."

"Thanks, Lucia. And please don't tell my Dad I said 'Shit.'"

"Your secret is safe with me. C'mon, I'll help you up the—"

Zane held up both hands. "Nah, you don't gotta. I can get up there myself. You go rescue some people who ain't as dumb as me."

"You're not dumb, Zane, you were just scared. With good reason. I'm just as scared, believe me."

Eyes widening, Zane said, "You? What for? You're a Phenomenon!"

"I'm still a person, Zane. And because I'm a Phenomenon, I'm in scary situations way more often than most people. And this situation is the scariest one yet, believe me."

"I guess. Well, thanks." He turned to head up to the perimeter. "Good luck!"

"You too!"

She watched Zane climb up the rubble pile in the same direction La Sombra had taken with the others in his group.

Then she turned around, preparing to check another spot that nobody could see from there, when suddenly the ground collapsed under her feet and she fell into the darkness...

Friday, 8:55pm
One minute after the disaster

The Garment Club had no external windows, so the power going out plunged the entire club into darkness, the only illumination provided by people's cell phones, many of which were quickly turned on and put into flashlight mode.

Lucia took those bits of light and expanded them, brightening the entire room.

"What was that?"

"It sounded like an explosion."

"Another blackout?"

"Damn!"

"Oh my God, you're Luminosity, ain'tcha?"

"Nah, that ain't her."

"Who else would make all this light, doofus?"

"You're the best, Luminosity!"

Someone came out of the rest room holding up her phone. "You're not gonna believe this! Somebody blew up Madison Square Garden!"

"Olivia, why you on the phone in the bathroom?"

"Really? That's what you focused on?"

Lucia looked over at the stage and locked eyes with Jojo.

Jojo nodded and lifted the bass over her head and put it on the stand. To the lead singer, she said, "Can you take care of my rig?"

The singer nodded. "Course. Be careful."

The guitarist asked, "What's going on?"

"I've got an uncle who works at MSG," Jojo said. "I gotta see if he's okay."

Without waiting for the guitarist to answer, Jojo ran off the stage, pushed through the crowd, and joined Lucia, who had altered the colors on her clothes to look like Luminosity's all-white costume with the prism motif.

By the time they got outside, Jojo had pulled down the mesh mask she wore over the bottom of her face. The rest of her stage outfit was pretty much the same as her Sarcastic Fringehead ensemble, including the rainbow hair.

Sometimes, Lucia thought, *I wonder how any of us keep our real names secret.* "I take it you don't have an uncle who works at MSG?"

Jojo shook her head. "But I had to say something. I've made too many enemies lately, I can't risk people knowing who I am."

For a moment, Lucia thought about explaining that lying to the people closest to you wasn't always the best plan. But Jojo was a teenager, and besides, it was *her* life, not Lucia's. On top of that, they had a situation.

Once they got out onto Eighth Avenue, they saw that there was a massive dust cloud where the Garden used to be. Lucia swallowed, remembering that awful day in 2001 quite clearly and trying very hard not to.

Cops were already setting up a perimeter when they got a few blocks north, and fire trucks and ambulances were already approaching.

Lucia looked for someone in sergeant's stripes, and found a familiar face from her days as a prosecutor in the Bronx. "R.J., when the hell did you make sergeant?"

Sergeant R.J. Butt turned to face Lucia. "Apparently, sometime after you became a Phenomenon." When last she'd seen R.J., he'd been a patrol officer in the 43rd Precinct in the Bronx. Now he had "MTS" on his collar in gold, indicating that he was assigned to Midtown South, the precinct that included MSG. "That why you quit the DA's office?" he asked her.

Sarcastic Fringehead was staring at R.J.'s nameplate. "Is your last name really "Butt'?"

Fixing the teenager with a fierce glower, R.J. asked very quietly, "Is that a problem, kid?"

Holding up both hands, Jojo said, "No, no problem."

"This," Luminosity said, "is Sarcastic Fringehead—how can we help?"

Now R.J. cocked his head. "You're really named after a fish?"

Jojo shrugged. "Is that a problem, Sarge?"

"No problem." R.J. shook his head. "Right now I'll take whatever I can get. Got no clue what happened here, but there's hundreds of commuters and MSG employees buried down there, so whatever you can do, go for it."

Friday, 10:47pm
One hour and fifty-three minutes after the disaster

It took a while for Luminosity's head to stop spinning and for her to be awake. But even when she opened her eyes, there was still total darkness.

Luckily, she never needed to be in the dark any longer than she wanted to be. Pulling light from other places, she lit up the area around her.

She was laying down on a train track, one of the many that radiated outward from Penn Station.

There was nobody alive nearby, which she confirmed by pulling the light reflecting off everything in the area and bringing it in front of her. All she got was empty spaces, piles of rubble, and more dead bodies.

She tried very hard not to focus on the dead, as well as on her fierce desire not to be one of their number.

First, she tried to get to her feet. This proved to be a horrible idea, as her left foot could not support her weight, and her attempt to get it to do so resulted in blinding pain shooting through her entire leg.

Gingerly, she sat back down on the rail, blinking the tears from her eyes, fuzzy from the pain.

She felt her heart beating like mad in her ribcage, and she knew she needed to calm the hell down. Utilizing the methods she learned at her grandparents' karate dojo—which she now helped her sister run—she inhaled through her nose for five heartbeats, held her breath for three heartbeats, and then exhaled through her mouth for five beats.

After a half dozen of those, she was almost calm.

Almost.

At the very least, she felt she could call for help.

As had been the case since the Garden collapsed, her cell phone had no signal. The nearby towers were probably overburdened, and possibly also damaged.

All right, so we go with powers. I've only been using them constantly for two hours, I'm sure I'll be fine. In truth, Luminosity had never used her powers for so long at a time before. Would she run out of proverbial gas?

Using her ability to move reflected light around, she was able to plot out a pathway from where she was to the perimeter. To her relief, there was a ladder she could take up to a higher spot, from which she could navigate the rubble to the street.

But there was no way she'd be able to climb it on her own with only one working foot.

So she pulled some light from all around and turned it into flares. Spaced every yard or so, they illuminated the pathway she needed.

Then she cast about for the other Phenomenons on site. She found Jansson first, but he was busy lifting more heavy things while some firefighters got people out from under. She still had no idea who he was, really—he'd just pulled up in a limo wearing a nice suit, talked to R.J, and started playing strongman.

Then she found La Sombra, who had just dropped a survivor off with an EMT—a fellow named Scott Crick, whom Luminosity had met before. Luminosity had read up on La Sombra, mostly stories in the very local *Queens Beacon*, and had also spoken with her friend Red Sky, another Queens-based Phenomenon, about La Sombra. She seemed pretty violent in the stories, but tonight she'd been nothing but amazing.

Luminosity sent the light that reflected off her to where La Sombra was so she could see that Luminosity was in trouble.

To her great relief, that plan seemed to work, as La Sombra made a beeline for the flares and followed them, climbing down the ladder to the rail that Luminosity lay on.

"You look like ass," La Sombra said.

Luminosity snorted at La Sombra's parroting of what De had said to her earlier that evening. *God, was that today? Feels like a year ago...*

"My left foot's messed up—might be broken, but I can't put weight on it. Give me a hand up?"

"Sure." La Sombra walked over and helped her to an upright position, then supported her weight as they moved to the ladder. "Nice trick with the flares and such. You realize you can fundamentally alter people's perceptions?"

"No, I can't," she said with a sigh. "I can just change what they see…"

It took them the better part of twenty minutes to get back to where the EMTs were, and to Luminosity's great sadness, she saw that Sarcastic Fringehead was being treated by one, on a gurney. An IV was attached to her right arm. The EMT moved off to help someone else, not having noticed Luminosity yet.

"What happened, kiddo?" she asked Sarcastic Fringehead.

The teen looked up at Luminosity, who was still being supported by La Sombra, and said, "That was gonna be *my* question!"

"She fell down a hole," La Sombra said, "but I got her out." She set Lucia down on the bumper of one of the many ambulances that were on Eighth Avenue, specifically the one closest to Sarcastic Fringehead. "You good?" La Sombra asked Luminosity.

"Not even a little, but I'll be okay here. Go do some good."

"That's why I'm here." La Sombra moved off.

"She's creepy," Jojo said.

Again, Luminosity snorted. "What happened to you, kiddo?"

"I fainted! It was *so* embarrassing!"

The EMT who'd been treating the teen—a tall man with a thick beard and long salt-and-pepper hair—came back to them, R.J. Butt by his side. "You fainted, young lady, because you're dehydrated. You need to go to a hospital."

R.J. turned to Luminosity. "What happened to *you*?"

"Fell down a big hole. Might've broken my left foot. I can't put any weight on it."

After checking Jojo's IV, the EMT examined Luminosity. Touching the left foot hurt a little, but not much, to her relief. "Feels like it's sprained," the guy with the beard said. "I'll bandage it, but you should go with your friend here to the hospital."

"We can't!" Sarcastic Fringehead said. "There's still people to save!"

Luminosity's heart warmed at the girl's words. Even after working herself to exhaustion, she wanted to do more.

R.J. said, "You guys are benched. Besides, we got pinch-hitters." He jerked his thumb behind his shoulder.

Following his thumb, Luminosity saw a woman growing to a great height. After a moment, she realized it was Noris Guerrero, a.k.a. La Colosa.

"Colosa and Particula showed up, and so did a whole bunch more firefighters and cops. And Sombra and Tangor are still here."

"Tangor?"

"Sorry," R.J. said, "Jansson. Long story. Anyhow, they can all take up the slack. You guys go get better."

Luminosity nodded. The EMT had only done a cursory examination—to be fair, he didn't have time to do much else—and she would rather have been properly looked over by a doctor. Once Luminosity's foot was bandaged, the EMT gave her a crutch and ran off to help someone else.

"C'mon," R.J. said, "I'll get you two to an ambulance That's leaving soon."

Using the crutch, Luminosity hobbled behind R.J., while Sarcastic Fringehead walked with the IV rack.

"Y'know," R.J. was saying as they navigated their way through the maze of ambulances, cop cars, and fire trucks, "they started callin' you guys Phenomenons' cause they didn't want to call you superheroes. Prob'ly figured it was too comic-booky or somethin'. Anyhow, after tonight—I'm callin' you guys superheroes, 'cause what you did tonight was pretty damned super and pretty damned heroic."

"Thanks, R.J.," Luminosity said with as much sincerity as she could manage while stumbling with a crutch. "Seriously."

"Me too, thanks," Sarcastic Fringehead added.

They climbed into an ambulance that already had four people in it—including Zane!

Upon seeing her, Zane's eyes went wide under his braids. "Holy shit, Lucia, what happened to you?"

Grinning ruefully, she said, "Right after you left, the ground fell out from under me."

He pointed at her. "I *told* you! I *told* you that was gonna collapse!"

"You did, Zane." She shook her head. "You did."

"And don't tell my Dad I said 'Shit.'"

She smiled. "I won't."

Saturday, 9:07am
Twelve hours and thirteen minutes after the disaster

"You *still* look like ass," De said as she approached Lucia in the emergency room at NYU Langone Hospital, having taken the 6 train down from the Bronx. Lucia, Jojo, Zane, and the rest of their ambulance-mates had been taken there. Lucia was sitting on a chair next to the bed on which Jojo was sleeping. Lucia's left ankle was thoroughly wrapped.

"Thanks, De. Ankle's sprained, so I'm gonna need to be off it for a few days. They even gave me a scrip for the good painkillers."

"So you're gonna be a *fun* roommate." De indicated the bed. "How's SF doin'?"

"She's okay now, just sleeping it off. She did *really* good last night, De."

"Yeah, I saw it on TV. Bitin' my nails down to nothin' since I ain't heard from you, just saw you riskin' your ass in a disaster area."

"I couldn't get a call through!" Lucia said defensively.

"Yeah, yeah," De said, making it clear she was just giving her childhood friend a hard time. "What about SF's parents?"

"She called them. Told them she was helping to drag people out of the rubble—which was basically the truth—and she's okay. They'll discharge her when she wakes up and I'll stick her in an Uber home."

"Sounds good." De pulled her phone out of her purse. "You were on the TV this mornin', too."

Lucia rolled her eyes. "Yeah, Len Dvorkin from New York 1 ambushed me when I hobbled down to the cafeteria to get some coffee. How bad did I look?"

"A lot better than that councilwoman did."

Frowning, Lucia asked, "What councilwoman?"

De turned on her phone and found the video she wanted, and played it for Lucia. The first thing Lucia saw was the New York 1 desk and the two anchors looking concerned at the camera.

"New York 1 caught up with Councilwoman Andrea Martinez, who was on the scene at Madison Square Garden this morning."

The camera cut to Martinez, who looked sweaty and dust-covered.

"This is a dark day for New York, losing hundreds of its citizens in the deadliest disaster here since September 11th, 2001. The good news is that a lot of other people were rescued, thanks to the heroic efforts of NYPD and FDNY, as well as several volunteers. But That's the only good news, unfortunately. We'll be working hard to recover from this."

Cutting back to the news desk: *"The entire City Council was at the Empire State Building for a speech by one of their number, Councilman Christopher Carothers, but interestingly Councilwoman Martinez was the only one who came to the disaster site."*

"Good for her," said the other anchor. *"The volunteers the councilwoman mentioned included several of the Phenomenons, including Lucia Maldonado, the former United Front member Luminosity, as well as Colosa and Particula, another local hero who has been tentatively identified as Ironic Figurehead, and a super-strong individual who has not been identified at all. New York 1's Len Dvorkin caught up with Luminosity at NYU Langone Hospital, where she's recovering from injuries sustained during rescue operations."*

Cut to Lucia, who looked haggard but decent, all things considered—the joys of being able to manipulate what you look like to the camera. Off-camera, Dvorkin asked, *'This is the second time you've been seen leading a team of Phenomenons—first that incident on Long Island that brought down Thomas Brincefield, and now this. Are you forming a new United Front?"*

"*I'm really not,"* Lucia said. "*Last night wasn't about teams or Phenomenons or superpowers, it was about New Yorkers coming together to help their own. It's unfortunate to have to say this, but NYPD and FDNY are* really *good at this stuff after 9/11, and I'm just glad that we were able to help out in our own way."*

"Ironic Figurehead? *Really?"*

Lucia turned to see that Jojo was awake. "Hey, kiddo, how you feeling?"

But Jojo was focused on her outrage. "It's a type of fish! It's a really, really *cool* fish! Don't these people Google? And that wasn't an 'incident,' we were *kidnapped.*"

Looking at De, Lucia said, "I guess she's feeling okay."

Noticing De for the first time, Jojo said, "Oh hey, Doc."

Jojo hadn't felt comfortable referring to De by her first name, and De herself balked at being called "Dr. Jones" by someone she'd been through a crappy experience with—Jojo and De were the ones who'd been kidnapped by Brincefield—so they'd settled on "Doc."

"I do feel okay," Jojo said, "and I just wanna get outta here. I never thought I'd say this, but after last night, I *really* wanna hug every member of my family."

"I feel that," De said emphatically.

"Has anybody found out *how* this happened?" Lucia asked.

De shook her head. "Ain't nobody got a damn clue."

"Really?"

"Really. The Garden just *collapsed.*"

Lucia, De, and Jojo just sat in silence after that, the noise of the ER all around them seeming inconsequential.

Looking down at her sprained ankle, Lucia said, "Maybe I won't be laid up for a few days."

"What do you mean?"

"Things are bad, De. We're gonna need more good guys out there, not fewer."

Jojo nodded. "I'm with you, Lumi." She grinned. "Maybe you *should* form a new United Front!"

"The existing one's fine," Lucia said, shaking her head. "But we definitely need to be on the ball before this gets any worse…"

PHENOMENON STORIES, PART II

BY MICHAEL JAN FRIEDMAN

"Wait," Better Angel said, leaning forward in her seat. "Are you telling us your *Counters* were responsible for what happened at Penn Plaza?"

"That's exactly what I'm telling you," said Georgina Pinkerton, including all of United Front except Torque, as well as Penny Trouble and her friend Deisha, in a single, sweeping glance. "You see, I maintained a backup headquarters at Penn Plaza, in case I ever needed it. My Counters went after the place. En masse, apparently. Just a few of them could never have generated the force necessary to destroy a structure of that size and integrity. But a couple dozen of them, working in concert? Having identified the weakest point in the building's makeup? That, I would think, could generate *more* than enough force."

Pinkerton's expression hardened. "My Counters have rebelled. Overthrown their creator, as it were. I should have seen it coming, but…" She shrugged. "I wish I could tell you what their agenda is, apart from ensuring I never give them or anyone else another order. Unfortunately, they're not all that predictable. And as We've seen, they're capable of anything. I repeat: *Anything*."

As the de facto leader of the superhero cadre United Front, Better Angel seldom felt that she was in over her head. But she felt that way now.

Had her life gone in a different direction, she would have been back in the house she grew up in at the corner of

Woodcrest Lane and Bob Stonehill Way, celebrating her acceptance into college with a cake from Big Bryan Geddes's House of Sweets. Not as Better Angel but as Emersen Terhune, honor student, member in good standing of the Rochester Fantasy Fans club, owner of a cat named Giggles.

She'd have been thinking about furnishing her dorm room, which meal plan to sign up for, whether to pledge for a sorority. Not the veracity of the crime boss of crime bosses sitting in front of her, piercing Better Angel with the intensity of her gaze.

Revek and Yoga had brought Pinkerton, Trouble, and Deisha to one of the United Front's satellite facilities, a shuttered boutique department store, as soon as Trouble told them the mastermind behind the war on Phenomenons was ready to deal with them—supposedly because her henchmen, the latest and most powerful generation of them, had turned on her.

With nowhere else to turn, Pinkerton was trying to ally herself with her worst enemies—the costumed heroes she'd been hunting for months.

Funny, Better Angel thought. She'd heard about Pinkerton from time to time, in the context of one news report or another, as often on the society pages as anywhere else. But she'd never suspected the woman of being the puppet master she was, or of being responsible for all the assaults made on Better Angel's fellow Phenomenons.

"You expect us to believe you're suddenly on our side?" Better Angel asked Pinkerton. "After you've overseen what amounts to a jihad against us?"

Pinkerton smiled a thin smile. "I wouldn't have used the word 'jihad,' but yes. Is that unrealistic of me? Perhaps. Unless, of course, I give you something meaningful." She indicated Penny Trouble and Deisha with a tilt of her impeccably coiffed head. "In addition, of course, to the life of their friend Silvercat."

"Something meaningful," Yoga prompted. "And what would that be?"

"Something you can use to defuse the threat posed by my Counters. That's the real prize here, isn't it? A weapon you can use against my creations, who've been beating you *at every turn*. Or are you going to claim otherwise?"

No one seemed inclined to do so.

"So," Pinkerton asked, "what's such a weapon worth to you—given how dangerous my Counters can be? If I can provide you with it here and now? A little pro quo for an enormous quid?"

Part of Better Angel refused to put her faith in anything Pinkerton promised them. This wasn't Michael Niosi they were dealing with, or Robert J. Sodaro, or the Boom Sisters. This was the top of the pyramid.

But another part of Better Angel—the one that acknowledged that she and her fellow Phenomenons were on a slippery slope—saw the need to at least hear Pinkerton out.

"What is it you want?" Better Angel asked.

"Protection," said Pinkerton, "from my creations. Shelter, preferably in a succession of secure locations. Your dedication to the priority of keeping me safe from them."

"You must have implanted in them a failsafe of some kind," Scopes ventured.

"Very insightful," Pinkerton said. "Unfortunately, they've managed to *disarm* my failsafe. But they have another weakness, one they can't get around so easily. One they don't know exists."

"And what's that?" Revek asked.

Pinkerton held up a long, slender finger. "Do we have an agreement?"

Better Angel looked around the room. No one objected to the idea. Not given the stakes involved.

She turned back to Pinkerton and said, "A conditional agreement: You hold up your end of the bargain and we'll hold up ours."

Pinkerton eyed her for a moment. Then she said, "Fair enough," and held out her hand. "Nice doing business with you."

Better Angel didn't shake Pinkerton's hand. She just said, "What have you got for us?"

Pinkerton took her hand back, her eyes narrowing. "You're not as innocent as you look," she told Better Angel, "are you?" But she didn't withdraw her offer. "Listen closely…" she said.

COUNTER ATTACK

BY ROBERT GREENBERGER

While there was a perfectly useful conference room, Victor Brenin held this particular meeting in the CED's operation center. While he spouted words about transparency, the truth was more complicated. He needed the rank and file to understand the urgency of the briefing, not just for the immediate danger, but so they shared the news, letting it seep into the Washington ecosystem. The latest presidential budget suggested cuts to the Cyber Engagement Division without pushback from the Senate Intelligence Committee, which told Brenin his clout had lost some luster. He needed a win, something to rub their noses in so they would approve instead, an *increase* in the budget. Brenin had plans for his relatively covert agency buried deep within Homeland Security; to accomplish them, there would be a need for lots of cash.

Attending and positioned closest to him were his Field Team leader, Fernando Rodriguez, and his number two, Sarah Morris. They were flanking the expansive operations console manned that morning by Molly Cafarelli, the CED's no-nonsense day shift leader. Standing directly behind her, his hand laying claim to the command chair, was the evening leader, Micah Warren, who had yet to go home and was clutching a steaming paper cup of coffee in his other hand.

"Our brethren at Fort Meade have kindly shared their intelligence about a series of encounters between a new class of opponents. In the field, they've been called Counters,"

Brenin said, his deep voice carrying beyond the clutch of people attending his every word.

"Accountants?" quipped Morris, earning her a disapproving quirk of Brenin's eyebrow.

"Counter, as in counter-agents, enhanced humans with superior strength, endurance, reflexes, and so on," Brenin said. "Think of your greatest Olympians, and they're three classes above them."

Brenin noted that that caught Rodriguez's attention. The field leader was an army vet who had seen his share of action in the field. The man's eyebrows knit in concentration, his eyes going unfocused, and he was already envisioning how to combat this new threat.

"Where'd they come from," Morris asked.

"Someone, somewhere, manufactured them and has recently unleashed an undetermined number. This clearly has been something in the works, but yes, the timing raises questions. If we can capture one, maybe we can ask politely."

"Where have they been?" Rodriguez asked.

"According to the NSA's Phenomenons desk," Brenin continued, "we have reports of Red Sky, Fringehead, and a newcomer called La Sombra all confronting them and surviving, but not unscathed. Word is, they walked away impressed by the level of threat the Counters pose."

Rodriguez refocused and quickly processed the abilities of the costumed vigilantes just named. To Brenin, they were an impressive bunch, but then again, he had no enhanced-powered people at his disposal, so he wondered if he might be a tad jealous. He idly thought about one day subsuming the United Front into the government but suspected that would not go over well with the personnel or federal bureaucracy.

"What are these…Counters…doing?" Morris asked, shuffling her weight from one foot to the other.

"It seems rampant destruction on a scale not seen since King Kong toured Manhattan," Brenin said. He looked around the room, knowing he was about to drop a bombshell in everyone's midst. "Intelligence has it that they're the ones who destroyed Madison Square Garden and Penn Station yesterday."

Eyes went wide, and even the murmurs behind the core team went silent as the severity of the threat became apparent.

"Molly, I want the footage for analysis," Rodriguez said, interrupting Brenin. "I don't know if the exoskeletons can match that kind of strength."

"On it," she said, tapping commands into her console, tasking someone to gather the available video. By the time the briefing ended, it would be loaded and ready for his study. Again, Brenin admired his team's efficiency, patting himself on the back for hiring well.

"We're still trying to understand how the suits were depowered," Morris added. She and the young operative Reese were in Brooklyn dealing with a set of illegally manufactured doppelgangers of their exoskeletons when the CED exoskeletons went inoperative. The technological outage was not limited to just them but also to other technologically enhanced Phenomenons.

"It's all connected," Warren interjected. The dark-skinned man was always looking for connections between events, finding a trail among the random breadcrumbs, making him among the first to spot threats. While sometimes written off as a benign conspiracy theorist, Warren had proven his value over the years.

"I concur," Rodriguez said, nodding, earning him an approving glance from Warren.

"To what end?" Cafarelli asked.

"Now that's a question I don't think we have an answer for," Brenin said. "Defend Today, Secure Tomorrow." That last was the agency's motto, plastered throughout their College Park, Maryland facility.

"What are we defending?" Morris asked.

"Right now, everything," the director replied. "These random acts of violence will make sense soon. But, we need to confront each Counter we find. You need everyone, Fernando, and every exoskeleton. Work with Kwan to coordinate assignments and alert the warehouses."

"You're not worried about another short circuit?" Morris asked. While the questions annoyed him, Brenin found she had a point. No rushing into danger without fully assessing the situation., He'd learned that lesson the hard way and more than once. "We're already down two suits after Brooklyn. I don't think the repairs are done."

"They're not," Cafarelli confirmed.

"But," Warren said, "Ke was showing me the work she'd been doing on the suits you found in Kansas." On a suspicious tip, Rodriguez and Reese had uncovered the illegal manufacture of the exoskeletons for some shadowy operation. They had damaged the lot of them and were still investigating the matter. Still, they had recovered the enhancements that had been made to the outfits and brought them back to their R&D department. Their head, Ke Ma, had been like a pig in shit, delighted to see her initial work improved upon in ways she hadn't imagined., She had commented just the week before how it forced her to think in new ways, which would make the next generation of suits even better. That was if Brenin could secure the budget funding.

"She's managed to repair those suits with the enhancements. Bit of a kludge, if you ask me," Warren continued.

"Good, we can use those in Cherry Hill," Cafarelli said. She gestured to a small screen on her console and then, with a flourish, transferred it to one of the overhead screens against the far wall. On it was a CNN news alert.

"What the hell's in New Jersey?" Morris said.

"At least one of these Counters has been spotted near an industrial park," Cafarelli continued.

Warren warned, "They haven't been field-tested. They haven't even been repainted."

"We're not posing for *Glamour*," Rodriguez said, his voice dropping even lower with disapproval.

"How quickly can you and Morris suit up?" Brenin asked.

"Put 'em on a van, and we can dress en route," Rodriguez said to the director.

Whatever was to be said next was interrupted by a commotion on the other side of the spacious ops center. Three people were now clustered around a console; the seated one was adjusting something.

"What's going on?" Cafarelli asked, pitching her voice in a way that instantly cut through the chatter and got their attention. That was a skill Brenin admired and wished he had.

Colleen Kwan, Cafarelli's young logistics administrator, instantly stood up, looking crisp in her CED uniform.

"We've received an encrypted data packet," she began. "It's addressed to us generically, and we're tracing the IP, but it's scrambled. It's going to take some time."

"Mysterious messages, just as there are all these Counters out there," Warren mused aloud.

"How long to crack it?"

"It's actually being decrypted now, Molly. It's clearly meant to be read."

Brenin finally left his position and walked toward the cluster, people getting out of the director's way. "What about security? Any trojan horses?"

"It looks clear," a tech to Kwan's left said, the director having forgotten her name.

"How clear?"

Without hesitation, the tech replied, "Clean as a whistle. It's meant for us despite the cloak and dagger pinging from servers around the world."

"What is it?"

"I'm putting it up now," Kwan said. She flipped two switches, and a screen near her station flared to life. A series of slides containing what was clearly scientific notation appeared. "It's about three megabytes of data. They're all biological formulas."

"I'm calling Greene," Cafarelli said, her hand already on the phone's handset.

Within minutes, Haywood Greene, the day shift's chief medical officer, arrived. He was among the older day-shift members, balding and with a pronounced paunch, his dark eyes already seeking out the screen. He wore his white lab coat over his CED polo shirt and scrub pants.

Everyone wanted instant answers. Everyone, that was, save Cafarelli and Rodriguez. They were each on phones, making arrangements for the two exoskeletons to be loaded and readied for transport, with a team ready to lend support.

"What's a Scopes?" the doctor asked, looking up from a screen.

"A member of the United Front," Brenin answered.

"Well, whoever he is, he did us a huge favor. I have here the biochemical alterations done to the humans you call Conduits."

"Counters," Brenin and Cafarelli replied.

"Whatever. This is some of the most sophisticated gene editing I have ever seen, way beyond what I thought CRISPR could do."

"What's CRISPR?" Kwan asked.

"It's a genetic engineering technique that's based on a simplified version of the bacterial CRISPR-Cas9 antiviral defense system," Haywood answered. "It's cutting edge, but this, this is bleeding edge."

"Why send it to us?" Brenin asked no one in particular.

"Think about it. These Counters are tearing up whatever they find, be it the Garden or whatever else they've targeted. If you found a key to defeating them, wouldn't you want it sent to the people who might be able to do something? Nothing says it was sent just to us."

Heads nodded nearly in unison, and a brief silence fell over the center as Greene studied screen after screen. He then rocked on his heels and said, "Holy shit!"

"What is it?" the director snapped.

"There's a formula here for developing a pathogen that might stop them," the doctor said.

"Where'd Scopes get that?" Rodriguez said.

"Same place he got their genetic makeup," Greene said, a wicked grin crossing his face. "Doesn't matter, but if this checks out, we have a way to take them down."

"How much time do you need," Brenin snapped. "There's one ripping up New Jersey."

"The whole state…oh…well, this gives me a tremendous head start. We have various pathogens in storage for research. If I can find one to use as a foundation…"

"Go find it and report to the garage. Change of plans, Fernando," Brenin ordered. "Load the suits in the mobile med center." Green practically ran to the doors leading to the medical center. Meanwhile, everyone else got busy preparing for the mission ahead, checking satellite uplinks, clearing comms traffic, and getting real-time reports on the danger awaiting the team in Cherry Hill.

"All the equipment won't leave room for more than one suit and operator," Kwan called out. "And the doc needs room to work. I can have the second suit and operator on the mobile tactical van. I'm recalling it from Reston."

"Reston? That'll take hours," Morris complained. "I want another shot at whoever is doing this."

"But you're going to wait," Rodriguez said authoritatively. "With one suit, I want the most experienced operator, and right now, That's Reese. Get them in here," he snapped to Kwan.

"Already called them," Kwan replied.

"That earns you a cookie," Cafarelli said, beaming at her with pride. "Today they're lemon blueberry."

"And what will you be doing," Brenin asked Rodriguez.

"Driving and being their backup," he said.

Less than two hours later, the team had assembled in the mobile medical center, a not quite state-of-the-art emergency response vehicle. While Rodriguez had waited for Reese and the exoskeleton to arrive, Greene's team had made certain it was prepared with Reese's blood type, plasma, and other surgical supplies. Optional gear was removed to make room for laptops and spare parts for the exoskeleton—just in case. It would be a tight fit for everyone until Reese donned the exoskeleton, but there would be just enough room for Greene to work with his pathogens. The elongated chassis of the vehicle had a section that could be sealed off, nominally, to prevent the spread of infection, but in this case, it would provide the doctor with a sterile environment for his experimental work. Rodriguez tapped another field agent, burly Christopher Brew, to ride shotgun—just in case. There were a lot of contingencies running through his mind as they prepared to rush into the unknown.

He'd been informed not long before that Reese had arrived at the base and had been hurriedly briefed by Cafarelli. Now, the young woman had turned up, brown eyes bright, their round face a mask of tension. They shook hands with Brew and Rodriguez before finally standing at ease. They peered into the open back bay of the vehicle, pursing their lips at seeing the prone exoskeleton, a jumble of familiar and unfamiliar pieces, a riot of colors, scratches, and burned sections.

"Think you can operate this thing?" Rodriguez asked Reese.

"'I shall not cause harm to any vehicle nor the personal contents thereof, nor through inaction let the personal contents thereof come to harm," they said.

Without missing a beat, Rodriguez replied, "It's what I call the Repo Code, kid!"

Brew merely blinked in confusion, causing the other two to laugh.

"*It's a movie reference*," Cafarelli said through their subdermal implants, one of several technological enhancements CED filed agents endured. "*They do that a lot, usually movies you're too young to know. You'll get used to it or be hopelessly confused. Greene's on his way; you roll in five.*"

"About time," Rodriguez growled. Brew went ahead and took his seat on the passenger side."

"Ready?"

"Charging into the unknown, facing Wonder Woman, and wearing a suit we're not sure works? Sounds like fun."

"At least this Counter doesn't have a magic lasso," Rodriguez said, heading for the driver's door.

As he entered the vehicle, Greene hurried into the garage with a backpack and two satchels. It was going to be a tight fit, but it needed to be done if he had any hope of creating an experimental pathogen to take down a colossus.

Rodriguez fired up the engine, causing Green to scramble into the rear, the reinforced steel doors slamming with finality.

While Greene worked in isolation, Reese spent the nearly three-hour drive from College Park to Cherry Hill reviewing the footage assembled by Kwan about the attack in New York City and what was happening at the industrial park, an unassuming collection of office buildings, warehouses, and one four-star restaurant that did boffo business at night. That had been spared—so far—while one office building had collapsed atop a second one, small fires spouting from windows and crevices. The Counter—a woman—was smart, tossing large, heavy pieces that were once buildings to block the various entrances to the park. State police had already been warned to keep their distance while fire trucks and other emergency vehicles were idling nearby.

Reese relished this, being an analyst. Their missions to date had been more active ones, covert ops, except for the public action in Brooklyn. They'd received good performance reviews and enjoyed being recognized for their actions, but there were times they thought Rodriguez only used them for physical pursuits, which demanded wearing the uncomfortable exoskeleton. As Ke Ma retrofitted the illegal gear into the suit Reese wore in Brooklyn, they persuasively argued to adjust it for female dimensions.

Reese preferred to analyze whenever possible, reminding everyone they had a brain, not just curves. Here was a perfect opportunity to study the opponent at length before taking action. The Counters were methodical with their destruction. The attack on Madison Square Garden was not random nor haphazard but methodical, starting with infrastructure before the showier façade. It meant cutting off power and water, taking out the HVAC system, and then going after the interior walls, letting it collapse inward. Despite the death toll, this was not designed as a mass casualty event. Each blow allowed people to flee.

The female Counter was doing much the same in Cherry Hill. She was a sturdy six-foot-plus, with impressive musculature from shoulders to calves. The neck was thick, with corded veins visible even from a distance. Her blonde hair was in a buzz cut, and both ears had steel bars, providing little to snag on. Her body had brightly colored tattoo sleeves, intertwining snakes that began at the wrist and writhed their way up her arms, coiling together under her t-shirt, the v-collar revealing symbols Reese couldn't identify. The woman's motions were smooth, fluid ones, as if she had dance training, but her rampant destruction also suggested an understanding of the architecture. Reese concluded the Counter had studied the building before taking it apart, a reverse architect of sorts. Again, people were allowed to run from the buildings as the rampage began. Not that they could drive away once the entrances were blocked, but they cowered, wisely keeping their distance.

"Facial recognition identifies your target as Terri Sponaugle, thirty-three. Long rap sheet, mostly petty stuff," Kwan reported from Maryland.

"Any combat training?"

"None, Reese. Maybe did something as a hobby because she looks practiced."

"I had the same thought."

As Reese watched, they began contemplating countering the Counter and what moves might neutralize someone with superior strength and agility. The exoskeleton was good for many things but was not responsive or fast, giving the Counter a decided advantage. Depending on what goodies Ke Ma had managed to install—even if they worked—Reese would be at a *dis*advantage until Morris and her second exoskeleton arrived an hour or two later. But by then, it might be too late.

From the driver's cabin, Brew, an olive-skinned with short hair in the military style Rodriguez preferred for his agents, announced, "We've been tracing the ownership of the buildings and its occupants. Once Colleen peeled away enough LLC layers, she was able to trace the ownership to Pinkerton Ventures."

That gave Reese pause, but her commander interrupted before they could say anything.

"That doesn't make a damned lick of sense. I thought Pinkerton was behind all this nonsense. That was the intelligence we received."

"I thought so too," Reese admitted. Why would Counters attack properties owned by Pinkerton? And obscure ones, too? How did that connect with the Garden? They spoke out: "Molly, are you there?"

"CED on standby," Cafarelli said in their ear.

"Can we find out what was scheduled to be performed or played at the Garden when the Counter attacked?"

"Standby." Less than a minute later, Kwan's soothing voice responded. *"The Knicks had a game against Milwaukee, and Archie Manning was giving a motivational lecture."*

"Who?"

"Father to Payton and Eli Manning, football greats," Rodriguez chirped from the front. "Great arms."

Ignoring him, Reese continued. "Who was Manning's sponsor?"

"*Power Button Limited, a subsidiary of Power Company Speakers Bureau, owned by...*"

"Pinkerton Ventures," Reese and Colleen Kwan said together.

"Attacks on anything Pinkerton-owned suggests something has changed, and the Counters are attacking their master," Reese said.

"That's *why we keep you around,*" Rodriguez said.

"I thought it's because I like your obscure movies," Reese shot back.

Whatever comeback he had was swallowed by Greene's emergence from his isolated space. He looked tired and worn, and a thin sheen of sweat was reflecting off his forehead. But he was smiling, which meant something positive.

"I've managed to use the data and have manufactured a pathogen that will attack the Counter's bioelectric system. It will be quick-acting or as fast as electricity moves."

"That's fast enough," Reese said with a smile. "How do I deliver it?"

"I can't make it into an aerosol; it diffuses too quickly, and I don't want you receiving a dose. It's geared for their bulk, and it'd fry you. It has to be a shot."

"So, I have to get up close and personal with Sponaugle. Great. The way she's taking down cinderblock and concrete, the exoskeleton will be tinfoil to her."

Greene gave her a tired shrug, which basically said he had done his part; now Reese had to do theirs. They nodded and turned their attention to the live feed now coming from a CED drone. The Counter had worked up a good sweat herself but wasn't slowing down. Her stamina was amazing, but it also meant that by the time they arrived, she might be tired and, therefore, slower.

"We'll be there in twenty minutes," Brew called out.

"Time to suit up," Reese said to Greene. "I'll need a hand."

The doctor nodded and followed their directions as they righted the suit and Reese began the laborious process of strapping, adjusting the fittings to their physique. Ma had done her work well; it was a better fit than the last time Reese wore this.

"I'm not crazy about biological weapons," Reese said, startling Greene, who was finalizing connections in the rear.

"Well, neither am I."

"Chemical warfare was banned after World War I for a reason. I think the same ethic applies here. Once you let that genie out of the bottle, there's no stopping it. Your CRISPR can be used for good or evil."

"Likely both over time," Greene admitted, coming around to face Reese.

"They just widen the gap between those with and without. Or, it'll take money needed to feed poor people and pour it into some banana republic's lab."

"Would you feel better if you knew the pathogen is being built specifically to the bloodwork I was shown, targeting the very environments that make the Counters a threat? On our accelerated timetable, even the computer models can't guarantee any sort of success."

Reese merely nodded, still dissatisfied. Their reverie was interrupted by the feeling of deceleration and rumbling over rough terrain. They had arrived, the van driving over curbs and grass, carving a path of its own, and it was time to act.

"I'm letting you out near the target. We'll be monitoring from here and staying out of your way," Rodriguez said from the driver's seat. "Morris is about ninety minutes out."

"Should've used a helicopter," Reese grumbled as Greene used Velcro strips to attach the two syringes to either thigh.

They looked down at them with a frown but gave the doctor a thumbs up.

Automatic locks clicked, and the rear door rolled open, letting Reese make the short jump to the ground. So far, the exoskeleton had been behaving smoothly and making all the right whirring noises. The next-gen enhancements improved flexibility and response time, making them better for combat than the CED specs. "I'm five by five," Reese announced.

"Go get "em, kid," Rodriguez said.

"I'll be monitoring your vitals from here," Greene said, opening a laptop and accessing the signals emanating from the tech buried throughout Reese's body.

Ignoring that, Reese began moving toward the scene of destruction. Terri Sponaugle had torn her shirt on rebar, exposing more tattooed skin and sweat. She'd been dismantling a three-story office building, which lay exposed; office furniture of all sorts had been belched out, wooden and metallic splinters littering the parking lot. She was making more than enough noise, so she had yet to register that she was no longer alone. Jersey State Police had kept civilians and media away and the former occupants were as far away from Sponaugle as possible. She hadn't even noticed when Rodriguez steered the van through the cordoned barrier.

Ideally, Reese would sneak up on the Counter, inject her, and watch the sparks fly. Instead, they gritted their teeth, knowing it was never going to be that easy. To inject her, Reese needed the woman behemoth stunned or immobilized, and needed the rubble to anchor her. After that, it was all going to be improvised.

Silently counting down to themselves, Reese launched themself on "One," rumbling forward and gaining whatever momentum could be generated. As they neared the Counter, Reese lowered their head, hoping a headbutt to the back would get things started. What they couldn't anticipate were the heightened senses that made Sponaugle swivel about, whipping both arms forward to catch the approach. With an audible grunt, the Counter seized Reese's helmet and twisted, throwing Reese off balance.

Already, the sound of twisting metal filled the air, and the exoskeleton was splayed on the macadam.

"Shit," Reese said, tasting the coppery blood from biting their cheek.

"*Elevated heart rate, pulse racing,*" Greene said.

"Shut up unless it's an imminent heart attack," Reese snarled. They rolled over, which was no easy feat with the heavy gear, but avoided being stomped. The Counter's move allowed Reese to reach Sponaugle's ankles and pound on them with her own enhanced strength. But all that got Reese was some irritated grunts.

"What do you want?" the Counter asked, her face a mask of irritation.

"I'd settle for your complete surrender, Terri," Reese offered. The use of her name surprised the woman.

"No."

"A fair fight? I'm Reese, by the way. Nice to meet you."

Sponaugle ignored her. "Not possible!"

She had a point. Reese was able to rise as the woman backed away, assessing the exoskeleton. Sponaugle's eyes studied the gear, not the occupant, which pissed Reese off. However, the assessment allowed her to trigger one of the experimental modifications from the recovered illegal armor. A high-pitched whine was emitted from embedded shoulder speakers, causing the woman to step back, hands going up to protect her enhanced hearing. That gave Reese the chance to charge forward and grab one of the woman's arms and twist it at a painful angle, hoping to force her to her knees. Instead, she whipped the other arm around and delivered a savage punch to Reese's midsection, forcing the CED agent to their knees. The exoskeleton didn't fully cover the human body, and this blow went right into their midsection.

"Any internal damage?" Reese wheezed.

"*None,*" Greene said. "*Yet.*"

"Thanks for the vote of confidence," Reese said, trying to rise but found themselves knocked backward by a brutal kick, which thankfully dented only the exoskeleton, not breaking any bones. Reese noticed that the kick was dangerously close to where one of the syringes was strapped. They needed to be protected because it was clear Reese could not win this battle hand-to-hand. The energy output showed battery life was down to seventy-two percent already. The fight was barely three minutes old, and Morris would never arrive in time without using a matter transporter. They had to invent those soon, Reese mused.

The agent rolled away from another kick and used the enhanced suit to right themselves and get back on their feet. They ached from the blows, especially the sore stomach, which would definitely be all sorts of black and blue in the morning, But that would have to wait because now they needed to stop a hulking human machine. Quickly, Reese assessed where they stood, the condition of the building they were standing beside, the debris scattered in every direction. A plan began to form, but they were distracted as, with a roar, Sponaugle charged, shoulder forward, trying to ram them.

Forcing themself to move, Reese planted their feet and twisted their torso so the woman missed her, and Reese grabbed handfuls of the t-shirt and used her attacker's momentum against them. The Counter was hurled forward, off-balance. Reese charged forward, rearing back and landing a swift series of blows against the woman's chest and back. The grunts and exhalations indicated they were causing some pain. While the muscles and nerves may have been enhanced, the skin seemed just as pliable as normal. Welts began to form, blood seeping into the sweat and dirt on the Counter's arms.

With a roar of rage, the woman charged at Reese, arms wide, to get them in a bearhug that would certainly crush the exoskeleton. Quickly, Reese changed their strategy and stepped backward, seemingly stumbling over a huge section of wall. That would require Sponaugle to also change her approach and lean down to grab her.

"*The suit's rapidly losing power,*" Cafarelli signaled. "*Save yourself and just buy us time.*"

"*I'm coming,*" Rodriguez added over the comms.

"I got this!" Reese said, loud enough for just the implanted mic to pick up.

The Counter approached cautiously, seeing sparks coming from one of the leg armatures, and wickedly smiled.

"Aww, is your little outfit malfunctioning? Shall I peel it off you?"

"Can't you buy me dinner first?" Reese said and winked, which seemed to annoy the Counter.

Sponaugle reached down, which was when Reese's arms swung in arcs that allowed them to stick both syringes in the attacker's arms. One was at a bad angle, but the other went into the soft flesh, and Reese depressed the plunger.

"What the fu--" the woman started to say, and then she violently convulsed. There was a pause, and then her body began to jerk spasmodically, a fish flopping out of the water. She fell to the side, unconscious.

"Got you, bitch," Reese said, scrambling to their feet. In the distance, they saw Rodriguez and Brew running like mad toward them. Raising a weary arm, they waved and then shouted, "Get something to secure her!"

"*You really did have it,*" Cafarelli said, impressed. "*You okay?*"

"*No, she's not,*" Greene cut in. "*I'm reading heightened pulse and heart rate and shallow breathing.*"

"That's what happens when you get the shit beat out of you. Tell Ke that the new suit's pretty good but needs repair. Again."

"And a paint job," Rodriguez said as he arrived to help Reese stay steady. Everything hurt, so the support was welcome. Brew leaned over the prone woman, whose chest was shallowly moving.

"The pathogen worked," Brew reported.

"This one's out cold. Pass word back to the United Front that it works and should be manufactured to stop the rest," Rodriguez commanded.

"*We're on it*," Cafarelli confirmed.

"*I'll write up my report in a few minutes once I tend to Reese here,*" Greene added from the van.

As Rodriguez and Brew secured the still-unconscious woman, Reese was gingerly removed from the twisted, charred, and depowered exoskeleton. It had done its job well but suffered great damage. The next model had to be made of stronger alloys and more tactical gear built in, Reese mused as Greene took their vitals, cleaned and bandaged various wounds, and gave them something for the all-over pain. Ke Ma had her work cut out for her.

"*I am so very proud of the work you did today,*" Brenin's voice whispered in their ear. "*I don't think we can consider you a rookie any longer.*"

"Thank you, sir," Reese said, too tired for quips.

"*Your work has been exemplary. We were wise to steal you from Quantico.*"

"Well, they didn't have your snazzy polo shirts," Reese said. "Easy decision."

Whatever Greene gave Reese was taking hold, and keeping their eyes open further wasn't an option. The mission was a success, even if the damage to the exoskeleton was going to be costly. Whatever threat Pinkerton had unleashed could at least be contained. There would have to be satisfaction in that.

Whatever came next could wait.

THREE POINT FOUR

BY PAUL KUPPERBERG

Bang!

The only reason Torque heard the retort of the sniper rifle was because he had paused momentarily on the eighty-fourth floor landing of the Empire State Building stairwell to catch his breath, allowing sound to catch up with him.

He knew he shouldn't have stopped. Not even for a millisecond, but he had to. Ever since the accident that night on the plaza of the ChronActive Building, running at speeds many times that of sound had been effortless, but now his lungs burned, his chest and sides ached, and his legs felt like lead. He had almost tripped on the seventy-ninth-floor landing and superspeed-stumbled up the next five flights, finally stopping himself, gasping and clutching tight to the handrail just to stay upright.

Damn it!

Everything hurt and he didn't think he could go another step. Not even to save a life.

Not even Dr. Dale Jurn's.

Then, maybe it was an echo or a reverberation, but Owen thought he heard the sound of the shot stretched by the Doppler effect, like the way things sounded when he was accelerating into super-speed, and he was running again, through the pain. His lungs burned and his chest tightened, but he ran. As fast as he could.

Which was no longer fast enough.

Not like it was before his speed became erratic, losing power, sputtering, and cutting out like a badly tuned car engine. Once, he could have raced up and down the exterior face of the building, outracing gravity's pull at almost twelve kilometers per second. Now, he was struggling to hit Mach two, each step more exhausting than the last.

But the gunshot.

A single bullet from a high-powered sniper rifle, fired from a height of one thousand feet above sea level, at a target on a boat in the Hudson River five and one-half miles away. Under normal circumstances—as normal as a circumstance can be with a sniper involved—he wouldn't have to worry about anyone making that kind of shot. The record for a sniper kill was two point three six miles, less than half the distance here, made by a Ukrainian marksman using a custom rifle. Five and one-half miles? Impossible!

But these weren't normal circumstances.

Bang!

***

Without realizing it, Owen Rogers had become a member of a club. Not in a sarcastic or metaphorical way, but an actual club, one that met regularly and for a common purpose, like a book club except in this one they fought crime and the sorts of international conspiracies they would have been reading about had it actually been a book club. On the one hand, considering he could run at unimaginable speeds and wore a costume (a one-piece sky blue get-up his scientific mentor Dr. Jurn called an "exo-reinforced sensor and containment bodysuit"), what other sort of club would he join but the United Front? On the other, with a background as an abandoned kid with trust issues after a series of abusive foster homes, who had only ever joined Alcoholics Anonymous, it was a miracle he could commit to membership in *any* group.

At first, his attendance at gatherings and participation in United Front joint efforts had been out of a sense of detached responsibility, the notion that since he had to run anyway—it was a physical need, to burn off the tremendous energy that built up inside him—he might as well put it to good use. He wasn't beholden to his teammates, nor they to him, and he never wanted to get caught up in causes or earthshaking affairs. He would help those who needed it that he came across in his travels, but he didn't want to go looking for trouble.

"You can run but you can't hide," Dr. Jurn had chuckled when Owen expressed sudden awareness of his feelings of comradery. "It was only a matter of time before you made friends, despite all your efforts to the contrary."

Owen wouldn't exactly call it friendship, but however he labeled the relationship, he responded to Revek's call when it came in. The United Front was at war with a faction of souped-up individuals called Counters, the now shattered Captains of Industry's next generation of powered hench-people. Unfortunately for Georgina Pinkerton, mastermind behind the Captains, she'd made her artificially enhanced foot soldiers too powerful—so much so that they realized they didn't need to take orders from Pinkerton or any general, and turned against their creator. When she ordered them destroyed, they returned the favor by targeting her for death, and she in turn ran straight to her until-then enemies of the Front for protection, for which she paid in information and tech support that was helping in bringing down her former enforcers.

Pinkerton left behind a mess. Whatever central command she'd established to control her fellow Captains of Industry had broken down and it was every criminal corporate chief for themselves. Her laboratory-engineered Counters were taking turns coming after her, the heroes of the Front absorbing the brunt of the attacks until some genius in some Washington, DC secret intelligence agency called the Cyber Engagement Division (CED) refined the biological agent that countered, on a genetic level, whatever it was that made the Counters Counters in the first place.

Owen had yet to encounter one of these super-dupers, but he'd read the reports of the Front members like Revek, Traction, and Yoga, who had, and knew the baddies shared a few characteristics: they were spooky, scary strong, fast, and resilient.

But Owen was faster and, while it usually broke every protocol the Front had set in place for the safety of the public and their members, he could sweep in too quickly to be seen and have the bad guys disarmed and restrained before they knew what hit them. No matter how fast or resilient these Counters were, he doubted any of them could stand up very long to a barrage of a thousand blows a second. Better Angel, the team's leader, had rolled her eyes at Owen when he said, "I usually win my battles before the other guy even knows he's in one."

It sounded egotistical but it was a fact. His speed made him one of the most powerful members of the Front. He'd only ever been physically challenged once, by someone he called the Smudge, the previously unknown eighteenth victim of the same illegal experiment gone wrong that released a barrage of energy called Quasons onto ChronActive Plaza in midtown Manhattan—an accident that gave Owen his speed and killed sixteen other innocent passersby. That nameless eighteenth person had been partially absorbed into the weird, other dimensional velocity zone he slipped into when he ran, and almost succeeded in pulling Owen inside it as well—before he outran the Smudge with the help of Dr. Jurn's science and Better Angel's assistance.

He'd heard Revek's emergency call over the headset built into the bulbous goggles that he thought made him look like some bubble-eyed insect but which Dr. Jurn insisted were necessary for aerodynamic purposes and to house the tech for sensors and cameras and the heads-up display. It was an SOS, a call for immediate back-up in Chicago. Owen was in

Singapore at the time, in the sprawling Lau Pa Sat street marketplace by the Central Business District, enjoying his third bowl of Hainanese Chicken Rice from a favorite vendor—super-speeding consumed a lot of calories—but he quickly answered, "I'll be there in a minute," which gave him time to finish the last bit of his spicy snack and still speed across the Pacific Ocean and two-thirds of the continental United States, and to arrive ten seconds early.

Torque came to a stop at what had once been Chicago's Grant Park's magnificent Buckingham Fountain, but which was now a mass of far-flung debris and a geyser of water shooting high into the air from the broken water pipes beneath it. The fact there hadn't yet been time to shut off the water main meant the damage was very recent. Torque looked around, but he heard the cause of this destruction before he saw it.

It was the sound of shattering brick and glass, coming from the far side of the meridian behind him and across Michigan Avenue. He turned to see twin trails of destruction smashed through asphalt and concrete and landscaping from the fountain west to the stately 19th-century Congress Plaza Hotel on the far side of the avenue. Faster than radioing Revek for a sit-rep, he ran towards the noise to see for himself.

And That's when things started to go horribly wrong.

This wasn't the first time something like this had happened to him. The last time he'd lost control of his powers had been in Detroit, sending him careening like a manic pinball that demolished everything in his path or generating devastating winds while spinning like a crazed top. This was a repeat of the incident, his legs taking on a mind of their own and sending him careening at twice the speed of sound on a swerving, looping path back across the park and into the icy waters of Lake Michigan. The shock of the cold broke his loss of control and he rocketed from the water with a flurry of super-speed kicks, then ran across the surface back to dry land.

Dr. Jurn had never figured out what caused that first misfire of his powers, citing any number of possible causes, from growing pains to solar flares. All they could do was wait to see if it happened again and it hadn't. Until it did. The only connection between the episodes was that they occurred in the Midwest and Revek was there both times. But those weren't meaningful data. They were coincidences.

Any hope his loss of control was over was dashed milliseconds later as Torque neared the Michigan Avenue hotel. The scarlet awning overhanging the front entrance had been torn away and flung into the roadway, the marble clad columns and revolving doors beneath it smashed as though a speeding train had run through it.

A man came hurtling through one of the street-level plate glass windows in a blizzard of safety-glass pebbles and flew into the side of a yellow cab whose driver had wisely fled the scene.

It was Revek. Torque had seen him come bursting through the window in slow motion, the way he saw everything when he was running at high speed. He had plenty of time to catch his teammate before he hit a kiosk touting a guy named Mark Anbinder for City Councilman—but suddenly, Revek's flying form accelerated to normal speed and Torque decelerated to the same. Revek hit the yellow cab, smashing in its side before bouncing to the ground and laying still.

"Revek!" Torque yelled and willed himself to run to his fallen teammate's side, but his legs wouldn't cooperate, and he suddenly could no longer hear it, the sound he hadn't realized had been in his head ever since the accident and only now in its absence realized how much he missed it now that it was gone. That hum. The soft, comforting sound of the velocity, the place the speed came from.

Then a human tank careened through the next plate glass window over, the force of the impact exploding the surrounding curtain wall and twisting the steel beams behind it.

The figure that emerged from a cloud of pulverized concrete dust was a bulked-up man-monster like some comic book steroid nightmare. He had to be close to seven feet tall and easily four feet wide at the shoulders, with no neck to speak of, and a face that looked like wet clay had been smushed permanently into a maddened scowl. His arms in a sleeveless t-shirt were like bridge stays of corded cables and his legs were thick stumps built for stability, not speed.

"Had enough, little man?" the behemoth bellowed and stomped through the debris toward the fallen Revek.

Torque took a deep breath and a step in the same direction, planning on getting his still-dazed teammate to safety, but his step took him only a few feet, as did the next one, and no matter how hard he focused and tried, he couldn't connect to the speed, and then he could but it was out of his control and instead of racing to Revek, he began running in a tight circle that created a whirlwind which picked up and rocketed debris from the hotel out in a deadly three hundred and sixty degree spray that smashed everything in its path.

Revek's powers were magnetic in nature and must have included an aura of some sort that cushioned him from harm, because despite having totaled the taxicab with his body, he was already rising to his feet to meet the charging behemoth—while all Torque could do was watch, trapped in his super-speed loop. The last thing he saw, before his legs took him racing off across Lake Michigan, was Revek and the behemoth slamming together with a force that would have been deafening if he wasn't already miles ahead of the sound.

He was moving fast, but nowhere near the velocities he was used to achieving. Something was between him and the speed, choking him off from the source, teasing him with the barest of tastes and putting it out of his control.

That loss ended as suddenly as it had started, just outside of Fort Good Hope in Canada's Northwest Territories, and Torque swept around Great Bear Lake, pouring every bit of

speed he could muster into it. As slow as he was, it took him more than three excruciatingly long minutes to cover the fifteen-hundred-mile return trip, arriving back where he started—to find Revek and the behemoth clutching one another in what seemed like a motionless embrace in the middle of Michigan Avenue. The two men were actually locked in a stalemate, their bodies trembling, muscles bulging, their feet literally digging into the asphalt as they struggled to gain an advantage over the other.

In past encounters, Torque had been able to see the minute oscillations of Revek's body, reminding him of the repulsive action of two magnets of the same polarity, continually pushing against each other but never able to touch. Now, his senses cut off from the wellspring of speed, he was limited to seeing only in the slow-motion visual spectrum, but he still had his magic bug-eye goggles which Dr. Jurn had packed with more nano-circuit bells and whistles than the speedster had bothered to learn. He blinked on the menu in the goggle's display, then selected sensors, and, lo and behold, "magnetic spectrum."

The two men turned into 3D silhouettes around which a series of magnetic ley lines swirled. They were both generating tremendous magnetic fields...but, no. Revek was generating the field, but it was flowing from him and around the behemoth, who was then channeling it back in an endless feedback loop.

Torque switched back to normal vision and charged at the motionless duo, still fast enough, he hoped, to break the deadlock and get in a few dozen blows before the behemoth recovered. Instead, he ricocheted off the very magnetic field he was trying to break up.

"Aluminum siding!"

The two words were delivered by Revek through gritted teeth over the radio in his goggles and caught Torque by surprise.

"What? Repeat that!"

"Aluminum!" Revek snapped. "Aluminum!"
Aluminum? Siding? It made no sense.

Torque looked around. Who the hell used aluminum siding anymore? It was all vinyl and wood shingles these days...and where was he supposed to find aluminum siding in the middle of downtown Chicago anyway?

His eyes stopped on the ruined front of the hotel and the debris spread around it. Shattered marble and concrete, twisted rebar and support beams, decorative panels, bent window frames and door surrounds...

Aluminum decorative panels, window frames, and door surrounds!

Non-magnetic aluminum.

Torque ran to the hotel entrance and selected a twisted length of what had once been a window frame and, holding it out before him like a knight with a lance, raced again at Revek and his opponent.

There was no sound or flashy effect, but as soon as the nonferrous lance interrupted the magnetic field, Revek and his adversary flew apart, and Torque charged in and swept Revek several blocks away to safety.

"What are you doing? I didn't call you in so we could run away faster," Revek demanded as soon as they came to a stop.

"Let's call it a strategic retreat, okay? Take ten seconds to come up with a plan."

"We had a plan," Revek said, "but the people making these monsters found a way to adapt to the pathogen the CED developed that shut down the Counters at a genetic level, so we're back to square one. I hit that brute with two doses and all he did was laugh at me. And not only is he quick and insanely strong, but he can throw my own magnetic forces right back at me."

Torque had heard some of the Counters had an extra power. This brute seemed to be one of them. "Does he have any control over magnetism on his own?"

"None that I've seen."

"That's got to give you some advantage."

"As long as I stay out of his reach so he can't channel the fields through me, I suppose, but…" Revek stopped, thought for a moment, then slowly said, "But, yeah. Maybe."

***

The showdown was over before it could begin. Torque sped Revek back to where the rampaging behemoth had turned his rage back on the hotel façade and the two came to a halt ten yards from him.

"Hey, ass face," Torque yelled, and the behemoth turned at the sound and, faster than the super-speedster would have thought the hulking figure could move, ran at them.

Seven yards from them, the behemoth stopped suddenly, shaking his head and grabbing at his chest, trying to take a few more steps but starting to sway, then, with a grunt of pain, swooning like an ingenue in an old Hollywood movie and crashing to the ground. He tried to push himself up but didn't have the strength. He collapsed in a twitching heap before, finally, falling still.

"Wow," Torque said, turning to his teammate with a wide-eyed look of admiration. "That is seriously gangster. What did you do?"

"I disrupted the electromagnetic activity of his brain and heart until his system scrambled and shut down. If I tried that on a normal person, it would seriously *murder*, but I gambled this beast was tough enough to survive it."

"Can you do that with all of them?" Torque asked hopefully.

Revek shook his head. "Only if they have that extra power he had. Which, as far as I know, they don't."

"So, what was his problem with the hotel?"

"His problem was with one of the hotel's guests. Georgina Pinkerton. She's been hiding out here since yesterday."

Moving Pinkerton from place to place was supposed to keep her safe. In this case, it had had the opposite effect.

Torque made a face. "Sucks we have to risk our asses for her."

"But it's appreciated...Torque, is it?"

Torque started at the sound of Pinkerton's voice in his headset.

"Quite a mess out there," Pinkerton said, "isn't it? They haven't exactly been subtle in their efforts to find me, have they?"

Torque didn't know what to say, so he thought he'd fall back on the best thing he'd learned in foster homes: shut up and listen.

Georgina barked a short laugh. "You're allowed to speak, Torque. Yes, of course, I know who you are... Owen Rogers, poor little orphan boy. ChronActive and Dr. Jurn did work for me, you know."

Torque was taken by surprise.

"You don't know, do you?" Pinkerton said.

She was like a taunting bully in a group home. Owen wouldn't give her the satisfaction of a reaction.

"Well, then," Pinkerton said, "I imagine you'd be interested to know that sometime in the next half hour to forty-five minutes—dear Dr. Jurn, while enroute by boat to Riker's Island under CED protection to consult with them on the Counter problem—is scheduled to be the victim of a sniper's bullet, as arranged by ChronActive's corporate security chief, a woman named Noel Croft."

"What?" Torque's response was reflexive, his cold façade be damned. "You're supposed to be giving information like this to the Front while it still can do some good, damn it."

"I'm sorry," Pinkerton said, "but my crime lord calendar is so full, sometimes I miss a few details. But you're supposed to be so damned fast, Owen. Forty-five minutes should be all the time in the world for you."

***

Chicago to New York. Only eight hundred miles, once the blink of an eye, but now it might as well have been a million. The harder Owen pushed himself, the more his exhausted system rebelled, the muscles in his legs seizing up and plaguing him with agonizing cramps, his lungs unable to gasp in enough oxygen, or his speed taking over and sending him racing off on time-wasting tangents or trapped in unbreakable bursts of manic energy. But he fought through it all, finding reserves of strength and will he never knew he possessed, and kept moving.

Georgina Pinkerton had provided him with enough intel to stop Dr. Jurn's assassin if he could get there in time. Even after her Counters overthrew her, she had maintained a measure of surveillance on many of her former lieutenants, including ChronActive's Noel Croft, who had, just before her own capture by the authorities, ordered Dr. Jurn's termination after the scientist had disobeyed orders.

She'd hired a cybernetically enhanced sniper-for-hire who went by the name Bersagliere, after a troop of 19th-century Italian military marksmen, for the job. According to Georgina, the shooter had a robo-eye linked to a high-tech sniper rifle, which fired a super-sonic smart cyber-load that locked unerringly on and tracked its target across great distances.

And now, irony of ironies, both Croft and Dr. Jurn were being transported together by boat to the all-but-shuttered jail facilities on Riker's Island in the East River, she to face incarceration, he to share his expertise with CED.

Time was ticking away.

In the middle of Manhattan, Bersagliere was in a north-facing office on the eighty-fourth floor of the Empire State Building, his sniper's nest secured with a bribe to someone on the building's staff. His weapon had been smuggled past security as a delivery of computer parts to the offices of a ChronActive subsidiary company, and he had been supplied with his victim's exact route, up the East River by boat in the company of CED agents to Riker's Island. Apparently, someone thought Dr. Jurn would be easier to protect on the open water where an attacker couldn't sneak up on him rather than by car across the much-traveled bridge to the island prison.

They hadn't counted on an assassin who could hit any target he could lay his cybernetic eye on.

Torque had lost all track of time. The innate awareness of time and space he experienced when connected to the velocity was gone, and he had been so focused on just staying on his feet that nothing but this moment and this next step mattered any longer.

And then he was there, in New York, at the Empire State Building, his lungs squeezed tight, dizzy from oxygen deprivation, heart pounding, but ramming his way through it all, up the stairs because no matter how diminished he was, he was still faster than the elevator, even with losing his footing on the seventy-ninth floor, and then--

Bang!

--the shot, and he was barreling through the stairwell door, faster now, fast enough to feel the speed energy again and to see the sonic ripples of the shot's retort as a wave rolling through the air that he ran towards, back to the source, a closed door with a pebbled glass window, too fast now to read what was painted on it and then he was on the other side, into a cramped little room filled with too much office furniture and a man dressed in a black suit kneeling in front of the office's single window, the elongated barrel of his high-tech sniper rifle poking through a hole cut through the glass.

Bersagliere's finger had yet to release the pressure on the trigger.

On the other side of the window, the air around the bullet exploding from the nozzle at nearly seven times the speed of sound expanded like a surreal bubble in time-space that burst into a sonic boom, but Torque had already left sound behind. He flung Bersagliere aside and was halfway down the side of the great granite edifice before the assassin crashed into the opposite wall of the office and then to the floor.

That's where the velocity faltered again, and he felt himself falling. He shouted, panicking for a nanosecond, but no, this wasn't the time to lose it, not as the killing bullet was flying with computerized precision towards its target five-and-one-half miles away at over 8,000 miles per hour.

Three point four seconds to impact.

That was the time he had to beat.

The speed was still there, just enough that he could whirlwind his arms and pump his legs fast enough to create a cushion of air that brought him safely, if jarringly, to the street below. Then the switch flipped again, and the power surged through him, and he was once again aware of everything in the velocity, including the assassin's bullet as it drilled through the atmosphere overhead on its arced trajectory over Manhattan.

Torque ran northeast, following the throb of the bullet's disturbance through the velocity. He was at Mach six. Mach seven. Mach eight.

He ran past Grand Central Station, under the Queensboro Bridge and the FDR Drive, and left land at 62nd Street to surge over the East River, then angle across Roosevelt Island and the river again before making landfall on the northeast tip of Queens.

He reached Mach nine as he sped off the end of the pier, nanoseconds behind as his boots hit the water for the final half mile. Mach ten. The government boat, the rest of the river traffic, the people and cars on the shore, the seabirds wheeling through the sky, everything around him froze between moments, except for him and the bullet, vibrating through the air...

Mach eleven!

The velocity twitched and he almost stumbled, but he was too close to fall. He couldn't. The speed was his and he wouldn't let it go, certainly not now when it was the only thing between Dr. Jurn and death.

"I'm *nobody's* goddamned victim," he growled to the wind, and pushed through the weakness, drawing the velocity to him.

Mach twelve.

Torque pulled ahead of the speeding projectile in the final instant as he swept onto the boat where the motionless form of Dr. Jurn stood on the deck with his phone to his ear, between the statues of two burly CED bodyguards in dark suits and sunglasses. A few feet away, at the railing, Noel Croft, a coldly beautiful, red-haired woman in a scarlet overcoat and handcuffs, caught between her own pair of burly federal escorts, watched Dr. Jurn with a slight, knowing smile on her lips.

Torque didn't know anything about munitions, but the four-inch brass cartridge that to his velocity-enhanced eyes appeared to be sliding sluggishly through the air looked frightening lethal, a ballistic nuclear missile in miniature. Its trajectory curved with precision on a line for its target. At this speed, it would vaporize a person's skull before they even knew what hit them.

Before he left Chicago, Georgina Pinkerton had said to him, "The reason Ms. Croft ordered the good doctor's termination was because of the mess he'd made of ChronActive's Quason plans."

"What are you talking about?" Owen said. "He wasn't even there the night of the accident."

"Dr. Jurn was on record as opposing the system, despite its being an outgrowth of his own research. He was monitoring the test run from a remote location, using it as his last chance to sabotage the program," Georgina said with a bark of sarcastic laughter. "They were meddling with forces they didn't understand! Tampering with disaster! Typical mad scientist doom and gloom."

"Except he was right."

"But," Pinkerton had said, "for all the wrong reasons. He was going to introduce a Trojan horse program into the Quason containment system that would have shut it down and neutralized the trapped particles. But at the last moment, a third party discovered what he was up to, overrode both ChronActive's and Dr. Jurn's remote systems, and executed the commands that caused the accident--and turned you into," she paused for effect, "what you are."

Owen felt the anger surging through him. "*What* third party?"

"Ms. Croft herself. She had too much invested in the program to let him destroy it at that stage. Unfortunately, her technicians had no idea what they were doing, resulting in the accident. And then, to have Jurn later turn against us by allying himself with the Front...well, she certainly knew I wouldn't have reacted kindly to that massive a failure of her leadership. Dr. Jurn's hide was supposed to mollify me." She laughed. "I went another way."

Owen could never hope to be anything but ambivalent about the accident on ChronActive Plaza. It was responsible for seventeen deaths, but had, in its way, saved his life. Before he became Torque, he was nothing more than a ghost, passing unseen, unfelt, and unrealized through the world. From that carnage he found a sense of strength and purpose he'd never thought was possible.

But that end could never justify the means, the cost of seventeen lives.

And three point four seconds after Bersagliere's bullet was fired, Torque reached up and closed his thumb and forefinger around it—stopping its progress less than one inch from the bridge of its target's nose. Then he held the now harmless munition up to Noel Croft's shocked gaze, as he rejoined the normal flow of time.

"What is—?" she said with a shake of her head, like she was seeing things.

"Torque?" Dr. Jurn said, stuttering in confusion.

Owen was as surprised as they were.

It had only been in the last slivers of a second that he saw the shot was aimed not at Dr. Jurn but at Noel Croft, and made the necessary adjustments to intercept it. There hadn't been time to think, only react.

But he got it now.

Dr. Jurn was accustomed to his sudden appearances from superspeed to zero, but the CED and federal agents were caught by surprise and fumbled for the guns under their jackets before they recognized the hero.

"Just a minute," Jurn said hastily into the phone at his ear in relief. "He just got here. I'll ask him." The doctor lowered the phone, a confused frown creasing his forehead as he looked back and forth from Torque to Croft. "I don't understand. I was learning about the attempt on my life, but..."

"I think this is Georgina Pinkerton's way of sending Ms. Croft her termination notice," Owen said darkly. He turned to Croft. "She must have bought off your own shooter to take you out as well."

"She wouldn't dare," Noel Croft said in a voice that sounded far less confident than her words. "I know too much."

"I think you just made Georgina's point for her," Dr. Jurn said. He turned his gaze on Torque. "Are you alright, Owen? You seem winded."

"I guess I am, a little," Owen said. "I'm still experiencing those power outages, but I had enough to make it here in time."

"Yes, thank you, my boy. It turned out different, but I know you did it for me," the scientist said.

Owen started to say, "That's what--" but stopped himself, embarrassed by the sudden rush of emotion that threatened to close his throat and choke his words.

Dr. Jurn smiled warmly and nodded. "Yes, Owen. That is what friends are for."

PHENOMENON STORIES, PART III

BY MICHAEL JAN FRIEDMAN

Better Angel looked across the meeting room at her United Front teammates—all of them except Scopes, who'd had personal business to attend to—and gauged their expressions, as what Professor Paracelsus had told them began to sink in.

Yoga was the first to ask a question: "If this <null> character had something important to tell us, why didn't he tell us himself?"

Paracelsus, pictured on a wall-hung video screen, just shrugged. As if to say *Your guess is as good as mine.*

Better Angel could see the professor wasn't happy. After all, he'd been given a message to relay by the mysterious <null>, and his words had to that point fallen on deaf ears.

On the other hand, Paracelsus had all but gone off the deep end—that wasn't a secret among his fellow Phenomenons. So whatever he'd had to say, Better Angel had taken with a grain of salt.

It was only after Pinkerton's scheme for defusing her Counters had failed in Chicago that Better Angel felt compelled to hear the professor out.

"It's too weird," Torque said. "Not that Pinkerton's been holding something back from us—that makes all the sense in the world. And if you're going to have a task force, you want to include Scopes. And Guardsman. But—"

"Some kind of lipstick woman?" said Revek, finishing his teammate's thought. "I mean…seriously?"

"Her name's Lipstick Lily," Better Angel said. "And she's a lot more capable than she sounds."

"She'd have to be," said Torque, "wouldn't she?" He turned to Paracelsus, who gazed back at them, sallow-faced, from the screen. "And no offense, Professor, but you don't look so good. I'm not sure I'd put anyone's life in *your* hands either."

Paracelsus didn't say anything in response. But then, he'd already said what he had to say—what he'd been *recruited* to say by <null.>

Someone none of us have ever heard of, Better Angel thought. Someone they weren't inclined to trust with their loose change, much less their lives and those of every other costumed hero.

Except this <null> seemed to know a lot about them. An *awful* lot. Like the fact that Grey Guardsman wasn't the *original* Grey Guardsman, but a stand-in named Gary Glover. Or that Yoga, in her secret identity as Jill Peters, had been a personal trainer to Finnish rock star Pekka Timonen before Peters got her powers. Or that Torque had spent his youth in a series of foster homes.

Information not known to the public, not at all easily obtained. Yet <null> had obtained it.

Clearly, if <null> had wanted to hurt them, he could have done so any number of ways. But he hadn't.

Still, they weren't talking about organizing a bachelor party. There were lives at stake—not just those of the individuals on the team <null> was proposing, but the lives of people everywhere. Because if Pinkerton's Counters were left unchecked, what happened to Penn Plaza could be just the beginning.

Which was why <null> had asked Paracelsus to speak with all of United Front, and not just the two members of the group he'd chosen for his task force. Because he had work for Better Angel and the others to do as well—strategies they could pursue that would at least slow down the Counters while

Scopes, Guardsman, and the rest of <null's> A Team disabled the source of the Counters' power.

If that was even possible, and not just something <null> wanted them to believe.

Torque held his hands out to the others in a bid for reason. "If we're sending a task force to pull the plug on the Counters, *I* should be part of it too. I mean, you've seen what I can do."

It was a departure for Torque to be volunteering for something. But then, Better Angel had seen Torque change since he'd hooked up with United Front. He'd become more selfless, more of a team player.

Unfortunately, selflessness wasn't all they needed at the moment. "Your powers are undependable," Better Angel reminded Torque. "Erratic. They can do as much harm as good." She glanced at Revek. "The same with yours, even if they've been better lately. And I don't have powers at all anymore."

"What about *Traction*?" Yoga asked. "He's one of our A-listers, and his powers are still intact."

"Damned right," Torque said. "If you're not going to send *me*, at least send Traction."

"He's still recovering from that beating he took," Better Angel pointed out.

Traction didn't argue the point. But then, he seldom argued *anything*.

"Then hell, send Yoga," said Torque. "She's not Traction or Revek, but she's got experience."

"Send Luminosity," Revek chipped in. "Send the C.E.D. For godsakes, send *everybody*."

Better Angel shook her head. "You heard the Professor. "It's not that kind of mission. It's got to be a small group so it can catch the enemy unawares."

Torque held his hand up like a kid in school. "Who's better at catching people unawares than *I* am?"

Yoga pointed to Torque. "What he said."

Better Angel shook her head. "I'd be lying if I said I understood every part of <null's> rationale. All I know is That's the team. Calculated to give us the maximal chance of success." She glanced at Paracelsus's image on the computer screen. "Or so We've been told."

"By whom?" Revek asked. "Someone who shows up out of nowhere and gives us our marching orders? For all we know, <null> is a kid with a tricked-out laptop and a knack for finding stuff on the Internet."

"If he is," Better Angel said, "he's better at what he does than anybody else. Which is why we need to take him seriously."

"What if we just take the information he's given us," Yoga said, "and send a different team? One we pick on our own?"

"Then he'll alert the Counters," said Grey Guardsman, who'd remained silent to that point. "At least That's what he said he'd do. Would he really? I don't know. But are we going to take the chance?"

The others looked at him, but no one wanted to state the obvious—until Guardsman put it out there himself: "And I'm not just saying that because <null> picked *me* for his team too."

Torque sighed in exasperation. Yoga folded her arms across her chest and looked away. Revek frowned and shook his head. But none of them said anything more.

Nor, for that matter, did Traction. Because he knew, as Better Angel did, that Guardsman had a point. <null> held all the cards. All they could do was play or fold.

And if they folded, the Counters would run roughshod.

Then Traction said something after all. "What if this <null> person is *right*? What if the team they're proposing really *does* have the best chance of succeeding?"

Better Angel looked around the room. Traction's remark seemed to be softening her teammates' positions.

"He was right when he told us about ourselves," Traction added. "Maybe he's right about the mission too."

No one took exception.

"It's not an ideal state of affairs," Better Angel remarked. "But we have to agree on a course of action."

"I know," Guardsman said, "that I'm not the original recipe. But I can hold my own. And I've learned a lot from the rest of you."

"And," said Traction, "you'll have the Guerreros with you. They know what they're doing."

Better Angel agreed. "Colosa and Particula have been at this longer than I have. They'll keep the mission on course."

"If they agree to go," said Yoga.

There was that, Better Angel had to admit. But to her knowledge, the Guerreros had never backed away from a challenge.

She hoped like hell they wouldn't start now.

"So we're together on this?" Better Angel asked.

First Traction nodded. Then Revek. Then Yoga, and finally Torque.

"Done," Better Angel said, and put in a call to Scopes.

THE MISSION

BY OMAR SPAHI

Steve Bloom—Scopes in his costumed identity—awakes, groggy. He feels his hand intertwined with another, and for a moment he thinks he's with one of his patients–the many people that he helped when he was an eye surgeon. Then reality hits him—hard.

Steve's mother, Diane, has been sick for a while now. She lays motionless on the bed in front of him. She's been going through chemotherapy since her breast cancer began to spread through her back. Each day it's been making her weaker and weaker, until recently she's been unable to do the simplest of tasks. The person he's relied on his whole life, now seems unable to function without his help.

His chest hurts, but it's not really his chest. What hurts is what's buried inside it, his heart. Except recently, his heart has felt hollow and cold. As if a part of his heart is missing, watching the person that raised him unable to function anymore.

The city's been in crisis since Georgina Pinkerton's powerful Counters have begun hunting Phenomenons. Steve's done his part to fight the threat as Scopes, but he's also felt compelled to help care for his mother. As a guy who was once a prominent surgeon, he's got the money to see to her care. But this is his mother, for godsakes, and she's dying. It's his duty to be there for her.

He's been driving her to every doctor's appointment, on the line in every phone call, and ready with food and every prescription. His mother has always shown him a strong mix of kindness and devotion. She supported him even through his toughest moments, without judgment, without the need for anything in return–working two jobs so he could go to college and then medical school, paying without question for the second-hand components he craved as he honed his skills at building high-tech sensory equipment, which at the time seemed only an expensive hobby. In turn, Scopes feels the need to be there for her as well, *until*…

Suddenly, he feels a buzzing–that of the United Front comm unit he wears on his wrist, disguised as an Apple Watch-style device. He looks down and knows who's calling him before he hikes up his sleeve to see the name. It's Better Angel, the young woman who's become the de facto leader of United Front.

"We need you," Better Angel says. "You and five others." And she describes the situation in very broad strokes because she doesn't quite understand it herself.

A computer entity–a person they can't identify, who somehow knows everything about them–has apprised them of the source of the Counters' power, and where to find it, and how to nullify it. And for reasons none of them can understand, he says six Phenomenons need to go on a mission to do so. Scopes is one of them.

"Grey Guardsman is, of course, ready to go. So's Professor Paracelsus, who seems to have some issues—just warning you. But we need you to contact the other four," Better Angel tells him. "That's the easy part. Then we need you to lead the mission. It's gotta be you. You're the one with the experience. I know you don't normally lead, but this time you have to."

Scopes's instinct is to say yes, of course. He looks down at his mother, lying in her bed. She needs him. He knows that. But the world needs him too. Once these Counters destroy all the Phenomenons, who knows what kind of hold Georgina Pinkerton will have over the world?

"On it," he tells Better Angel.

But as soon as she signs off, Scopes has second thoughts. He fights an inner battle–pacing across his mother's room, going back and forth in his mind, from his duty to his mother on one hand to his duty to the United Front and the world on the other.

Better Angel said that it had to be him. She isn't one to say such things lightly. What if he says no and innocents get killed because of his decision? How will he live with himself?

The stakes are just too high. His mother would be the first to tell him so.

He sneaks into another room so as not to disturb his mother's sleep and contacts Particula, who will in turn contact her sister Colosa. Then he contacts Lipstick Lily, who knows of Scopes and has met Better Angel, but is shocked she's been selected for this mission. "Are you sure you've got the right crime fighter?" she asks.

The rest of the team is surprised as well. They wonder why it's them that's been chosen. Scopes wonders the same thing. But this is the gig he signed up for, isn't it? To save people, hardships or not?

He has made his decision. He's going to go on the mission. Consequences be damned. What's one life compared to the many that'll be saved once he succeeds? It's far from a no-brainer, and it's an emotional decision that rocks him to his core, but it's the right thing to do.

Still, he can't leave his mother alone. His being an only child means there are no brothers or sisters for Scopes to lean on when times get tough. And times can't be tougher than this.

He looks at his mother, the fragile landscape of her. He's been around death before in his line of super-hero work, but this time it feels different. It feels slow, inevitable, as if watching paint dry were an Olympic sport. Hell might be easier than this, he thinks.

There's only one person he can call on since his dad passed away a few years earlier. Scopes calls his mom's on-call caregiver and tells her he needs her right now. He wishes he had someone else who cared for his mother the way he does, but the best he's been able to do is get paid help. It's better than no help at all, but still Scopes feels like it's not enough. His mother deserves more.

Then again, she has barely gotten up from her bed in over a week. What's the good of Scopes sitting around there anyway?

The phone rings, one ring, then another. The caregiver answers "Hello?" and without a moment of hesitation Scopes lets out a big sigh of relief. She can be there, she says. *Thank goodness.* She can be over in five minutes. *Five minutes,* Scopes thinks. It occurs to him that it may be the last five he ever spends with his mother. He doesn't want to miss a moment with her. His eyes get watery. *What if I don't make it back in time?* He stops himself. *Don't let the bad thoughts in,* he thinks. "She'll be okay. She'll be okay," he mutters to himself out loud.

He goes into the next room to say what might be goodbye to her. But he finds her shockingly out of bed, and she's fallen on the floor in an attempt to get to the bathroom. She's thrown up on herself from the chemo medication. Scopes races to her side, and yells out "Mom! Are you okay?" But she's so very far from okay. Her body is failing her.

She'll be gone soon. Maybe very soon.

His mother wipes off her mouth and pushes herself up against her bed. As he watches, stricken, she starts to fall over again. But this time, he manages to catch her just before she hits the floor. She's so light in his arms, so pale, so clearly at death's threshold…he realizes then that he's been fooling himself.

He can't leave her after all.

Despite what he thought, the right thing isn't saving the world. This time the right thing is staying there with his mom.

Scopes picks her up and puts her in bed, and kisses her on the forehead. "I love you, Steven," his mother mutters to him.

He straightens and smiles and says, "I love you too, Ma. More than you could ever know."

Then he calls his mother's caregiver and tells her not to come after all. This, he reflects, regarding his mother, is what he needs to do. This is mission critical.

He sends out the message in a group chat, so as not to rob his mother of the time it would take to inform his teammates in a conversation. He is forthright and honest and explains the situation as directly and clearly as he can.

His mom has cancer, he says. She doesn't have long left to live and he can't take part in the mission. He waits for a response. He doesn't know what they'll say. Will they be compassionate? Will they try to talk him into going? Demand he show up?

Then he gets a message from Better Angel. We get it, she tells Scopes. We're with you in spirit. Let us know if there's anything we can do.

Scopes begins to cry. His teammates…they're better to him than he deserves. He's still torn, still feels the need to go on the mission after all. But he's made his mind up. He's got to follow his heart on this one.

Scopes just hopes the other five can accomplish their mission without him.

OVER THE MOUNTAIN

BY MARIE VIBBERT

In the wake of strangers, Lily trudged up an incline that was mostly loose chunks of rocks. *Talus.* She remembered that term from the geology field camp she'd taken in undergrad, thinking it would be an easy A. It wasn't, and what she remembered about talus slopes was you didn't go walking on them, but the four folks ahead hadn't asked her opinion. Why would they? She was a beauty product developer wearing a bandolier of lipsticks. What was she even doing here?

"Every member of the team is essential, and they say it must be the five of you," her assistant, Lam, had said when he gave her the message. "They don't say who the other four are, though." He gave her a hopeful look, like she knew?

Who were "they"? Lam clearly didn't know. The message had been encrypted, sent to her work drop-box that no one had access to but her… and Lam, because she had given him all her passwords in case of emergency.

She really hoped "they" didn't hold that against her.

Twenty minutes earlier, a helicopter had dropped them in a mountain meadow. At the time, she'd only recognized two of the others on the team. Grey Guardsman was one, of course. Clearly, he was the one who was going to be in charge.

Lily still couldn't believe the famous hero had shaken her hand and said, "Call me Gary."

At the moment, he was frowning down at a topographic map. A few yards behind him was Colosa—even more intimidatingly gorgeous in person than on TV. The slighter woman bickering with her must have been her sister, going by the familiarity. She kept injecting strings of Spanish that Lily didn't get but could assume were insults.

Colosa was wearing platform heels styled to look like the love child of timberland hiking boots and stilts. The thick rubber soles were clearly only for looks because they were doing nothing to help Colosa balance as she slipped and slid on a bunch of rock slabs.

Rock slabs that had no business being there, Lily couldn't help thinking. She was no expert, but as far as she could tell this part of the country wasn't supposed to be so craggy.

I have to be wrong about that, don't I? We're climbing mountains here. I'm not imagining them, right?

Or maybe she misread the helicopter route. *Yeah. That has to be it. Absolutely.*

As she thought that, she saw Colosa wave at Gary. "You're going to have to stop and ask for directions," she said.

Gary turned to look with more patience than Lily would have been able to exercise. "We have to get up over this mountain. This is the gentlest slope in the area."

"With a cliff on top of it," Colosa's sister pointed out. Lily had already forgotten the name she'd greeted her with. P-something? Particle? No. That wasn't a name. There was, indeed, a wall of stone marching along atop the talus slope.

Gary was unconcerned. "We'll get to the base of the cliff and head toward that low point."

Lily followed his pointing finger and sighed. It was a cut full of rhododendron. Probably a stream. Ugh. This was turning out just as bad as Geo 101, only there wasn't some septuagenarian professor scampering up like a mountain goat to put them all to shame.

Lily glanced at the one person lagging behind her. The professor. Wan and strange, he'd returned her handshake with listless pressure and said, "I'm not a hero. All I do is kill people."

He was at least well dressed for the cool weather, with gloves and a long coat and hat. His face was pinched, and he kept muttering to himself, looking down and to his left at something the rest of them couldn't see. What was *he* doing here?

The United Front had so many weird and unlikely powers; it stood to reason they knew someone with second sight, who had conjured up this motley crew, each of them with a purpose. Lily hoped her purpose wasn't "cautionary tale of failure."

Lily's thighs were burning by the time they reached the cut. Predictably, it was full of fast-moving water that would probably be freezing. Gary folded his map and looked helplessly around. "I guess we go up the stream."

"These are suede," Colosa stated, like that ended all discussion.

Lily's field camp had hiked up a stream. In snow. It had not been the fun spring break vacation she'd hoped for. She peered up the cliff. "That's only about twenty feet," she said, "couldn't you, um, grow tall enough to lift us over?"

Colosa picked up one foot than the other. "I'm barely staying upright at the size I am."

"It's the talus slope," Lily muttered. Then they were all looking at her. She hadn't meant to say it out loud. She grimaced. "What we're standing on; it's the loose rubble that eroded off the cliff. I took a geology course once." Oh no, now they were looking like they were going to expect, like, expertise. Grey Guardsman was holding the map toward her.

"Cover girl is right," P-something said. "We need Colosa to get us up there. Quit grouching, Noris. There's plenty of room for your big feet here." She moved to a largish boulder and started kicking away the loose rubble around it.

Colosa huffed, but with a smile. She must like showing off. Her sister made sure there was a good, steady place to stand, and then Colosa began to grow. It was… fascinating. Lily felt carsick, like she was shrinking, or falling toward the woman.

Then she really was falling, as was Colosa, like a tree, the scree-slope too unstable to support her larger form and sliding away like so many stacked cards.

Lily landed atop a rapidly diminishing Colosa. The slope over them was disturbed, moisture-darkened in a rut down from where they had been. At the top, against the cliff, Grey Guardsman and the professor looked tiny.

"That," huffed Colosa, "was a terrible idea. Get off me. Ofelia! Help me up!"

P-something was named Ofelia? Anyway, Ofelia had managed to surf down the slope, keeping her feet, so she was on hand to grab Colosa's arm and hoist her up. "Maybe we can try again, over that way? It looks more stable?"

Then Colosa cried out, crumpling as she first put weight on her left leg.

***

The P-something was Particula, Ofelia's code name, which made sense, and Lily repeated it to herself over and over to remember. Particula was pretty good with a bandage, and gloomy Professor Paracelsus said it was just a sprain, though he also said that he wasn't a medical doctor.

Still, they had one limping person, and it was starting to get dark, the temperature dropping fast with a ground wind that smelled like rain.

Gary approached Lily as she was trying not to cry. "Find us a sensible path over the mountain. You're the most qualified to read this map."

"I took one geology field camp, and I got a D."

He gave her a sad smile, "D is for diploma?"

"My last idea got Colosa hurt."

"I think we can blame those fancy boots for that." He put a hand on her shoulder. It was broad and heavy, and reminded her of her father's. "We're all here for a reason. Maybe this is yours."

Reluctantly, Lily took the map and held it open. Fat raindrops plopped on it from the branches overhead. Lily bit her lip.

Colosa and Particula approached. Particula had one arm around her sister's waist, supporting her as she limped. Colosa waved her free hand. "So, where are we going? How do we get out of this rain?"

Another squeeze on her shoulder from Grey Guardsman. Lily sighed. "I hate to say it, but our best bet is to go up through the stream. Water always finds the lowest path."

"We go up the stream," Gary stated, and strode away, leaving Lily with the map.

"He's buying me new boots," Colosa muttered.

Particula muttered back, "Callate. You'd be better off barefoot."

Crossing the base of the talus slope, they found the stream. Gary stepped right in and marched uphill. It was only ankle-deep, but biting cold, fast-rushing mountain water. "Look out for loose rocks," Lily said, and Colosa snorted.

"At least we're already wet," Particula said as the rain sped up.

This was pure misery, cold rain and cold water sloshing in the tops of her boots, but Lily started to feel optimistic when they passed the top of the talus slope, entering a narrow cleft. She could just touch both walls of their little canyon. She looked behind her to see how the sisters were getting on. They were not able to be side-by-side anymore. Particula was behind, guiding Colosa forward as she stumble-hopped, both of them looking down and concentrating on footing. They definitely had it worse than Lily. Behind them, the professor stood in the middle of the stream, looking like a morose post.

Colosa reached Lily. "How much further do we have to do this?"

Gary was about ten feet ahead. It looked like the cleft went forever at this point, but that was just the perspective playing tricks. She checked the map and tried to figure it out. There were the tight little v's of the stream cut. She laid her thumb on them and compared its width to the legend. "Another thirty feet?"

Colosa groaned. Particula patted her side. "I-it's a-already half-f-way."

Particula was shivering, and her face had gone pasty. Lily shoved the unfolded map messily into her pocket. "Here, I hope this helps. Um… yes, "Campfire Glow.'" She pulled out one of her tubes of lipstick.

The sisters looked at her like she was… well, like she was offering lipstick in the middle of a rainstorm in the middle of a mountain stream. She twisted the tube up a little more. "It's a heating compound. The colloid matrix will shift when you put it on, allowing the chemical reaction to… uh, never mind. Just try it?"

Colosa snatched the lipstick and smeared it messily.

Lily briefly thought how this would be the worst possible social media post for MarveLush cosmetics.

Colosa smacked her lips and straightened. "I feel… warmer." She twisted to hand it to Particula.

Lily felt warmer, too. "I know it's lipstick but go ahead and put some on your cheeks and nose. No one to see but us, right?"

In a few minutes they all had stripes of dark orange war paint, and something had softened between the sisters and Lily. They continued up to where Gary was waiting. The cut was getting wider and the streambed less steep. Lily suspected that meant the rock layers were changing, the more massive, hard-to-erode rock that formed the cliff giving way to something else. They were doing this. She pushed forward, past Gary, to see if she could … yes, there was a spot where they could easily scramble out of the stream and onto dry-ish land again. They were nearly over the cliff! She turned to call down to the others, and that was when she noticed that Professor Paracelsus wasn't in sight anymore.

Then, as if the sky heard her think, "It can't get worse," there was an ominous rumble of thunder and the rain picked up a notch, slashing down hard.

She skittered down to Grey Guardsman. He frowned at her. "This doesn't seem like the season for thunderstorms," he said.

"It's not," she agreed, and the unspoken worry hung between them. Possibly, this magical gateway place they were heading toward was having unexpected effects on the weather. She sighed and slipped around him, backtracking. "The professor dropped back," she told the Guardsman. "I'll find him. You keep going. When you can step out of the cut on the right side, go there and wait for us."

The Guardsman looked at her for a moment. Then he said, "Agreed,"

Lily didn't want to see the confused looks as she passed Colosa and Particula, but they took her instruction to follow Grey Guardsman with stoic calm.

Every step she was taking down in search of the professor was one she was going to have to repeat going up again, and her thighs were quaking from all this unaccustomed exercise. Please, she prayed to no one in particular, let me get through this and I'll never skip leg day again.

She slipped, and her heart caught in her throat, but she didn't fall. There was the professor, another ten feet down or so, sitting in the stream, his arms around his knees.

What the absolute hell?

He was freezing, of course he was, soaking wet and shivering, his bloodless lips moving in silent syllables like he was praying. She hovered a moment, then shook his shoulder.

He blinked at her and said, absurdly, "I shouldn't be here."

"You were chosen like the rest of us. Come on, hypothermia is going to take a lot longer than you like."

He didn't answer, but he let her pull him to his feet. "Do you have ghosts, Lillian? Does anyone haunt you?"

"Nope. I live in a fun place called "reality."" She grimaced at herself, but he didn't react. He really was icy cold, clammy as a dead fish. "Also, um, I'm going to put some lipstick on you."

That, he reacted to. He pulled out of her grip. "I beg your pardon?"

As much as she wanted to explain her brilliant breakthrough in colloidal compounds, she cut it to, "It's magic heating lipstick. And I'll put it on like war paint, like I have it."

It might have been his depressive passivity, but he let her slash his face with Campfire Glow.

The color really worked for him, but she decided not to tell him that.

At the top of the cleft, Gary and the others had made good use of their time, cutting and stripping walking sticks, including a stout branch for Colosa to lean on. The raw wood shone brightly in the gathering gloom. Here, above the cliff, the slope was gentler to the top of the mountain. All around them were tall pines, the ground covered in a soft carpet of needles. Colosa took one look at the professor and said, "We have to stop and build a campfire. No maquillaje magico can take the place of drying him off."

Particula breathed out heavily through her nose and stared up the hill. "I suppose we have time. But how? There's no shelter."

At least the cover of thick pine boughs broke the rain into tiny spitting drops and heavy collected pearls. Lily noticed, though, that she could see everyone's breath. They needed heat. Any firewood they could find would be soaked. "Do any of you have, um, fire-starting powers?" Three annoyed looks and one blank one.

Gary looked to Colosa, "You could peek over the trees?"

"Don't make her trip again," Particula said. "Toss me up." And with a spring, she was jumping and shrinking.

Grey Guardsman seemed prepared for this because he held out his hand for her to land on, a tiny, doll version of herself. "Ready?" he asked.

Her voice came tiny and high, "Ready." She crouched like a sprinter in the blocks.

Lily was terrified at the idea of Particula flying through the air, but the small woman seemed calm. Gary shifted his feet and threw. Lily flinched, reaching out, just in case, but quickly lost track of Particula in the rain and branches.

"Relax," Colosa nudged Lily. "If she falls, she's got physics on her side now. You think flies worry about hitting the ground?"

Oh, right. Small body, small inertia. Still, Lily blinked against the rain, keeping herself ready.

The professor sat cross-legged on the ground. He sat there like he wasn't interested in anything, not holding himself like a cold person would, though it was clear he was shivering. "No," he said, to the air at his right, "we're not going to make it."

Gary squatted next to him, putting a hand on his shoulder.

Colosa grew a foot, peering up in the tree, steadying herself on the trunk.

Something small bounced down, landed, and grew into Particula. "There's a cabin! Not far at all." She pointed uphill.

Lily felt her stomach unclench. They *were* going to make it.

They all felt better, it was clear. Even the Professor stood and joined the march uphill, everyone chattering about how much they were looking forward to warmth and dryness.

Which was why they weren't paying as much attention as they should have. They trooped together over a hump of land, just an ordinary rise and fall, some harder stone underground, perhaps, separating this area from a rivulet feeding the stream. It was that and a brake of rhododendron interrupting the steady tree trunks that blocked their view until it was too late. Gary had hung back with the professor, minding him, so it was

Particula in the front who brushed the glossy rhododendron leaves back and gasped, "Madre de Dios!"

Lily stumbled into Particula's back, and that was when the bear stood up on its hind legs, huffing at them. A living, stinking wall of fur.

Shit. What had her professor said to do if you saw a bear? Hold still? Get on the ground? There was something about how you should move sideways to be non-threatening and no matter what, never, ever—

"RUN!" Gary pushed her sideways. The bear roared and dropped its massive paws on Grey Guardsman's shield, which he'd put in its path. The… the absolute idiot!

But then Colosa was scooping her up, loping at a giant limp, crashing through the rhododendron. She had Particula under her other arm and was cursing with each step.

Smart; her giant size would discourage the bear, probably send it running. Lily tried to see over her shoulder.

"There!" Particula shouted, and then Lily was being dropped like a sack of groceries on a wooden plank porch. The cabin!

Particula shook the door handle. "It's locked!"

Lily popped Firestarter Red out of her bolero and scrambled to apply the iron-melting compound when the door opened in front of her—just wide enough to display the double barrels of a shotgun. Behind which was a stout woman with straight blonde hair. "This is private property!" She shouted.

"Lady," Particula gasped, "We're being chased by a bear!"

The lady was staring at Colosa, who was resting her weight with one hand on the top of the cabin, the other hand massaging her ankle. "Bajate," Particula hissed up at her.

Thankfully, then, Grey Guardsman came jogging up, the Professor leaning against him, holding his arm. There was blood on Gary's grey uniform.

The woman stepped back, "Oh. Oh my. Mr. Guardsman. Oh, come inside."

Norma Storms was the name of the owner of the cabin. She came up to the mountain top to hunt in season, and to work on a novel. She had a well-stocked first aid kit, and took over tending to the professor, who had a nasty gash on his forearm, parallel lines of claws rending skin.

"I didn't recognize you in hiking clothes, Ms. Guerrero," she apologized deferentially to Colasa. "You took on a bear?" Norma shook her head over the bandage she was wrapping around the professor's arm. "I hope it wasn't Juno. She's got two young cubs. There are two males that sometimes cross this area when Juno's down in in the valley for fish. I hope it was one of them."

"I thought if I could just get in the way long enough for the others to run," Gary said.

"Never run," Lily and Norma said in unison. Norma gave her a look of approval.

Gary grimaced, clearly aware of his error, "But the bear turned on the professor."

"You're lucky you all got out of there alive," Norma said, tying off the last of the bandage.

Lily said, "Thank you, ma'am. We won't be here long. Getting this wound treated, and getting the professor out of the rain, it's going to save us. We need to get to the other side of the mountain by tomorrow morning. The, well, fate of the world is in the balance. I think?"

Everyone gave her annoyed looks at her delivery of that line. "It's very important," Gary translated.

Norma sucked her teeth. "Well, you're almost to the top. About five, ten minutes. But there's no easy path down. I go along the ridge, east, and there's a nice trail that switches back."

"I don't think we have time for that." Lily laid out the map on Norma's rough-hewn table. Their destination was far enough that it would take a flat-out run to get there in time if they followed the path down the easy, eastern side of the mountain, even if Colasa carried all of them, and that seemed unlikely as she was currently sitting with her foot propped up on the sofa under a bag of ice. Lily traced the ridge, and up and down the contour lines, and found a place where the lines widened out a little. "Maybe here?"

That was when the front door of the cabin THUMPED, with the unmistakable huff of a bear.

Norma ran to the front window and pulled back the curtain, which she promptly closed. "It is Juno. Her cubs are with her. You all are not leaving this cabin tonight."

Gary approached the door, only to flinch back as it was hit with bear-weight again. "We, um, need to. It really is the fate of the world."

"She's pissed and she probably smells the blood. Grizzlies mostly scavenge, but if they come across a wounded animal, they have no qualms about adding it to their diet."

Lily turned to Colosa. "You could scare her off with your size."

Colosa narrowed her eyes. "And how scared will she be as I'm stepping through the door and under the porch with no room to grow?"

"Professor," Gary said, "this might be the time for your skill."

Paracelsus frowned. "I don't think so."

Gary addressed the rest of them. "The professor here can transmute one element to another, from anything he has ever touched. He specialized in transmuting the iron in blood into gold, killing from afar. And he sure did touch that bear."

"You can't kill a female grizzly out of season!" Norma said. "They're endangered! She has cubs to feed!"

Paracelsus straightened, lifted his chin. "I'm not a killer anymore. I told you I'm useless."

Lily stared at him. "One element to another, regardless of where on the periodic table? Iron and gold ... I mean, never mind the difference in bonding valences..."

"Does that mean," Particula interrupted, "there are these bodies out there … if they decomposed, the gold would be left like in all these branches?"

Colosa rolled her eyes. "NOT the point, hermanita."

Lily knelt in front of the professor and took his hands. "Stinkdamp," she said.

There was an awkward silence as everyone stared at her. Oh, right. She'd been thinking so fast she had forgotten to say things out loud again. "You touched a lot of wet things out there. Pick one and transmute the hydrogen in the water into sulfur. That'll make the water sulfur dioxide, commonly called "stinkdamp'—it's a smelly gas. It won't be dangerous in the open, but It'll drive the bear away."

The professor stared at her, then slowly nodded. "I… I can do that."

Lily stood up, proud. "Seems my special purpose was being a chemist, after all!"

There was a moment when she felt like, not just a hero, but smart, and everyone was admiring her, but then they all smelled it at the same time, like Godzilla had farted.

Lily gasped and covered her nose. Norma cried "Pheeeew" and glared at Lily. "This had better go away, young lady."

**

Twenty minutes later, they were looking down the other side of the mountain. The rain was letting up, and the air was sweet. They were on a slight promontory, with a clear view. Lily sighed, folded the map, and pointed. "See the depression, there? It's a swale—the head of a stream that hasn't formed yet. We'll follow it down."

Gary nodded. "Let's go."

Lily took a moment, though, letting the others go first. Colosa was walking better now. Paracelsus had transmuted her cotton bandage into a firm, rubbery polymer. He was the last to pass Lily, and he paused. "Thank you," he said. "For reminding me that every weapon was once a tool."

He wasn't frowning or talking to his shadow. Lily's chest swelled with pride.

THE BRIDGE

BY DAN HERNANDEZ

As it turns out, the problem with hitting the big time is taking the big-time hits. And nobody's bigger than me. Colosa, the Girl Who Grows, the 7th, 8th, and 9th wonder of the world, with legs up to here and there and waaaaaaaaay up there, a little bit vain, a little bit dense, but goddamn, she wears it well. It's true, too. I wear everything well. Everything except pain.

As I wedge my body across this ravine, farther than I've ever pushed it before, far enough I can feel my bones beginning to snap like the cables connecting the Tappan Zee bridge, or whatever they're calling it these days, I know I'm going to have to wear this pain just a little bit longer.

There's a dead drop of a few hundred feet beneath me, jagged rocks grinning up like leering fans. My teammates are somewhere around my bellybutton, running as quickly as they can manage. It isn't a pleasant tickle. Feels more like the gross and unwelcome presence of bugs on your skin, errant creepy-crawlies working their way up your body, and in my current position, there's nothing I can do about it. I have to maintain a united front, or maybe I should say, I have to maintain The United Front. I'm in a proper bridge position, also known as a wheel in Yoga, which sounds nicer but hurts the same. An old-fashioned plank would have been more comfortable, but it was easier to extend my leg forward, using the joint of my ankle to lift everyone up and onto the human highway that is me.

With my head upside down and tilted backwards, I can see the secret facility we're trying to infiltrate, and I know if my arms give out, if my feet fail me now, more people will die than just the five costumed weirdos who hoofed it out into the woods of Nowhere to save the world.

I don't really understand much about our mission. Not even where the heck we are, with all these mountains and such. I'm not what you might call a detail-oriented person, which is to say, I rarely pay attention, and even when I do, I'm vaguely bored. This is why I wore the wrong damned shoes on this trip.

But when the Grey Guardsman asks you to use your growing powers to become a living passageway across a deadly chasm, creating a backdoor into the bad guy's secret base, good luck saying no. It would be like trying to say no to your sweetest high school boyfriend, you know, the one you don't look back on and cringe, if your high school boyfriend went on to be the greatest Phenomenon of them all.

The others aren't so bad either. Professor Paracelsus is giving off a little bit of an unhinged vibe, but he's powerful, courageous to keep going despite his nutbar status. Cover Girl's kind of great, actually, and I am hoping if we survive this experience, we can do some kind of collab. It's nice to meet another person who has a sense of style, or at the very least, who can contribute to mine. And then there's Ofelia.

I can hear her in my earpiece. "Noris, how are you doing this?! I thought your limit was sixty feet? Your body must be at a hundred! A hundred and twenty!" I can't even risk grunting back at her. At this size, any sound from me would echo off the rocks and alert every baddie this side of Lake Geneva or wherever the hell we are. Maybe I *should* pay more attention during the briefings.

Luckily, Dana, The Timeshaper, our man in the proverbial van, chimes in, perpetually connected to his favorite sisters, even though he's sitting pretty back in the Bronx. "When we examined Figurine's headquarters after Noris, uh, squished him, we found his notes on your father's work. He was actually pretty brilliant even if he was hopelessly insane. Figurine managed to enhance your father's nanites so they could support Colosa's body at even greater sizes than ever thought possible. We were going to tell you, but things kind of escalated…"

I don't need to see my sister's face to picture her displeasure as clearly as if she were standing in front of me. I grew up with that sour, sour puss. But what I don't tell either of them, what they'll find out soon enough, is I can feel myself weakening. My wheel position is starting to go flat, sagging; my wrists are getting tired. Maybe the blood in my body is diluted just a touch too much. Maybe I'm getting the bends, or maybe I should call it The Bigs. All I know is I have to hold on, no matter what it costs me, and what it costs me could be everything.

That's called being a hero, I guess.

Ofelia, or should I say Partícula when we're on duty, never really believed my hero's heart was in the right place, which is funny, because my heart's usually so much bigger than hers. My sister thought in her typically dour way anyone interested in clothes that actually fit or pedicures or glamour of any kind couldn't possibly care about the little guy. The incredible shrinking Ofelia should know. She's a little guy professionally.

Of course she was wrong. Orencio Guerrero was my *papi*, too, after all. He taught us to care about other people with the time he had to give us, which ended up being a lot less than we ever could have anticipated, less than we deserved, less than we can forgive.

That's why I went undercover to see who at NeoWork was responsible for his death. That's why I pretend to be stupider than I am in public, why I go on degrading reality shows, why I agree to be Mayor Gary Wolf's arm-candy at fabulous galas where I get the amorous old fella drunk enough to howl at the moon and introduce me to all the fabulous and sophisticated people who might be responsible for murdering my father. It's why I don't care the entire world saw me naked, rampaging down the Avenue of the Americas, an all-new, all-different,

X-rated experience that has, I'm told, impacted the psychological and sexual development of an entire generation of teenagers. Shame can only hold you back. Nothing is ever holding me back again.

If I make it off these rocks, that is. My friends are somewhere mid-sternum now. My arms and legs are on fire. Out of the corner of my eye, I notice a tiny, flying speck coming closer. It looks like a drone, but not like any drone I've ever seen. Its camera lens projects some kind of high-tech scanning laser, don't ask me what kind, that sweeps the surrounding wilderness in looping arcs. Do Georgina Pinkerton's super-powered flunkies know we're here…? Even if they don't know yet, if that drone spots us, we're finished, dead, dead, dead, dead, dead, one for each of us. And how could it *not* spot us?

Ofelia's in my ear again. "I see it, Noris. We're handling. Just be ready for me." I have no idea what Ofelia means, but I do know my fingers are starting to lose their purchase on the ground. I dig deeper, physically into the ground, spiritually down into myself. I steady. For now. If I don't shrink back to my normal size soon, I won't be doing my little turn on the catwalk ever again. A tragedy for me, and quite frankly, the world.

I can feel motion around my upper ribs. I can just barely see Cover Girl taking out one of her fabulous weaponized lipsticks, and suddenly, a heavy mist rises into the air, obscuring our presence, at least for a little while. The feeling of skittering bugs increases, closer to my neck now, disconcerting, intolerable. But I <u>do</u> tolerate it. I'm a model.

"It's coming toward you, Colosa!" Timeshaper's voice sounds a little more hysterical than usual, which makes me think the situation must be even worse than I realize. The drone's darting through the fog, a hunter, the electric seeing-eye dog of our doom. Cover Girl bought us time, but it won't be long now.

Something's running up my chin. My first instinct is to
stick my tongue out and try to shoo it away, but I restrain
myself. I'm not going to tongue one of my allies to death.
That's for the bedroom, tee hee. Just kidding. But what's no
joke is that my fingers are slipping again, and now my feet are
sliding, too.

I lurch to one side, forcing myself to hold my weight with
whatever reserves of endurance I've built up over many years
of Pilates and kicking criminal ass. Ofelia's screaming at me.
"Hold on, Noris! Just open your mouth, and when I tell you,
spit me out!" This is, I think it's fair to say, not the way most
sisters talk to each other. For us, it felt as natural as breath, as
teamwork, as our shared blood flowing through different sized
veins.

Ofelia's inside my mouth. I can taste the iron grit of the
dirt from her boots, earthy notes across the palate, the world's
worst tasting menu. The drone is almost upon us now. The fog
is beginning to dissipate, proving to be a temporary friend,
indeed. If the base is alerted, Pinkerton's goons will tear us
apart before we can do anything about it. I guess I was paying
attention in the briefing!

"Do it." Ofelia's not always a good time, but she's also the
best of us. Tiny terror, brave li'l bitch. I suck in as much breath
as I can manage, more than enough to inflate a blimp or put
out a brush fire, and I expel the air with all the force I can.
Ofelia goes flying out of my mouth, high into the sky, and a
moment later, I hear a clanging sound.

"Partícula's inside the drone!" Timeshaper's voice still
sounds anxious; however, he's also impressed with what
Ofelia is willing to ask of herself, the ferocious commitment
that girl has from molecule to atom to quark to whatever
comes after. Cover Girl and Professor Paracelsus rush past my
left eye, shimmying down my hair. Look at me, a post-modern
Rapunzel, *edición Cubana*. But where's Grey Guardsman? If
I accidentally shook him off my body, and he's down there,

impaled on the rocks, I'm for sure getting kicked out of the club.

The drone sputters, sparks shooting out from its chassis. I picture my sister inside of what must be a multi-million-dollar piece of technology, ripping into it like a raccoon into a bag of marshmallows. Things get less funny when the drone begins plummeting toward the rocks with my sister still inside. "It's gonna crash! I'm not gonna make it back! Noris! Keep fighting! Never stop fighting!" Those are the last words my sister ever said to me.

At least, they would have been if not for something impossible.

No one's ever asked me why I think Phenomenons do more good than harm in the long run. All the accusations are true. We can't all control our powers. Some of us turn heel, *rudo*, as my father would have said, in the most devastating ways imaginable. We make ourselves targets, and sometimes the collateral damage is just too damned high a price to pay.

But we foster hope when there is none. We give people facing death, destined death, a little voice whispering in their minds, "Maybe just this once it's my day to be saved by something beyond imagining, something I dare not hope could be real, something fantastic, uncanny, spectacular, amazing, something truly phenomenal. If anyone ever asked me, I'd say this is the gift we give the world until we have nothing left to give. I've experienced it from the 30,000-foot view, but I never thought one day the miracle would happen on my behalf, far closer to the earth.

The Grey Guardsman arcs through the air, propelled by a grappling hook and zipline. My microscopic sister I can't see, until there she is, appearing in mid-air, returning to normal size, enveloped by muscular arms, the arms of a savior, a warrior rescuing a warrior. But they're going too fast. Another few seconds and they'll be upon the sheer rock of the ravine wall and…

I have one chance. I put all my weight on one hand, hearing the bones snap one after another, the pain magnified. I feel the Grey Guardsman and my sister slap into my hand, the palm skin peeling back, lacerating, an open wound, but a wound that will heal, unlike the grievous wound that would be my broken heart if I let Ofelia die. With a final effort, I fling them up onto the far wall of the ravine, watching them land with a thud, battered but still intact. Finally, I return to myself, no longer colossal, just normal Noris using the last of her strength to pull her body to safety.

Now, I seem to be resting on a platform of iron or copper or some other element conjured by the hand of the esteemed Professor Paracelsus. We all made it across, and the base looms before us. Nearby, Cover Girl stands next to the Grey Guardsman, a little look of reverence in her eyes despite the leadership position she seems to have taken among us.

My sister's face is looking down at me, filling the frame of my eyes, her head shaking in annoyance, as if answering in the negative a question no one has posed. For Ofelia, annoyance and love are so often the same thing. She should unpack that. Maybe she'll have a chance. Maybe we both will.

The Grey Guardsman asks me if I can go on. Of course I can. Partícula, my partner, my sister, my everything, helps me up, and I tell her, when this is all done, after we win, I'm looking forward to going home and falling into a giant-sized sleep.

But not yet.

DUM ANMALS

BY ILSA J. BICK

DUM

i wusnt alwaze DUM.

i no whut peepul think. peepul say A LOT a lot in fronuv me and

my frens say A LOT a lot in fronuv me becuz they think i am onlee a DUM DOG. so they dont worree abowt wuht they say becuz my frens think im DUM.

witch is not troo.

now DUM is a straynge wurd. Beecuz DUM is not all the time the sayme as not so smart.

a persun mite not haf a veree good brayne and okay that meens a persun is dum abowt sum things. some peepul cant lern so good. a persun can also be not so book-smart if he didnt go to skool or the lieberry. so he is book-*stoopid* but not *stoopid*-stoopid or DUM. gif that persun a book and help him reed new ideaz and then he lerns to think bedder.

now whut *is* troo is that DOGS *can* be stoopid. DOGS can doo stoopid things but mostlee when we are puppees. beecuz puppees are preddy stoopid. puppees will chu a sliper. or piddul on the rug. or leev a big gloopee *doo-doo*...altho sum peepul call it sumthin wurst...on the floor whitch *is* the *wurst*.

but beeng stoopid doesnt make DOGS any wurster than peepul. peepul can be very stoopid and doo very stoopid things and be meen for no reezon. or maybe peepul just forget they got braynes sumtimes.

also DOGS *luv* peepul. DOGS want to *pleez* peepul.
DOGS do work, play fech, go hunt. peepul luv us. peepul say
we are there bes fren.

witch issen troo. not bye a long shot.

becuz u dont kick yer bes fren. u dont drown him. or burn
him. or choke him or mayke him fite anuther DOG—or *enny*
anmal and maybe *kill* anuther anmal—jest so *u* mayke monee.

no.

i may be onlee a DUM DOG. but even *i* no bedder than that.

***

peepul think anmals are moslee DUM. that is becuz anmals are
a misstery. we see and heer and do things they cant. but peepul
think that becuz anmals dont think lyke *them* and since peepul
think onlee *peepul*- thinking is the most importent thing...then
that meens anmals are DUM and stoopid.

now...that is sort of troo. anmals braynes are smaller. we
are diffrent. sum anmals...we will not fly rockets.

but that duz not meen we are DUM. there are all sortz of
wayz of beeing smart.

***

DUM also meens sumthing else. a persun whoo cannot speek
is also DUM. now that persun can *think*. that persun has got a
brayne. that persun mite even be SPEHSHULL. that persun
mite be a GEE-NEE- US but speek a languache u will never
unnerstan.

so u will never no...unless u can reed his mynd. unless u
haf a way of getting into his *brayne*.

well.

i mite bee DUM. and i mite bee onlee a DOG. but that duzint
meen that *i*...am not *spehshull*.

This Just In

"This, just in." Newsman Jim Arrowood's yammer drifted in from the next room. His tone had taken on the manic urgency of a chipmunk on speed. (At least that's what Sarah said. Although Layal knew what a chipmunk was—had even eaten a few that hadn't been watching their backs—she had no clue about speed. She didn't think chipmunks had anything to do with driving a car.)

"An earthquake measuring a whopping five-point-six on the Richter scale," Arrowood rapped, *"has rippled through the Appalachians."* He wasn't exactly shouting, but even Layal heard the panicky excitement as the announcer rattled on. *"The tremor was felt from Huntsville, Alabama to Rochester, New York and is yet another anomalous occurrence in a string of such events sweeping..."*

"Sarah!" A woman's voice, shrill, sharp, just as anxious, her words as spiked as the stiff wires of an old bristle brush. "Honey, stop whatever fool thing you're doing and get in here! There's been another—"

"I *know*, Mom." Sarah sounded exasperated. "Why do you think I'm packing?"

"I still don't understand where you think you're going or even how." Sarah's mother lifted her voice to a bray to counter Arrowood. "There's two feet on the ground and unless you're planning on taking a snowmobile, which you don't have—"

Layal. Darya's voice cut through the chatter. *You there? You were saying about the van? Where it was found?*

Right. The cat jerked herself away from memories of disarticulated chipmunks. *Sorry.* What had Layal been telling the wolf? Right...the van.

They found Homer and the van in Ohio but close to West Virginia. Layal was perched on the sill of the cabin's northwest window—*making like a loaf of bread* was what Sarah said whenever the black cat tucked all four paws beneath her body to keep her toes warm. They were into May and yet, for the last seven days, the weather had turned brutal. Temperatures plunged into a deep, hard freeze. Worse, this particular room got almost no sun at all. Squatting here was like trying to get comfortable on ice-glazed sidewalks and alleyways, something with which was much too familiar. *Sarah told her mother that the only reason they found Homer in time was because whoever stopped the van forgot about Homer's cellphone. When he didn't pick up, she had a feeling something was wrong...*

Arrowood, again, derailing her thoughts: "*Roads are out in multiple municipalities as well as power in small communities and the larger urban centers of—*"

And? Then what? Darya's words fizzed with impatience. *What about Qudamah?*

Right. Sorry. Through a layer of thin ice frosting the window, Layal could just make out the wolf-shaped blotch hunkered beneath the low boughs of a Norwegian spruce. From an animal's point of view, the nice thing about the spruce was that the areas beneath those large boughs, which brushed the earth, were virtual caves: mostly dry even in winter and very dark. Perfect camouflage for a black wolf who'd come to call. *So, then—*

She was interrupted by another shrill imperative from Sarah's mother: "Just hold your horses, young lady!"

"Mom." Sarah, shouting to be heard over the television. "I'm sorry, but I've got to go. I need to pack!"

Floating above the women, Arrowood said, "*I'm joined now by Dr. Mark Struthers, professor of geomagnetic physics at Cornell University...*"

Layal? Darya. *What happened next?*

What had she been talking about? Sarah and her mother were still arguing. All that noise was giving the cat a headache. Layal eyed the door, wishing she was strong enough to bull away the doorstop and then push the darned thing—

Benny do.

What? She looked down at the beagle, who'd been snoozing on a braided rug.

Benny do. The beagle heaved himself to all fours, padded to the door, worried the doorstop free with a paw, then nosed the door until the metal tongue clicked. *Good?*

Yes, Benny. The effect was instantaneous, though Layal could still make out the announcer's yammer and the women sniping at one another as a muted, manic gabble. Still, better than full blast. *Thank you.*

Layal friend. Limping back to the rug, the beagle turned three circles then settled down with a slight groan. *Benny luv Layal.*

Layal? Darya, again. *You said that Sarah had a bad feeling and...?*

Right. Sorry. What had she been saying? *Del was supposed to call at midnight, but the place in Ripley where they were going to stay called Sarah an hour earlier because Homer and Del hadn't shown up...*

Del. Darya interrupted. *Who is that?*

Was, she said. *Just a human.* Did that sound brutal? Dismissive? Fine, so sue her. Take away her catnip. Because many times had someone said, *oh, it's just a dumb cat.*

Layal? Benny raised his head from his forepaws then clambered to all fours. *Layal mad?*

Is that Benny? Darya asked.

Yes, she said at the same time the beagle's tail thumped. *Darya!* the beagle shouted. *Darya, Darya, hi, hi!*

Hey, Benny. Darya's tone was even, though Layal could hear the wolf's unspoken question. The conversation was supposed to be private, just between the two of them.

He followed me in, she said to Darya.

Benny heered you call Darya. The beagle's mouth split in a wide grin. *Benny heers lots.*

Oh. Layal was a little flustered—and, well, puzzled. The only time when they had heard one another—when they'd been a collective mind with virtually no privacy—was when

Mother was in their heads. But Mother was gone. The implants which Rahul and Hana had slipped in to control, punish, and condition them to obey had all been removed. Darya had been their leader—the Queen Bee as Rahul sometimes called her (and which made no sense)—but Mother had been what united and goaded them to action. Even united, however, they could not fight Mother.

Now, though, Mother was gone and that mesh...that common thread...had been broken. Each now spoke alone, *thought* alone. For Layal, silence—a quiet spot in one's own mind—was a good thing.

So Layal calling Darya should've been just as private. Benny shouldn't have known. In fact, Sarah had taken Benny out to keep her company as she shoveled a path from the house to the driveway and *that* was when Layal came to this window and called. A mental shout, really, because a wolf's territory is vast and Darya had been very far away, at the limits of Layal's abilities.

But Benny heer. When she looked down, the beagle's grin was, if anything, wider. As if he were in on some private joke. *Benny*, the dog said, *heered you call Darya.* The beagle gave himself a mighty shake that set his long ears flopping from side to side. Then he plunked back down on the rug and yawned. *Benny heers lots now. A LOT a lot.*

Okay. She didn't know what else to say. She directed her attention back to Darya. *Where were we?*

Ripley. There was a gap and then Darya said, *Isn't that from a movie Rahul liked?*

Yes. She had to work not to spit, something at which, being a cat, she excelled. She hoped Rahul was at the bottom of a deep, dark hole. A grave would be just the thing. If she could handle a shovel, she would be happy to dig his.

Rahul is. Benny, again. *Rahul awreddy has.*

Wuh... And then the thought fizzled like the bits of too-wet kindling Sarah's mother sometimes added to the fire. Instead, there was a breathless moment—a very long one—during which neither Layal nor Darya said anything. Layal wasn't even sure she was thinking.

And then Darya said, *Benny, how do you—*

But she got no further.

Because the beagle—Benny—began to howl.

HULP
1

I know. I hurt, too. Qudamah dredged the words from what felt like a mind reduced to mush. He was exhausted, drenched with sticky sweat. His mouth tasted of blood. *It will go away, Chester. Just hang on and let it—*

This time, Chester actually moaned. Chester wasn't good at words and the few he could hang onto seemed, to Qudamah, stand-ins for all the thousands of words the chimp could never express. The few Chester did know, he crammed with emotion and at full volume: **QUDAMAH HULP. QUDAMAH HULP.**

Chester's pain and his thoughts had bled through to the other two chimps, Huey and Louie, and now they picked up the chant. **QUDAMAHQUDAMAHQUDAMAH—**

Please. Stop. The mental cacophony felt as if someone were taking a thick stick and swinging it: *whackwhackwhack* against his skull. The sensation was a little like Mother's punishments had been, actually—though *that* comparison didn't do him a lot of good and gave him no comfort. Because there was nothing he could do to make this better for himself or them. They were all virtually mummified by a series of straps and buckles and clamps and rendered incapable of much in the way of movement. Qudamah couldn't see the others or even crane his head for a look. *Please. Stop. Stop.*

They didn't. If anything, the chants grew louder.

He tried to think of what to do. These three chimps had been unlucky enough to make the cut. Of all the test subjects—ten other chimps and the clutch of tamarins with whom

Qudamah had shared that ill-fated ride in Homer's van—Huey and Louie...not their real names but what the hell; humans did whatever they wanted...had shown enough intelligence, enough spark to slot into their little club. Rahul and Hana had apparently decided that they needed four subjects this time. Perhaps because they weren't using Mother but, more likely, because there was no Darya to lead their pack.

Although—once he *had* overheard Rahul and Hana talking, just the two of them, their voices low and hushed, as if worried they'd be overheard. He'd wondered why, then learned that the two were held in separate quarters, under guard. Just in case they *conspired*, as the colonel put it: *conspired to derail this particular project.* From the fist-sized bruise on Hana's cheek Qudamah had spied one morning and a day after Rahul's upper lip had puffed to the size of a small sausage, Qudamah thought that probably both had done their share of stalling and *derailing.*

The colonel, a big beefy guy who called the shots, would insist they try again soon because this time around, the experiment—to open some kind of door—had worked. Not for as long as the colonel would have liked, but it had worked.

And making it work was all that mattered to the colonel and the people who were *his* masters.

2

The portal loomed, nearly filling this access chamber Qudumah and the chimps lay, separated from the humans because, well, if this portal *did* stay open, who knew what might happen then? Wouldn't do for the humans to be hurt and maybe killed. Although Qudamah thought they had very conveniently forgotten that if something horrible *did* happen, he and the others might be reduced to hamburger. Or maybe worse.

Or could it be better?

Because a door went two ways. Maybe life was better on the other side and not the horror show all Rahul's movies imagined. Heck, Qudamah's real life was a horror show and he would never end up on the little or big screen.

The portal was a strange contraption, though. The look of it put him in mind of a place Sarah and Homer had once visited: an iron mine in Minnesota, a place called *Soudan.* Sarah had been once before; Homer had not and she was trying to convince him to go.

But it's just an old iron mine, Homer had said, his tone quizzical. *What's the point of going down to see something I can see in any old mine open for tourists?*

Because of this. Sarah had produced a picture of a gigantic metal ring, rilled with wires and connected to some complicated array. *It's a far collector. For neutrinos. They shoot the neutrinos from the Fermi Lab in Illinois and the beam travels underground all the way from Illinois through a little bit of Wisconsin and on up to Minnesota, to the mine, where the hits are recorded.*

Looks like something from Stargate, Homer had observed before nodding. *Sure, we can make the trip. Maybe when I'm done taking your little friend...*He'd hooked a thumb at Qudamah...*down to that sanctuary.*

That trip had cost them all. He had wound up here and Homer was...Qudamah cut off that thought. He felt crappy enough as it was.

The thing was: the door, this *portal*, they were supposed to keep open was somehow encompassed within a ring very much like the one Sarah had shown Homer. The portal, on this side anyway, required a strong magnetic field. That—as Keefer, the head scientist, had explained to Hana and Rahul— was something they had discovered by trial and error. That was also the reason they'd relocated deep within a deserted iron mine, much like the one Sarah wanted Homer to visit. The big difference was there was still a fair amount of ore here which had, over the millennia, become magnetic. *It's the reason,*

Keefer said, *that the magnetic line here follows the line of an ancient strike-slip fault.* In some ways, this deep under the Earth's skin, the magnetic forces were stronger even than at the Poles. This also posed some problems for the scientists in terms of calibration and their instruments.

But all that was beyond Qudamah. He'd had a hard enough time just following Keefer's explanation. At the time, he'd also wondered why he bothered, but ignorance was, he had discovered, not bliss. He'd left bliss behind a long time ago: as soon as that trapper's net had closed around, ripped him up and away from the wet greenness of a tropical forest, and left him dangling, screeching his lungs out for help.

Except no one came running but the poachers.

3

HULP. The thought was an endless loop, a circle much like the metal ring enclosing the invisible door or whatever the humans were trying to open and keep open. That word, hulp, swirled in Qudamah's mind the way an ant might try to find its way out of a basketball only to travel forever, looping round and around again and again and again. **Hulphulphulphulp.**

He had to do something. Otherwise, whatever fresh pain lay in his future wouldn't matter because his brain would be so much oatmeal.

Try this. Think of this. Qudamah muscled the thoughts through the cacophony, aiming squarely at Chester. Chester, he knew best, although that was relative. Their languages were still too different even if their emotions were the same. *Stop. Don't think about* **hurt**. *Think about* **this**.

Digging deep, he dredged up a memory: a sunny day at Sarah's cabin, the smell of evergreens, the sun dazzle from snowpack bright enough to cut tears. Benny, wriggling and making a dog-angel in a fluffy fall of new snow.

No. Chester must never have seen this. Not white leaves. That is snow. It's cold. Like very, very cold water on a hot, hot day. Think **this**. He *thrust* the images at Chester, at Huey and Louie: of Layal, tail stiff with indignation, trying her best to walk without her paws touching the ground. *That* had actually made Qudamah—

"Say." A human. One of the two hazmat-suited techs sent to clean up the mess. Pain not only wreaked havoc with the chimps' minds, but also with their bowels and bladders. Cupping a smeary clot of runny feces in a plastic bag, he looked over at the animals, still restrained on their couches. "That was Louie, wasn't it? Making that sound?"

"I thought it was Huey....naw, listen, look at them. It's both." The other tech tilted his head. "Did they...did they just laugh?"

"Naw, that was a hoot." Another tech. "See, Chester just did the same thing. The little guy, that tamarind, you know all they can do is chirp."

The first tech: "Wait, ain't tamarind a kind of fruit or something?" A pause. "Say, are they laughing *more?*"

They were. Because humans could be so incredibly dumb. As long as they could laugh...they would be all right. As long as they could laugh at these stupid humans, the screams in his head went away. The images of Qudamah's friends and pain which replaced them hurt, too, but the hurt was good because that hurt was also of a piece: of belonging and love.

See this, feel this. Hurt like this. *The other hurt will go away, but this is a memory to hold onto. Make a fist of your mind and hold on,* Qudamah told the others—and himself. *Just hold on.*

Dreams

By the time Sarah and her mother banged through the door into the west room, Benny had stopped screaming. That didn't stop Sarah's mother from grabbing Sarah's shoulder. "You see?" she cried. "You can't leave now! What do you expect me to do with a sick animal?"

"He's not sick, Mom." Although Sarah's voice was shaky. Cuddling the beagle to her chest, she gave a little laugh as Benny licked her fingers, then squirmed to get free. "You see, it was just...maybe a seizure, I don't know. That happens sometimes. He had a head injury, you know, and—"

Benny? Tuning them out, Layal jumped from her perch on the windowsill and hit the floorboards

Darya chimed in: *Are you all right?*

Benny fine. The thought was a bit breathless after Sarah gave the beagle another squeeze before letting him wriggle free. He even sounded a little embarrassed. *Benny just...feel hurt.*

Whose?

"I think he's fine, Mom." Pushing to her feet, Sarah turned on her heel and started for the outer room where the television was still yammering. "I have to finish packing."

Her mother gave Benny a doubtful look before trailing after her daughter. "I still don't understand—"

Benny, Darya pressed. *Whose hurt did you feel?*

Qudamah's. The beagle gave himself a mighty shake that began at his head and rippled all the way to his tail. *Qudamah hurt bad.*

It was on the tip of Layal's tongue to ask, yet again, how Benny could know this, but Darya muscled in first with something more productive: *Is he with Rahul? Down deep underground?*

Yes. Rahul and Hana and Qudamah in a deep deep hole. Benny just no. The beagle paused, as if considering. *And there is ohnlee two ways owt. Going up— and then going akross. Ohnlee the akross door keeps clozing.*

Going up must mean an elevator, which would make sense if the others were in a deep hole. But across? Layal's nose wrinkled. What was that about?

Darya: *Rahul and Hana are being held prisoner with Qudamah?*

Yes...not in jayl, but not free eether, Benny said. *Rahul needed Qudamah and Qudamah's friends to open the akross door. Now it's open.*

A door? Layal asked. *What's on the other side?*

Don't know. But I have dreams.

No one said anything for a long moment. In the silence, Layal could hear the voices of the women. Sarah and her mother were still arguing, but that ebbed and flowed as the women moved through the cabin. Jim Arrowood wasn't on the television anymore, though, at least not by himself. Another man was talking and probably that professor who'd come on the broadcast to explain something important. *"...and we've collated the data. Each occurrence has been along a magnetic line. Now, as you can see, Jim, this latest and most prolonged distortion lies squarely along a very strong magnetic line of a very deep and ancient slip-strike fault running from New York and Alabama—"*

Benny found something in his ear to scratch. Layal was aware only of how cold the floor was and how she wished she could just close her eyes and forget all this.

Benny. Darya almost seemed to clear her throat. *What dreams?*

Just dreams. Benny inspected his paw, licked it, then dug at his ear again and hard enough to set his tags jingling. *I heered before but not so good.* The beagle was silent a moment as if searching for an analogy. *I heered them like Darya does. Like fingers?*

Fingers? Layal was interested despite herself.

Demons, the wolf said. *I dreamt about them...well, most of the time.*

Real demons?

No, of course not. Jinn. They're from old Iraqi fables that Rahul and Hana knew. Some are out to trick you. Some can be good. Most are evil, though. The stories say that a wolf at the door is something you want, good luck, a charm against the bad jinn...against demons...that come up from the ground at night. The wolf at the door bites off their fingers and drives the jinn back underground.

You never mentioned dreams, Layal said.

I didn't think they were important. In the stories, a wolf is a, well... Darya gave a mental shrug. *A guardian at the threshold between one world and the next.*

Darya not onlee gard there is, the dog said.

You—But Layal was cut off by Sarah, pitching her voice louder to be heard over the broadcast in the next room: "*Mom, I can't explain it, but I just have to go. This is important!*"

"But who *are* they? And *whyyyy?*" Sarah's mother was very good at wailing.

The professor, still yammering on the television: "*And these magnetic fluctuations are quite interesting. They've been very unstable, winking in and*—"

"How can you leave Homer? How can you leave *me?*" Sarah's mother's voice was watery.

The professor: "*But the longest and strongest fluctuation is located just a few miles east of Ripley, West Virginia where the magnetic line is*—"

"Sarah, where are you *going?*" Sarah's mother demanded.

"I just..."

Benny. Layal looked at the beagle. *You said you called for help. Did you...did you also tell Sarah*—

Layal broke off at a sudden rumbling coming from somewhere outside the house. An engine, and a large one judging by the vibrations shuddering up from the floorboards and into her paws.

Who is that? Layal asked Darya. *You're outside. Can you see? Darya, who is it?*

Breach

Hunkering down onto his haunches, Gary moved aside a leafy branch—and spotted what he and his team had been sent to find.

"That's it?" Colosa asked. "A house?"

"I guess so." Though he was also surprised. Checking his watch, he shrugged. "These are the coordinates."

"Not what I expected." Particula, like her sister, seemed unimpressed. "At all."

"Okay, but we're here now," Gary said. Here was a steep, once-heavily wooded slope which looked as if it had been through some kind of cataclysm. Or maybe more than just one disaster, something similar to a couple tornadoes, a couple earthquakes. Felled trees, dislodged boulders, cracks in the earth—and of course, there was all this snow to wallow through.

And yet, there was the house: a simple high-ceilinged, slate-shingled, dark gray ranch. The house seemed to be undamaged. In fact—Gary ran his gaze over the surrounding landscape—the house, intact and almost placid-looking...yes, that was the word. The house was that breathless, deceptive calm before a storm or the eye around which a hurricane raged.

"Are we sure?" Colosa asked. "I mean, I'm not up for charging into someone's living room."

"Unless we're being chased by a bear," Particula added.

"Which we're not at the moment." And thank heavens for that. "Anyway," Gary said, holding up the watch he'd snatched from Scopes's tech stores, "this thing seems to think we're here, so I guess we are."

"If that's true," Lily said, "where are the guards? Where's the barbed wire or surveillance cameras? There's not even a picket fence. And it's small, you know?"

"Considering that none of us has ever seen a trans-dimensional portal, I don't think we know anything about size. But I'll grant you, this is not what I expected. That color is just weird. Just off, know what I mean?" Except he wasn't sure he exactly knew either...but then he had it. The siding's off. He'd seen plenty of vinyl siding in his life; Costco sometimes stocked what Home Depot didn't. But, even at this distance, he thought the material wasn't vinyl at all.

*I think it's metal. Lead? Could be, but...*Gary shook his head. "Man, this is where we could have used Scopes. He'd know how to figure this out."

"Wellll," Colosa drawled, "considering that he isn't here, we just gotta make do."

"No argument from—" He broke off as the professor leaned in so close, the man's breath, like his words, tickled Gary's ear.

What? Gary felt the tiny hairs prickle along the back of his neck. Yes, he heard what the guy was saying, but he didn't understand...

"A dog?" The words were nearly as quiet as the susurration of a light rain and so soft that, for a split-second, Gary could almost imagine he was only thinking, not saying anything but pushing his thoughts into Paracelsus's skull. "A dog?"

The professor nodded but said nothing else.

Terrific. Gary gritted his teeth hard enough to hurt. Of all the times to get all Buddha on me, he thought, pulling back from the man so he nearly stumbled. All of the effing times to come at me with this—

"You okay?" He looked up to find Lily's eyes searching his. "What's the matter?"

"Nothing." He turned aside with an abrupt, almost dismissive gesture he regretted an instant later. "Just..." He forced his mouth into something that felt—and probably looked—like a skull's rictus grin. But he had to maintain control. He couldn't allow for their doubts now, not when they were this close. So, get ahold of yourself. These people were counting on him. He even allowed for a thought about what the real Grey Guardsman might do in this situation but that only made him angrier.

Grow up. His jaws were so tense, he thought his teeth might crack. *Stop thinking about the real Grey Guardsman. You are Grey Guardsman now. So suck it—*

"Cover me."

What? Gary's head snapped round so fast he ought to have broken his neck. That was the professor, again, and really, hadn't the guy bothered him enough already with his crazy talk about a dog—

But then, one look downslope...and he could only gawp.

Because Paracelsus was already out in the open—and moving. Neither fast nor slowly. More...deliberately: moving in a considered sideways shuffle, like a crab picking its way over a particularly gnarly tumble of splintered boulders and fissured rock.

"What the eff," Lily asked no one in particular, "is he doing?"

"Trying to get himself killed is what," Colosa observed.

That, Gary thought, was just a little too close to his exact thoughts. He knew Paracelsus had issues, and serious ones at that. But suicide? He couldn't picture it.

"And what's he want us to cover him with?" Particula asked. "Harsh language?"

"Come on, guys, think. We got to help him." Then Lily looked at Colosa. "You know, a diversion would be really good right about now."

"Singing my song, honey." Colosa's lips curved into a fierce grin. "Just give me a hot minute."

Pivoting, she moved away fast, sidestepping along the tree line, growing as she went. In a matter of seconds, Colosa had sprouted to a height of at least forty feet and nearly as high as the snow-laden trees. Grabbing one, she shook the tree by its trunk, first hard and then harder still...

Oh, my god. Gary watched, a little slack-jawed, as the wind whipped the now-airborne snow into a swirling white cloud. Not quite an avalanche but too heavy to remain suspended, the snow-cloud barreled downslope. Okay, that was certainly something else to look at.

"Aw-right." Particula pumped a fist as her sister moved to a second tree and repeated the maneuver. "No way anyone on watch will miss this."

"Even better than that," Lily observed. "Because now any guard will be looking the wrong way."

All true—and speaking of the wrong way, where was the professor? Peering down the slope to his left, Gary spotted the man. The professor's movements were considered, careful, almost casual, as if he had all the time in the world to pick his way over rocky and gnarled tree roots. Gary was pretty sure he would've made like a jackrabbit, but Paracelsus seemed in no hurry.

Problem was...time was kinda of the essence—

A sudden sound that did not belong and was not the wind: a high whine followed by a crack and a whing and then a distant spang of metal against rock.

A fraction of an instant later, Particula cried, "Colosa!"

"What?" Startled, Lily whirled on her heel. "What was—?"

"High velocity bullet breaking the sound barrier. You don't hear it until it's past." Gary swung his head toward Colosa, who'd reared back. She'd managed four enormous snow clouds which were still rolling downhill, but now whoever had spotted her in that house was pumping bullets up the slope. He watched as Colosa clambered away from the edge in two giant-sized strides. As it happened, gravity and distance were on her side—or the guards had crappy aim, take your pick. In the next second, he let out a huff of relief when the woman gave them all a thumb's-up.

Lily put a hand on Particula's arm. "Relax, she's good." To Gary: "You see the professor?"

"Yeah. Look." He pointed with his chin. "He's on the near side of the house."

"Wow, talk about slow mo," Particula said, her voice still a little shaky. "He doesn't hear all those guns?"

"Probably doesn't even notice," Lily muttered as the professor neared the bottom of the slope. "Man, that is one odd dude. You gotta wonder what he thinks he's doing—"

As if he had heard her, that odd duck of a professor did what only he could.

Still unhurried, perhaps even oblivious to the pop-pop-pop of gunfire, he crossed the remaining forty feet of level ground between him and a corner of the house. There, he stood for a second...more like a millisecond or two...then stretched a hand and let his fingers rest on the corner.

"What's he up to?" Particula asked.

Gary shook his head. "I don't—"

The wall shimmered. A split second before, the wall, like the house, had been the color of a bit of graphite snapped from a discarded pencil. But now...

"Whoa." Lily gawped. "Do you see—?"

"Yeah," Gary breathed. "I do."

The wall changed and rippled, its color shifting from that drab gray to a shade that reminded Gary of the bellies of thick clouds right before that first clap of thunder—and then, finally, a pale, nearly translucent silver: something that appeared so thin the wall actually rippled and crinkled. Gary thought of his mother, in their kitchen, ladling leftovers into a bowl before ripping a sheet from a roll of—

"Oh, my God," Lily said. "Is that aluminum foil?"

"Yeah, I think so. Close enough for government work anyway." Hefting his shield, Gary was just about to suggest they get a move on—

When Paracelsus turned, cupped his hands around his mouth, and beat him to it.

"What are you all waiting for?" Paracelsus bellowed. "An engraved invitation?"

Phenomenons
1

The wall Paracelsus had transmuted came down like silver-colored tissue.

As soon as that happened, a barrage of bullets whip-cracked through the air. So many bullets flew so fast, anyone in the line of fire would have been reduced to mush and bloody socks.

Lucky for them...they weren't there.

Oh-kaay. Huddled at the right corner of where the house's wall used to be, Gary spared a glance at Lily on his left and then across to the place that had been the wall's left corner where the sisters and Paracelsus crouched. So, great, he'd thought ahead and gotten them split up, one group left, one group right—and out of the line of the fire that was sure to come.

But now what?

Only a matter of time before those guards call for reinforcements and then they all come out blasting. He didn't want to think about the mess—

All of a sudden, a guard darted through the opening where the house's wall had been. A split second later, a swarm of bullets buzzed in pursuit. Many rounds spanged against rocks or buried themselves in the earth, sending up small brown geysers. But just as many smacked into the guard's body sending up jumps of blood. The man did a herky-jerky stutter-step, dropped his weapon, and then toppled face-first. His body hit with a heavy thump, followed by an audible crunch that reminded Gary of the sound crushed eggshells made as he fed them into the garbage disposal. Probably the impact had broken the poor guy's nose, although the guard was well past caring about such things. Being kinda dead and all.

"Why?" Lily said in an appalled whisper. She'd paled, her skin bleaching to the color of bone left to bake under a desert sun. "Why are the other soldiers' shooting at their own guy?"

"Beats m—" Gary broke off as another guy blistered through into the daylight. He was running fast but not fast enough to outrun a second volley. This one spun a little pirouette before crumpling, though his feet didn't seem to have gotten the memo. Instead, they continued in a spastic little herky-jerky shuffle that was getting them nowhere fast.

What the... But then Gary saw Paracelsus. Saw the man touching the near corner of where a wall had once stood not five minutes before.

That's when Gary understood. What had Paracelsus called it? Yes, transitive power: one that enabled him to affect the thoughts and emotions of those who touched what he did. It worked even if that person or persons had touched an object well before the Professor.

The guards were in the house. At least a few had touched that side along the wall, which was still standing and where Paracelsus was now. Monkeying with their brain chemistry or some such. Back at United Front HQ, Better Angel had briefed him on the prof and his abilities. Gary hadn't understood a word of it then and he didn't get it now.

But seeing is believing. He just didn't know if he liked it. Okay, there was bound to be a bit of carnage when you were breaking into someplace others would really rather you not be. But there was necessary and then there was—

Two more guards bulled out side by side. They made a dozen yards before the bullets followed. The one on the left got a little further, but he was a lanky guy. Then, again, well-placed rounds were excellent levelers, and they went down one after the other in a fresh flurry of high-velocity rounds.

And then...nothing. And more nothing for a very long three seconds.

Good. Following his spine, sweat tripped down the rungs, a vertebrae at a time, to pool at his waist. His pits were damp and so was his neck. He blotted sudden sweat beads from his upper lip but furtively, with the back of one gloved hand. Wouldn't do for the others to see how much those dead guys—how they'd been slaughtered by their own men—got to him. Did the real Gray Guardsman get all wobbly? Probably not. So, he had to stiffen up, get a grip. Soldiers were thrust into combat all the time—and this was a fight for the world that only he could finish.

I'm the only one who can save us.

And yet...what Paracelsus had said only to him, about some sort of very special dog...did that make any sense? Unless that was the way this was supposed to go down. Because there was a legend, wasn't there? There'd been a kid in his class...what...seventh-grade? What had the kid said?

"Stinks." He looked down at Lily. "The smell," she murmured. "You know, of..." She fluttered a hand. "Like someone set fire to a butcher shop."

She was right. The wind had changed, bringing with it the mingled aromas of fresh earth, burnt clothing, the meaty fug of fresh blood that always reminded him of raw liver.

"So now what, Boss?" she continued. "I don't think anyone else is coming—"

"Hush." He put a finger to his lips then cocked his head. "Hear that?"

"That buzz?" Her face cleared. "Yeah, they're talking it over. Trying to figure out what to do next."

Which meant they had to do something, and fast. He wondered how many were left. Hard to tell. Too many overlapping voices. A lot of guys, though, he figured. The house was big, and this might even be where the men bunked. So...maybe two squads? That meant around twenty guys. Well...he slipped a quick look at the dead men...make that sixteen, all of whom had presumably not come near that missing wall. Which sort of sucked.

How to take them all? They couldn't use Colosa's powers; the interior was too small, only a single story. So, what?

He was chewing on that one when, out of the tail of an eye, something blurred. Jerking his head up, he was in time to see a twinkle, a flash of black hair—and then Particula vanished.

What the—? Across the divide, Colosa gave him a thumb's up. But a thumb's up about what?

"Where did Particula—?" Lily began then stopped at a sudden yelp that came not from him or Colosa—

That came from inside the house. Just as that thought bloomed at the front of his mind, he flinched at the sudden loud report of a gunshot. This was followed almost instantly by a glassy crunch and a loud thump. Someone, he thought, had just hit the deck.

"Oh, my God." Lily grabbed his arm. "She might be hurt. We have to—"

"No, wait." Colosa isn't worried. In fact, the woman was beaming. Praying that the top of his skull remained where it was, he risked a quick peek around the corner—

Lying in a loose-limbed heap, a guard was sprawled in a halo of blood and something brittle and brighter that caught the light. The blood was coming from the guy's nose, which seemed to have undergone a sudden and radical surgery. Out cold. His eyes tracked to the ceiling where the nub of a fixture dangled by a single cord. Probably the guard had inadvertently popped off a shot when he got popped.

Gathered round the guy were four other men, eyes buggy with fear, trying to look in all directions at once.

Parti—

Before he'd even finished that thought, Particula was there, among the men: first small then swelling fast, sprouting from the floor like some malevolent mushroom on speed. She came up, ready, fist cocked, elbow back and then as she drew level with another guard, her fist pistoned out, smashing into the man's throat. Dropping his rifle, the soldier grabbed at his neck and his knees kinked and he dropped, eyes buggy, face going a ghastly shade of purple. His mouth gawped like a fish stranded on a dock—an apt description for a man trying to pull in air through crushed cartilage.

Sucker punched. Gary was glad the guy was down, but he didn't feel good about it. His gaze ticked to the first guard. Be glad, man; you're going to wake up at least. A little uglier, but at least you'll be alive to look in the mirror.

The house was in pandemonium: men shouting, all of them turning in wild circles, looking for the woman who had just been there, hadn't she just been there, she was just here, where the hell was she?

"Here," Particula said. This time, she'd timed her transition from tiny to full-sized so she came up beneath a guard. Wrapping both hands around the rifle's barrel, she gave that a mighty jerk. The guard lost his grip, and then he was backpedaling but not fast enough. Hands still clamped on the barrel, Particula swung hard, digging out that breaking ball before that sucker crosses the plate. If she'd been a batter, that ball would've blasted right out of that ballpark. As it was, there was a solid thunk of wood against bone; the man's head snapped to one side so hard and fast, the guy probably could've played the stunt double for that old movie about exorcisms. Gary wasn't a fan of such movies, though he'd watched tone on a dare at a sleepover when he was ten. The pea soup was just that: pea soup. But that old head-twisting trick was probably the scariest, pee-in-your-pants thing he'd ever seen.

By now, the guards were in a panic, bunched together, eyes wide, trying to look every direction at once—and that was when Lily shouted over the babble, "Particula, get out now!" Slipping a lipstick from her bandolier, Lily gave the cap a twist then slung the now-open lipstick into the guard house. An instant later, a custardy, egg-yellow cloud hissed out in a thickening spume.

"What is that stuff?" Peeking around the corner, Gary counted good half dozen men writhing and flopping on the floor. About four more had clustered near a window they'd apparently opened and were sucking air. Pulling back, he looked down at Lily. "Smells like battery acid."

"Close enough for government work," she said then turned as Particula shimmered up from the earth to her full height. "Have fun?"

"Yeah, until you just had to get involved." Particula was by their side. She rubbed the knuckles of her right hand. "I could have done a few more."

"Save your strength," Gary said. "You'll get your chance. We got a long way to go before we find this lab. Speaking of which—"

"Hold your horses, boss." Lily put a hand on Gary's arm. "I know you're itching to flatten those guys, but you should wait a couple seconds for the gas to air out."

"When you do, want company?" Particula asked.

"What? And let you get all the glory? Besides, we got a long way to go." Gary hefted his shield. "I can do a quick mop."

Which he did—and very well.

2

After, when they'd all moved inside:

"This is just the weirdest space." Lily turned a circle. "No rooms. Just some chairs, boxes of supplies. A fridge. No cots, so they don't sleep here."

"Which means they have to rotate and pretty frequently. There's not even a toilet," Gary thought about that a second then added, "Or were dispatched here as a last line of defense against a breach. Could have been dropped off here from some other location."

Particula groaned. "If that's right, we just did a whole lot of work for nothing."

"Those guards didn't behave as if they were defending nothing. Boss says we're close, we're close." Lily flicked a sideways glance at Gary. "Although this place is kinda spooky."

He knew what she meant. No vehicles. No rooms, no beds. He eyed a half-finished can of soda, evidently taken from a small minifridge humming in one corner. Which begged another question: where was the—

"Where's the power coming from?" Colosa frowned up at the ceiling. "There are lights. The fridge has power."

"No TV," Particula observed. "No computers. Not even a deck of cards. How did these guys end up not going stir-crazy and killing each—"

"Hush." Gary raised a hand to shush them all. He waited a beat then another. "You hear that?"

The three women tossed looks at one another and then at Paracelsus, who only stood with hands in his pockets and seemed more intent upon studying his shoes. Eventually, Colosa turned back and gave a shrug. "No?" she said with a little question mark at the end, like a student who just knows the answer to that equation is dead-wrong.

"What do you mean?" Lily asked. "What are we supposed to hear?"

"There's this sound. Kind of comes and goes." He looked from side to side, a gesture that put him in mind of a German shepherd he'd once known: the way its ears could swivel independently. At the time, he'd thought that was a pretty nifty trick. Now, he was all too aware of his very human limitations. There were a lot of things animals just knew.

Like that dog. The dog the Professor said was the key.

"It's a hum, really," he said to the others. "Very low and a little irregular. Like…it seems to cycle. Just listen a couple seconds."

The others—and, yes, even the Professor—cocked their heads like obedient spaniels, closed their eyes, and went quiet. After a few seconds, eyes still closed, Colosa raised a finger. "Wait." She paused for a heartbeat then two. "There. You hear it? That...well, it's kind of a ripple. Like water ebbing and flowing. I don't know how else to describe it, but—"

"Yeah, I hear that, too." Her sister looked left and then right. "There." She pointed to a far corner into which a stack of three boxes had been wedged. "Coming from there."

They all gathered at the spot. "Nothing on the wall." Lily looked at Gary. "Underneath?"

"A good a suggestion as any. Got to move these boxes first, though." Bending, he gave the first a mighty heave—and then went staggering back, suddenly off-balance.

"Whoa, Nellie." Colosa and her sister grabbed at an arm which saved him from falling on his ass and then Colosa continued, "Why would anyone leave a stack of empty boxes here?"

"Because of this." Kneeling, Lily ran a forefinger around the four seams of a very large square incised in the floor which the empty boxes she'd pushed aside covered. "There's something under here." She paused. "Sound's louder, too. But how do we get down there? This is a hatch, so there's got to be a way."

"Here." Gary pointed at a spot on the righthand wall. "It blends in so well you have to know it's here."

They all drew together in a tight cluster to stare. "That's a control?" Colosa wrinkled her nose. "Looks more like where the paint's bubbled up."

"But the other walls are smooth," Particula countered. "No bubbles. Not even a light switch."

"Well..." Gary scrutinized what he thought must be, for lack of a word, a call button: a barely perceptible dimple at about shoulder-height on the facing wall. "Might do for everyone to back up."

"You say that as if you expect a ka-boom," Lily said as she scuttled back to huddle with the others.

"Always a first time." He mashed the dimple with a thumb. The bleb gave; there was an audible click followed by a hum that was lower than the one they'd all heard and then...

"Ohhh, boy," Lily said as the square on the floor levitated, pushed up by what appeared to be a free-standing elevator.

"Sorta like that show, the one with the goofy spy who talks into the bottom of his shoe?" Particula observed. "But in reverse."

He knew the show. Good thing there wasn't a phone inside, or they might end up in free-fall. The elevator was like something out of a science-fiction movie: a huge rectangle wide enough to accommodate about ten people at a time, and maybe fifteen if everyone held their breath. Or wasn't carrying a rifle, Gary thought. The thing was a little futuristic but only because it slid up to meet them instead of coming down from above. As soon as the car slotted into place the hum, which had intensified, returned to that same low oscillation Gary had picked up. A second later, the doors parted noiselessly to reveal an interior car bathed in soft light.

"Should we?" Particula, again. "I mean, there's only one way to go and whoever is below us…"

"Knows we're here. I don't see we've got another option." Then Gary thought of something else. "You know, these guys," he said, hooking a thumb over a shoulder, "there were a lot of them, right? Armed to the teeth? Except here we are, calling up an elevator, and there is no one coming up with it. You have to imagine that Pinkerton designed her system to keep an eye out for trouble."

"Cameras around here somewhere? I can believe that." Colosa favored him with a narrow squint. "You're saying, this was all they got left? They threw everything they had? These guys we just mopped the floor with?"

"I'm saying it's a possibility."

"Even so, two of us could stay up here." Particula moved a little closer to her sister. "Keep an eye out."

"To what end? Not like we've got walkie-talkies." Come to think of it, he'd seen none on the soldiers or guards or whatever they were. Last gasp, maybe, the way Colosa put it. So, cameras and a constant video surveillance complete with surround-sound and in glorious technicolor, but he bet no one below was really enjoying the show. "Listen, the fact that no one's come rushing up here would suggest that there may not be more surprises below."

"Always the possibility of an ambush," Particula said.

"Yeah." Colosa arched her left eyebrow. "Come into my parlor, said the spider to the fly."

"Very funny," he said.

"You see me laughing?" Colosa shook her head. "I am not."

"Our mom always did say she had kinda this gallows humor," Particula put in.

"Well, I vote we stick together, and we go," Lily said. "Otherwise, what's been the point of coming here in the first place?"

There didn't seem to be anything more to say to that, so they piled in, Paracelsus first and then the sisters and Lily and, finally, Gary with his shield at the ready.

"Say," Lily said, as Gary searched for the down button, "I sure hope that shield of yours is bullet-proof."

Poking the only button he could fine, he turned to grin down at Lily as the doors slid shut. "Wellll…"

3

The elevator went down a long way, though they had no way of knowing just how far. The ride reminded Gary of the time his uncle had taken him to an abandoned coal mine down around Pittsburgh. That seam had run in a diagonal and so the elevator had, too, something that was only evident if you looked at the slant of the elevator rails on the surface. Once inside, there was no sensation of falling to one side: just the whir of machinery and the flash of lights whipping past as they went past one seam level after another.

This elevator was a little bit like that but mostly different. For one thing, the walls were opaque. For another, the mechanism was virtually silent as if the car was gliding into the guts of the Earth on frictionless rails.

After thirty seconds, Lily said, "My ears just popped."

"Mine, too." Particula waggled her jaw. "I hate that. Airplanes are the pits, let me tell you."

"Change in air pressure." Colosa looked at Gary. "Wherever this is going, it's pretty far down."

"Considering our location and all things being equal," Paracelsus put in, "an abandoned mine would be the best place to set up the portal."

"Coal was big here," Gary said. "Iron, too."

"Iron, I think," the professor said in his soft, mild way and then lifted a chin toward the elevator's doors. "And I do believe that we are about three seconds from finding out just what lies beneath."

"Wait," Lily said, "wasn't that a movie with—"

But then the elevator settled with a sigh and the inside of the car grew so quiet, Gary heard Lily swallow.

I feel that. Pulse thrumming, Gary tensed and held his shield at the ready, and as the doors split, he braced for—

A whole lot of nothing. No people milling about. No one brandishing a weapon.

Particula broke the silence first. "Okay, that was a little anti-climactic."

No one laughed. Probably just as nervy as he felt but maybe for different reasons. They were worried only about whether or not Pinkerton's people had thrown all they had into a last-ditch defense through which they had just broken.

But he...Gary...he was so close to what he had come to believe was his destiny...he was keyed up, on high alert. Stepping from the elevator, he said, "Okay, everyone stick—"

"Oh." Lily's vocalization of wonder might have come from a very small, very dazzled child. Ducking around Gary's shield, she stepped into a very wide, very high cavern and stared up. "Guys, would you look at this?"

Okay, fine, get yourself mowed down in a hail of bullets. See what— And then that stumbled to a halt as he got a good look. "Wow," he said, taking in the banks of computers and other machinery about which he hadn't a clue but all of which were festooned with winking lights and a lot of buttons and knobs. But then as he moved further into the room, he caught yet one more...well, it wasn't quite a hum, was it?

What is that? He searched for an analogy and for some absurd reason, he thought of a beach and a seven-year-old boy holding a shell to his ear because his father said that the sound he heard...*Well, son, that's the sea. All the sea that ever was and ever will be on Earth, that's what you're hearing.*

An entire world. He now followed the sound, with its endless susurration, that soft ebb and flow, that hoosh. *All the sea in the palm of your hand.*

He circled around the elevator, the entrance to which had slid shut and now showed only a tiny green light, and then stopped dead.

It took him a full twenty seconds to work up enough spit to get out even a word. "Guys," he croaked. "Back here."

The clap of running footfalls heading his way on the double, at first echoing and then flatter as they neared, careered around the corner, and then he heard Colosa, out of breath: "What? What's the ma—"

She stopped.

Silence.

Then, someone...Lily, he thought...said, "Oh, my Lord."

4

The bay was very large and not really an alcove: more like sectioned-off from the enormous cavern by machinery and workstations. On this, the near side, were four metal beds arranged like the points of a compass. The beds reminded Gary of surgeon's gurneys, except each of these were also outfitted with five stout-looking leather straps: two for each arm, two for the legs, and one at the head. Also at the head of each was an odd skullcap, bristling with wires and leads.

Two beds were empty—presumably because their occupants currently stared out from the depths of two of a quartet of cages nested a short distance away. Which left the other two beds and both were occupied.

A chimp, arms and legs tethered, lay in one. Gary knew the animal was alive only because at the sound of their voices, the chimp slowly opened puffy lids to reveal eyes choked with blood. At the sight of them, the chimp's lips peeled away in a snarl, revealing incisors that were a peculiar shade of orange from the blood the animal either had coughed up or drew from its own torn and ravaged lips.

Strapped to a second bed was much smaller, golden-haired monkey. Unlike the mute chimp, the monkey let out several weak chirps.

Yet all that was not what held and drew Gary, and he let himself be carried past the others who were exclaiming over the chimp and monkey. He moved away and deeper into the high cavern: toward the source of that quiet yet inexorable aural tide.

Well, hello. Gary stopped well short of the device. He would give that thing plenty of distance for the time being, thanks. He might be hurtling toward what he thought of as destiny, but he wasn't a maniac. One step at a time. His gaze traveled from the Portal's base and on up into the high ceiling. This cavern was so enormous, he had to crane to see all the way up and still unsure there wasn't more of the rocky ceiling hidden by a deep well of shadows in the high darkness. The Portal, a strangely drab-looking metallic ring, sprouted coils of wires which led to a phalanx of computers, all of which hummed with activity. And why not?

They're monitoring you, he thought as his gaze came to rest on the ring's center, and you are most certainly—

"Wow." Startled, he turned to look back over his right shoulder. Colosa was staring, open-mouthed. "Just...wow."

"Oh, that poor thing." Lily, behind them in the bay with the animals, her voice echoing a bit. Looking past Colosa, Gary saw her moving toward the small, golden tamarin. "What did they do to you, honey?" she asked.

"Careful," Particula warned. "I wouldn't go fiddling around or let them run loose or anything."

"I'm not fiddling." Lily sounded offended. "I'm only letting it go."

"Girl, don't you watch movies?" Particula shook her head. "Chimps are nasty. Eat your face, pop your eyes like grapes."

"Well, this isn't a chimp. It's a tamarin and—"

"Looks kinda alive, doesn't it?" Colosa said, bringing him back. "The inside of it, I mean. The way it ripples. And it's so blue, why is it blue?"

"It is quite lovely, isn't it?" Gary turned to his left as Paracelsus slipped from a wedge of shadow. The man was as stealthy as a panther; Gary wondered how long the professor had been there studying the portal. Or had the man been studying him? "Quite the remarkable feat to open this and keep it that way. Think of the energy that thing's harnessing as we speak. Enough to power...well...let's say that limitless feels like an understatement."

"That's why the middle's like that, right?" Gary asked. "I've never seen anything like it. Is it...aqueous? No," he answered his own question. "It's energy. It can't be, can it?"

"Sure looks like water to me. It's got those ripples. Only..." Colosa scrunched her nose. "It's too thick, know what I'm saying?"

"Listen, Lily." Particula, again. "I really don't think you should be playing around with these animals. Let's get some professionals to come in and take care of—"

"And just leave them like this? Absolutely not." Lily's tone had turned a little snippy. "You don't want to help, don't help."

"I'm not saying that. I'm only pointing out—"

"Gelatin." Gary snapped his fingers. "That's it. The energy ripples the way a half-set bowl of gelatin does."

"I'll take your word for that. Jell-O's never been my thing. The way it moves...like eating something alive." Colosa paused. "Me, it looks a lot more like the gauze curtain used to hang in my abuela's kitchen. The way it kind of ripples like there's some kind of wind."

From the bay, Lily crooned: "Take it easy, boy, just take it easy. Let me get these nasty old straps—"

"Or," Paracelsus said, "a particular fusion of space-time loci, all correlating to a specific resonance frequency."

"I love it when you talk dirty," Colosa said.

Paracelsus ignored the gibe. Or perhaps he simply had no sense of humor. "It fits the theories. Of course, given that energy and matter are essentially interchangeable under certain—"

A skin, Gary interrupted. "No, a eyelid. That's what it reminds me of, those third set of eyelids a lot of animals have."

"Okay, that's a little creepy." Colosa shuddered. "Seriously? It's looking at us? There's some kind of giant eyeball underneath going back and forth the way it does when you're dreaming?"

"You're anthropomorphizing because you don't understand," Paracelsus said, at the same moment Gary said, "Sure feels like it."

"Can you both be right?"

The men looked at one another, then back at Colosa and Gary said, "I don't know."

"I will concede the point," the professor said. "The questions are many, I would think. Is this...eye, as you call it, truly open or is that a protective covering that might part and give way to an alternative reality if the right person were to approach?"

There are no ifs about it. I'm the right person. Gary knew that in his bones. Aloud, he said only, "I guess that also depends on who's doing the deciding."

"True. There is the Eye we see and the Eye which sees." The professor fell a silent a moment then said, "But you are still attributing human qualities to what is, in essence, an energy vortex. This is a barrier, nothing more, and sentience is absolutely out of the—"

A sudden shrill, something impossibly high and primordial, made them all jump. What the— Turning, Gary was just in time to catch a blur of something small and bright orange scuttling out of the bay to dart under a series of workstations, spaced several feet apart, were snugged against a rock wall.

"Now you've gone and done it," Particula said. "I told you to be careful."

"Well, it's not like I meant for that to happen." Lily's voice was cross. "He was just really fast and then I was afraid of grabbing him too hard."

"Which is why I told you to wear gloves."

"And I told you, the gloves were too bulky. Made me feel like Mickey Mouse," Lily replied. Turning to Gary, she said, "I didn't mean to let him loose."

"Little late," Colosa observed. "Horse kinda outta the barn, if you know what I'm saying."

Gary cut through the bickering. "It is what it is. All that matters now is we secure the animals." Although...his gaze flicked to the chimp still on its metal bed, the ones in the cages...how they were going to do that, he hadn't a clue. For its part, the chimp only regarded him with a baleful glare that Gary thought was probably as close to what an animal with murder in its heart might give.

"There's no way I'll be able to reach under and grab it." On hands and knees now, Lily was peering under the workstations. "I hear him moving, but I can't see him. It's too dark."

"Even if you could, he'll probably just run somewhere else. He's one fast little guy," Particula observed. "You keep poking around like that, he maybe bites your fingers or something before he does.”

Lily sat back on her heels. “I don’t suppose you’d consider maybe making yourself kinda small...”

“You consider right about that.” Then, as Lily groaned and again lowered herself until she was belly to the ground, the better to see under the workstations, Particula continued, “How about some fancy knock-out gas from one of those lipsticks?”

“Yes, I have some. I just—” Lily’s voice cut out for just a moment and then she was pushing up to a crouch and turning. “I’m just saying that there’s no way,” she said, but her eyes were very wide and then she was up and moving to a neighboring workstation. Grabbing a pen, she scribbled something on a pad then turned and held up the pad for them to read.

not rock

air through crack

someone inside

“Really?” Gary just knew a completely empty complex was too good to be true. After a quick glance at the others, he said to Lily, “So what do you suggest?”

“I dunno,” Lily said. “do what Particula said and call someone to take charge of the animals?”

“How many people do you think we’d need?”

“Oh, maybe about four or five,” she said—but held up two fingers then waggled the hand back and forth.

Two or three. Too few to be guards. Station staff, more likely than not. If they were armed, of course...that was another matter. Still, he had a feeling...

Lily was dashing off something else now: Particula.

“This is revenge, that’s what,” Particula murmured. “That monkey comes after me...”

Speaking of that monkey...that was when Gary noticed the most peculiar thing. Or rather, felt it. Turning a look toward the workstations, he saw that the tamarin was sitting, very quietly, very calmly on a desk to the right of a rocky slab which Gary now realized wasn't rock at all.

Lily was right. Rock's fake. Synthetic. He peered more closely and spotted seams delineating a rectangle about six feet high. Like the fake floor for the elevator. That's a panel. Probably leading to a panic room of sorts. If there was a mechanism to open the room from the outside, he didn't see it. Although he bet there had to be something readily accessible. And of all places to perch, the monkey chooses that desk.

"What are you—" Colosa began then stopped when Gary raised a warning finger to his lips then used that to point to the monkey before taking the pad and pen from Lily, scrawling something, then tapping the paper with a finger for emphasis.

panic button desk monkey

He saw from their expressions that they understood what he'd just figured out. The tamarin didn't run to someplace random. Readying his shield, he gestured for the others to fan out to either side. If the people in that hidden room were armed, there was much less chance they'd all take a bullet...but he also bet things wouldn't come to that. He would put down good money that Pinkerton had already bet the farm on stopping them topside. Someone interested in aerating them would've come out blasting just as soon as that elevator opened.

As they approached, the animal did the most curious thing. It didn't move away. Instead, it kept to the edge of the desk and stretched a hand underneath.

As if reaching for something. Gary watched the animal perform the same maneuver twice. All the while, the animal's eyes never left his face. Showing me how to open the door.

"Well, I'll be a..." Colosa stopped herself, but Gary finished the rest in his mind.

A monkey's uncle, he thought as the tamarin jumped to a nearby shelf and settled onto its haunches. The animal looked...relaxed? No, pleased. How did he know that? He wasn't clear about that, but he did understand that the tamarin didn't want to miss this. Had, in fact, settled into a front row seat. And why not? Gary would lay good money on the people responsible for abandoning that poor thing were now hiding behind that panel door. Shield firmly clasped in his right hand, he felt beneath the desk with his left and was unsurprised to find the same kind of soft dimple that served to call the elevator.

Pushing it, he quickly stepped back as the panel door slid open.

5

"I told you." Letting go of a weary sigh, the man hung his head and stared, almost listlessly, at his hands. "The colonel and most of his personnel evacuated. They ran. They left us, my sister and me, and the animals behind, and that's all I know."

"But the portal's still active, Doctor," Gary said.

"Please." The man rubbed a temple and gave another of his sighs, although this one sounded more exasperated than exhausted: as if his life would be so much better if only Gary weren't so dim. "Just Rahul."

"Okay, Rahul, so let me get this straight. The portal's open and stable because your animals..." He waved a hand in the general direction of the cage where the chimp—Rahul's sister said its name was Chester—slumped. The animal was fast asleep. The woman had injected the chimp with a sedative then waited until the animal's eyelids slid shut and its head lolled. Then, pulling on thick gloves and other protective gear, she'd expertly released the chimp's restraints and hefted the sleeping animal the way a mother might a small child, and carried it to a waiting cage. "The animals made this happen?" Gary asked.

"Yes, working together as a unit." It was Rahul's sister, Hana. She inclined her head toward the golden tamarin who seemed content to remain perched on that shelf. "We couldn't have done it without Qudamah. He'd already been part of a, well..."

"A collective," Rahul said. "A trio, in lockstep, performing the single imperative we gave them."

"Because resistance is futile." Hana lifted a shoulder then let it drop. "From an episode of an old show. Where he got the idea."

Rahul's expression turned petulant. "It was a fine episode."

"And you're saying the monkey's brain was altered?" Paracelsus cocked his head. "You fashioned some sort of neural network?"

"Amongst a quartet of animals, initially. One was..." Rahul cleared his throat. "One was what you might call a common denominator: a donor species, if you will. We then cloned and grafted the relevant cerebral components—"

"Can we just cut through all the scientific woo-woo?" Colosa rapped. "Bottom line, you two mucked around in these animals' heads until they could, what? Talk to that portal? Convince it to open up?"

"And remain open and stable," Paracelsus. "Which I would imagine was the point."

"Without getting into the specifics," Gary said, "is there any way to shut it down from this side?"

Rahul looked offended. "Whyever would anyone want to?"

"Oh, I don't know," Particula said. "A couple earthquakes, a few hurricanes."

Rahul scrubbed the air with the flat of a hand. "But things have settled down now, haven't they? Those other occurrences...they were hiccups. Bobbles along the—"

"Guys." Lily pointed to the elevator. The indicator was red. "Someone's coming down."

"It wasn't us," Hana said, quickly. "We didn't call for help."

"But help is coming." When Gary turned, Paracelsus continued, "The ones I told you about. They're friends and no threat."

Particula frowned. "How do you—" she began then broke off as the elevator sighed open.

They all took a long look, and then Lily said, "Just when you think things can't get any stranger..."

"Don't shoot." The woman was young and had eyes that were a deep, intense blue. Hands raised in surrender, she stepped from the elevator and tried on a wobbly smile that keep slipping from her lips. "Hi. My name's Sarah." She was talking fast, her words tumbling over one another. "I don't know we're here, but this guy...<null>? He came, said we all had to come and then <null> just left, dropped us off, and there are all those men, those dead men..." She swallowed, her blue eyes suddenly shimmery and wet. "And that...that..."

"Was pretty awful, I bet," Gary said, gently. Sarah's eyes, so blue and watery, were like the Portal. "And then?"

"Yes." Sarah's head moved in a brisk nod. "And then we found the elevator—"

"We." Colosa interrupted. "That's three times you've said we or us."

"Four." When Colosa turned a look, Particula shrugged. "She said us twice."

"Competitive, much?" Lily said.

"Whatever. Fine." Colosa rolled her eyes. "So, who's we, who's us—"

A sharp screech knifed the air. The sound made them all jump...and Gary half-turned, but the golden lion tamarin had already leapt to the floor and was bulleting across the lab as, from the depths of the elevator, came—

"Whoa," Colosa said. "That's us? A cat." Then repeated that as a question. "A cat? You brought—" She broke off as the tamarin leapt—but not for the woman. Still screeching, the monkey bulled into the cat, knocking it from its feet before locking its own arms around the cat's neck.

Oh boy, a cat-monkey takedown. That's all we need. Gary started forward before he was sure how he'd even break them up, but then Paracelsus hooked a hand around Gary's right elbow.

"Give them a minute," the doctor said. "They won't hurt—"

"Whoa!"

Colosa. What now? Gary's head whipped back toward the elevator. Colosa had shot up a full two feet and looked poised to get even taller—and he saw why.

"Oh...my God." Particula backed up a step as a very large, very muscular, very black wolf slipped past the woman's legs. "You got a wolf, too?"

"Yes, but it's fine, it'll be fine!" The woman held her hands up, palms out now, like a cop at a traffic cop. If she was fazed by Colosa's sudden grown spurt, she didn't show it. (On the other hand, there was a lot going on. She might not even have noticed.) "Her name's Darya, she's fine, she won't hurt you, the cat's Layal and..." She slicked her lips as a dog trundled from the elevator. "This is Benny."

"Of course, you've got a dog. Of course, why not?" Having recovered from her surprise, Colosa was now back to her normal height. "And let me guess. He doesn't bite."

"No." They all turned, and Paracelsus continued, "He doesn't."

"And they all know each other?" Lily asked.

"Obviously." Then Rahul continued, not pleasantly, "All for one and one for all. Just one biiig happy family."

"Rahul," his sister said, "for once in your life, please do shut the eff up."

<h1 style="text-align:center">6</h1>

I'll be damned.

Gary watched as the animals crowded round Sarah and the small tamarin. Purring as loudly as a small outboard motor, the cat rubbed its head against the monkey's own while the beagle, its tail inscribing frenzied circles in the air, put its front paws on Sarah's knees—the better to get at the monkey—and plastered the tamarin from head to toe with one long and very thorough lick.

"You ever seen anything like this?" Lily murmured.

"Nope," Gary said as even the wolf nosed the tamarin. If that animal...Darya, was it?... if she wanted a snack, the monkey would be just the ticket. "But that guy, Rahul, is right. Looks like one hell of a family reunion."

"Because it is." When they both turned, Paracelsus continued, "All are quite...remarkable." Then added, "The dog, in particular."

"The beagle?" Lily looked skeptical. "It's just a dog. Have you seen how it limps?"

"Books are not to be judged by their covers—and neither," Paracelsus said, his gaze locking onto Gary's own, "should any man or animal. The cover isn't important. It is what lies beneath, in here." The professor placed a palm over his heart. "What we are made of is what matters and these animals are as remarkable as we can be."

If we act from the heart. Gary's chest was suddenly tight. He couldn't quite catch his breath. Because that dog was the one: the dog Paracelsus told him about on the mountain before they'd even set foot in this place. This is the dog that he said will help me disable the portal.

Either the dog felt Gary's gaze—or maybe heard him somehow; it didn't really matter which—because the animal suddenly turned a look over a shoulder. For a weird, almost surreal moment, Gary thought the dog could see through his shell of flesh: into his eyes and through to his mind and all the hidden nooks and high shelves where Gary stored his doubts and fears and what he felt to be his destiny: to cross the portal's threshold and cut off the Counters' power at the source.

Or die trying? Or succeed but still die? Was he ready for that? Was this where the river of time and all his yesterdays narrowed to a singular, crystalline pivot upon which he—and the world—turned?

Well, no time to find out like the present.

Only the dog noticed when Gary crossed the chamber. Kneeling a short distance away, Gary tugged off a glove though he kept his eyes on the dog's own, which were a soft caramel flecked with black. Like amber, and Gary thought that was appropriate somehow. Because amber once was the living blood of ancient trees in which relics from a long-ago past—a fly, a bee, a beetle, even a frog—were perfectly preserved.

Will I age once I'm through the Portal? Will I die? Or will the dog and I become relics, miracles in amber for someone somewhere else to find?

He didn't know. These were questions with no answers—and he was only stalling.

Heart. That's what the professor said. It didn't matter that he wasn't the real Gray Guardsman, whatever that meant. Because real was as real gets.

And it's what I'm made of that counts. He extended a hand. *What we're made of.*

"Hey, boy," he said. "How you doing?"

The Eye
1

Everything down here is so…quiet and clean and clear. Even, for the first time, my mind. My thoughts.

I think that is because I have been moving towards this moment for years: ever since Rahul decided that bits of me, my brain cells, cloned and grafted into the others, were essential. That I was the final ingredient, the secret to his success, the common denominator: the one animal whose history is inextricably linked to humanity's own. We dogs are the stuff of stories and legends and, even in a few, we are brothers. Those are the stories Rahul drew on to reach his conclusions—and he wasn't wrong.

Because everyone knows: a dog is a man's best friend.

2

Like me—like Darya and Layal and Qudamah—the five people who came before we arrived are special. I just know it. (Besides, one woman lost control and grew suddenly much taller. Even the Benny I was before would've caught that clue.)

One, though…that Man in Gray is different. I've felt him watching and now I turn as he approaches. The way he stares…it is as if he's been expecting me.

"Hey, pup," he says, extending his fist so I can sniff his knuckles. (I do this, but only to be polite. I already know he's no threat, but since he has gone to the trouble of meeting me where he thinks I am, the least I can do is return the favor.) "How you doing, boy?"

Fine. I give his knuckles a little nuzzle, a small lick. We're both fine now. I'm the one you're looking for. I don't know how I know…but I think I am here to help you close the Eye.

I'm not sure how he and I will do that. But I am here to— what is it humans say? Ah, yes. Die trying.

I don't think that will happen. In all the television shows and movies Rahul made me watch, the dogs don't die. Well, unless they were very bad.

Although I do recall a movie in which a very loyal German shepherd did die...but even I saw that coming. If you live around monsters such as vampires, eventually...you'll be bitten. Trust me on this. I know monsters.

After all, I lived with Hana and Rahul.

3

There is a show Rahul liked about people stepping into a circle of watery light and ending up on another planet or, sometimes, a ship. Hana always thought the first two series—one that was on Earth and the other that was underwater—were a little silly.

But the third one, where people went through the circle and ended up on a ship, she liked. She said she liked it because it showed people at their worst and their best and because they didn't have control of the ship. They only had control over themselves and so whatever happy ending they might find, they would have to make.

The other thing: even though the show only ran for two seasons, there was nothing neat or tidy about it. Nothing wrapped up in a bow, Hana said. At the end, the ship continues on into the empty space between galaxies, a space that will take more years to cross than the crew has air. The only choice is for the crew to go into...I'm going to get this wrong...suspendered animayshun. Except one person can't. There aren't enough pods. So, at the end of the show, he stays awake while everyone else sleeps—and even though it's sad because he might die, he's also excited because who knows what new things he will be the first human to see?

Like this. Here. Now. If I step through...what new things will *I* see?

4

Dogs are not color-blind. We see shades of blue and green and yellow, but the colors are muted because our eyes aren't as important as our nose.

The Eye shimmers and ripples and I think it is a bright, impossible blue. Like something out of one of Rahul's movies, I guess.

What my nose tells me, though...I gulp a bit of air and taste blood and scorched hair and the stink of fear...but that is my past; that is behind me. That is not what is ahead and on the other side of

The Eye. Yet, if I tried to explain how that smells to you, well...I'm a dog and you're not and you wouldn't understand.

That's okay. You can't help being human.

But what I smell is...the future.

5

The Man in Gray stands beside me. I can't tell what he's thinking, but I smell his excitement. I think he believes this is what he was born to do. That his life has been leading up to this one moment or that it will finally prove something.

Me...I know that mine has, and this will.

"What do you say, pup?" The Man in Gray squints down. He's smiling, but his mouth wobbles just enough that I know he's also a little scared.

Makes two of us.

There's this saying that if a lion could speak, a person wouldn't understand. So even if I did, I don't think the Man in Gray would get it—or like it if he did. But I might be wrong.

Let's go, I say, though this comes out as a bark.

We start forward. We don't run. The Eye will wait. The Man in Gray doesn't look back and I'm sad for him because I don't think he has anyone to look back for or who will care if he is gone. Maybe that's why he's willing to leave here for whatever waits. Maybe that's why he wants me to stick close.

Because everyone needs a friend. Everyone needs a family.

Benny!

Layal. I know she's crying. If I were a human, I'd want a camera so I could take a picture and tease her with some day. I probably shouldn't look back either. Isn't there some story about a woman who turns to salt?

But I do turn and look over a shoulder. I can't help it. Maybe I shouldn't, but I'm only a dog and these are my friends, this is my family.

Sarah's cradling Qudamah in her arms. Darya's on her right and, snugged between Darya's front legs is Layal, looking very small.

Be careful, Layal says, her voice watery. *You dumb dog*.

She doesn't say try to come back in one piece...but I hear her anyway. Because I hear all of them if I put my mind to it. I wonder if I will still be able to once I am on the other side? Or will I come to them in a different way?

I don't see Rahul or Hana; I don't care. They were never my friends, never my family. But the others...they've all got a little piece of me inside. Because resistance is futile.

As for me...

I once saw a movie with a very funny man made of tin who said he knew he now had a heart because it was breaking.

So, yes, that. I don't say good-bye either. What a stupid expression, anyway. There is nothing good about leaving a part of your heart behind.

"Let's go, pup," the Man in Gray says.

Yes. I turn from my past. It's time to step into my future.

Coming, I say. *Coming*.

PHENOMENON STORIES, PART IV

BY MICHAEL JAN FRIEDMAN

For a moment—maybe several moments, it was hard to tell—Gary didn't know where he was.

Then he saw the plastic containers of chocolate-covered treats sitting next to him on a table, and the people milling around in front of him behind their shopping carts, and the immense, metal-skeleton ambiance of the place, and he got it: He was back at PriceCo.

With sheer rubber gloves on his hands to keep things sanitary. With a hairnet on his head for the same reason. And a freebie station in front of him, all set up with a plastic sneeze guard and a red plastic tray, and a sign advertising the kind of treat he'd be giving out—in this case, chocolate-covered almonds.

People loved chocolate-covered almonds.

Somewhere off in the distance—outside the store, Gary guessed, miles away—there was a howling, like a storm whipping up. Odd, he thought.

The only sounds he should have heard were the hum of the HVAC system and the chatter of the customers. No music, because that was PriceCo policy. And definitely no howling.

Anyway, it was far away, so nothing to worry about. Gary was sure of it.

Where he was, in the candy aisle, it was safe. And calm—no wind. A nice temperature, too.

In the store's freezer aisles, it was cold. Even in the summertime. But not in the candy aisle. There it was comfortable all year 'round.

And all Gary had to do was put the chocolate-covered almonds into little paper-doily cups. Ten to a cup—that was what Chad, his supervisor, had told him the first time he got the chocolate-covered almond assignment.

"It's not supposed to be a meal," Chad had told him. "Just a taste. Just enough to whet the customer's appetite so he looks for the chocolate-covered almonds on the shelf and buys a container full of them. Maybe two, if we're lucky."

Chad hadn't told him how many chocolate-covered treats to put in the doily cups this time. But that was probably because he figured Gary already knew.

Because that was one thing Gary was good at: Remembering stuff. He didn't know how, considering he spent half of every night patrolling the streets, looking for a mugger or something else Grey Guardsman could help with. But even with that stealing his sleep, he remembered how many chocolate-covered treats to put in a doily cup.

Ten. Ten was the number.

Also, Gary remembered the procedure after he filled each cup. Because his responsibility didn't end with putting the almonds into the paper cups. PriceCo had its hygiene protocols, which dictated that he could offer stuff to the public only after he'd extended it to them under the sneeze guard.

That was the biggest rule, the one that was hard and fast, Gary thought as he opened a container full of chocolate-covered almonds and poured ten of them into a doily cup. No exceptions, he mused as he poured out ten almonds into the next cup.

He was filling a third cup when he saw a man's hand reach around the sneeze guard and try to snag one of the cups Gary had already filled. "Hey," Gary said, pulling his red plastic tray back where the hand couldn't reach it. "You can't do that."

He traced the hand to a guy with a jowly face and a thick, grey mustache. The face looked disapproving. "Why not?" it asked.

Funny…the guy's face had a rainbow aura around it. Like Gary was looking at him through a prism. Must be the lighting, Gary thought.

"Sorry," he said, "but you've got to wait till I put them out front."

"I can't," the guy with the mustache told him. He jerked a thumb over his shoulder. "My wife's at the register already."

Gary sympathized with the guy. But PriceCo didn't give him a lot of leeway.

"Sir," he said calmly, "I'm not here to argue with you. We've got rules we have to follow. Otherwise, they'll shut us down and nobody will get anything."

The guy looked astonished. And his aura…it got bigger all of a sudden, and it rippled around him.

"You kidding me?" the guy said. "It's gonna make a difference if I take one freakin' cup of chocolate almonds?"

Gary bit his lip. The last thing he was supposed to do was piss off the customers. He was there to make the customers feel at home. "Make them feel loved," Chad said one time, "because the last time someone gave them a treat it was their mother, and that was probably a long time ago. You put out a tray of freebies and they get that that feeling all over again. Like somebody cares about them. Like somebody wants to put a smile on their face. So it's not just food you're giving them. It's love."

Unfortunately, this customer wanted his love in a hurry, and the kind of love they gave out at PriceCo didn't come that way. Which was why Gary found himself saying to the guy, "That's right, sir. Because if you take a cup from the back, everybody's going to want to do it that way. Then we'll have chaos. And when we have chaos, they shut us down."

That was how it worked at PriceCo. And not just at PriceCo. It worked that way all over. There were rules about who got what and how they got it. And when somebody broke those rules, Gary had to step in. He had to take a stand against the chaos.

Like there was more at stake than a doily cup full of treats. Like there was an order to things, and he was the only one who could maintain that order.

"Look," the guy growled, "I don't give a crap about your rules. I'm the customer. The customer is always right." He looked at the other folks gathered around Gary's station. "Isn't that what they say? Isn't the customer always right?"

Something weird happened then. Really weird. Everything jumped. The way things jumped sometimes on a video screen, when the feed was interrupted for a moment.

And when the feed came back, everything had a rainbow aura around it. Not just the guy with the mustache, but the metal structures on which the store's boxes full of containers and jars and bags were stacked. And the other customers, and their carts. Even the paper cups full of chocolate-covered almonds had shimmering rainbow auras.

Something's wrong with my eyes, Gary thought.

But it wasn't just what he saw that was different. It was what he heard: The howling that had been so distant was getting louder. Louder and closer. Like it was right outside the door to the store.

"Do you hear that?" he asked the customers.

They just looked at him, their auras playing around them. With growing apprehension in their eyes.

"Nobody?" Gary asked.

How could that be? It sounded like the world was crying in pain. A whole lot of pain.

He was so focused on it, he almost failed to notice a hand reaching for the treats on his tray. The same hand that had reached for them before.

Gary looked into the face of the guy with the mustache and pulled the tray back again. "I told you," he said to the guy, whose aura was going crazy, sizzling and erupting the way the surface of the sun sizzled and erupted on TV sometimes, "you've got to wait!"

"I'll freaking have you fired!" the guy snapped, his features twisting, his face turning apple-red. "Who are you to tell me what to do? A goddamned sample clerk? Are you kiddin' me? Give me that--"

And he reached even farther for the chocolate-covered almonds, so far his fingers brushed one of the paper cups on Gary's tray.

But Gary drew the tray back again, behind him this time so there was no chance the guy with the mustache could get at it. "You've got to wait," Gary insisted, steel in his voice, "just like everybody else!"

The guy with the mustache glared at him, his aura whipping and shooting rainbow tendrils in the direction of the ceiling. "Wait and see," he snarled. "Your ass'll be on the pavement before closing time!"

Gary didn't care. He had a job to do and he'd done it. He'd held back the chaos. He'd done what he was born for.

He watched as the guy moved in the direction of the checkout. If he wanted to find the store manager, it wouldn't take much. She was talking to a woman on the fresh-pizza line just past the registers.

Suddenly, the store jumped again. For a second, or just a fraction of a second, it looked to Gary like the walls were waterfalls and the ceiling was flying away into the sky, and the air was sparkling like sunlight on a lake.

Then everything snapped back to the way it was. Solid walls, solid ceiling. The sparkles in the air were gone.

The auras too. People just looked like people. Sounded that way as well. No howling, not even a little.

Gary took a deep breath and thought, Thank god.

Suddenly, he got a weird feeling—like his blood was rushing around his body faster than it was supposed to. Really fast, like it was setting new records for high-speed circulation.

He felt lightheaded, like he was going to faint. Then flushed, like his face was going to explode. Then lightheaded again.

Gotta tell Chad, he thought.

That was what he'd been told to do. If you feel sick, call Chad. Get yourself out of there before the customers think they're going to catch something from you.

Or worse, that it was the stuff you were doling out—the stuff they were all eating—that had made you sick.

Gary reached for his cell phone to make the call. But he couldn't get to it. His hand couldn't get under his apron.

Then he realized why that was: He wasn't wearing an apron. He was wearing a uniform. Something purple and silver-grey.

The colors of Grey Guardsman.

Because That's who he was, who he really was, who he had become slowly, gradually, night after night until finally the transition was complete—Grey Guardsman.

He looked around again. The customers who had crowded around his station were gone. In fact, the whole store was gone. He wasn't in PriceCo anymore. He was somewhere else.

A blank place, featureless, devoid of detail. As if it were waiting for someone or something to come and fill it up.

It was then that he remembered: <null.> The mission. The task force. The portal.

That's where I am, he thought. He looked around, and a feeling of nauseousness came over him. *I'm inside the portal…*

He had to shut the thing off. Take the Counters off the board. That's why he was there.

Funny that he'd thought he was back at PriceCo. He'd never see that place again, would he? Or any other.

Can't think about that now, he told himself. He had a job to do. He had to shut off the portal. <null> had told them so.

The only problem was…how? It wasn't like there was a lever with a sign that said Shut Portal.

Then he saw the dog. The beagle. He was sitting at Gary's feet, looking up at him as if he'd been there all along.

Gary remembered now—the dog had entered the portal with him, had been part of what he had to do. Though he hadn't known how, exactly. But now, somehow, he knew.

Gary knelt and scratched the dog behind the ear and said, "You can do this, can't you, boy?"

The dog looked back at him, and something in his eyes said yes, he could do this. But he needed Gary to do something too.

To…protect him while he was busy doing what he had to do. Protect him from what? Gary wondered.

And in that moment, as Gary tried to figure out what they were up against, the dog disappeared. Gary looked around for him but he was gone. A pang of sadness and more than that lodged in Gary's gut.

The dog, he thought. The poor dog.

But it wasn't just the animal he mourned. He mourned his world as well. Without the dog, there was no way Gary could shut down the portal, or the threat the Counters posed to his world.

Suddenly, he started to go numb. Like the ability to feel was draining out of him, and not a little, and not slowly.

Am I dying? he thought wildly.

It was like whatever connected his skin to his brain had been cut. He couldn't feel the floor under his feet, or the shield on his back, or…

Or even himself. His arms, his chest…it was as if they belonged to someone else.

Then he did feel something.

It felt like hands grabbing him—not just a couple but a bunch of them, grabbing him and holding onto him. So hard, so terribly hard, he could feel their fingers digging into his bones.

At the same time, he knew it wasn't hands he was feeling. It couldn't be. Where he was…it was where no one could stay for very long. <null> had said so.

Gary was alone, horribly alone, without even his friend the dog to stand with him—facing a reality no one had ever seen or heard or imagined. So there was no way anyone could be grabbing him with anything even approaching a human hand.

Something else, then. A predator? Latching onto him with things that felt like hands and fingers, holding him steady so it could consume him?

He didn't know. And maybe he wouldn't until it was too late, until the thing used its teeth or whatever it had in place of teeth to tear the life out of him. He just didn't know.

What he did know was this: Whatever it was and whatever was holding onto him, it hurt.

And that wasn't the only pain he felt. More and more, it wasn't just a matter of fingers—or something like fingers—digging into him. There was something else, something that had started in the background and become the center of attention.

It felt like his body was being stretched on an invisible rack, more and more with each passing second, like everything that held him together—the bones, the cartilage, the ligaments, and even the skin, for crying out loud—was being pulled apart.

They didn't want to be pulled that way, the bones and the cartilage and the ligaments. They weren't built to do that. But whatever was pulling kept it up, making the pain worse and worse…

And worse…

Finally, Gary screamed. He couldn't help it. He screamed at whatever cruel dynamics of the universe made it possible for a human being to experience such agony.

And he kept on screaming until he realized, with a start of relief, that the pain had stopped.

Just like that. One moment he'd been caught on the horns of a searing red nightmare and the next he was free of it.

He drew a ragged breath. He whimpered from the deepest parts of him. And he cringed at the thought of the torture starting all over again, because he didn't trust this respite—not at all.

But the pain didn't come back. After what seemed like a long time, he dared to open his eyes—and found himself looking up at a woman with high cheekbones and dark exotic eyes and flawless brown skin. Maybe the most beautiful woman he had ever seen.

They weren't in the place beyond the portal, either. They were in the room where he and his team had found the damned thing.

I'm…back? he wondered.

It wasn't possible. And yet there he was. He looked around.

There was no sign of his teammates. They're gone, he thought.

Of course they were. What was the point of staying there if they didn't think he was coming back? The animals were gone too—where, he didn't know. How long had he been away, anyway?

He turned to the exotic-looking woman again, her fingers enmeshed in the fabric of his uniform, as if she could give him answers. Even one. That was when he realized they weren't alone, the two of them.

There were others standing behind her. Two men and another woman. They stared at him for a moment, then they looked at each other.

One of the men—the bigger one—indicated Gary with a gesture and said, "What the—?"

As if that were a signal, the woman opened her hand, releasing Gary. Without her hold on him to keep him upright, he dropped to the ground like a sack of potatoes, too crushed and run over and spit out to even try to break his fall.

The woman looked down on him with disdain, like he was garbage or worse than garbage. Like she was skeeved out just by the thought of having touched him.

Then she turned to the others and said, "This ain't Rascal."

ACKNOWLEDGMENTS

This vessel would not have reached safe harbor without the special dedication and generosity of the following brave hands: Christopher D. Abbott, Mark Anbinder, Lorraine Anderson, Rob Armstrong, Jim Arrowood, Stephen Ballentine, Paul Balze, Steven Bloom, John H. Bookwalter Jr., Jeremy Bottroff, Wayne Brown, Chris Carothers, Casey Chambers, Andrew Cherry, Alexandra Corrsin, Scott Crick, Rhiannon Crothers, Michael Donnelly, Len Dvorkin, Roscoe Fay, Colleen Feeney, John Fitter, Lynda Foley, Bryan Geddes, Giggles, Bill Glasgow, Frank J. Hernandez, Mary Jane Hetzlein, Dino Hicks, David Holets, Brad Jurn, Peggy Kimbell, Karen Krah, krinsky, Chris LaBanca, Tom Longstaff, Denis MacDougall, Eric Mesa, Edgar Middel, Kevin Miraglia, Bill Moe, Gail Morse, John Nacinovich, Thomas Nelson, Michael Niosi, Brandy Pastore, Mary P. Perez, Jill Peters, Stephen Peterson, Yankton Robins, Lenny Rock, Andy Santoro, Rahadyan Timoteo Sastrowardoyo, Julia Scott, Linda Silverman, Robert J. Sodaro, Liz Stonehill, Norma Storms, Corey Terhune, Pekka Timonen, T.J. Walsh, Matthew Wang, Gregg Whitmore, and Gary K. Wolf.

ABOUT OUR AUTHORS

ILSA J. BICK is a child psychiatrist, as well as a film and television scholar, surgeon wannabe, former Air Force major—and an award-winning, best-selling author of dozens of short stories and novels. Her work spans established universes such as *Star Trek, Battletech, Battlecorps, Mechwarrior Dark Age*, and *Shadowrun* as well as stories for the shared *Pangaea* universe from Crazy 8 Press. Her original novels include such critically acclaimed and award-winning books as The *ASHES* Trilogy, *Drowning Instinct, The Sin-Eater's Confession,* and *White Space* (longlisted for the Stoker).

Ilsa's also written in *New York Times* best-selling author Elle James's *Brotherhood Protectors*. Her four-part Soldier's Heart series features Kate McEvoy, a cybernetically enhanced Afghan vet and Sarah Grant, a veterinarian struggling to help her dead lover's traumatized war dog, Soldier. *Protecting the Flame* follows photojournalist Emma Gold after a plane crash in a snowy mountainous landscape where the odds of survival drop with the plummeting temperatures and her realization that those searching for the plane aren't necessarily out to rescue the passengers.

Most recently, her story "Dheeb," which follows an unlikely quartet of enhanced, sentient animals, marks her third outing for a Crazy8 anthology.

Currently a cheesehead-in-exile, Ilsa has recently moved to London which is…an adventure.

Drop by for a visit at **www.ilsajbick.com** or check out her Friday's Cocktails (such as they are because all her barware has been packed away and won't see the light of day until she finds

a permanent place to live) and other assorted effluvia on Facebook
https://www.facebook.com/ilsa.j.bick and
https://www.facebook.com/ilsajbickauthor
Twitter *@ilsajbick*, and Instagram *@ilsajbick*

MICHAEL A. BURSTEIN has earned ten Hugo nominations for his short fiction, which is collected in the volume *I Remember The Future*. He is a winner of the Astounding Award and the editor of the anthology *Jewish Futures*. Burstein lives with his family in the town of Brookline, Massachusetts, where he is an elected Town Meeting Member and Library Trustee. However, he grew up in Forest Hills, Queens, home of Spider-Man, about whom he wrote "The Friendly Neighborhood of Peter Parker" for the book *Webslinger*. He has two degrees in Physics, once worked at Los Alamos National Laboratory on secret research, and has appeared in two Woody Allen movies as well as one Iron Man novel.

RUSS COLCHAMIRO is the author of the Sci-Fi thriller novels *Crackle and Fire*, *Fractured Lives*, *Hot Ash*, and *Blunt Force Rising*, the four books featuring hardboiled intergalactic private eye Angela Hardwicke. A member of author collective Crazy 8 Press, Russ is also the author of the SFF novels *Crossline*, *Finders Keepers*, *Genius de Milo*, and *Astropalooza*, editor of the SciFi mystery anthology *Love, Murder & Mayhem,* and co-author and editor of the noir anthology *Murder in Montague Falls*, and has contributed to more than a dozen SFF anthologies. Russ is also a member of the Mystery Writers Association of America and is host of the *Russ's Rockin 'Rollercoaster* podcast, interviewing a who's who of science fiction, crime, and mystery authors. You can follow him on Facebook, and Twitter and Instagram @authorduderuss, and on his website russcolchamiro.com.

PETER DAVID is a prolific author whose career, and continued popularity, spans nearly two decades. He has worked in every conceivable medium: television, film, books (fiction, non-fiction, and audio), short stories, and comic books, and acquired followings in all of them.

In the literary field, Peter has had over forty novels published, including numerous appearances on the *New York Times* Bestseller List. *Publisher's Weekly* described him as "a genuine and veteran master." Probably his greatest fame comes from the high-profile realm of *Star Trek* novels, where he is the most popular writer of the series, with his title *Imzadi* being one of the bestselling *Star Trek* novels of all time. He is also co-creator and author of the bestselling *New Frontier* series for Pocket Books. A partial list of his titles include *Q-Squared, The Siege, Q-in-Law, Vendetta, I, Q* (with John DeLancie), and *A Rock and a Hard Place*, plus such original science fiction and fantasy works as *Knight Life, Howling Mad*, and the *Psi-Man* adventure novels. He also produced the three *Babylon 5 Centauri Prime* novels. He has also had short stories appear in such collections as *Shock Rock, Shock Rock II*, and *Otherwere*, as well as *Isaac Asimov's Science Fiction Magazine* and the *Magazine of Fantasy and Science Fiction*.

Peter has written more comics than can possibly be listed here, remaining consistently one of the most acclaimed writers in the field. His resume includes an award-winning twelve-year run on The Incredible Hulk. He has also worked on such varied and popular titles as *Supergirl, Young Justice, Soulsearchers and Company, Aquaman, Spider-Man, Spider-Man 2099, X-Factor, Star Trek, Wolverine, The Phantom, Sachs & Violence*, and many others. He has also written comic book related novels, such as *The Hulk: What Savage Beast*, and co-edited *The Ultimiate Hulk* short story collection. Furthermore, his opinion column *But I Digress* has been running in the industry trade newspaper *The Comics Buyers Guide* for nearly a decade, and in that time has been the paper's consistently most popular feature, which was also collected into a trade paperback edition.

Peter is the co-creator, with popular science fiction icon Bill Mumy (of *Lost in Space* and *Babylon 5* fame) of the Cable Ace Award-nominated science fiction series *Space Cases*, which ran for two seasons on Nickelodeon. He has also written several scripts for the Hugo Award-winning TV series *Babylon 5*, and the sequel series, *Crusade*, as well as the animated series *Roswell*. He has also written several films for Full Moon Entertainment and co-produced two of them, including two installments in the popular Trancers series as well as the science fiction western spoof *Oblivion*, which won the Gold Award at the 1994 Houston International Film Festival for best Theatrical Feature Film, Fantasy/Horror Category.

Peter's awards and citations span not only an assortment of fields, but the globe. They include: the Haxtur Award 1996 (Spain), Best Comic Script; OZCon 1995 award (Australia), Favorite International Writer; Comics Buyers Guide 1995 Fan Awards, Favorite Writer; Wizard Fan Award Winner 1993; Golden Duck Award for Young Adult Series (Starfleet Academy), 1994; UK Comic Art Award, 1993; Will Eisner Comic Industry Award, 1993. Recently, his work was again nominated in two categories for the Eisners. In the 1999 SFX Readers Award he was the sixth most popular author in the field, with four of his books finishing in the top ten in their category ("The Peter David Midas touch continues," wrote the SFX editors.)He is also a founding member of **Crazy 8 Press**, the internet publishing venture launched at Shore Leave 33.

KEITH R.A. DECANDIDO first created Luminosity about thirty years ago, and is very grateful to Michael Jan Friedman for giving him a place to finally give her form and substance, not just here, but also in the prior two *Phenomenons* volumes. He has written a metric buttload of superheroes in prose over the years, including the Spider-Man novels *Venom's Wrath* (written with José R. Nieto) and *Down These Mean Streets* (recently reprinted as part of *The Darkest Hours Omnibus* along with Spidey novels by Jim Butcher and Christopher L. Bennett); the "Tales of Asgard" novel trilogy that includes *Thor: Dueling with Giants, Sif: Even Dragons Have Their Endings*, and *Warriors Three: Godhood's End*; short stories in the anthologies *The Ultimate Spider-Man, The Ultimate Silver Surfer, The Ultimate Hulk, Untold Tales of Spider-Man, X-Men Legends, With Great Power, The Side of Good/The Side of Evil*, and *Tales of Capes and Cowls*; the *Heroes Reborn* novella *Save the Cheerleader, Destroy the World*; and novels and novellas featuring the Super City Police Department, including *The Case of the Claw, Avenging Amethyst, Undercover Blues*, and *Secret Identities*. Keith has written sixty novels, both media tie-ins (in more than thirty different licensed universes from *Alien* to *Zorro*) and in worlds of his own creation (the upcoming *Supernatural Crimes Unit* series, the long-running *Dragon Precinct* series, the Adventures of Bram Gold series, etc.), and he also has more than a hundred works of short fiction and more than fifty comic books to his credit. He also writes about pop culture for many places, but mostly for the award-winning web site Reactor Magazine (formerly Tor.com) and his Patreon (patreon.com/krad). With Wrenn Simms, he's formed the very-small-press publisher Whysper Wude, and he also is an editor, a musician, a martial artist, and devoted New York Yankees fan. There may be other stuff, too, but he can't recall due to the lack of sleep. Find out less at his web site at DeCandido.net.

MARY FAN is a sci-fi/fantasy writer hailing from Jersey City, NJ. She is the author of the Jane Colt sci-fi series, (Red Adept Publishing), the Starswept YA sci-fi series, (Snowy Wings Publishing), the Flynn Nightsider YA dark fantasy series (Crazy 8 Press), and *Stronger Than a Bronze Dragon*, a YA steampunk fantasy (Page Street Publishing). She is also the editor of Bad Ass Moms, an anthology from Crazy 8 Press. In addition, Mary is the co-editor (along with fellow sci-fi author Paige Daniels) of the Brave New Girls young adult sci-fi anthologies, which feature tales about girls in STEM. Revenues from sales are donated to the Society of Women Engineers scholarship fund. Her short fiction has appeared in numerous anthologies, including *Pangaea III: Redemption* (edited by Michael Jan Friedman), *Keep Faith* (edited by Gabriela Martins), *Thrilling Adventure Yarns* (edited by Bob Greenberger), *Magic at Midnight* (edited by Lyssa Chiavari and Amy McNulty), *They Keep Killing Glenn* (edited by Peter and Kathleen David), *Tales of the Crimson Keep: Newly Renovated Edition* (edited by Bob Greenberger), *Mine! A Celebration of Liberty and Freedom for All Benefitting Planned Parenthood* (from ComicMix), and *Love, Murder & Mayhem* (edited by Russ Colchamiro).

In her spare time, Mary can usually be found at choir rehearsal, in the kickboxing gym, swinging off a flying trapeze, or tangled up in aerial silks.

MICHAEL JAN FRIEDMAN is the author of 81 books, nearly half of them set somewhere in the wilds of the *Star Trek* universe.In 1992 Friedman wrote *Reunion*, the first *Star Trek: The Next Generation* hardcover, which introduced the crew of the *Stargazer*, Captain Jean-Luc Picard's first command. Over the years, the popularity of *Reunion* has spawned a number of *Stargazer* stories in both prose and comic book formats, including a six-novel original series.

Friedman has also written for the *Aliens, Predator, Wolf Man, Lois and Clark, DC Super Hero, Marvel Super Hero*, and *Wishbone* licensed book universes. Eleven of his titles, including the autobiography *Hollywood Hulk Hogan* and *Ghost Hunting* (written with SciFi's Ghost Hunters), have appeared on the prestigious *New York Times* primary bestseller list, and his novel adaptation of the *Batman & Robin* movie was for a time the #1 bestselling book in Poland (really).

Friedman has worked at one time or another in network and cable television, radio, business magazines, and the comic book industry, in the process producing scripts for nearly 180 comic stories. Among his comic book credits is the *Darkstars* series from DC Comics, which he created with artist Mike Collins, and the *Outlaws* limited series, which he created with artist Luke McDonnell. He also co-wrote the story for the acclaimed second-season *Star Trek: Voyager* TV episode "Resistance," which guest-starred Joel Grey.

In 2011, Friedman spearheaded the establishment of Crazy 8 Press, an imprint through which he and other talented authors publish their purest and most passionate visions. Crazy 8 Press currently features 10 authors and more than 75 original titles. Follow him if you dare at crazy8press.com,, or on Facebook as Michael Jan Friedman.

ROBERT GREENBERGER is a writer and editor. While at SUNY-Binghamton, Greenberger wrote and edited for the college newspaper, Pipe Dream. Upon graduation, he worked for Starlog Press and while there, created Comics Scene, the first nationally distributed magazine to focus on comic books, comic strips, and animation.

In 1984, he joined DC Comics as an Assistant Editor and went on to be an Editor before moving to Administration as Manager-

Editorial Operations. He joined Gist Communications as a Producer before moving to Marvel Comics as its Director-Publishing Operations.

Greenberger rejoined DC in May 2002 as a Senior Editor-Collected Editions. He helped grow that department, introducing new formats and improving the editions 'editorial content. In 2006, he joined *Weekly World News* as its Managing Editor until the paper's untimely demise. He helped revitalize *Famous Monsters of Filmland* and served as News Editor at ComicMix.com.

He is a member of the Science Fiction Writers of America and the International Association of Media Tie-In Writers. His novelization of *Hellboy II: The Golden Army* won the IAMTW's Scribe Award in 2009.

With others, he cofounded Crazy 8 Press, a digital press hub where he continues to write. His dozens of books, short stories, and essays cover the gamut from young adult nonfiction to original fiction. His most recent works include numerous short stories, essays, and articles, plus *Superman: The Definitive History* (cowritten with Ed Gross).

Bob teaches High School English at St. Vincent Pallotti High School in Laurel, MD and is an adjunct professor at Maryland College Institute of Art. He and his wife Deborah reside in Howard County, Maryland. Find him at www.bobgreenberger.com or @bobgreenberger.

GLENN HAUMAN is an American editor, publisher, writer of novels and short stories, and colorist. As an editorial consultant to Simon & Schuster Interactive, he contributed to a number of *Star Trek* CD-ROMs such as the *Star Trek Encyclopedia*, *Star Trek: The Next Generation Companion*, and the *Star Trek: Deep Space Nine Companion*, as well as those for other properties, such as *Farscape*. Among Glenn's books are the eBooks *Star Trek: Starfleet Corps of Engineers: No Surrender* and *Star Trek: Starfleet Corps of Engineers: Creative Couplings*, which he co-authored with Aaron Rosenberg and which is noteworthy for dramatizing the first Klingon/Jewish wedding ceremony. Glenn wrote the short stories "On The Air," which appeared in the anthology *Ultimate X-Men*, and "Chasing Hairy," which appeared in the anthology *X-Men Legends*. Both were featured on the Sci-Fi Channel's *Seeing Ear Theater*. Glenn is a founder of ComicMix. He also provided the color art for Mike Grell's *Jon Sable, Freelance*. He is quite tall, and so notoriously overworked that he has been known to crib his author's biography from his own Wikipedia page.

DAN HERNANDEZ is a writer-producer who recently served as co-showrunner and executive producer of the upcoming *LEGO Star Wars: Rebuild the Galaxy,* as well as Hulu's adult animated comedy *Koala Man.* Along with his writing partner Benji Samit, Hernandez also created the Disney Channel original show *Ultra Violet & Black Scorpion*. Other television credits include the Peabody-nominated *One Day at a Time, The Tick*, *Central Park, Super Fun Night*, and *1600 Penn*. Dan and Benji are developing multiple shows under their overall deal at Disney.

In film, Dan and Benji's credits include the critically acclaimed *Teenage Mutant Ninja Turtles: Mutant Mayhem, Pokémon Detective Pikachu*, which was the first adaptation of a video game to receive a "Fresh" score on Rotten Tomatoes, and *Addams Family 2* for MGM. Dan and Benji are working on features for multiple studios, including Netflix and Disney, and in 2019 were spotlighted as one of *Variety*'s "10 Screenwriters to Watch." To date, Dan and Benji's movies have grossed over half a billion dollars at box office.

Dan graduated from Brown University with an Honors degree in Fiction. His short fiction has most recently appeared in the science fiction anthologies *Pangea III: Redemption* and *Phenomenons: Every Human Creature* (Crazy 8 Press).

Brooklyn-born, **PAUL KUPPERBERG**, is the author of more than three dozen books of fiction and nonfiction for readers of all ages, including his memoir *Panel by Panel: My Comic Book Life*, *Direct Creativity: The Creators Who Inspired the Creators*, *Direct Conversations: Talks with Fellow DC Comics Bronze Age Creators*, *The Devil and Leo Persky*, *The Same Old Story*, and *In My Shorts: Hitler's Bellhop and Other Stories* (Crazy 8 Press), *Supertown* (Heliosphere Books), *Paul Kupperberg's Illustrated Guide to Writing Comics* (Charlton Neo Press), *JSA: Ragnarok*, *Direct Comments: Comic Book Creators in their Own Words, The*

Unpublished Comic Book Scripts of Paul Kupperberg, and *Son of the Unpublished Comic Book Scripts of Paul Kupperberg* (Buffalo Avenue Books), *Kevin* (Grosset & Dunlap), and *Jew-Jitsu: The Hebrew Hands of Fury* (Citadel Books), as well as short stories and essays for anthologies published by Crazy 8 Press, Simon and Schuster, Ace, DAW, Titan Books, Sequential Arts, and others. Paul has also written over 1,400 comic book stories featuring such characters as Superman, Supergirl, Vigilante, The Doom Patrol, the Simpsons, and Archie, including the 2012 Eisner Award and 2013 Harvey Award-nominated (and the 2014 GLAAD Media Award winner for "Outstanding Comic Book") *Life with Archie* series that culminated in the controversial "Death of Archie" storyline. A former editor for DC Comics, *Weekly World News*, and WWE, Paul is also the creator of *Arion Lord of Atlantis*, *Checkmate*, and *Takion* for DC Comics. You can follow him online at PaulKupperberg.net and on Facebook, Twitter, and BlueskySocial.

ALEX SEGURA is the bestselling and award-winning author of *Secret Identity*, winner of the Los Angeles Times Book Prize for Mystery/Thriller and a *New York Times* Editor's Choice and an NPR Best Mystery of the Year. He's also the author of the Pete Fernandez series, as well as the Star Wars novel, Poe Dameron: Free Fall, and a Spider-Verse adventure called Araña/Spider-Man 2099: Dark Tomorrow, in addition to a number of comic books for Marvel, DC, Dark Horse, Image, Mad Cave, and more. He lives in New York City with his family.

HILDY SILVERMAN primarily writes genre fiction (science fiction, fantasy, horror and mystery). In 2005, she became the publisher and editor-in-chief of *Space and Time* (**www.spaceandtimemagazine.com**), now a five-plus decades old magazine of fantasy, horror and science fiction. She is also a past president of the Garden State Speculative Fiction Writers, a current member of Crazy 8 Press, and a frequent panelist on the East Coast science fiction convention circuit. For more information, please visit **www.hildysilverman.com.**

OMAR SPAHI is a TV animation writer whose past work includes Ben 10, Hello Neighbor: WTRB, and Sonic Prime. After spending years making independent comics, Omar began producing films including Code 8, which has been featured as the #1 movie on Netflix

GEOFFREY THORNE began his writing career placing stories in Simon & Schuster's prestigious Strange New Worlds anthology series. Since then he's had short stories and novellas in multiple magazines and anthologies, including *Steamfunk* and *Ellery Queen's Mystery Magazine*. He's written and produced multiple TV series both in live-action and animation, as well as several series for Marvel and DC comics, including *Mosaic* and *Green Lantern*. In 2019, Thorne was the co-executive producer of Starz channel's *Power: Book II: Ghost*, the first sequel to the global phenomenon, *Power*.

Hugo and Nebula nominee, **MARIE VIBBERT**, has sold over 90 short stories to top markets such as *Vice*, *Nature*, *Amazing Stories*, and *Analog*. Her debut novel, *Galactic Hellcats*, about a female biker gang in outer space rescuing a gay prince, was long listed for the British Science Fiction Award. Her third novel, *The Gods Awoke*, came out in 2022 and is about a powerful telepathic space entity who thinks she may be a trickster goddess, and how she figures out what to do about that. Marie's work has been called "Everything science fiction should be" by the *Oxford Culture Review* and has been translated into Czech, Chinese, and Vietnamese. She once played defensive end for a women's professional football team and by day she is a computer programmer in Cleveland, Ohio. You can learn more about her at MarieVibbert.com.